Muscles ri**e
worked, a

Stop it, she told herself. *Stop acting like an idiot.*

"Liz."

She whirled around and found him standing far too close to her. She tried to step back, but the bookcase stopped her.

"What?" Her voice was damnably breathy. She tipped her head back to look up at him and for a crazy moment wondered if he would kiss her again.

He dashed her ill-formed hopes. "Staff meeting an hour after lockdown."

He hesitated another moment, and she waited for his touch, like an idiot, still hoping. Then he backed away and headed for the door.

As his footfalls faded, a rumbling started, vibrating the rock walls. A sudden formless terror gripped her. She was glad that Ethan had left, that he wasn't witness to her fear.

"It'll be all right, Miss Lizzy. You'll see."

She scrambled to her feet. When she saw who stood grinning in the doorway, she gaped.

"Uh . . . Uh . . . " She flapped a hand at the red-haired young man.

He smoothed the front of his coat, then hiked his trousers up a bit. *"Howdy, Lizzy."*

"I . . . uh . . . ." She cleared her throat, tried to keep her eyes from bugging clear out of her skull. "I know you." She blinked, a laborious process. "You're him. That guy."

"Which guy would that be?"

"The miner. Noah Simmons."

He grinned more broadly. *"That I am."*

Liz swallowed once, twice. "And you're dead."

Titles by Karen Sandler

UNFORGETTABLE
NIGHT WHISPERS

NIGHT WHISPERS

KAREN SANDLER

JOVE BOOKS, NEW YORK

To Linda, Debbie, and Shari—the best sisters a girl could ever have.

HAUNTING HEARTS is a registered trademark of Penguin Putnam Inc.

NIGHT WHISPERS

A Jove Book / published by arrangement with
the author

PRINTING HISTORY
Jove edition / September 1999

The Penguin Putnam Inc. World Wide Web site address is
http://www.penguinputnam.com

ISBN: 0-515-12584-9

A JOVE BOOK®
Jove Books are published by The Berkley Publishing Group,
a division of Penguin Putnam Inc.,
375 Hudson Street, New York, New York 10014.
JOVE and the "J" design
are trademarks belonging to Penguin Putnam Inc.

PRINTED IN THE UNITED STATES OF AMERICA

10 9 8 7 6 5 4 3 2 1

Prologue

Noah Simmons took another step into the blackness of the Hoyo del Diablo Cavern, the scrape of his leather bootheel loud in the vast space. Lantern tight in his hand, he held it out before him. The flame burned steadily, sending its glow barely beyond the reach of his arm.

How deep was he now? Far beyond the searing heat of the desert above him, beyond even the faintest touch of light. He'd begun descending from the moment he'd stepped inside the yawning entrance of the cavern. Now a chill bit deep into his bones, despite his heavy sack coat. His eyes strained at the meager light.

A sound brushed at his ears, sifting inside like a whisper. The echo of his footsteps, maybe, or his own breathing. But danged if it didn't sound like his own name.

In spite of himself, his hand trembled. The flame within the hurricane glass guttered and flickered, twisting his shadow along the floor of the cave. A trick of his light-

1

starved eyes drew a devilish image just at the edge of the flame's reach. Noah gripped hard on the lantern's handle, eyes squeezed shut a moment to drive away the illusion.

Hoyo del Diablo. Devil's Pit. Dang it, he wasn't a superstitious man, but now, folded so deeply into the darkness, he could believe the tales. This wasn't a place for a man. It might not be Satan's abode either, but Noah could swear something lived in the endless black beneath the Arizona Territory desert. Something that didn't want him there.

He longed for a drink, even a swallow of whiskey. But he'd finished his flask last night, passing it around the fire at the Pima village. Now it lay empty in his hip pocket, not even a drop to wet his whistle.

Another whisper. It *was* his name. Sweet Jesus, was it calling him? Coming for him?

He struck a rock with the toe of his boot, launching it across the floor. It clattered as it went, *chitter, chitter, chitter,* then the sound cut off. As if a hand had reached out to stop its progress.

Shrugging off the urge to shiver, Noah edged forward, lantern extended. As he shuffled along the rocky floor, an image rose in his mind's eye of his sour-faced mama, the day he'd seen her last.

She'd stood on the shady front porch of her Philadelphia home, in a starched white shirtdress that didn't dare show a wrinkle, her hair pulled back so tight it was a miracle it didn't come clean off her head.

All the proper young men had gone off to fight the rebels and here he was haring off to find treasure. Mama swore she'd never forgive him. Not because he wouldn't defend the Union, but because he wouldn't take her with him.

He hadn't wanted to look at her as he left; she had a way of tearing strips off him with just her hard black eyes. So he gave her just a quick glance, then climbed on his mule and left her behind.

The mule was dead now, on account of the heat, its body broiling in the sun somewhere back in the desert. And Noah had yet to find even a trace of the silver he'd come seeking. Mama would be right pleased.

But now, surely his luck had turned. Two days ago, half-dead of thirst, he'd stumbled across a Pima village by the Gila River. The Indians gave him food and water and that night by the fire, they told him about Hoyo del Diablo. About the silver all through its limestone walls, and gold, too. Riches ready for the taking.

Riches, and a monster.

Another wisp of sound tickled his ears, brushed against his skin like a spiderweb. A whimper seemed to want to make its way up his throat and he swallowed it back. Surely, there was nothing there. He just had a touch of the crazies, from too much time alone. From dreams of Mama and her wagging finger.

When his toes first tipped over the lip of the abyss, Noah thought he was done for. He flapped his arms in a panic, the lantern light shuddering and flickering. Sheer luck he fell back on his behind instead of pitching forward.

Once he'd gathered his wits and pulled himself up onto hands and knees, he crept to the edge of the drop-off. He grabbed up the lantern and swung it out over the empty space, looking for the bottom. His straining eyes saw nothing but blackness. Hand shaking, he picked up a pebble and tossed it in; he listened for a long while before he heard the faint clatter of the stone striking the walls of the pit.

Well, now, that explained the rock he'd kicked. No monster hand had picked it up; it had simply fallen into the abyss. And the whispery sounds, well, they must be on account of the big empty space twisting his footsteps around and echoing them back to him.

Noah struggled to his feet and brushed off his baggy trousers, knees still shaking from the near disaster. He would have to step carefully around the yawning hole, to look for a way around it. He bent slightly, lantern hung low, to see what he could of the edge.

It didn't feel like hands on him, exactly. More like a bump

or a shove, almost as if the cavern's rock wall had squeezed in tight against him. Before he knew it, his feet flailed in empty air as he hurtled past the sheer face of the abyss.

In those last moments of terror, he couldn't be sure what hung above him on the precipice. A formlessness, blacker than the darkness around it. The heaviness of evil dripping from it.

His name whispered one last time.

Chapter One

Lordy, how could a dead man be so danged happy?

Noah Simmons drifted along the twisty narrow corridor deep within Hoyo del Diablo, his ghostly self fair to bursting with joy. After more than a hundred years of isolation, with only bats and spiders to break the loneliness, he was back among the company of civilized folk.

When the first group had climbed down the tangled passageways of Hoyo del Diablo, he'd thought they might be devils, sent by the monster. They had carried lanterns without flames, the brilliant light chasing away the dark. Unfamiliar words littered their speech—*computers, telecommunications, environmental control.*

When he'd realized they were people—ordinary men and women—he'd been beside himself. Human noise surrounded him again, filling up his empty soul.

Then he'd found *her*. His Lizzy.

She wasn't like any woman he'd ever met. In fact, he

5

hadn't known right off she was female, with her short hair and men's clothes. But when he'd seen her face, her blue eyes, he'd turned all soft inside. He'd been smitten, sure as rain.

And danged if he wasn't glad Mama wasn't around to poke her nose in and put a stop to it, like she had with Beulah Brown and Nessie Williams. He could love Lizzy with all his heart if he wanted and Mama couldn't do a blasted thing.

He'd watched Lizzy work with the others, day by day, bringing down equipment, machines like nothing he'd ever seen. Sometimes when her back was turned he would touch the things, surround them with his energy. After decades of practicing with stones and pebbles, it didn't take much more energy to shift a jug or a box across the floor.

She hadn't liked it—he'd seen that right away. She'd get all het up and return the thing to its proper place. She'd scowl at the thin air, never seeing him, but maybe knowing something was amiss.

Lordy, he loved her.

She was gone for now; all of them were, gone in groups in that newfangled elevator. He'd never had a chance to ride on an elevator, so when he first saw them use it, he followed them inside. He oozed through the door, found himself a place. But when the elevator started up, he slipped right through the grate at the bottom. The car carried the folks up to the surface, but left him behind in the dark shaft.

He guessed the elevator was off-limits, as were certain other pathways within Hoyo del Diablo. Then there were those places he would not go, where the *thing* still waited for him.

It didn't do to dwell upon those old memories. Instead, he'd think about *her*. With Mama long dead, nothing could stand between him and Lizzy. He loved her. And he knew once she saw him, she would feel the same for him.

That is, if he didn't scare the holy bejeezus out of her first.

PHOENIX, ARIZONA, PRESENT DAY

"To BioCave!"

Liz Madison raised her glass, her fingers tightening on the delicate crystal of her water goblet. As passionate as she was about the self-contained underground community of Bio-Cave, she couldn't bring herself to add her voice to those ringing around the banquet table. Not when she wanted nothing more than to toss her sparkling water into Ethan Winslow's drop-dead gorgeous face.

"And to the BioCave team!" Aaron Cohen added to his salutation, the maze of lines on his seventy-something face crinkling in delight.

Damn lucky for Ethan Winslow that he'd parked his six-foot-four at the other end of the table. Liz would have needed a hell of an arm to baptize him with her Perrier from where she sat.

She might have tried it, but she'd risk hitting Ethan's fiancée. Cynthia was too sweet to bean with a crystal goblet. God only knew why a woman as nice as her had hooked up with the surly geologist, no matter how tall, dark, and handsome he was.

"Hey, Ethan," Aaron said, his frail, bony frame dwarfed by the taller man's. "Getting nervous?"

It was pre-wedding jitters rather than Ethan's imminent descent into BioCave's underground caverns the old millionaire referred to. As if anything as trivial as tomorrow's nuptials would shake cold-as-ice Ethan Winslow. In her nastier moments, Liz suspected it wasn't love that drove the geologist to wed Dr. Cynthia Welles, but the fulfillment of Aaron's marrieds-only requirement for BioCave.

Damn, she should have tried that trick. Except there wasn't a man out there with whom she could spend six months in close quarters deep beneath Arizona's Sonoran Desert.

Certainly not Ethan Winslow. She despised Mr. Gorgeous, from his thick, dark hair to his size-twelve feet, and all parts in between. Sharing a tiny room in BioCave's subterranean community with Ethan Winslow would be a disaster.

Hell, the man must be psychic. He'd turned to look down the table at her, his steel-gray eyes fixed on her as if he knew she'd been thinking of him. Liz's hand tightened on her glass until it trembled and she felt the cool splash of liquid on her fingers.

Damned if she would look away first. She kept her gaze focused on him as her mouth went stone dry and her insides turned to jelly. Only Ethan Winslow could make her feel so unworthy, so like a child. Only he knew the buttons to push that set off all the old insecurities.

She felt stripped bare as his gaze burned into her, but she maintained eye contact. And finally, it was he who turned away, when Cynthia leaned in to whisper something to him and he had to give his attention to his fiancée.

Liz set down her glass, then lifted it again to drink, then nearly upset it when she returned it to the table. He'd done it to her again, despite her abhorrence of him, despite all her pent-up anger at his lordly arrogant ways. With one look he'd shaken her to her core.

"It's really too bad you won't be joining us," the man to her left said, drawing her attention from Ethan.

She smiled at Dr. Nishimoto, swallowing back her irritation. "Aaron promised me a spot as an aboveground monitor."

"Yes, but you deserve to be belowground with the rest of us." The elderly doctor patted her hand.

Liz forced herself to keep smiling. "I don't know that I'd get along with the resident ghost."

Dr. Nishimoto laughed, then turned to his wife to share Liz's joke. Actually, Liz would face the spirits of a dozen dead miners if it guaranteed her a spot in BioCave.

She swung her head back around to gaze at Aaron Cohen. She'd hoped her special relationship with the eccentric old millionaire would have been enough to persuade him to let her go belowground as a single. But he'd been adamant, insisting that married couples provided the most stability, that six months out of contact with the outside world would be too stressful without a life partner to face it with.

So in three days, Ethan Winslow and his soon-to-be wife would be taking up residence in Hoyo del Diablo, while Liz would be nursemaiding the staff from the aboveground monitoring station. Never mind that she had participated in every step of the planning stages, that the hydroponics lab had been designed with her needs in mind. As a single woman, she didn't meet the requirements.

"Please, Ethan!"

Cynthia Welles's hissing whisper carried clearly down to Liz, snapping her attention back to the geologist and his fiancée. Cynthia sat staring down at the table, her hand over her mouth. A curtain of silver-blonde hair half-concealed her face.

Ethan glowered down at her, his steel-gray eyes dangerous. Liz resisted the urge to spring to Cynthia's defense; she knew what it was like to be on the receiving end of his arrogant intimidation. He murmured something to his fiancée, the words lost in the noisy dinner conversation.

Cynthia dropped her hand, her delicate face set. "I can't." Her soft-spoken words were barely audible despite Liz's focused attention.

Liz gave up any pretense of listening to the chatter of those near her and turned toward Ethan Winslow. She knew that look on his face, like a storm growing in wrath. It was the same one she'd seen before he'd dressed her down in front of a roomful of people at a staff meeting. That had been the last straw; she'd quit GeoCore that afternoon, despite Aaron Cohen's pleading that she stay with his corporation.

"I never wanted to, Ethan," Cynthia said, her voice louder now. "It was always your idea."

Ethan must have sensed Liz watching, because he flicked his gaze at her, his hard eyes burning into hers. Tipping her chin up at him, she let a slight smile curve her lips. His anger bubbled in his face like a geothermal pool, sending a twinge of alarm down Liz's spine. She stood her ground, but relief washed over her when he returned his attention to Cynthia.

He cupped a hand under her elbow. "Let's go."

Cynthia, God love her, jerked her arm away. "No! Let's have this out, here and now."

That was enough to create a lull in the din of voices so that Ethan's piquant response dropped into the room, clear as crystal. "Damn it, Cynthia!"

A collective gasp circled the table followed by an avid, expectant quiet. Towering over his fiancée, one large hand again circling her arm, Ethan Winslow sent a thunderous look around the room. Gazes fell to the table, one by one. Except Liz's. Her smile widening to a grin, she tossed her head, sending her short brown hair back out of her eyes for a better look.

She didn't miss Ethan's low growl. And she might have let it be, looking away like the rest of them, out of respect for Cynthia's privacy, anyway. But then Ethan's fiancée rose to her feet, dignity around her like a cloak.

"Excuse me," she said into the continued silence of the room. "I have something to say."

Her voice trembled, and she kept her eyes averted from her fiancé's cold-as-steel gaze. "As much as I believe in BioCave, as important as I consider its goals of self-sufficient communities, of proving alternative energy sources . . ."

"Cynthia," Ethan interjected, his tone a warning.

Cynthia rolled right on, and Liz grinned in unabashed delight. ". . . I am declining my position on the BioCave staff. I cannot in good conscience leave my clinic or my patients."

Jaws dropped around the table; Liz's grin faded. Without Cynthia, BioCave would be short a physician. Liz tried to remember the specialties of the other two M.D.s on staff— Dr. Nguyen was a research pathologist while Dr. Nishimoto—

If Cynthia dropped out of the BioCave experiment, Ethan Winslow would have to, too. Liz was certain Aaron Cohen would enforce the marrieds-only rule for Ethan, in spite of how crucial the geologist was to the alternative energy aspect of the project. Aaron would have a hell of a time replacing someone of Ethan Winslow's stature.

As Ethan sank back into his seat, his rage visibly fraying his usual elegance, Liz tried to muster up some glee at his downfall. But somehow, sour grapes didn't seem to apply here. It took only one glimpse of Aaron Cohen's crestfallen face to realize that the entire experiment could be jeopardized by Cynthia Welles's backing out.

The buzz of voices resumed, no doubt chewing over Cynthia's bombshell. The blonde woman had moved to stand behind Aaron, and she leaned close to speak to him. A sudden thought sparked its way into Liz's mind as she watched the conversation. Had Cynthia only backed out of BioCave? Or was she jilting the great Ethan Winslow as well?

A preposterous notion filtered into Liz's mind and she had to smile at the insanity of it. If Ethan was back on the market, maybe she ought to snap him up. There would be nothing to bar her from joining the BioCave staff if she and the mean-tempered geologist wed. In fact, with Cynthia out, there'd be space for Liz, and Aaron wouldn't have to replace Ethan, and—

Liz slammed a lid on her line of thinking. It was making entirely too much sense.

She sneaked a peek at Ethan. What craziness it would be, marrying a man she'd despised for nearly five years, spending six months isolated with him in Hoyo del Diablo . . .

She caught sight of Aaron Cohen seated next to Ethan and her stomach clenched. The old man's gray pallor worried her, the anxiety in his rheumy blue eyes broke her heart.

You could fix everything, Liz, a little voice whispered inside.

Sure, just by marrying the devil, she retorted silently.

And yet . . . Liz returned her attention to Ethan Winslow, and forced herself to lock her gaze with his. The man damn well looked at her as if the whole thing were her fault, as if she'd somehow induced Cynthia's deviant behavior. Then, when she didn't look away, he raised one dark brow, as if daring her to do the unthinkable.

Then and there, Liz decided.

She was going to ask Ethan Winslow to marry her.

Liz gripped her Toyota's steering wheel, feeling like an utter fool. An hour after the BioCave celebration sputtered to an unlamented end at ten, here she sat like some kind of pervert outside Ethan Winslow's posh Scottsdale condo.

They were in there together, Ethan and his suddenly rebellious fiancée. Maybe by now the arrogant geologist had coaxed Cynthia into his arms and was now changing her mind in the most graphic way possible.

The thought of Ethan and Cynthia lying with limbs entwined in his bed started a wrangling in the pit of Liz's stomach. The insanity of her purpose for being here settled on her. Suddenly she wished her Toyota Camry was a time machine in which she could vanish into another century.

She must be a lunatic to think Ethan Winslow would be willing to marry gangly, strong-willed Liz, when he had the option of the sweet, incomparable Cynthia. BioCave or no BioCave, Ethan would no more agree to marry her than to—

The click of a closing door caught Liz's eye. She hunched down in her seat as Cynthia strode from the lobby entrance of Ethan's condo complex and headed for her Mercedes. Ethan watched her leave from inside the glass door. He'd discarded his suit jacket and rolled up the sleeves of his pale blue dress shirt. Night and the dimly lit lobby shadowed his expression.

The set of his shoulders told the story, though, as his gaze followed Cynthia's progress to her car. He was still angry; every tense line of his body blared it. Liz's spirits lifted as Cynthia's Mercedes tore off down the street.

Ethan turned from the door, sending Liz scrambling from the Toyota. She just managed to reach the glass door and rap on it before Ethan exited through the inner lobby door.

He turned again and slowly retraced his steps across the lobby toward her. She hadn't let herself be nervous until now, hadn't even given herself much chance to think of what she was going to say. It wouldn't have mattered if she'd rehearsed every word, because Ethan Winslow's steel-gray eyes, filled with a mix of suspicion, curiosity, and some indefinable other emotion, drove every thought clear from Liz's brain.

He tugged the locked security door open and tipped his head down toward her. "What is it?"

Staring up at him, she felt like such a wimp in her coral silk blouse and matching skirt. Why hadn't she gone home first to change into a T-shirt and jeans?

She stood up straighter, wobbling a little in her heels. "Can we talk?"

"What about?"

"About BioCave," she managed.

He quirked an eyebrow at her. "BioCave seems to be a moot point for me at this juncture."

Relief flooded Liz. "You didn't persuade her then?"

His brows drew together, the storm threatening again. "What is this all about?"

A chill trembled up Liz's spine despite the lingering Arizona heat of early June. "Could we go inside?"

One corner of his luscious mouth curved up in a sardonic smile. "Are you planning to ravish me, Ms. Madison?"

Liz tightened her arms around herself to keep from planting a fist in his amused face. "I just want to talk," she said through clenched teeth.

He hesitated, eyeing her as if seeking out the tasty parts, then opened the door wider. "Come on up, Ms. Madison."

His smug tone, as well as his formal use of her last name, irritated her. Despite their enmity, they'd always been on a first-name basis, even during those black days when he was her supervisor at Aaron Cohen's engineering firm. Addressing her by her surname was probably meant to get her goat.

Liz followed Ethan through the lush courtyard of his condominium complex, passing massive saguaro cactus and well-irrigated hibiscus. The mix of native and exotic plants produced a stunning effect of shape and color. *The water bill here must be staggering,* Liz mused, *just to keep those exotics alive in the desert sun.* One of the perks of living in a glitzy condo, she supposed.

"Ms. Madison?" Ethan pulled her attention from the profusion of purple-flowered drosanthemum.

He stood at his open door, one hand outstretched in invitation. Liz stared at his elegant fingers, the large, upturned palm. What would it feel like to draw her hand across his, trace her fingers up his wrist, to the crook of his elbow where his sleeve was rolled?

The sound of his feet shifting brought her mind back to where it belonged—to BioCave and the reason she'd come here. Cheeks flaring with heat, she ignored his proffered hand and swept past him through the door.

If the extravagant garden hadn't been indication enough of the richness of this place, Liz's first brief scan of Ethan's condo clinched it. The entryway floored in pillowed limestone, the oak moldings accenting the walls, the acres of oatmeal Berber carpet in the living room. She'd known Ethan Winslow came from money—he couldn't live here on a geologist's salary—and the opulence of this setting confirmed it.

Liz stepped into the living room and turned to take in the butter-soft leather sofa, its dove gray a shade lighter than his eyes. She itched to scan the titles in the bookcase that spanned the whole of the far wall. What kind of books would Ethan Winslow read? *How to Make Enemies and Intimidate Your Subordinates?*

"Adding up my net worth?" his low voice rumbled in her ear.

Liz nearly leaped out of her pumps. How did such a large man move so quietly? She whirled to face him, putting an extra foot or two of space between them.

"I don't give a damn about your net worth," she said.

He crossed his arms over his chest, the beleaguered cloth of his shirt straining at the shoulders. "I guess you wouldn't. You've already got yourself a millionaire."

Liz took a step toward him, hand clenching at her side. "What the hell is that supposed to mean?"

He just stared, his gray eyes chill with disdain. "Why are you here?"

The words scrambled in her mind, scattering like panicked children. She closed her eyes a moment, shook her head to clear it.

When she opened her eyes again to his intense gaze, she realized she couldn't do it. She couldn't frame her audacious proposition in any sensible way, couldn't produce the proper words to persuade Ethan Winslow to consider such a ridiculous notion.

She wished she could leave, or better yet, simply melt into the carpet and disappear. But she couldn't; she'd talked her way into Ethan Winslow's condo and she had to say something.

"You know we both want the same thing," she blurted out.

He gave her a wolfish grin. "Do I?"

Ignoring his innuendo, she shook the tension from her hands and paced away from him. "We both know how important BioCave is, the questions it can answer about increasing the world's food supply, developing cleaner energy sources—"

His large hands gripped her shoulders, cutting short her nervous rambling. She drew a trembling breath as he turned her toward him.

When she kept her gaze fixed on his chest, he cupped her chin in one warm hand and tipped it up to him. "Tell me why you're here."

When she would have tugged herself free, his grip tightened. Irritated with him, annoyed with her own reaction to his touch, she tossed out the words. "We should get married."

That got his attention. His taunting smile faded and his hands dropped from her. "We should get married," he parroted back.

"Right," she said. "To each other."

The smile returned, slightly bemused. "You and me."

"Yes," she said.

He seemed to swallow back a laugh. "And we should get married because . . ." He waited for her to complete the equation.

Run. Run out the door. But she stood her ground and pushed the words out in a rush. "So that we can both be part of BioCave. I qualify to be on staff, but I'm single. You're Aaron's golden boy, but without Cynthia . . ." Alarm settled in Liz's chest. "She *is* still out of the picture?"

"As far as BioCave is concerned, yes."

"But you still plan to get married?"

His cheek dimpled, startling her. "Of course."

"Right. Of course." Liz ignored a twinge of disappointment. "That makes it even better."

"Our getting married, you mean," he said, bracing one shoulder against the wall.

As he shifted his arms, the play of ropy muscles drew her eyes from his face, distracting her for a moment. She snapped her gaze back up.

"If you and Cynthia still plan to wed, we'll have a clear understanding we're marrying for convenience sake only. To allow both of us to achieve an agreed upon goal."

"BioCave," he said.

"Right." She was pleased that he hadn't refused her out of hand.

"So there wouldn't be any . . ." He raised one brow evocatively. ". . . between us."

Liz took an involuntary step backward. "No. Of course not. It'd be a marriage of convenience. We wouldn't need to . . ." Liz fluttered a hand at him.

". . . be intimate," he finished for her.

"No." Her eyes widened when he pushed off from the wall and moved toward her.

"Despite the fact that we'd be man and wife." He moved closer, eyes steady on hers.

Liz retreated another step, felt the soft leather sofa stroke her calves. "In name only."

"We'd be sharing a space smaller than this living room." He stood over her now, his broad shoulders filling her field of vision. "Sleeping in the same bed."

That complication hadn't even crossed Liz's mind. "Maybe it wouldn't be such a great idea, after all."

He tipped his head down so that she could feel his breath warming her face. "Yes."

"It was ridiculous to even suggest it." Liz shrank back against the sofa, trying to eke a fraction of space between them. "I'll just go now." She feinted to the left.

He curved his hand around her upper arm. "Yes, I'll marry you."

She froze, the flesh under his fingers burning with his imprint. "You'll what?"

His thumb shifted, tracing a path along her sensitive inner arm. His gray eyes seemed to darken. They flicked down to her mouth, his gaze skimming her lips a moment before they returned to her eyes.

He backed away, releasing her arm. "I agree, we should get married." He shoved his hands into the pockets of his dress slacks, rocked back on his heels. "Cynthia's adamant— she won't abandon her patients. I know you've paid your dues as far as BioCave's concerned; you deserve to be part of it. And I damn well won't be shut out for lack of a willing spouse."

Liz crossed her trembling arms around her middle. "But what's Cynthia going to think when you tell her you're marrying me?"

He shrugged. "She'll understand the arrangement will be for convenience sake only. She knows there's no great love lost between you and me." His gaze sharpened on her.

"What about Aaron? How will he feel about it?"

Liz drew her brows together, puzzled by the intensity of the question. "He won't like the fact we're doing an end run around his marrieds-only rule. Other than that, why would he care?"

Ethan's gray gaze raked her from head to toe. "Why indeed?"

His hidden message set off a warning in her that she chose to ignore. "So what about . . . the sleeping arrangements?"

He smirked. "You think I can't resist your charms for six months?"

Heat rose in her cheeks. "Of course you can. It's not as if I'm any great beauty like Cynthia."

He tipped his head at her, his faint smile more genuine. "Don't sell yourself short, Ms. Madison."

Now what was *that* supposed to mean? Liz was dying to ask, but didn't dare. She had what she'd come for—an agreement from Ethan and an entrée to BioCave. She could leave now.

She edged toward the front door. "We'll need to get right on the marriage license, the blood tests."

"I can pull a few strings." He followed her progress to the door.

She laughed, an edgy sound. "I suppose it would be tacky to just erase Cynthia's name from the license."

The dimple winked in again. "I'll take care of it. I'll let you know where to go for the blood test."

She groped for the doorknob. "Is there time? The BioCave experiment starts in three days."

"I'll handle it," he told her. "Don't worry."

Liz's fingers grazed the sleek oak of the door, then grabbed the handle like a lifeline. "But Cynthia . . . how's she going to feel when you cancel your wedding tomorrow?"

He sighed, then closed the distance between them. "We'd already agreed to postpone the wedding. We hadn't planned any great ceremony, just a justice of the peace and dinner with a few friends." He reached out and swept a lock of hair from her eyes. "It'll work out, Liz. I'll take care of it."

Before she could react, before she could even think, he leaned close and pressed his lips to her forehead, letting them linger there for a long, warm moment. Then he straightened and backed away.

"I'll call you tomorrow," he said brusquely.

Liz felt like Dorothy in *The Wizard of Oz* when the good witch Glinda marked her with her kiss. She was certain when she looked in the mirror, she'd see Ethan Winslow's brand.

But there was nothing good about Ethan Winslow, especially now when an inexplicable anger clouded his face. What the hell was he so mad about?

"Listen," Liz said, "we don't have to—"

"I'll call you." He reached around her to open the door. His hand covered hers on the handle, lingering even after the door was open.

Liz retraced her path across the courtyard, the warmth of the Arizona night suffusing her, the scent of honeysuckle teasing her with its sweetness. Although she didn't dare look back, she could feel his eyes bore into her with each step. She allowed herself one sidelong glance as she slipped through the security door and saw him standing rigid in his doorway, his hard face in silhouette.

What have I done? she asked herself as she started her car with trembling hands. *What in God's name have I done?*

A marriage of convenience, she told herself. *That's all it is.*

But as she threaded her way through the dark streets toward home, she couldn't help but think she'd made a deal with the devil.

Chapter Two

How could that man be marrying his Lizzy?

Noah stood in the yawning main cavern of Hoyo del Diablo, glaring at the tall, dark-haired man called Ethan. He was good-looking, Noah supposed, one of them big, brawny types. But Noah didn't like the way this Ethan treated his Lizzy, nor how he looked at her when he thought no one was watching. Noah watched him, all right, and he dang well didn't like what he saw.

Lizzy shivered in her pretty rose silk dress, her face pale and her eyes scared. Sure as anything, that Ethan fellow had put that fear in her face. Noah might not know the how or why of it, but he would take it upon himself to keep Lizzy safe. From bullies like Ethan, from things that burrowed deep in the dark.

A tremor passed through Noah. Pushing away the memories, he turned his focus to the words the reverend spoke.

Liz tipped her face up to the wan sunbeams filtering down the light shaft high above her. The faint sunlight glittered off the stalactites stretching down from the ceiling, but couldn't chase the chill that had settled deep within her, couldn't begin to warm her soul. She'd thought she'd come to accept her deal with the devil, but now, standing beside him . . .

Her bare arm, goose-pimpled by the cool air, lay snugged against Ethan's arm. He'd curved his other hand over hers, and his thumb was unexpectedly restless against the back of her wrist.

Maybe it wasn't too late, Liz thought. Maybe if she gave Ethan a shove and kicked off her low-heeled leather pumps, she could sprint for the exit of the vast cavern and to the elevator before he recovered. She might lose BioCave, but she'd retain her soul.

She stayed put.

The bodies crowded into the echoing space shifted in Liz's periphery like multicolored blobs. In the mix of sixteen belowground staff and a dozen or so of the aboveground monitors, only Aaron Cohen's face seemed distinct. He gazed at her, his pale blue eyes troubled, his aged face lined in sadness.

Maybe she shouldn't have been honest with Aaron. Maybe she shouldn't have revealed the truth about her marriage of convenience. It might have been better to tell him the same story they'd told the others—that she and Ethan had fallen in love during the planning of BioCave, and Cynthia had stepped graciously aside in favor of Liz.

Hah! As if Aaron would have ever believed such a fairy tale. That was nearly as lunatic a concept as marrying a man she hated.

The justice of the peace droned on. It seemed so callous to treat the marriage vows this way, to join a man and woman who would doubtless be at each other's throats the moment the knot was tied.

Restless, she looked past Ethan into the crowd beyond. Dr. Nishimoto stood beside his misty-eyed wife, Wendy, the Jacksons just beyond them. A man wedged between the

Nishimotos and the Jacksons stared at her intently, his unfamiliar face teasing a faint memory.

Where had she seen that boyish face before? Mentally, she went through the list of aboveground staff, but she couldn't place the red hair, the brown eyes. And that hat—it looked like a porkpie from the 1800s.

Ethan's low, solemn rumble, "I do," pulled Liz from her reverie.

Good God, they were halfway there. Now it was her turn. The justice of the peace directed his attention toward her and the words spilled from his lips in a garble. She comprehended not a one of them until he finished with, ". . . as long as you both shall live?"

Liz gasped, the shock of the words knifing through her. There was nothing lifelong about her commitment to Ethan; why hadn't he asked to have the vow cut from the ceremony? She glanced at Ethan sidelong. He'd just promised forever, without batting an eye.

If Mr. Ethics could do it, Liz supposed she could, too. She opened her mouth, but nothing but air sifted out. She swallowed, tried again, and muttered, "I do."

The justice of the peace beamed. "You may kiss the bride."

Run away, her panicked brain screamed. *Run away.* Her feet remained rooted to the spot, as if the stone floor of the common room had melded to them.

Warm hands curled around her upper arms, tugged her around. Her traitorous feet moved obligingly enough at Ethan Winslow's command, shifting so that they stood toe to toe with him. As his hands glided up to cup her shoulders, Liz rested tentative fingers against the front of his dark, elegant jacket.

She tipped her head back, bracing herself for the mocking smile she knew she'd see on his face. It was there as she'd expected, the faintest curl of his lip that spoke volumes about how little he thought of her. Yet another message roiled in his gray eyes—confusion, puzzlement, a reluctant heat.

Just a quick peck on the lips, that was all that was necessary. She rose a little on tiptoe, leaning her head back farther to give him better access. She pursed her lips as she
would when kissing Aaron's weathered cheek and closed her
eyes.

His hands tightened on her shoulders, the imprint of each
finger plain. She waited for the brush of his lips. And waited.
Until her lips felt cramped from their tight pucker. She relaxed her mouth and let her eyes drift open.

Terror filled her.

She'd stood up to Ethan Winslow countless times. During
those hateful two years she'd worked under him at GeoCore.
On the rare occasions she'd crossed his path at environmental
conventions. And in the last nine months of planning
BioCave, when he seemed to find every excuse to challenge
her.

But she'd never before had to contend with what she saw
in his face now. Desire so raw it set every limb to trembling,
a fire in his eyes she was sure would consume her if she
didn't back away quickly.

He pulled her closer.

He seemed angry with his passion, as if it was somehow
her fault. Indignation rose, ire that he blamed her yet again
for something she'd had no part in. There was nothing particularly sexy or sensual about her; how the hell could she
have had anything to do with arousing him?

She thought his gray eyes would ignite. They burned into
her, searing along her nerve endings, sensation pooling like
warm honey between her legs. Anticipation flared in her,
sharp and impatient.

"Well," she whispered, chin tipped up, "are you going
to kiss me or not?"

The wildfire jumped its boundaries. With a growl, he
dipped his head and covered her mouth with his. Surprise
parted her lips—shock at his assault, not the heat of his
mouth, the groan rumbling low in his throat. His tongue

thrust inside and Liz clutched at the lapels of his suit jacket to keep her knees from giving way.

She heard his rumble of satisfaction as he cupped the back of her head with one hand, fitted the other into the small of her back. She felt him along her full length now, her breasts against his chest, her legs against his powerful thighs, her hips pressed against the tantalizing hardness in between.

He pulled back, just far enough for his face to come back into focus. What she saw in his eyes startled her—a softness, a tenderness that seemed incomprehensible in Ethan Winslow. She lifted her hand, brought it against his cheek, an involuntary caress.

He turned to press a kiss into her palm, his eyes closing for a moment. Then he stepped back, and the mocking smile was back, erasing the gentleness she'd seen before. Hell, she'd probably just imagined it.

The sound of shuffling feet and the murmur of laughter intruded, bringing the heat of embarrassment to her cheeks. God, how could she have stood here and pawed Ethan Winslow in front of all these people? As she scanned the crowd surreptitiously, Aaron Cohen's grinning face caught her eye. What the hell was he so happy about?

Beside her, Ethan cleared his throat and tucked her hand back into the crook of his arm. He turned to the crowd gathered in the common room. "I'd like to introduce my wife," he said, his voice booming through the cavern, "Mrs. Ethan Winslow."

Liz shot him a dark look. "The name is Liz Madison."

He smiled at the justice of the peace as he shook the man's hand. "It's Liz Winslow now."

Liz pasted on a smile and greeted a well-wisher. "Madison. I'm keeping my maiden name."

Ethan accepted the congratulations of the next in line. "Not as long as you're married to me."

"You know damn well this isn't a real—"

His warning squeeze on her shoulder cut her off. "Dr.

Nishimoto,'' he said as the elderly Asian man stepped up next.

Ethan patently ignored Liz's glare. She might as well leave the issue of her name until later when they could be alone. She turned back to the line of people, offering her hand.

And nearly snatched it back when she saw the man who stood there. ''Richard. What are you doing here?''

The baby-faced botanist compressed his mouth into a thin-lipped smile as he grasped her hand limply. ''I'm on staff.''

''You can't be,'' Liz said. ''Joe Miller has the other botanist slot.''

His grin wasn't friendly. ''His wife turned up pregnant. I'm taking his place as head botanist.''

An unease settling in Liz's stomach had her groping for Ethan's hand. ''*I'm* head botanist. I'll be running the hydroponics lab.''

Richard's eyes narrowed on her. ''Who told you that?''

Liz locked her fingers with Ethan's. ''Aaron. He gave me the assignment yesterday.''

''He promised that to me,'' Richard hissed. He leaned close, craning his neck up so that a few pale strands of his sparse hair slipped into his eyes. ''Cohen told me I could run the lab.''

''I'm sure he intends for us to work together.'' Just the thought gave Liz heartburn.

''But you'd be the lead.'' His mouth twisted into a nasty frown. ''You've pushed me aside, just like before. Just because you and that filthy old man—''

Liz gasped, outrage thundering through her. She clenched her free hand into a fist, determined to plant it in Richard Niedan's face. But before she could so much as cock her arm back, Ethan had whirled and shoved the botanist aside.

''Do you have a problem with my wife, Niedan?'' Ethan said, his voice calm and measured.

Liz shivered at the threat beneath the layers of control. Richard, obviously too dense to recognize it, puffed up his chest in indignation. "Only when she steals something that belongs to me."

Liz tugged at Ethan's arm. "Leave it, Ethan."

He shrugged off her hand, his focus fixed on Richard. "And what would that be?"

"The lead position in the hydro lab. Cohen promised it to me."

"Because we didn't have a better qualified candidate," Ethan told him. "Now we do."

Richard's gaze raked Liz from head to toe. "Better qualified?" He smirked. "You know damn well her best qualification is that she and Aaron Cohen—"

Ethan's fist shot out before Liz could so much as blink, and connected with Richard Niedan's face with a satisfying smack. Richard hit the deck with his nose spouting blood, hollering as if he'd been killed.

Phoebe Niedan, a woman far too nice to be married to a jerk like Richard, hurried to crouch at her husband's side. "What happened?" She pressed a handful of tissues against his bloody nose.

"I slipped," Richard said before Liz or Ethan could answer.

Ethan rubbed his knuckles as he towered over the botanist. "Yes, you did," he said quietly. "Be careful, Niedan. Don't let it happen again."

Richard gave Liz a hateful look over the wad of tissues, then focused his attention on his wife who was clucking over him. "We'd better have Dr. Nishimoto look at this," she said.

He pushed off her hands and rose. "It'll be fine. It's just a bloody nose."

One last venomous glare at Liz and Richard headed out of the common room, Phoebe at his elbow. Liz took a long breath and released the tension in her shoulders.

She looked up at Ethan. "Thank you."

He shrugged, his expression impenetrable. "Six months is

a damn long time to have Niedan questioning your authority at every turn.''

Aaron approached, his jacket discarded, his dress shirt baggy on his skinny frame. He bobbed his head toward the exit that Richard and Phoebe had just passed through. ''He going to be a problem?''

''Actually, Aaron—'' Liz began.

''I think we've set him straight,'' Ethan cut in.

''It's not too late to make a substitution. Now that we've got the best heading the hydro lab,'' he nodded toward Liz, ''we can cut some slack on the back-up botanist.''

Liz tried again. ''Aaron, I—''

''Not necessary,'' Ethan said. ''I'll make sure Niedan won't give her any more trouble.''

''Excuse me, can I say something, please?'' Liz asked.

''Of course, Lizzy.'' Aaron turned to her with a smile. ''I'm all ears.''

Ethan's gray eyes held a message, a warning maybe, or a challenge. As if he expected her to demand that Aaron remove the annoying botanist from BioCave. She turned her back on Ethan, her focus on Aaron.

''Richard Niedan's a pain in the butt,'' Liz told Aaron, ''but I can deal with him.''

''Great.'' Aaron rubbed his hands together. A pleased smile lit his face as he looked from her to Ethan. ''This is all going to work out just fine.''

Ethan murmured something noncommittal, then turned to Liz. ''Why don't I meet you in our quarters in a bit? There's something I have to discuss with Aaron.''

''About BioCave?''

''Nothing that concerns you.''

Irritation roiled inside her at his dismissive tone. She nodded curtly. ''I have to check supplies in the hydro lab anyway.''

Ethan traced a finger along a strand of dark hair that had fallen across her forehead, his touch melting her annoyance.

"Later, then." His fingertip continued along the line of her jaw.

"Later." Damn that tremor in her voice.

His smile seemed almost tender as he gazed down at her. The kiss he brushed across her lips sent a shiver straight through her. But when he pulled back, his gaze seemed shuttered, almost angry. He strode away from her, heading toward Aaron without a backward glance. Deep in conversation, the two left the common room.

What the hell had that been all about? Liz wondered. She gulped in a lungful of air and rubbed her hands over her arms to cast off the rest of Ethan's touch.

Should she go to their quarters first to change? She was dying to get out of that damn dress and into jeans. But she'd just as soon put off as long as possible her first encounter with Ethan in the small space of their quarters.

Lord, what had possessed her to do this? How could she have thought she could live side-by-side with Ethan Winslow for six months underground?

Thank God Wallace Nishimoto would be heading up BioCave, and not Ethan. Before she could push them away, memories of her days at GeoCore closed in on her. The dread she'd felt walking in the door each morning, uncertain if before the end of the day, Ethan Winslow would tear into her, belittling her every effort, leaving her ego in shreds.

Thank God that nightmare was over. It would be enough of a challenge sharing quarters with him without having him call the shots in BioCave.

But what would she do about these rampant fantasies? Those wedding vows had been curiously liberating for her libido. If she couldn't keep her wandering thoughts under control she might be sleeping in the lab tonight.

As she turned toward the exit, the back of her neck prickled, as if someone watched her. The red-haired young man with the intense brown eyes? She scanned the room, searching for him, but it seemed he'd gone.

A trace of unease tickling up her spine, Liz left the common room and headed for her hydro lab.

Ethan strode down the corridor toward his quarters, barely controlling the urge to put a fist through the limestone wall. He'd end up with broken knuckles and a bloody hand, but right now he could use that kind of distraction.

It was tempting to blame his savage mood on Aaron's disturbing news. But he knew his foul temper had nothing to do with the latest peril to BioCave and everything to do with Liz Madison's mile-long legs.

Liz Winslow, he corrected himself as he stepped inside the tiny quarters. *My wife.*

Who would soon be sharing this minuscule space with him, a twelve foot by twelve foot square room carved out of rock. Who would be sleeping by his side on the pull-down Murphy bed now stowed against the wall. Who would be showering in the tiny bathroom, water coursing down her lean, tanned body . . .

With a growl, Ethan flung his suit jacket across the room, trying with the force of his throw to drive the erotic image from his mind. He pitched his duffel bag after it, and it slammed against the Murphy bed with a satisfying crunch.

What the hell have I done?

He could still feel the touch of her hand on his cheek, the feel of her lips against his. The tissue-thin silk dress had seemed to melt when he held her so he could almost feel her bare skin against his palms.

Ethan muttered an obscenity under his breath, cutting off the memory. He'd always prided himself on his self-control where women were concerned—which was why he'd chosen cool, reserved Cynthia. But Liz, with her lean, athletic body, the dark silk of her short hair and the fire in her blue eyes . . . Anger roiled in him again, that she so easily took away his self-control.

And self-control was something he would need desperately during the BioCave experiment. Aaron's report of more missing supplies and damaged equipment had the old millionaire a heartbeat away from indefinitely postponing the experiment. Only Ethan's repeated assurances that he could handle the potential problems persuaded Aaron otherwise.

He took in a calming breath, easing away the last of his agitation. For the hundredth time, he wished he and Cynthia hadn't left things so unsettled. She'd seemed almost relieved when he'd told her about his proposed marriage to Liz. The six months apart would give them some breathing space, Cynthia had said. She trusted him completely with Liz.

Ill-placed trust, Ethan thought with a grimace. With his engagement on the verge of dissolving, and neither he nor Cynthia caring much about that, he didn't even have a promise of fidelity to hold him back. Not when Liz rubbed every nerve ending raw with nothing more than a smile.

Ethan pondered the enigma that was Liz Madison. Despite the way she'd risen so rapidly in the ranks at GeoCore, he'd come to admit reluctantly that she was a top-notch botanist. By the time she'd left the company two years ago, he'd realized her relationship with Aaron Cohen might have had less to do with her fast progression than her ability.

Ethan didn't like to speculate about the closeness between Liz and Aaron. She was fifty years his junior—surely the relationship stopped at the bedroom door. But when Ethan considered the extensive financial help Liz had accepted— her tuition at the University of Arizona, the Phoenix condo, her new car—it left a bad taste in Ethan's mouth.

Aaron deserved a little comfort in his sunset years—especially after losing his beloved wife last year to a stroke. What the old millionaire didn't need was a gold-digging opportunist like Liz.

Turning restlessly, Ethan scanned his and Liz's cramped quarters. The living/sleeping space boasted a built-in desk, the pull-down double bed, a small closet and dresser. The natural rock walls had been painted a light, soothing shade— not just an aesthetic consideration, since the special paint acted as a vapor barrier. The vivid cushions on the built-in rough-sawn wood bench and the wash of color in the Native American wall-hangings accented the otherwise drab room.

Ethan grabbed his duffel and carried it to the dresser. The top drawer was already full—neatly folded T-shirts were crammed next to a colorful array of tightly rolled panties. She'd appropriated the second drawer for sweaters and jeans, leaving the bottom two for him.

He quickly unloaded his duffel into the dresser, then stuffed his jacket inside the empty bag to take back above-ground. His gaze fell again on the Murphy bed, stowed vertically against the wall.

He laughed, a dry, humorless sound. He was ten times a fool if he thought he could sleep beside Liz in that narrow bed without reacting to her. He'd be hard as the rock walls surrounding him imagining those endless legs wrapped around him in the dark. It would only be a matter of time before the powerful attraction between them exploded.

Ethan stripped off his shirt and trousers, dropping them into the duffel before heading for the tiny bathroom. They had only a few hours before lockdown, when the last of the traffic to and from the surface would cease. He had another load to bring down before then.

Unwilling to take the time to shower, he dashed a couple handfuls of water onto his face and let them drizzle down his chest. Thoughts of Liz's long legs still vivid in his mind, his body reacted predictably, thrusting against the navy knit of his shorts. He wasted another handful of water on his face in a useless attempt to cool himself down. Not even the constant mid-fifties temperature of Hoyo del Diablo could chill his overactive libido.

He heard her footsteps in the corridor outside and briefly considered sliding the bathroom door shut. But hell, she was bound to see him dressed in even less sooner or later; they might as well get the awkwardness out of the way now. Scrubbing his face dry with a towel, he strode from the bathroom.

The plant in her hands nearly took a nose dive to the rock

floor. She only just managed to steady it, spilling some kind of fluid from the pot as she did so. Her blue eyes wide and startled, she didn't seem to know where to look, fixing her gaze first on his bare chest, then skimming past the danger zone to his legs, then settling on his face.

By God, she was blushing! He would have laughed at the notion if the throbbing between his legs weren't so damn painful. She seemed to sense his discomfort and the cause of it, because her gaze drifted down to the swath of blue fabric that barely contained his erection.

If anything, the rose of her cheeks deepened. He heard the catch in her breath, sensed the fine trembling in her hands. Her lips parted, making him want to taste what lay within, to run his palms across her sensitive nape bared by the short cut of her hair.

He took a step toward her before he stopped himself. He'd damn well better think of something else, or he'd have her on the floor with her long legs around his waist, thrusting deep inside her.

He crossed to the dresser and dug through it for a pair of jeans and a T-shirt, drew them on. "All set in the lab?"

She turned away from him to set the plant on the desk. "I'm short a case of nutrient solution."

They were already on the list of missing items Aaron had given him. Replacements were on their way. "Maybe it's still aboveground."

She shook her head. "They were all accounted for yesterday. Now one is missing." She brushed at the dark stain spreading across the front of her dress. "Damn. You think this stuff will come out?"

The wet silk clung to her breasts, shaping their curve. Her bra seemed a scarce barrier to the most intimate details of her body.

He reached into the bathroom for a towel and tossed it to her. "I have another load to bring down. I can check for your case in the last shipment."

As she swiped at the front of her dress with the towel, the

friction brought her nipple out in sharp relief. Ethan watched, figuring he might as well enjoy the view. He was a damn glutton for punishment.

She caught him looking. With a strangled gasp, she whipped her arms across her breasts. "Let me change. I'll go with you."

She hurried to the small dresser and pulled out a handful of clothes. Clutching them to her chest, she raced to the bathroom and slid the door shut. A useless gesture, since he could vividly picture her undressing in the small room. Tearing his eyes from the closed door, he bent to the task of pulling on his Nikes.

She reappeared a few minutes later in a red camp shirt and khaki shorts that ended at mid-thigh. It was impossible to avoid looking at her; he might as well look all he wanted. So as she seated herself at the desk to strap on her sandals, he ran his gaze from her trim ankles up shapely calves to her tantalizing thighs. Gooseflesh had risen on her tanned skin in reaction to the cool subterranean air. "You'll freeze to death in those shorts," he told her.

Her head swung up and her eyes locked on his. It might have been courteous to pretend he hadn't been watching, but since when had he been the noble type? He trailed his gaze again down her legs.

"I only brought the one pair," she said. "I thought since I'd be going up to the surface again—"

"Two more hours until lockdown," he said, suddenly impatient to leave. "We'd better get going."

She unfolded herself from the chair, a wary look in her eyes as she moved past him out the door. Swinging his duffel bag to his shoulder, he followed her into the narrow rock corridor.

He might have thought Liz less tempting outside of their quarters. But just being at her side was damned erotic. The nape of her neck, bare from the top of her collar to the short wedge of her sleek dark hair, begged his fingers to touch it, his tongue to taste. Ethan dragged his eyes away and focused on the overhead low-voltage fluorescents that illuminated the corridor.

"Are the photovoltaic cells up to capacity?" Liz asked as they turned down a side corridor toward the elevator.

"Not yet. I found a glitch in the wiring, spent all day yesterday to correct it."

"I'd wondered why the hydroponics pumps were on standby." She tapped the elevator button, then turned to Ethan. "What about the wind generators?"

"On-line."

He stood aside to let her enter the elevator first. When she turned to face the corridor, her eyes widened as if she'd seen something peculiar. Before he could follow her gaze, the doors slid shut, cutting off their view.

"What?" he asked when her brow furrowed.

She shook her head. "Nothing."

As the elevator rose the one hundred feet to the surface, Ethan entertained a brief fantasy of making love to her here, hot and quick. He grit his teeth against the image.

The elevator opened onto BioCave's main aboveground observation post, a glass and wood atrium built onto the mountainside's rock face. Although the elevator shaft was man-made, the entrance itself and much of the underground living and working space took advantage of Hoyo del Diablo's system of natural caves.

Liz paused to take in the half-dozen large-screen video displays that eavesdropped on BioCave's public areas—the mess hall/common room, the kitchen, Liz's hydroponics lab, Ethan's energy center. Ethan supposed he should be grateful Aaron hadn't set up cameras in the private quarters.

Liz gestured to the monitors. "How do you feel about being on display?"

"It's only from nine to five while the tourists are here. I can keep my language clean for that long." Unable to resist, he lay his hand on the small of her back, guiding her to the exit. He felt her shiver before she shrugged away from his touch.

When they entered the airlock, the temperature rose a good twenty degrees, auguring what awaited them outside the second door. After the coolness of BioCave's subterranean chambers and the air-conditioned atrium, the Arizona heat nearly stole Ethan's breath away with its intensity.

"God, it's only June." Liz hurried to one of the four-wheel-drive pickups Aaron had provided to transport supplies and equipment. "Makes me glad I'm spending the summer underground."

Ethan watched her stride toward the truck, the supple movements of her arms and legs tantalizing. She hesitated briefly when she saw the large cardboard box in the truck bed, then reached over to tug it closer.

"You were right," she said, puzzlement in her tone. "Here's the last case of solution. But I could have sworn . . ."

"We've all been working hard." He tossed his duffel into the back of the truck. "You probably just miscounted."

Liz turned to him, speculation clear in her gaze. She had to sense he was keeping something from her, but he hoped to hell she wouldn't push the issue.

She shrugged, then wrapped her arms around the cardboard box. She lifted it, staggering a little under its weight.

"Let me get that," he said.

"You have your own stuff to carry," she gasped, trying to blow her damp bangs from her eyes.

He tugged the box from her arms. "My gear's lighter. If you'd grab that red duffel and the backpack . . ."

She reached into the truck bed, her shirt already plastered to her back by sweat. She slung the duffel and backpack over her shoulders, then headed back to the monitoring station.

He followed, shifting the box to hold it more comfortably. She pulled open the door for him and stood aside. Even the still-warm air of the airlock was a relief; the chill air of the atrium itself even better.

Liz sighed and eased duffel and backpack to the cool tile floor. She wiped beads of sweat from her brow, shaking the drops from her bangs.

Ethan watched her, wondering what her heated flesh would taste like against his tongue. A drop of moisture lay on her temple and he contemplated brushing it clean with his lips.

The edges of the cardboard box cut into his hands, dragging him back from his wayward thoughts. Angry that she so easily distracted him, Ethan had to resist the urge to hurl the box across the atrium.

"I've got work to do," he said. "Where do you want this?"

She gave him a sharp look, her eyes narrowing. "The hydro lab."

He brushed past her and headed for the elevator. "Let's go."

Liz glared at Ethan's retreating back. "Didn't take long for Mr. Personality to show his true colors," she muttered under her breath.

One of the techs looked up from her monitoring post. "What's that?"

"Nothing." Liz slung Ethan's gear back over her shoulders and followed him.

"Come on." He waited in the elevator, one broad hand holding the door in place.

She slipped past him, not particularly concerned when the duffel banged against him. He slapped the button to take the car down, then leaned against the elevator wall, arms across his chest, one foot propped on top of the cardboard box.

"When do they kill power to the elevator?" Liz asked as the car glided belowground.

He waited until the elevator stopped and the doors opened before he answered. "At lockdown."

She exited the car, trying to squeeze past without touching him, but he seemed to fill the space and her arm grazed his. From just that slight touch, arousal washed over her like a wave of Arizona heat.

She bolted down the narrow rock corridor, trying to outrun him, outrun her emotions. Adding to her unease, a prickle started down her spine, as if someone besides Ethan followed her. She resisted the urge to turn and look. God forbid Ethan should think she was looking for him.

He caught up with her, the heavy box barely a burden in his powerful arms. "Having second thoughts?"

And third and fourth. Between her clamorous libido and strangers, real or imagined, dogging her footsteps, who wouldn't? "Of course not."

"If you do, tell me now. We only have another hour or so to return aboveground."

She halted at the door to the hydroponics lab, gasping for breath. "I'm not backing out now." She pushed open the door. "Not after all I went through to get here."

He followed her inside. "You'd think you'd sold your soul to the devil."

She couldn't stop the shudder that shook her. "If I have, this would be the place to do it."

He stared at her intently. "Are you afraid, Mrs. Winslow?"

"It's Madison." She was terrified, but damned if she'd let him usurp her name.

He dropped the box of nutrient solution to the rock floor of the lab, the plastic bottles inside rattling with the violence of his action. Whirling to face him, she tossed duffel bag and backpack at his feet.

"Thanks for your help," she snapped.

He took a long breath, as if groping for patience. "Where do you want these?" He gestured at the box.

"I can handle those myself," she told him. "I'm sure you have your own work to do."

She saw his jaw tighten in barely suppressed anger. Then without another word, he bent to rip open the box, his strong hands making short work of the packing tape.

"I said I don't need any more of your help."

Ethan didn't answer. He pulled the jugs in pairs from the box and stowed them under a worktable. Muscles rippled across his broad back as he worked, a mesmerizing display.

Stop it, she told herself, *stop acting like an idiot.* Aloud, she said, "Suit yourself," and turned to a cardboard box full of reference books. She kept her back to him as she loaded the volumes onto a bookcase.

"Liz."

She whirled around, dropping the book in her hand, and found him standing far too close to her. She tried to step back, but the bookcase stopped her.

"What?" Her voice was damnably breathy. She tipped her head back to look up at him and for a crazy moment wondered if he would kiss her again.

He dashed her ill-formed hopes. "Staff meeting an hour after lockdown."

Her gaze slid from his face to focus on her toes. "Thanks, I'd forgotten."

He hesitated another moment, and she waited for his touch, like an idiot, still hoping. Then he backed away and headed for the door. Pushing aside her ridiculous disappointment, she crouched to pick up the book she'd dropped and turned away from him to fit it on the shelf.

"Later, then," he said from the door. Then his footsteps retreated down the corridor.

As his footfalls faded, a rumbling started, vibrating the rock walls. She knew the sound—they'd powered up the air-circulation system, one of the last steps in the sequence before lockdown.

A sudden formless terror gripped her. For all her dreaming and planning to be part of BioCave, the reality of six months underground caught her unaware, squeezing a mortifying whimper from her throat. She was suddenly glad that Ethan had left, that he wasn't witness to her fear.

"It'll be all right, Miss Lizzy. You'll see."

She scrambled to her feet, whacking her elbow on the metal bookcase as she turned. When she saw who stood grinning in the doorway, she gaped.

"Uh . . . uh . . . " She flapped a hand at the red-haired young man.

He smoothed the front of his coat, then hiked his trousers up a bit. *"Howdy, Lizzy."*

"I . . . uh. . . ." She cleared her throat, tried to keep her eyes from bugging clear out of her skull. "I know you." She blinked, a laborious process. "You're him. That guy."

"Which guy would that be?"

"The miner. Noah Simmons."

He grinned more broadly. *"That I am."*

Liz swallowed once, twice. "And you're dead."

Chapter
Three

"Well, yes, ma'am." Noah looked a little troubled by her statement. *"I'm afraid that's true."*

Her mouth hung open as her brain scrambled frantically for something to say. But what do you say to a ghost? "Ah, how are you?" Besides dead, that is.

"Well, mighty fine, now that we've met."

He took a step into the lab—well actually, he glided—and stood before her. He wore a houndstooth sack coat and matching pants, an ascot neatly tied at his neck. A porkpie hat sat on his head, gray felt with black ribbons dangling.

She might have believed he was real—if not for the sight of her worktable, dimly visible through his middle.

But of course he couldn't be real. Her exhaustion coupled with the stress of dealing with Ethan, mixed with her fascination for people from a long-dead past had conjured up an illusion of Noah Simmons. This was no doubt some kind of waking dream.

He took off his hat and tucked it under his arm. *"I am*

mighty curious about one thing. How do you know my name?"

"I'm kind of a history nut." As she spoke, she wondered at the wisdom of making conversation with an illusion. "I'd read about the Emma Simmons's temperance movement—"

"Emma Simmons?" He lost his grip on his hat, snatched it back before it floated to the floor. *"My mama? That Emma Simmons?"*

Neat trick the way he grabbed the hat, as if it were real, as if he were real. "She stormed out to Arizona looking for you. When your body was discovered, she started the temperance movement in your memory."

He seemed a little confused. *"A temperance movement. In my memory?"*

"Well . . ." Liz hesitated. Noah might not like the picture history had painted of him. But this was a dream, what did it matter? "It was because of how you died."

His eyes went so wide she saw the whites all around the irises. *"How I died?"* he asked hoarsely.

"The drunken fall down into the pit."

Outrage replaced the fear in his face. *"But I wasn't drunk!"*

"They found the empty flask on you."

"But I wasn't—" He seemed to bite off the words. He rubbed at his Dundreary sideburns, his expression troubled. Then he fixed his earnest brown gaze on Liz. *"I got to go. I'll come back when I can."*

In the blink of an eye, he disappeared, the air seeming to collapse into the space he'd occupied. In the next moment, reality seemed to take hold again.

There, see, she told her befuddled brain. *Nothing to be worried about here. It was a dream and now we're awake.*

She turned back to the boxes of supplies still spread across the floor of the lab. Pulling rolls of plastic sheeting from the nearest box, she turned to place them next to the nutrient solution under her worktable.

And stuttered to a stop. The rolls of plastic thudded to the floor. She counted, just to assure her brain that her eyes weren't lying.

A bottle was missing. Of the twelve she'd watched Ethan unpack, only eleven remained.

Drunk! His mother thought he'd died a drunk! And told the world about it, no less.

Noah reached the wall of the tiny space that was his own special cave, and turned to walk the other way. He'd come here often in the long years since he'd died, to think his thoughts through, to fight off the loneliness. The place felt safe—if the monster came here, Noah never sensed its presence.

So his sour-faced mama had had the last laugh. Spreading false tales about her only son, writing him into history as a drunken fool. He would've preferred obscurity over this sullying of his good name.

And what would Lizzy think? This revelation dashed all his hopes for a good impression. He would have to somehow get back in her good graces, to start over with her. Because he could not possibly reveal the true reason for his death.

It might be foolish hope, but he'd come to think over the years the monster had gone to sleep and no longer posed a threat. He didn't dare speak its name, even to Lizzy.

For it might yet wake.

Liz stepped into the cavernous common room, on the lookout for Ethan. She'd found the missing bottle back in the far corner of the lab, and she wanted to know why he hadn't put that jug with the others. Even more important, when had he done it? She never saw him in the back of the lab.

Of course, if Ethan hadn't put the bottle there, then who had? It didn't bear thinking about.

Liz moved through the vast room and found Ethan standing at the far end, by the tables still laden with food from the wedding feast. He towered over Dr. Nishimoto who stood beside him, his head bent to listen to what the doctor had to say.

Liz shoved up the sleeves of the sweater she'd grabbed from their quarters and threaded through the tables toward Ethan. She waved to the Jacksons as she passed them, recalling the middle-aged couple from her time at GeoCore. Her gaze skimmed over several unfamiliar faces, paused on Richard Niedan's scowl, then locked back onto Ethan as she reached his side.

The mocking smile was back, accompanied by an arrogantly cocked brow. "Mrs. Winslow."

Liz swallowed back the urge to correct him. "Ethan."

His gray gaze fixed on hers a moment, then drifted down her face, pausing at her lips, then settled with fascinated attention on the pulse at her throat. A line of heat followed where he looked, and Liz had to force herself to keep from squirming.

He jerked his head back up, retreated a step. "If you'll excuse me . . ." Barely waiting for Dr. Nishimoto's farewell, he strode off across the common room toward a group clustered around one of the far tables.

Liz watched him, confused and flustered, then turned to the elderly physician. "When can I show you the hydroponics lab, Dr. Nishimoto?"

"In a day or two, when I have the clinic in order. Ethan tells me he's given you the lead position."

The audacity of the man. "Aaron gave me that assignment, not Ethan." She flicked an irritated glance at him across the room and caught him staring at her. Ethan looked away, turning his back on her.

Stewing, Liz did the same, focusing her attention on Dr. Nishimoto. "Ethan doesn't have the authority to make staff decisions."

The physician gave her a puzzled frown. "Of course he does. He's heading BioCave."

"Ethan?" Her too-loud voice echoed against the high ceiling. She continued in a near whisper, "Heading up Bio-Cave?"

"You didn't know?"

"I thought you . . ." Liz unclenched her hands that had fisted at her sides. "Aaron told me he picked you."

Dr. Nishimoto's dark eyes narrowed on her face. "I bowed out in favor of Ethan. I felt the project deserved someone with more vigor than this old bag of bones."

She gave him a wan smile, her throat tightening in response to the old fears. She glanced over her shoulder at Ethan, still in conversation with the Jacksons. As if sensing his eyes on her, he looked toward her and held her gaze for a long moment. He smiled, just a bare movement of his lips.

He knows, Liz realized. *He knows that I know.*

And he damn well can't wait to lord it over me! Liz thought with a sudden surge of anger.

"Excuse me," she gasped out to Dr. Nishimoto, and stalked across the common room. She tugged at Ethan's arm. "Could I speak with you, please?"

"Can it wait?" he asked. "The meeting's about to start."

"No," she bit out, then headed off toward the kitchen.

A side room carved out of a small cave adjacent to the common room, the kitchen was blessedly empty. Liz whirled to face Ethan the moment he stepped into the room.

"Let me make this clear," she said without preamble, "I am in charge of the hydro lab. You will not usurp my authority."

He moved to the end of the stainless-steel work island, one large hand resting on its corner. "Why would I?"

Liz circled the island, placing it between them. "Because that's what you did every chance you could at GeoCore. But it's damn well going to be different here. You may be in charge, but I demand you respect my abilities and keep an open mind to my ideas and suggestions."

He nodded, but Liz couldn't help but feel his acquiescence was a sham. "As long as you continue to demonstrate you deserve my respect."

Liz gripped the edge of the island, the steel cool under her fingers. "I will not have you treat me as you did at Geo-Core."

He eyed her coolly, his gray gaze colder than the soulless bite of metal under her hands. "Then be certain your actions in BioCave are more professional than they were at Geo-Core."

"I don't know what you mean."

He paced the length of the counter, rounded it so that they stood toe-to-toe. "Then I'll spell it out for you. You're married to me now. I will not have you seeking more profitable opportunities with any other men on staff."

"How dare you!" She flung up her hand to strike him.

He grabbed her wrist easily, gripping it in his large hand. "If it's any consolation," he said as he resisted her attempts to free herself, "I'm wealthier than anyone else here. So you've already made the best deal possible."

She tugged once more at his hand and he let her go. "Damn you, Ethan Winslow." She slapped her palms against his chest in frustration.

Before she could draw back, he trapped her hands, covering them with one of his. The other hand curved around the back of her neck and pulled her toward him. Before she could think, before she could protest, he covered her lips with his and stole a savage kiss.

Then he let her go, backing well out of her reach. For a moment, she thought he might apologize. But he didn't, turning on his heel and heading toward the exit.

"Ethan!" Liz called before he'd slipped into the common room.

He faced her, his gray eyes hooded. "What?"

Knees still shaking from his kiss, she steadied herself against the counter. "Why did you give me the lead botanist's position?"

Silence stretched for long moments as his hard gaze fixed on her. "Because I knew you were the best," he told her finally, then continued on through the door.

She uncurled her fingers, surprised at the crescents the nails had dug into her palm. Dragging in a calming breath, she forced herself to relax.

Hell, she'd thought she'd left behind the ugly gossip about her relationship with Aaron when she'd left GeoCore. She'd suspected the closeness between her and the old millionaire had been at least some of the source of Ethan's animosity, but it still distressed her to have it confirmed.

And how could she defend herself? She'd promised Aaron to keep their secret. Preserving the old man's dignity far outweighed her own discomfort.

She could deal with Ethan Winslow and his misplaced self-righteousness. Let him believe what he wanted. Resolved to stand up to him, Liz followed him from the kitchen into the common room.

He flicked a quick glance at her as she entered, then turned to the rest of the staff. "If I could have your attention please." His request bounced off the ceiling and walls of the vast room.

Liz marveled at how Ethan could take command with such ease, in the tone of his voice, the lines of his body. No one would second-guess him as leader.

He held out an imperious hand toward her. "Liz."

She would have liked to defy him, but she knew it would be unprofessional, as well as a useless gesture. She supposed he wouldn't hesitate to stride over and drag her to his side.

She threaded through the tables to stand beside him, close enough to feel his body heat, yet out of reach of his touch. No matter how she felt about Ethan privately, she would put on a front of unity. She owed Aaron that much.

Because BioCave was more than the creation of a viable, self-sustaining underground community. Ethan's experimentation with alternative energy sources and Liz's attempts to increase plant yields were vital issues. But Aaron's greatest interest lay in creating a cohesive team from a crowd of disparate, competitive individuals.

Aaron fully expected they'd all be one big happy family

by the end of the experiment. Of course, he didn't realize Liz would probably strangle Ethan long before that.

"—introduce ourselves first," she heard Ethan say when she tuned back in to what he was saying.

He started with himself, laying out a brief autobiography, as well as an overview of what he hoped to accomplish in the next six months. Liz found herself mesmerized by his voice, the movement of his lips as he spoke, the rhythm of his words. "Light, wind, and water," he said, as if they were talismans from which all the world's energy needs could be derived.

Even if she hadn't already bought into BioCave's ideals, Ethan's conviction would have persuaded her. She didn't want to respect him, to believe in him, but she couldn't resist the pull of his influence. You can respect him professionally, she told herself. That doesn't mean you have to like him.

So when he turned to her, enfolding her hand in his to urge her to speak next, she left her hand there for the minimum time necessary to give the impression of a loving wife. Then, giving him a patently false smile, she tugged her hand free and put a good three feet between them before facing the others arrayed around them. She could sense his annoyance with her as she began to speak and she felt a small triumph in it.

With genuine enthusiasm, she described her own hopes for BioCave, her intentions to prove out a myriad of hydroponics methods to determine which would produce the best results. "The good news is, we'll have the opportunity to try a dozen variations on zucchini and tomato casserole," she said, then added in response to the groans around the room, "I suppose that's the bad news, too."

She finished with an invitation to all to visit the lab, then gestured to the Nishimotos to go next. After the doctor and Mrs. Nishimoto spoke, the Jacksons introduced themselves, then the Niedans, the Smiths, the Vuchoviches—the names started to blur in Liz's mind. Some of them had come in late in the planning stages so she knew them by reputation only.

Ethan scanned the room. "Is that everyone, then?"

Liz sank back onto the edge of the table behind her, relieved that the ordeal would soon be over. The strain of playing wife wore on her. She wanted nothing more than to escape to her lab.

Rubbing at the tension between her eyes, she gazed through her fingers at the assembled couples. She envied them their unity, the strength of their bonds. Even the Bradshaws, with their legendary yelling matches, had maintained their marriage well into a second decade.

A glimmer of movement caught her eye. She lowered her hands to focus and nearly fell from her perch on the table.

Noah Simmons. Standing in the common room.

She glanced up at Ethan who was methodically laying out the "house rules." If he saw that red head bobbing between the Niedans and the Bradshaws, she saw no sign of it in his face.

She looked back at the group. Noah was gone.

Or had never been there. She swiped a hand over her face. These nutty dreams had to stop or she'd go straight from BioCave to the loony bin.

"That's it, folks," Ethan said when he'd finished. "See you in the morning."

Murmurs of goodnight mingled with the scraping of chairs and shuffling of feet. Trang and Qwong Nguyen, who among their other duties had volunteered to be the BioCave cooks, headed for the kitchen while the rest of the staff called out their goodnights. Soon, she and Ethan were alone.

Liz surreptitiously scanned the common room for roving ghosts. Ethan stroked a finger along her arm, sending a shiver through her. "Something the matter?" he asked.

The bright fluorescent lights lining the sides of the cavern flickered, then dimmed. Another hour and they'd go out entirely to conserve their precious electricity.

For a moment, she considered telling him her crazy dreams. But prosaic Ethan would never see the harmless whimsy in ghost sightings.

"Nothing," she said. "Just tired."

He gazed down at her, his gray eyes steady. "What am I going to do with you, Liz Winslow?"

"Work with me," she answered softly. "Respect me. Just as you would any other member of the staff."

"You're not any other member. You're my wife."

He tipped his head down to her and her eyes drifted shut. A dim voice inside wanted to remind her she was wife in name only, that they'd agreed their relationship would not be physical. But when his lips first brushed her cheek, the voice silenced.

A faint moan slipped from her throat. Somehow, her hands found their way to his muscled forearms, the fingers curling around the hair-roughened skin.

His lips moved to her temple, pressing kisses along the way. His hot breath roiled against her skin, easing a sigh from her lips, and sharp sensation chased up and down her spine.

His tongue wet her temple, then trailed along to her ear. A warmth started inside her and she knew if he kept touching her she'd end up a puddle on the rock floor.

He flicked his tongue in her ear and she had to grip his arms to keep standing. "Liz."

"Yes?"

"The bed is down."

His tongue traced the shell of her ear, effectively wiping her brain clean. "What?"

"The bed," he repeated. "It's ready for us."

The bed, she thought dimly, *the bed.* Now why should that word set off an alarm?

It wasn't until his hand curved around her rib cage and his thumb teased the side of her breast that she woke up. Liz shoved at him, stumbling a step or two back until she'd cleared a space between them. She shook her hands, trying to shake loose his heat, but it had burrowed bone deep.

She tried to still her body's trembling. "I'm not going to bed with you."

A mocking smile curved his lips. "There *is* only the one bed."

"Which is for sleeping, period."

His smile broadened and she knew he was laughing at her. "Did I suggest anything else?"

"You know damn well—" she said hotly, then cut off her words as they echoed around the cavern. "We had a deal. A marriage of convenience. That doesn't include the convenience of having my body."

He tipped her head up and she waited for another punishing kiss. But although his fingers tightened on her jaw so that she was sure they'd leave a mark, he didn't kiss her. He snatched his hand back as if touching her had offended him and strode from the common room.

Liz closed her eyes against the surprise of tears. Why did he despise her so? Why could she do nothing right in his eyes? It couldn't just be her relationship with Aaron. Ethan's displeasure with her had started before that scuttlebutt had surfaced at GeoCore.

She racked her brain, tried to think back over the years to what might have started their enmity. Was it that she stood up to him, that she didn't kowtow to him? If that was so, they had a long, long battle ahead of him. Because she would always stand for what she believed was right.

She shuddered again, thinking of how he'd touched her. Why, when he'd never before shown the least bit of interest in her, was he pursuing her now? Convenience, she supposed. The same convenience that had bought her a position in BioCave made her handy as a sex partner. And Ethan apparently had no qualms about taking advantage of her proximity in Cynthia's absence.

One thing was sure, Liz thought as she zigzagged through the tables toward the exit. She wasn't returning to their quarters yet. She hadn't quite finished assembling all her hydro setups before the meeting; she'd complete them now instead of leaving them until tomorrow as she'd intended.

When she reached her lab, she noted with irritation that

the door was slightly ajar. She'd told Richard to be sure to shut it. The hydro lab required a specialized environment; it was difficult enough to maintain without leaving the door open to the drafty corridor.

She pushed the door open and was about to step inside when the hair on the back of her neck prickled up. She remembered her peculiar dreams as she looked around the lab, searching for the source of her unease. Everything seemed to be in place—the lumber for the hydro tanks, the plastic sheeting to line them, the bottles of nutrient fluid beneath the worktable . . .

Two bottles were missing.

She moved quickly to the worktable. Maybe Richard had rearranged the bottles so that those two only appeared to be missing. But no, she realized as she did a swift mental count of the neat rows, two were definitely gone.

Richard must have taken them to perform a side experiment in his own small lab. Although why he would have needed two bottles of the highly concentrated fluid, she couldn't fathom. She really couldn't spare that much—she had carefully calculated what she'd need for food production and hadn't requisitioned much extra.

She'd have to talk to Richard in the morning; with any luck, he hadn't used the bottles yet and she could get them back. Putting aside the problem of missing supplies, she scanned the floor for the hammer. Somehow, it had ended up over by the bookcase; she must have kicked it there in her hurry to get to the meeting. Grabbing it up, she returned to the task of building grow tanks.

An hour later, her arms ached from pounding nails and her eyes burned from the tedious task of fitting plastic sheeting into wooden frames. She glanced at the clock—midnight, surface time. She was exhausted and desperately needed sleep. Yet every time she imagined crawling into bed beside Ethan, a cold shaft of cowardice stabbed her.

Maybe she should sleep in the lab. She gazed down at the cold rock floor, wondering facetiously if it was as hard as it looked. Maybe if she slipped back to their quarters and snitched the spare blanket from the bed, she could fashion a pallet that wouldn't be too horribly uncomfortable.

Her bones might tolerate the rock floor for one or two nights, but for six months? She'd be bruised and battered in a week, not to mention what her disturbed sleep would do to her already volatile temperament. She couldn't possibly set up camp there permanently.

There was nothing for it but to climb into bed beside the man. With any luck he was already asleep.

Liz pushed her stool back from her worktable and, after stretching out the kinks in her lean body, headed for the door. She slapped the manual control for the lights, dimming them to low-voltage use before stepping into the corridor. The far end of the corridor dissolved in shadows, the faint overhead illumination just sufficient to light her steps.

Although the low light was disorienting, Liz made her way unerringly through the turns to her own corridor. She fixed her eyes on the blackness that hid her door and quickened her pace, looking forward to a good night's sleep.

"Lizzy."

She stopped short and turned. The faint whisper of her name seemed to hang in the air. She strained to see in the dim light, listening.

"Lizzy."

As soon as the sound faded she wondered if she'd even heard it. The memory of it throbbed in tandem to her heartbeat, her quick breathing, making her doubt it had been anything more than her own imagination.

Then something bumped against her, once, twice, so that she banged knees and palms against the rock wall in a desperate attempt to keep from falling. The lights flickered, strobing between dimness and utter black.

Another shove, pushing her backward. Arms flailing, she groped for support. But there was nothing to grab for to save her and her head struck the rock floor. A flash of light behind her eyes punctuated her own startled scream. Before her shout finished echoing on the walls, she heard the tread of answering feet thundering down the corridor.

As she lay there in the intermittent dark, before unconsciousness took her, she realized her dream had returned. Noah Simmons stood over her in the corridor, the sadness and worry of his expression overlaid with a sharper emotion. Terror.

Chapter Four

Before Liz could even register the sharp pain battering her skull, a large, warm hand caressed her cheek, soothing the ache. Instinctively, she turned to that hand, maintaining the connection as if it were a lifeline.

"What happened?" a concerned voice buzzed in her ear. Dr. Nishimoto?

"I don't know," Ethan answered, "I found her like this."

"Fell . . ." she muttered, gasping against the pain when strong fingers probed her head.

"How could she have fallen?" Dr. Nishimoto asked. "There's nothing in the corridor."

"Can I get her off this damned hard floor?" Ethan growled.

"Go ahead," Dr. Nishimoto answered. "Carefully now!"

She felt a muscled arm cradling her head, another hooked beneath her knees. Then she was flying, a pleasant sensation until the world chose that moment to spin and buck. She groaned, clutching at the strong chest she was snugged against.

"Better put her down quick," Dr. Nishimoto warned, "she's looking mighty green about the gills."

"Kill that light!" Ethan barked as the dim light of the hallway gave way to brightness. Liz squeezed her eyes shut against the lance of light until the brilliance eased and her nausea with it. She chanced opening her eyes then and faced a landscape of firm male skin dusted with dark hair.

If she turned her head just slightly, she mused, she could press her lips to his chest. She thought she'd try, arched her neck slightly. But a moment later she was set gently on the bed.

"A concussion," Dr. Nishimoto announced as he flicked an examining light from one eye to the other.

Liz narrowed her eyes against the glare, grateful Ethan had laid her down before she'd committed a foolhardy, concussion-induced act. Eyes half-lidded, she gazed at him surreptitiously.

She felt his hip pressed against her thigh where he sat beside her on the bed. A strange expression lit his face, softened the edges of his cold gray eyes. Worry . . . and fear.

"How bad?" he asked Dr. Nishimoto.

Dr. Nishimoto probed her head again, eliciting another gasp from her. "Not much swelling. Fairly mild, I'm guessing."

"Speak for yourself," Liz rasped.

Another prod of Dr. Nishimoto's fingers had Liz groping for comfort. In a heartbeat, Ethan's hand linked with hers. He didn't even flinch at her death grip in response to the pain.

"Think you can sit up, Liz?" Dr. Nishimoto asked. "I can give you a couple aspirins. I don't dare give you anything stronger."

Ethan moved swiftly to place a supporting arm behind her shoulders and eased her up. She accepted the aspirins from Dr. Nishimoto, then took the glass of water his wife, Wendy, brought from the bathroom.

After she swallowed the pills, she gazed around the room.

The Jacksons stood just inside the door, Richard behind them. The Vuchoviches hovered in the ill-lit corridor with another couple—the Smiths?—in the shadows beside them.

"What happened?" one of the onlookers asked.

"She tripped and fell." Ethan carefully lowered Liz back onto the bed, although she would have just as soon remained in his arms.

"I still don't understand what you tripped over," Harlan Jackson said, a perplexed frown on his dark face. "There are no obstacles in the corridor."

"It happened when the lights went out." Liz brought a shaky hand up to her temple, trying to remember. "I must have stumbled over something in the dark."

Ethan's gaze sharpened on her. "The corridor lights went out?"

Liz nodded. "Evening shutdown, I guess. Should have activated the manual override."

"The corridor lights are programmed to always stay on," Ethan said. "They have to, for safety reasons."

Liz rubbed at her temple, something else teasing the edge of her memory. "I know it went completely dark."

Dr. Nishimoto gave her arm a gentle squeeze. "Concussions can scramble your recall of what led up to the blow. That blackness you remember may well be the moment you were unconscious."

Liz tried to focus on what had happened. She remembered the lights flickering, remembered . . . hands on her? A shove? But she saw no one in the long corridor with her. She had to be mistaken.

"You're probably right. It's all pretty foggy." She looked up at Dr. Nishimoto. "I'm awfully tired. Can I go to sleep now?"

"You can," the doctor answered, "but Ethan will need to rouse you every hour to check your condition."

Marvelous, Liz groused to herself. That would really endear her to Mr. Grouch, losing a night's sleep to protect her from the consequences of her own clumsiness. She sneaked a sidelong peek at Ethan, expecting his dark wrath at the inconvenience she'd caused.

But instead she saw concern in his gray eyes, and that perplexing softness. He reached out to brush a lock of hair from her eyes, his fingertips like a whisper across her brow.

"No problem," he said. "Just tell me what to look for when I wake her."

While Dr. Nishimoto went over his instructions with Ethan, Liz tried to puzzle out the enigma of Ethan Winslow. He should have been angry with her for causing him so much grief, yet he'd seemed damn near human about it.

The shuffling of feet reminded her of the crowd arrayed in their quarters. Of course, he wouldn't have appeared as anything but the doting husband in front of the other staff. No doubt, that explained why he'd treated her like precious crystal.

"Party's over." Dr. Nishimoto shooed away the gathered staff members. Picking up his medical bag, he turned to go. "I'll come check you in the morning. Bed rest for you all day tomorrow."

He was gone before she could complain that her work couldn't wait a day. She scowled at Ethan. "I have to be in the lab tomorrow."

"No." He scooted onto the edge of the bed facing her feet. His fingers began working the buckle of her sandal.

She tugged her foot away. "What are you doing?"

He grasped her foot again. "Taking off your shoes."

She would have tried once more to pull her foot free but by then the heat of his fingers moving across her instep and sensitive sole started a lassitude that stole her energy. What did it matter if she let him take her sandals off? How risky could that be?

Very, she realized a moment later when he began massaging her bare feet. Energy crept into her limbs again, but energy of a different kind that urged her to snake her legs around his waist and tug him closer.

She snatched her feet free of his enfolding hands. When

she might have expected him to grab them again, he rose and crossed to the small, built-in dresser.

She watched aghast as he opened one of her drawers and plucked a midnight blue nightgown from it. "Put that down," she said.

He obliged, tossing it beside her on the bed. But then he snuggled up beside her and tugged her sweater from her arms. Easing the garment over her sore head, he reached for the buttons on her blouse.

She slapped his hands away. "What do you think you're doing!"

His fingers returned implacably to the front of her blouse. "Helping you undress."

She crossed her arms over her chest, thwarting his attempt to slip a button free. "The hell you are. I'm perfectly capable of undressing myself."

"You have a concussion, Liz," he told her patiently. "You have to take it easy."

"Not that easy." She rolled to the other side of the bed and swung her feet to the floor.

An ill-advised move, she realized when the room commenced spinning. She squeezed her eyes shut to still the motion, one hand on the rock wall just beyond her knees.

"Let me help you." Ethan put his arm around her shoulders. Somehow he'd moved beside her, his body providing an anchor for a world that insisted on tilting.

"I'll be okay in a minute." She risked opening her eyes and was relieved to see the room had leveled out. She tensed to rise and had to swallow back the swell of nausea.

"Damn it, Liz," Ethan said, his voice low in her ear, "you're acting like an idiot."

Inexplicably, tears pricked at her eyes, tightened her throat. "I don't want you undressing me," she forced past the constriction.

Ethan sighed, and Liz could swear she heard his slow count to ten. "Lay back in bed. I'll go into the bathroom. Call me when you're done."

"Thank you," she murmured, feeling like a child.

He helped her back down onto the bed where she had to admit she felt much better. She looked up at him where he stood between the wall and the Murphy bed and for the first time she saw he wore a pair of pajama bottoms, their muted gray stripes matching his eyes.

She fiddled with the top button of her blouse. "I would never have guessed you wore pajamas."

"I don't. I bought these two days ago."

His eyes didn't quite meet hers. With sudden insight, Liz realized he was watching her restless fingers as if in his mind he'd pulled away her shirt and could see what lay beneath.

She snatched her hand away from her blouse. It fell on the silky knit of her gown, the smooth brush of it against her sensitized skin as evocative as Ethan's touch. She could imagine all too well him sliding the gown up past her hips, her waist, above her breasts . . .

"Well?" Her breathlessness sounded far too much like an invitation.

Ethan seemed to shake himself, then he turned on his heel and strode into the bathroom. The door rolled shut with a clatter, then moved open again just a crack.

"So I can hear you." His voice seemed thick and hoarse. It must be the echo of the confining bathroom, or the filter of her blood pounding in her ears . . .

Her hands shaking with more than the aftereffects of concussion, Liz released the buttons on her shirt and slipped her arms from it. Grateful for the front closure on her bra, she released it, then shimmied out of her shorts in slow steps. She left her panties on, although the turquoise strip of silk seemed scant protection.

She worked the nightgown on over her head, fighting dizziness when she had to lift her hips to pull it down. She tried to swallow back her weakness, but when she called out, "Ready," she sounded pretty pitiful.

Ethan shoved open the door immediately, as if he'd been

waiting on just the other side. "Are you all right?" He knelt on the bed beside her.

"I will be as soon as the guy with the hammer lets up." Her blouse and bra still lay under her. She wanted to rid herself of them, to scoot under the covers, but the thought of moving even the slightest inch daunted her.

Ethan seemed to understand. He eased her to her side and pulled her clothes free. Tugging down the covers, he lifted her from the bed and placed her gently between the sheets. Then he pulled the blanket to her chin.

"I'm in the middle of the bed." She closed her eyes against the relentless ache. "Where will you sleep?"

"I doubt that I will," he said.

She slanted a look up at him. "Because you have to check on me, you mean?"

"Something like that." The corner of his mouth quirked up; the mocking smile, but she had the sense he was its target, not her. "Go to sleep."

"You need to turn out the light," she said querulously.

"Of course." He circled the bed to the control. With a touch, he dimmed the room, a great relief to her throbbing head.

"Go to sleep," he murmured again.

And she did, without further objection.

Ethan sat in the desk chair, feet propped up on the bed, watching Liz sleep. Her headache seemed to have followed her into her dreams, furrowing her brow, tightening her mouth with a faint tension.

He wanted to kiss away her pain, to brush his lips against hers until she relaxed into a gentler sleep. But he knew damn well any kiss he gave her wouldn't end in comfort.

Ethan closed his eyes and rubbed at his face. Damn, he was tired. But he didn't dare sleep, just as he didn't dare stretch his body alongside Liz's and pull her against him. She'd fallen asleep in the middle of the bed, but after he'd woken her briefly to check her response, she'd rolled over to the far side near the wall.

So now there was ample space for him on the bed. If he lay there, if he didn't move, didn't breathe, he could avoid touching her. But of course, he wouldn't want to keep from touching her.

Ethan sighed, the sound rough with frustration. He might have every intention of making love to her before the six months were out, but even he wasn't fiend enough to take her when she had a concussion. That he even considered it, tried to rationalize it in his mind, spoke to the way Liz inflamed him far beyond the bounds other women had barely tested.

His gaze fell on the timer he'd propped on the desk. Afraid he might doze in the chair, he'd set it to go off each hour. He could close his eyes for a few minutes, assured that the alarm would wake him. But if he tried to sleep folded in the stiff-backed desk chair, he'd be a mass of knots when he woke.

Which left the bed.

Ethan pounded his fists on the arms of the chair, angry with himself. How did she turn him into such a damn animal? He had always enjoyed sex, took pride in his partner's pleasure, but a piece of him always stood back, restrained. Liz tore loose the restraints, shook him to his very core. Just the thought of his hands on her body aroused a violent need that appalled him.

Liz shifted slightly, and the blanket slid low enough to expose the rise of her hip. Folds of midnight blue concealed her golden skin from his eyes, but the thin knit hugged her curves faithfully. He could reach over and slide his hand up along her body, pushing the gown as he went, exposing her sleek, lean body . . .

He was on his feet before he even realized. If the timer hadn't squealed in the next moment, he would have been on her in a heartbeat, stripping the gown and panties from her, driving himself into her body.

Setting his teeth against his lack of control, Ethan kneeled beside Liz on the bed and shook her gently. She pouted and complained, but she roused enough to assure him the concussion hadn't worsened. He let her turn over again and fall back asleep.

Sitting back on his heels, Ethan eyed the awkward chair, then the expanse of mattress before him. No contest, he realized as he eased the blanket out from under him. After ascertaining that the timer would go off in another hour, he slid down onto the bed, every muscle tense as he held himself away from Liz.

Hell, that wouldn't last long. As soon as he drifted into sleep, his subconscious would seek her out, draw her body close to his. Might as well do it now and enjoy it while still awake.

Moving carefully so as not to jostle her sore head, Ethan slid one arm under her and dropped the other over her waist. She backed up immediately into him, spooning against him. He fisted his hand as her hips squirmed against his aching erection and dragged in slow breath after slow breath.

Finally, she stilled and sank into deeper slumber. Pillowing her head on his arm, Ethan tipped his head to rest his lips against her hair. The faint sweet scent of her shampoo mingled with her own natural scent. His senses full of her, Ethan slept.

Liz woke with a start, her heart rattling in her chest as if she'd leaped headlong from dream to awareness. Her hand crept across the mattress, seeking out Ethan before she was consciously aware that was what she was doing. She skimmed the cool sheet next to her with her palm before pulling her hand back to her side.

She had her eyes squeezed shut and memories tapped at her brain. A fall in the corridor, Ethan carrying her to their quarters, his body beside her on the bed. Dim images of him leaning over her, shaking her to the edge of wakefulness, then letting her sag back into sleep.

She readied herself to open her eyes, fearful that the dull ache at the back of her head would flare into sharp pain. But when she eased her eyes open, gazed around her at the artificial early morning light seeping into the corners of the room, the ache let up a bit. She sighed, relaxing even more of the pain away.

Then tension gripped her head again. She wasn't alone after all. "You," she squeezed out.

Noah Simmons, hat in hand, peered anxiously at her from the foot of the bed. *"Miss Lizzy, are you all right?"*

"I would be if . . ." She struggled to sit up, managing to prop herself onto her elbows. ". . . if I wasn't hallucinating."

Noah drifted around the bed to hover over her. *"Is that like the vapors? I know ladies is always getting the vapors. My mama—"*

"You are a figment of my imagination." Liz scooted herself upright, scrubbed at her face with her hands. "Relax, Liz. He'll be gone in a moment."

She tipped her head back up. He wasn't gone.

She didn't know whether to laugh, scream, or cry. If she didn't find a way to make sense out of what she was seeing, she'd probably do all three.

"Listen," she said, putting on her most rational tone. "I've had a fall, hit my head—"

"I know that, Miss Lizzy, and I'm mighty sorry."

A faint memory fluttered. "Was it you that pushed me?"

"No!" Noah seemed offended. *"Course not. I would never push a lady."*

"Then who did?" She asked the question of herself, but when she glanced up at Noah, or rather the illusion she'd persuaded herself was Noah, he got a mighty guilty look on his face. "You know, don't you?"

He seemed ready to tear apart the porkpie hat in his hands. He backed away from the bed, looked around him.

"Where's this light come from? Don't see no windows."

"It's recessed lighting, set to mimic normal daylight

hours.'' She shook her head. "Why am I talking to you? You're not real.''

He turned back to her. *"I am, Miss Lizzy. As real as that fella you're married to. I just happen to be . . . to be . . ."*

"Dead," she finished for him. She threw back the covers and rose carefully. "I'm going to the bathroom. When I get back, I want you back in whatever part of my subconscious you emerged from."

Shutting the bathroom door behind her, she took care of the bare necessities, wary of the ache in her head. A pair of aspirins from the bottle next to the sink, a quick job with her toothbrush, and she felt almost human.

She stared at her reflection in the mirror, working up the nerve to return to her room. What if he wasn't gone? What if that knock on her head had shaken something loose, making her see things that weren't really there? But it couldn't just be the concussion. She'd seen Noah before her fall.

So was she nuts? Or was he really the spirit of Noah Simmons?

She rubbed at the bridge of her nose, trying to think. Ethan Winslow might be driving her to distraction, but she damned well wasn't crazy. So if she opened the bathroom door and still saw Noah, she would just have to start believing in the supernatural.

She slid the door aside, peeked into her room. Noah hung suspended over her bed, his porkpie hat at a jaunty angle on his head.

"You're real then," Liz murmured, stepping into the room.

Noah spun to face her, his broad smile revealing a set of truly atrocious teeth. *"That I am, Miss Lizzy."*

"Why me?" She flapped a hand at the apparition, urging him from the bed. "Couldn't you find someone else to haunt?"

Noah obligingly drifted away, settling beside the desk. *"But no one else suits like you do, Miss Lizzy."*

With a weary sigh, Liz crawled onto the bed, scooted under the covers. "Suits?"

Noah grinned at her from beside the bed. *"For courting, Miss Lizzy. I aim to make you my sweetheart."*

Liz sat bolt upright in the bed, setting off a clamoring in her head. "Sweetheart?"

"I didn't aim to bring it up so sudden, but I—"

"I can't be your sweetheart."

His grin faded. *"I know you're married and all, but—"*

"Noah, you're dead." She lay carefully back in the bed. "A ghost can't court a living person."

He took hold of his hat again, twisting it in his hands. *"It's true we got more obstacles than most folks."*

She wanted to laugh at his understatement, but his woebegone expression suppressed her impulse. "I'm sure you are . . . were a fine man. But I truly don't think—"

"Got to go!" Noah whirled away from her and in an instant blinked out of sight. But his hat remained and after a moment, fluttered toward the floor like a feather.

A soft rap sounded on the door. "Noah!" Liz watched the porkpie settle to the brightly colored area rug beside the bed.

"Liz?" Dr. Nishimoto called from the other side of the door.

Liz scrambled across the bed stretching her fingers out toward the hat. "Just a minute!"

Just before she reached the porkpie's brim, Noah's hand rematerialized. His fingers closed around the hat and snatched it into oblivion.

"Sorry!" his disembodied voice cried just as Dr. Nishimoto nudged open the door.

He peered into the room, caught her sprawled across the bed. "Are you okay?"

She scrambled back under the covers, the fast motion rewarding her with a sharp ache at the back of her head. "More or less." She pressed fingertips to her temples.

As Dr. Nishimoto circled the bed to examine her, he glanced toward the open bathroom door. "Is Ethan here?"

"I don't know where Ethan is." The admission that she didn't know the whereabouts of her own husband came out more irritably than she'd intended. "I mean, I assume he's in his lab."

Dr. Nishimoto nodded as he prodded the back of her skull. "Most likely. Just thought it was him I heard you talking to. Although I didn't hear his voice."

"I guess you found me out." She tried to laugh, but the elderly doctor had found a tender spot and she winced instead. "I was talking to myself. Helps me work out problems sometimes."

Grasping her chin, he checked her eyes with a penlight. "Pupils even and reactive. You're doing fine."

She tried to push herself up. "I can get back to work, then."

Hands on her shoulders, Dr. Nishimoto urged her back down. "One day of bed rest, Liz. That's a nasty goose egg on your head. I can see it's still causing you a great deal of pain."

She sighed and shut her eyes. "It is. I'm just anxious to get my experiments started."

"Tomorrow will be soon enough." She heard Dr. Nishimoto's footsteps as he crossed the room. "Shall I get Ethan for you?"

She dearly wanted to say yes. But somehow having him dragged here under doctor's orders didn't mean as much as having him come because he wanted to be with her. She'd just as soon be alone.

"Don't bother. I think I need a nap, anyway."

She heard the door shut softly as the doctor departed. As she lay quietly in bed, doing her best to relax away the throbbing in her head, a different ache insinuated itself inside her. A tight knot of loneliness settled in her middle, coupled with a yearning for a hand nestled in hers, fingers stroking along her brow.

Ethan's hand, Ethan's fingers. The tension eased in her as she thought of him and she drifted into sleep.

• • •

His porkpie hat tugged firmly onto his head, Noah eyeballed Ethan from his vantage point near the ceiling of the room the geologist called "communications." Had he looked, Ethan would catch nary a glimpse of the ghost above him. It hadn't taken Noah long to master the trick of invisibility when the BioCave folks first turned up in his domain. If Noah wanted no one but his Lizzy to see his ghostly form, he knew just how to accomplish that.

The hat, though, that was a wonder. He'd never before lost his grip on any part of his ghostly person. But something about Miss Lizzy just made him lose his concentration.

He glared down at Ethan moving about below him. He'd been here a good long time since leaving Lizzy's room, wondering just how he could defeat this rival for his sweetheart's affection. There was no doubt Ethan had the advantage. He was fair-to-middling handsome while Noah was just as homely in death as he had been in life. Ethan was already wed to Lizzy, giving him a mighty strong claim. And there was that little matter of his being alive while Noah was assuredly dead.

Noah hadn't quite worked out a way around that problem.

Giving his fingertips a twitch, Noah floated a bit lower to get a better look at Ethan. The dark-haired man stood at a tall worktable, studying the innards of a large metal box. Noah slipped low enough to brush against Ethan's shoulder and perused the colorful tangle of what he now knew were called wires.

A noise at the door to the lab caused both man and ghost to turn around. The doctor entered and wound his way between the stacks of equipment arrayed across the room.

"You're a hard man to track down," the doctor said as he reached Ethan's side.

Ethan returned his attention to the metal box. "I've been here all morning."

"Not enough to keep you busy in the energy center?" Dr. Nishimoto leaned an elbow on the workbench. "I thought communications was the Vuchoviches' domain."

Face still buried in the box, Ethan groped for a tool just beyond his reach. "Had some time on my hands."

The doctor plucked the tool from its holder, wary of its tip. Noah had seen that white-hot tip melt clean through metal. A soldering iron, one of the cave folks had called it.

The doctor held out the tool to Ethan, its thick wire trailing. "Thought you might have used that time to keep Liz company."

Ethan's groping hand seemed to hesitate. He glanced over at the doctor, then back into the box. "I can't waste my time entertaining my wife."

Outrage arose in Noah. Here was poor Lizzy, injured and suffering, lying alone in her bed. And her beast of a husband couldn't even take time out to visit.

Watching Ethan reach for the soldering iron again, the devil seemed to take hold of Noah. Just as Ethan's hand neared the handle Noah reached in to nudge it ever so slightly. Ethan's fingers brushed against the tip of the tool instead of the handle.

Snatching his hand back, Ethan yelped in pain, bumped his head on the inside of the box. "Damn it!"

The doctor set down the iron and reached for Ethan's hand. "God, I'm sorry. Are you okay?"

Ethan pulled his hand away. "Fine. It's nothing." He grabbed the handle of the soldering iron and dove back into the box.

The doctor watched for a while, then seemed to figure out he'd been dismissed. "If you need anything for that burn, let me know."

Ethan grunted a response. After a moment, the doctor left the room. As the door shut behind him, Ethan emerged from the box and slammed the soldering iron on the worktable.

His two burned fingers in his mouth, the geologist looked to Noah like a foul-tempered little boy. A little boy who needed another lesson.

Leaning in close to Ethan, Noah reached into the tangle of wire inside the box. Focusing hard, he gripped a handful and gave a sharp tug.

Chapter
Five

After two long days and nights of convalescence, Liz felt ready to jump out of her skin. When Dr. Nishimoto arrived on the morning of the third day, she leapt from the bed. "Tell me you're going to clear me for work."

"Most likely." He urged her into the desk chair. "Let me look you over."

As he examined her, Liz could barely sit still. She was tempted to blame her restlessness on worry over lost time, the delay in getting her experiments started. Or on her fear that Richard Niedan had mucked everything up in her absence, despite his insistence he'd followed her every instruction to the letter.

But she knew better. She had more on her mind those two long days in bed than hydroponics and Richard Niedan's incompetence. Those concerns paled beside the real worries—that Noah Simmons's ghost might at any moment reappear. And that her own, very much alive, husband never would.

"Eyes look good," Dr. Nishimoto said, flashing his penlight. "Headaches?"

"Not since yesterday. I feel fine."

Neither Noah nor Ethan seemed to want to show their faces. That should have been a relief. But while she was glad enough not to be haunted by the dead, her every fiber seemed to ache for Ethan.

Dr. Nishimoto's fingers found the knot on her head, but she scarcely noticed his probing. She was too busy entertaining vague memories of a large warm body close to hers in the night. The crease in Ethan's pillow each morning verified what she'd suspected—he'd slept beside her the last two nights. But why was he only willing to be close to her when she was dead asleep? When the Jacksons had dropped in yesterday, Harlan had volunteered that Ethan was waist-deep in alligators working out bugs in the energy systems. But could those problems really occupy his every waking moment?

Dr. Nishimoto rose, stethoscope looped over his neck again, penlight back in his pocket. "I hereby pronounce you ready for duty. Just take it easy. No heavy lifting."

After Dr. Nishimoto left, Liz dressed quickly in a butter-yellow sweater and jeans. As she hurried down the corridor to the hydro lab her overactive imagination plied her with images of Ethan's body laying beside her in bed. Had he touched her during the night? Had his body by happenstance rolled against hers?

Heat flared in her cheeks. She might have put it down to mortification, to embarrassment over the awkwardness of the situation. But that didn't explain the ache in her chest, her yearning to see him again.

When she reached the hydro lab, she peeked inside and took a quick look around. She was pleased to see the grow tanks filled with nutrient solution and dozens of seedlings started. Richard had been true to his word.

Closing the lab door again, she continued down the corridor toward a small storage cavern near the common room. She'd managed to squeeze a few moments of productive work into the hours of enforced bed rest, brainstorming al-

ternate methodologies to distract her from her preoccupation
with Ethan. She'd actually devised a useful technique to try
and would need some of the spare lumber to build an addi-
tional tank.

The storage room door was partway open when she arrived
and the light from inside spilled into the corridor. Hoping
someone else hadn't already claimed the lumber for another
project, she hurried into the room.

Liz jolted to a stop at her first view of the storage room.
Richard crouched at the far end of the narrow room, surrounded by a tumble of broken lumber.

Liz moved farther into the room, scanning the disarray.
"What the hell have you done?"

Richard whirled, rising to his feet. "Nothing. I didn't do
anything."

Not a stick of lumber remained unbroken. Liz tried to tamp
back her anger. "What the hell happened here?"

Richard thrust out his lower lip like a recalcitrant child.
"It was like this when I came in."

Liz took in a breath to calm herself. "Who did this, Richard?"

He blinked, as if startled she wasn't accusing him. "No
one. It was an accident. Take a look."

Then she saw, under the tumble of wood, a chunk of
grayish-green rock the size of a medicine ball. Her gaze flew
up to the arch of rock above her where a cavity matching
the size of the boulder gaped.

Bending, Richard scooped up a pea-sized piece that had
broken off when the rock fell. "Whoever quarried the storage
room didn't do a very thorough job checking its structural
integrity." Rising, he held the fragment out to Liz. "It must
have been pretty unstable for a chunk that size to fall."

In spite of herself, Liz's shoulders tensed, as if more rock
could fall at any moment. "We'd better have Ethan take a
look at this."

"I'll finish cleaning up while you go after him." Dropping
the bit of gravel in his pocket, Richard turned back to the

rock, bent, and grasped it. All his straining to move it didn't budge it a millimeter.

Liz walked over and tugged at his arm. "I want you out of here, now. I'm not taking any chances."

He bristled at her order, then seemed to swallow back his wounded pride. He left the storage room, mumbling something about getting some reading done in his quarters.

At the door, Liz watched him hurry off down the corridor. Satisfied he was gone, she reached for the light switch.

"Lizzy."

She banged her wrist turning back to the room. "Who's there?"

Taking one step back inside, she scanned the narrow storage space. The crates stacked against the rock wall, the boxes and cans of supplies left no room for anyone to hide.

And yet, she could almost hear the echo of her whispered name. Had it come from the corridor?

Something prickled up her spine, a grazing touch, an infinitesimal pressure. The sensation teased a memory, of a shove, a push. Then a fall, and her head striking the floor.

"Noah?" she rasped out. But she knew instinctively the malevolence clinging to her had nothing to do with the bumbling ghost.

She tried to step back from the room, to escape the inexorable touch. But fear rooted her to the ground so that she could do nothing more than squeeze her eyes shut. "Ethan," she whispered, wishing for nothing more than to have him here.

With the speaking of Ethan's name, the pressure eased, the ribbons of terror released her. With a trembling hand she slapped off the light, then shut the door behind her. She pressed in the emergency lockout code—she didn't want anyone coming in while she went after Ethan. He was the only one who knew the override code.

As she headed for the energy center, tremors of reaction overwhelmed her. She had to stop, to lean against the rock wall of the corridor as she dragged in long gusts of air. But with each calming breath, her memories of what had happened in the storage room seemed to fade.

She continued on down the corridor, trying to remember. She'd felt something, something that frightened her. But now, in the dim glow just outside Ethan's lab, the source of her fear eluded her.

A piece of the rock ceiling had fallen, that was it. And she'd been afraid another might fall, might injure her or Richard.

That answer didn't quite sit right, but she couldn't seem to shake loose anything better from her subconscious. Fingertips on Ethan's slightly ajar door, she tensed to push it open.

She stopped herself as a different kind of trembling chased along her skin. Good God, just because she hadn't seen the man in nearly three days was no reason to behave like a besotted schoolgirl. All her pent-up longing seemed ready to explode. If she didn't rein herself in, she'd make a complete fool of herself.

She took a breath and eased the door open. Twenty or so networked computers lined the walls, each displaying colorful images of the status of the solar, wind and water energy production. Four worktables crowded the center of the room, each one laden with a haphazard tumble of equipment. And behind the leftmost worktable, hidden by a boxy piece of electronic equipment, Ethan uttered a low-voiced stream of curses.

She cleared her throat and he emerged from behind the metal box, slamming a soldering iron to the worktable. "What?" Then he seemed to register it was her. He swiped a hand across his brow, then gestured to her. "Sorry. What is it?"

Determined not to let him intimidate her, she moved closer to the worktable, stepped around it to face him. "We have a problem."

He laughed, not a pleasant sound. "Hell, stand in line."

For the first time she took in his unshaven face, the way

his dark hair looked as if he'd run frustrated fingers through it numerous times. "What's the matter?"

He rounded on her, his gray eyes harsh. She thought he might swallow her whole.

Then he turned away, his jaw working as he stared into space. "I've got connections coming undone for no apparent reason. Components unplugged. Computer hard drives inexplicably wiped out." He sighed, digging another furrow in his hair with his fingers. "Thank God for backups."

Liz resisted the urge to stroke his face, to comfort him. Then she thought, to hell with it, and cupped her palm against his cheek.

A bad move, because whatever was eating at him seemed to rocket into overdrive at the contact. Tendrils of fear and excitement tangled in her middle.

Covering her hand with his, he tugged, pulling her away. Disappointment gave way to a melting heat when he brought her hand to his mouth and pressed a kiss there. She stepped nearer, her other hand running up his chest, across the soft knit of his T-shirt, to curve over his shoulder.

He brushed his lips against her fingertip. "This would not be a good time to test my powers of resistance."

When his tongue flicked out to wet the pad of her finger, she moaned, a low, soft sound. She shook her head. "We shouldn't."

"Why not?" He drew her finger into his mouth. "We're husband and wife. This is what married people do."

"Because . . ." At the pressure of his lips on her finger she threw back her head. "Because . . ."

There was a reason, she was sure of it. She just couldn't frame it in that moment.

"Because it's not a real marriage," he filled in for her.

Her gaze flew to his face, tried to gauge the odd tone she'd heard in his voice. But she saw nothing in his harsh, gray eyes. They seemed as opaque as the rock walls surrounding them.

She pulled away from him, skimmed her bangs back from her face. "It's not a real marriage."

He stared at her, some emotion playing across his face. Liz wished she had a translator into his mind, his soul. A way to unravel the message hidden behind his eyes. Then he grabbed up the soldering iron and buried himself back in the piece of equipment he'd been repairing.

She touched a tentative hand to his elbow. "Can I help?"

He hesitated, then emerged long enough to grab her hand. "Hold this, please."

He closed her fingers around a bundle of wires. "What are you trying to do?" She peered inside the exposed electronic innards.

When he turned his head to answer her, his face was inches from hers. He flicked a glance at her lips, then returned his attention to the box.

"Several connections were broken here. I was having trouble holding the wires in place to solder them back in." His hand brushed against hers as he manipulated the soldering iron and she jerked in response. "Keep your hand still."

"How did so many of them get loose at once?" Liz held herself rigid, doing her best to keep her fingers clear of the hot soldering iron. Watching Ethan work, she allowed herself the luxury of admiring the ropy muscles of his arms at close range. The way he filled his navy T-shirt was downright breathtaking.

He uttered a pungent oath, then gripped her hand to move it a fraction closer to the solder joint. "If I told you, you'd think I was nuts."

She shifted to ease the tension in her arm. "Try me."

He cocked one eyebrow toward her at her injudicious choice of words. Heat arced between them, a palpable thing. Then he bent back over his work, leaving her with her heart rattling in her chest.

"If Ivan Vuchovich hadn't seen it too, I would wonder if I was loony. One minute I've got perfect connections, the next, pop! They're all broken. It's as if an invisible hand grabs the whole mess and jerks them loose.''

Invisible hand. Liz's pleasant perusal of Ethan's body short-circuited as she realized just whose invisible hand that had to have been. "Maybe there's a problem with the solder.''

He shook his head. "I've tested the joints myself after I've repaired them. Gave each one a good, strong tug. Nothing wrong with the solder. But an hour later, those same connections are broken.''

"I'm sure you've got it this time. It won't happen again.'' Especially once she had a conversation with a certain ghost.

"One more. Hold on.''

Fatigued, Liz pivoted slightly and rested her free hand on Ethan's back. His arm jerked and Liz sucked in a breath when the tip of the soldering iron brushed the back of her hand.

"Sorry.'' Ethan kept his eyes focused on the insides of the box. "There.'' A moment later he pulled the soldering iron clear.

Liz backed away, relieved to put some space between them. He dropped the soldering iron in its holder, then reached for her hand, cradling it in his palm. His touch sent a skittering sensation up her arm, distracting her from the pain.

"I've got some aloe somewhere in here.'' Keeping a hold of her hand, he dug through a drawer under the worktable, came up with a green-filled bottle. "How are your hydroponics experiments coming along?''

"Richard got a good start on the seedlings.'' She gasped when Ethan dabbed aloe vera gel on her burn. "And I brought down some mature plants. And since hydroponic plants grow so much faster, we should have a consistent fresh food supply.''

Although he'd finished smoothing the gel into her skin, he didn't released her hand. "So tell me the bad news.''

His touch coupled with the soothing aloe scrambled her

thoughts. It was an effort to remember why she'd sought him out. "There was an accident in the storage area by the common room."

His grip tightened. "What happened?"

"A chunk of rock fell from the ceiling and smashed the spare lumber."

"Was anyone hurt?" His gaze roamed over her as if seeking injury.

She shook her head. "It must have happened sometime during the night."

Tugging at her hand, he rounded the worktable. "Show me."

Liz waited while he shut and locked the door to the energy center. She half-hoped he'd take her hand again. When he didn't, she did her best to ignore her disappointment.

"Richard discovered it," she told him as they hurried along the corridor.

He puffed out a sigh as he raked his fingers through his hair. "I've gone over all these caverns with a fine-toothed comb, checking for stability. Everything was rock solid."

"You must have missed something," Liz said.

He scowled as they rounded the last curve. "I damn well better not have."

When they arrived at the room, Liz gestured at the locked keypad. "I entered the emergency code."

Ethan's fingers brushed her arm. "It's not locked."

She saw in a moment that he was right. Not only was the door not locked, it was slightly ajar and the light glowed inside.

A sensation traveled up Liz's spine, like a memory of a touch. She couldn't seem to bring herself to push open the door. "Maybe Richard came back. But I told him to stay out."

"And Richard doesn't have the override code."

"Maybe I didn't program the lockout correctly."

Ethan nudged the door open. "Niedan, are you in there?"

But there was no one in the room. And although the rubble

of broken lumber still lay on the floor, the massive rock was gone.

With a bare touch on her shoulder, Ethan urged her into the room. "Where's the piece that fell?"

"I don't know. It was there." Liz pointed. "You can still see a bit of crushed rock."

Ethan knelt to run his fingers across the floor, coming up with bits of gravel. Then he tipped his head up to inspect the ceiling.

"Your rock couldn't have come from there," he told her.

She looked up at the gaping hole. "Of course it did. How could it have not?"

"Because that hole was already there. There *was* a loose piece, but I pried it out myself more than a month ago."

Ethan watched the emotions chase over Liz's face as she looked from the ceiling to the mess of broken lumber. "Then where did the rock come from?"

Crouching again, he sifted his fingers through the grayish-green remnants of the boulder. "Good question. Especially since this gravel looks like peridotite. It's an igneous rock. You might find it in a cave formed by volcanic activity, but not in a limestone cavern like Hoyo del Diablo."

She sank to her knees beside him, the full implication of what he'd said seeming to weigh her down. "Then it was brought from outside BioCave. But who? And how? That was a hellacious big rock."

"Someone could have wrestled it onto a dolly. As to who . . ." Ethan narrowed his gaze on her. "You say Richard discovered it?"

"Yes, but you don't think . . ."

"There's bad blood between you two."

"That's true, but why would he smash the lumber?" Settling back on her heels, she scooped her hair back from her brow. "I didn't even know I wanted to use it until yesterday when I came up with a new methodology. And I certainly didn't tell anyone about it."

"But you'd be the most likely staff member to use the wood."

She shook her head. "I saw him try to move the rock. He couldn't shift it even an inch. I don't see how it could be Richard."

"Hell, you're probably right." As much as he wanted a neat solution to at least one of his never-ending streams of problems, he saw the sense in what she'd said. He still intended to grill Niedan about it, but he didn't expect results. "So where does that leave us?"

Her expression thoughtful, she plucked a bit of gravel from the floor. "Until today, I don't know that anyone's been in here since lockdown. Could it have been one of the workers?"

"The question would be why." Ethan rose, held out a hand to help Liz up. She accepted his assistance, but pulled her hand away as soon as she gained her feet. "Aaron kept the workers pretty happy. Well-paid, plenty of perks."

She nudged a piece of the broken lumber with her sneakered toe. "And it still wouldn't explain why the rock is gone now. I don't know who would be strong enough to . . ." Something changed in Liz's face, an uneasy light of realization coming on.

Ethan gripped her arm. "What?"

"Nothing." She stumbled back from him, pulling her arm free. Hand outstretched, she stared at the bit of peridotite in her palm.

He caught a flicker of something in her face, something that dug at his insides. Fear. Outright terror.

Then it was gone as if a veil had dropped. She seemed puzzled by her own reaction.

Ethan swept the pebble from her hand, dropped it into his pocket. "Come on." Gesturing toward the door, he waited until she preceded him out of the room before following. Pulling a screwdriver from the back pocket of his jeans, he unlocked the circuitry box of the electronic lock.

"What are you doing?" Liz asked

He studied the circuits, then pulled out a palm-sized black case from his jeans pocket and plugged it into a jack inside the box. "Downloading all the key codes that have been entered in the last several days."

"Good idea. We can figure out who's been in here."

When he'd downloaded the codes and relocked the door, he turned to Liz. "You figured something out in there. What was it?"

Her brow furrowed as if she was trying to remember. "I don't know. I just . . ." She shrugged, a quick raising and lowering of her narrow shoulders.

Ethan wanted to press her, to force the information from her. But when he looked into her clear blue eyes, he saw no guile, no deceit. Only a trace of confusion.

Still uneasy, he pocketed the black storage device. "If you remember, let me know." He lay his palm against her cheek, feeling some sort of urgency, a faint danger. Then he dropped his hand. "I'll go talk to Aaron."

She smiled. "Tell him hello for me."

The light in her eyes ate away at him. He nodded abruptly. "Keep quiet about the damage. I want to see if someone comes forward on their own."

Turning on his heel, he strode away from her, irritated, angry and worried all at once. Hell, why was nothing about Liz ever straightforward?

"That's the last of them." Ethan shifted in his seat in BioCave's communications center, his gaze fixed on Aaron's image on the center color monitor. "All the entry codes stretching back over the last two weeks."

Aaron's lined face filled the monitor, his image surrounded by eleven others displaying the common room, the hydro lab, the energy center and various other locations throughout BioCave. Ethan found his attention drifting again to the display of the hydro lab, where Liz moved in and out of the screen, her supple body a constant distraction.

"Give me a minute to pull the names from the database,"

Aaron said, drawing Ethan's focus back to the business at hand.

Gaze fixed off-screen at his computer beside him, Aaron ran a hand over his brow, smoothing back the thin hair on his pate. For the hundredth time Ethan wondered how a vibrant woman like Liz could carry on an affair with a man fifty years her senior. If the rumors were true.

With an effort, he pushed aside his straying thoughts. "Even if the vandalism occurred before lockdown, there's still the question of who moved the rock since."

Aaron sighed, a hiss over the faint static on the monitor. "We should know in a moment. I have to say, I'm glad you insisted on individual key codes for all the employees."

"I'm just glad all the lock boxes store a record of entry." Ethan's voice trailed off as Liz's tall, graceful form snared his attention again.

"So, how are things between you and Liz?"

Ethan snapped his gaze back to the monitor displaying Aaron's face. A crafty smile curved Aaron's thin lips and a devilish glow lit his pale blue eyes.

"Fine," Ethan said, wondering what was going on in the old man's mind. "Things are fine."

"That's dandy." Smug smile still in place, Aaron turned back to his keyboard, rapped away at it. "Here it is. Huh . . ."

"What?"

"I'll download these names to you, but . . ."

Impatience pricked at Ethan. "But what?"

Aaron gestured at his screen. "I can account for everyone here, vouch for them. Other than Richard's and Liz's, they're all aboveground folks. Except . . ."

Taking in a breath, Ethan waited in silence. Aaron turned to face him from the center monitor. "There are two unidentified codes here. One preceding Richard Niedan's and one following Liz's lockout."

"Unidentified?" Ethan leaned forward in his seat, caution strumming along his nerves. "What do you mean?"

"They're invalid codes. Garbage." Aaron scraped back his hair again. "They're not in the BioCave computer. There's no way they could have been used to gain entry."

Ethan let out a puff of air as he eased back in the padded swivel chair. "And yet they were."

The unease in Aaron's eyes echoed Ethan's own. Invalid codes that had allowed entry into a secure room, that overrode a lockout. Destruction wreaked by Lord only knew whose hand.

Ethan absently returned Aaron's good-bye as the center monitor went blank. He didn't know which was more distressing—that there was a glitch in the Vuchoviches' security software or that someone among them might be capable of the vandalism in the storeroom.

Needing the distraction, he returned his attention to watching Liz. For ten minutes, he followed her every move, enjoying the grace of her slender arms, her long, tanned legs. Then she strode to the door of the hydro lab and disappeared from view.

Ethan knew instinctively she was headed for the communications center. His anticipation of her arrival irritated him, made him feel vulnerable. He tamped down his excitement ruthlessly. When she entered, he swiveled in his chair to face her.

She slipped inside the communications center and shut the door behind her. "What did Aaron say?"

He considered withholding the information from her, oddly loathe to upset her. But he needed her informed, needed her on his side.

He quickly explained about the codes. "I'm going to ask the Vuchoviches to do a stress test on the security systems, track down the bug."

She moved closer and her scent drifted toward him, something light and floral. His brain seemed to freeze as it processed her delicate fragrance.

He registered her lips moving and suddenly realized she was speaking. ". . . how's Aaron?"

Running a hand over his face, Ethan strove to reorder his thoughts. "Great. He's great." He flicked a glance at her. "I could page him again. So you could talk to him yourself."

Ethan realized he was holding his breath, waiting for her response. He forced himself to breathe.

She shrugged. "I'm sure I'll get a chance to talk to Aaron soon."

He should be relieved that she didn't seem to care one way or the other. But what did her *laissez-faire* attitude really mean? That there was nothing between Liz and the seventy-eight-year-old millionaire? Or that her relationship with Aaron was nothing more than a loveless affair of convenience?

Just as he was a husband of convenience. What would he prefer? A legal document binding them? Or the chance to have her in his arms, in his bed?

His lips stretched into a mirthless smile. Now *that* was a no-brainer.

He sprang to his feet, the tight space of the communications center suddenly stifling. "I have to get back to work."

When she didn't move, he brushed past her, enjoying the way she tensed at the slight contact. He wondered how it would feel to trace the neckline of her yellow V-neck sweater, then slip a hand inside to cup her breast.

She shuddered, as if she'd read his thoughts, then turned her back on him to scan the monitors. "Too bad there isn't a camera in the storage room. We'd have a tape of what happened."

It was one of the few spaces besides the personal quarters without a monitoring camera. Even the communications center had one, perched up above the door. He was damned grateful cameras didn't record dirty thoughts.

He pulled open the door. "I have to go," he told her again, gesturing for her to lead the way out of the room.

She turned and stepped around him, nothing but her fresh scent brushing against him. With hands that trembled ridiculously, he shut the door and locked it.

She walked beside him to the energy center, no doubt headed for the hydro lab. Something seemed to bubble beneath the surface in her, like an unasked question.

As they moved along the corridor, she tucked her hands into the back pockets of her pale denim jeans. "When are you going to tell the staff?"

He suspected that wasn't what she really wanted to say. "I'll speak to the Vuchoviches this afternoon. The rest will be notified at dinner tonight."

She nodded, then took a long breath. The action pushed her breasts out, making him want to test their weight beneath the soft knit of her sweater.

They'd nearly reached the energy center when she turned to face him. "Why haven't you come to see me since the accident?"

Head tipped up, color rising across her cheeks, he knew what the question had cost her in pride. His first impulse was to throw a biting comment back at her, but something inside him, a soft spot he didn't even know he possessed, tempered his response. "I've been to see you."

"When?" She narrowed her gaze on him. "While I've been awake?"

He had to smile at that. "No. At night, when I've come to bed."

The color in her cheeks flared darker. "So you have been sleeping with me."

He felt compelled to needle her, just a little. "You seemed to enjoy it, even asleep. I'll admit, it's always seemed a bit kinky to have a woman that way, all but unconscious, but after trying it—"

Her sharp gasp warned him, but as sharp as his reflexes were, he barely caught her wrist before she laid her hand across his cheek. As it was, he could feel the strength of her and realized if she'd made contact he'd be wearing the imprint of her hand right now.

He locked his fingers around her wrist to prevent her taking another swing. "Even I'm not so low as to have sex with a sleeping woman."

He didn't bother to add that he'd been sorely tempted over the last two nights. That the sight of her laying beside him stirred an ache inside him that he crassly chose to identify as merely sexual urgings.

When she tugged against his grip, he released her. She breathed deeply, her chest rising and falling with the effort, until the rage in her blue eyes finally cooled.

"You might not be my first choice of a companion," she said, her anger still edging her voice, "but I think it would be useful for both of us to have someone to talk to in the evenings. As a sounding board, if nothing else."

He slipped his hands into his jeans pockets, displaying a nonchalance he didn't feel. "And what about sleeping together? Have you resigned yourself to that inevitability?"

Her jaw worked, but she gave him a clipped nod. "I can see there's no way around it. And you've obviously demonstrated you can manage to sleep beside me and keep your hands off." Her glare punctuated her final words, more effectively than the slap she might have given him.

"I'll be more than glad to give you your space in bed." He couldn't resist adding, "As long as you want it."

She didn't bother responding to that. "Shall we meet for dinner then? I'm looking forward to having a meal outside the walls of our quarters."

He nodded. "I'll see you in the common room at seven."

She turned away, started down the corridor.

"Liz."

She looked back over her shoulder, wary. "Yes?"

"If you know anything more about what happened in the storage room, even a hunch, you'll tell me." He didn't bother to make it a request.

"I don't know any more than you do."

Even in the dimness of the corridor, he detected a hesitancy in her. She wasn't exactly lying, but there was something beneath the surface she wasn't sharing.

She continued on her way and he watched her, as beguiled by the sway of her hips as by the layers of complexity he kept uncovering in her. Like the twisting passageways of Hoyo del Diablo, a man could get lost within Liz Madison's tantalizing secrets.

Smiling at his own whimsy, Ethan unlocked the door to the energy center and tried to turn his focus back to his work. After an hour of entertaining more thoughts of Liz's soft lips than the status of the wind generators, he set the systems on automatic and left the energy center to seek out the Vuchoviches.

Chapter
Six

Liz felt a twinge of guilt that she hadn't been strictly honest with Ethan. She did have a suspicion as to what might have happened in the storage room. But since the answer involved a man who'd been dead one hundred-plus years she was reluctant to share with Ethan what she knew.

The trick would be finding Noah. How do you go about summoning a ghost, anyway? Call his name? Chant a spell? No way would she do any heebie-jeebie stuff. If Noah wouldn't come when called, she'd just wait until he next appeared.

Tapping out the entry code to the hydro lab, she slipped inside and locked the door behind her. She used her personal lockout code to prevent Richard from entering. He'd be royally ticked to have to knock, but she didn't want to chance him barging into her conversation with Noah.

The last thing she needed was a witness to her lunacy. Brushing back her hair, she took a breath, ready to call Noah's name. Then slapped a hand over her mouth as the camera over the door caught her eye. She'd gotten so used to it she'd nearly forgotten—her every move in the lab would be displayed on monitors aboveground and in the communications center.

She'd have to place a manual block on the transmission. As she stepped behind the worktable that held her computer, she wondered what Ethan would make of it if he happened into the communications center and saw the hydro lab monitor blacked out. Then she recalled he'd been in the com center earlier while she'd worked in her lab. Had he watched her then?

She shuddered at the thought of his intense gaze on her. It didn't bear thinking about. Forcing her focus to the keyboard, she tapped in the video blocking code. A moment later the ready light on the camera blinked out.

"Okay, Mr. Simmons, you'd better be listening." Liz turned away from the computer. "Noah!"

She tensed, listening, slowly scanning every corner of the room. "Noah!" Her voice echoed off the arch of the high ceiling, setting off a tremor of sound. "Noah," she said more softly.

The pressure seemed to change in the room. She felt it shift in her middle ear, resonate along her jaw. She'd never noticed those sensations before, but then she'd never before had a warning he was about to appear.

He seemed to blink in with a rush of air, although nothing stirred in the lab, not the papers on her main worktable or the wisps of hair on her brow. She was relieved to see his porkpie hat squarely on his head.

"You called me, Miss Lizzy?" He seemed quite pleased that she had.

"I need to talk to you," she said quickly to forestall any amorous notions on his part. "About what happened in the storage room."

Noah faded briefly to a shimmer before rematerializing. *"I don't know nothing, Miss Lizzy."*

"You're a terrible liar, Noah." She moved closer, intrigued by the drop in temperature near the ghost. "I happen to know you've been bedeviling Ethan."

His guilty look confirmed her guess. *"Needed a lesson,"* Noah mumbled.

"It has to stop, Noah. You could put us all in danger by pulling the wrong wire. And that rock, you could have hurt someone—"

"I didn't have nothing to do with that rock!" He swept off his hat, clutched it between his hands. *"I did take it away after, threw it down the pit. The creature gets its power from rocks such as that. I couldn't let it stay—"*

"The creature?" She circled him, aware of the waves of distress coming off him. The disturbance, mixed with his chill aura, set off a faint resonance of fear within Liz. "What creature?"

He slammed his lips shut and looked away. She waited, listening to her heart beat, to her own breathing. Noah kept his eyes downcast as he turned the brim of his hat around and around in his hands.

When he spoke, it was to his porkpie. *"Miss Lizzy, I admit to the broken wires and such. And I did take the rock away and drop it down the pit, though it took all my energy to spirit it through the door."*

Mouth dropping open, Liz stared at him. "You pulled the rock through the door?"

He sneaked a glance at her, a bit of pride in his brown eyes. *"Under it, really. Through that itsy little space at the bottom. You wrap yourself around it, see, and squeeze yourself down flat so you . . . well, that part would be right difficult for you live folk."*

She laughed. "I imagine it would."

"But it wasn't me that put the rock there, Miss Lizzie, or broke the lumber." He met her gaze now, seemed desperate for her to believe. *"I never broke a thing that I didn't figure could be fixed."*

She had to take a breath, to gather her nerve to ask in a near whisper, "Was it the creature, then?"

He faded again, glittering along his limbs a moment before returning. *"That was foolishness, what I said. Ain't no creature."*

The stubborn set of his face told Liz he wouldn't say anything more on the subject. Just as well, because she truly didn't want to hear the answer.

"Noah." She waited until he looked at her. "Will you stop pestering Ethan?"

He looked mutinous, but he nodded. *"I will. If you will allow me to come visit you now and again."*

"You can." She smiled at him. "But you know there can't be anything between us."

"Because you love that mule's behind you're married to?"

She would have laughed at the ridiculous notion, if Noah didn't look so solemn. She put out a hand toward him, deep into the coolness of his aura. "He's my husband, Noah."

"If you say so, Miss Lizzy." Keeping his sad, soulful eyes on her, Noah backed toward the wall behind him. His fingers wiggled a farewell before he melted into the rock and disappeared.

Pausing at the entrance to the common room, Liz searched the room for Ethan. Her raspberry silk shirt, the one concession to femininity she'd brought down to BioCave, seemed to cling to her as she moved. She shouldn't have worn it— it wasn't nearly warm enough. Even worse, it seemed to bring her nerves to the surface, when she was already on edge from the tumultuous events of the day.

She scanned the food line, but Ethan wasn't among those filling their plates. As she entered the room, the slide and flutter of the silk shirt, the sensual way it stroked her skin, disconcerted her. She realized the real mistake in putting it on was not its impracticality. It was because it reminded her far too much of Ethan's touch.

Keeping one eye on the entrance, she stepped into the food line behind William Bradshaw. Trang and Qwong had managed to concoct an appealing meal from the food stores and the small crop of herb plants they'd brought with them. But when Ethan finally entered, Liz lost all interest in the pasta and sun-dried tomatoes she'd been scooping onto her plate.

Why did the man have to look so damned good? He'd changed into forest-green corduroy pants and a cream-colored flannel shirt. Exposed by rolled-up sleeves, his muscular forearms kicked off a myriad of fantasies.

He spotted her and headed straight for her. "We have to talk." Plucking her plate from her hands, he set it aside on a table.

One hand on her elbow, he continued with her smoothly to the kitchen where Trang and Qwong were just untying their aprons to go get their own dinners. "I'll bet you're glad you're not on clean-up crew," Ethan said as the two cooks headed for the door.

"Darn right," Qwong said as he slipped out into the common room.

Ethan urged Liz to a back corner of the kitchen where they wouldn't be seen from the common room. "The Vuchoviches just finished their check of the security systems."

Watching his mouth move as he spoke, she had difficulty focusing on his words. "And?"

"No bugs. The system is working perfectly."

In spite of herself, she reached out for him, lay a hand on his arm. "How can that be?"

"You tell me." His fingers closed around the silk sleeve of her shirt, interlocking their arms. "How could garbage codes have opened that door? Who dropped the rock there? Who carried it away?"

Her grip tightened on his arm. She knew the answer to the last question. Had Noah somehow mystically opened the door as well? But no, he'd said he had to transport the rock under the closed door. And he'd insisted he hadn't brought it there.

"What?" Ethan asked, his eyes fixed intently on her face.

She shook her head. "Nothing."

He cupped her chin with his free hand. "You know something."

The impression of his fingertips seemed to burn into her skin. "No. I'm just worried, that's all." She kept her eyes on his, willing him to believe her.

After a moment, he sighed, a half-smile curving his lips. "I must have just missed you in our quarters when you went to change." He drew a fingertip along her jaw, then grazed it across her lower lip.

As relieved as she was that he'd changed the subject, his touch wound her nerves so tight, she thought she'd jump out of her skin. She shivered as his stroking finger wiped every concern from her mind.

"Must have." The words came out shaking, trembling as he passed his thumb across her lips.

"You look luscious in that color." He cradled the side of her face with his large hand. "Delicious," he murmured, lowering his head. "I'd like a taste."

"Our dinner's getting cold," she said against the roil of his warm breath.

He skimmed his lips across hers. "I love cold pasta."

Her breath caught at the contact. "The clean-up crew will be in here soon." The last word drew out on a sigh as his mouth trailed along her jaw.

"Clean-up crew's already here," he whispered in her ear. "We're it."

Annoyance pricked at her that he'd committed them to the job without even telling her. Then sensation washed away every feeling but pleasure when his tongue flicked into the shell of her ear and traced its whorls. Her knees trembled and she had to grope for Ethan's broad shoulders to hold herself up.

"I want you," he rasped into her ear. "I'd take you now, right here if I could do it without anyone seeing."

She was on fire, from her toes to the tip of her head, the furnace emanating from the center of her. When he nudged his thigh between hers and pressed against her, she cried out softly. His thigh flexed against her again and again, his hard muscles stroking her, teasing her. . . .

With a rush of shame, she realized what he was trying to do. Shoving as hard as she could, she pushed him away, amazed when she succeeded in backing him off. She knew he could have held fast if he'd wanted to, could have continued his sensual assault. Retreat was his decision.

She couldn't face him for a moment. Fire still licked along her veins, pooled between her thighs, agonizing her. She took two long, shaky breaths, then slowly ran her eyes up the length of his body.

Her gaze snagged on the front of his corduroys, at the hard bulge pushing against the placket of his pants. Her trembling hands ached to cup that hardness, to rub along its length, to feel him shudder in response.

Tearing her eyes away, she tipped her head up to meet his gaze. His gray eyes were shuttered, resilient as steel as he flicked them over her body.

"Why are you so afraid of your own pleasure?"

"I'm not afraid," she said, too quickly. Had she been afraid? She tried to parse out her feelings, but his looming presence scrambled her brain. She lifted her chin. "I just didn't want to."

He laughed, a deep rumble of scorn. "You lie terribly."

"It's the truth," she insisted.

He took a step nearer, although he didn't touch her. "I can still see the tremors in your arms. The swell of your lower lip." He brushed his thumb along it, then leaned close to whisper, "The way your nipples jut against the silk of that blouse."

With a gasp, she ducked away from him and hurried across the kitchen. "I'm going to eat."

"Liz," he called, stopping her, turning her around. Arms crossed over his chest, he gave her his mocking smile. "It will happen. It's simply a matter of time."

Her eyes widened and she knew no amount of lies could hide the fear in them. "I won't let you force me."

Anger clouded his eyes. "I won't have to." There was a wealth of inference in those few words.

Then he strode past her out of the kitchen, leaving her to follow behind him.

They accomplished the kitchen clean-up with silent efficiency. Liz might have thought Ethan would see scullery work as beneath him, but he scrubbed pots without complaint or comment, with as much attention to detail as he would give a faulty solar panel.

After toting in the leftover food, Liz worked beside him, drying each piece he washed. She waited each time for him to set the item down in the dish drainer, not wanting to risk touching his hand. Her arms and shoulders ached with tension by the time they'd finished.

When Ethan stood during dinner to announce an emergency meeting before lights-out, Liz was relieved that it would forestall their return to their quarters. The meeting gave her a respite from Ethan's pursuit of her. She didn't know what angered her more about his stalking her—his insolence or her own very real excitement at the prospect.

Longing for escape, she tossed the damp dishtowel over the towel rack and tried to flex the tension from her shoulders. Ethan watched her with rapt fascination, his gaze dropping briefly to her breasts. Heat rose in her cheeks as he started toward her, a look of determination on his face.

But he stepped past her. Irritation warred with relief as he hefted the mop and bucket and came back toward her.

He lifted the bucket to the sink. "I'll finish up. You go ahead."

Her baffling emotions rooted her feet to the ground, made her reluctant to leave him before he'd finished. "Are you sure?"

He swung the filled mop bucket to the floor, raised his brow at her in a decided leer. "Unless you'd like to finish what we started earlier. If we went into the dry stores and shut the door behind us—"

She didn't stay to hear the rest of what he had to say. Shoulders back, chin up, she entered the common room and headed for the table where the Jacksons, Smiths, and Nishimotos sat.

"Suppose I could squeeze in here?" With smiles and a shifting of chairs, they made room for her. Since the table seated six, seven in a pinch, Ethan wouldn't be able to sit beside her.

He saw through her ploy when he entered from the kitchen, defeating her attempt to keep her distance by tugging another table closer. He perched on its edge, near enough to lay a hand on her shoulder if he chose.

He didn't touch her, but just his proximity was unsettling. She would have risen and moved to another table if she didn't think it would cause a scene. Not to mention the fact that Ethan might well follow her there, too.

So she stayed where she was, her shoulder aching with the expectation that he would touch her. Perversely, he didn't; in fact, he didn't even look at her. He didn't have to. She got the message quite clearly. She was his—and there was no use in trying to avoid him.

He shifted, propping one long leg on the chair in front of him. "I've gathered everyone to report an incident in the storage area by the common room."

Ethan proceeded to describe what had happened, as well as informing the staff about the invalid codes. "I thought it best to keep everyone informed."

Janet Vuchovich spoke, her dark eyes worried. "I didn't think to mention this before but I've noticed a few problems in my lab—minor things, like books out of order, files missing from my hard drive—"

"Me, too," Harlan Jackson put in. "A toolbox disappeared one day from the engineering lab and turned up the next day in my quarters. Neither Benita nor I moved it."

Oh, Lord—Noah. Liz didn't realize the ghost's mischief extended to the rest of the staff. She'd have to call him again, give him another talking to.

She was suddenly aware of Ethan's silence, of his eyes on her. Feeling like a deer caught in the headlights of a semi, she smiled gamely and turned away. After a moment, she could feel his attention shift back to the staff.

"I've had some problems as well." He leaned his elbow on his propped knee, so his hands dangled millimeters from Liz's shoulder. "Which means we're going to have to heighten security."

A murmur rippled through the crowd. It was Richard Niedan who voiced what the others were reluctant to mention.

"Are you saying someone among us is responsible? That one of the staff is vandalizing equipment and supplies?"

Ethan's gaze was on her again. "At this point, I don't know what to think. We might have to consider the possibility of a stowaway."

That set off a further clamor among the staff. Ethan gestured to quiet the group and his fingertips brushed Liz's blouse, sending the air straight from her lungs.

"I want supplies inventoried," Ethan said. "I want unattended rooms locked at all times. If you see anything suspicious, you're to notify me at once."

The meeting broke up. Liz sprang to her feet, beyond the tantalizing proximity of Ethan's large hands, and headed straight for the exit. She sensed Ethan turning to follow.

Just as she increased her pace, she heard Dr. Nishimoto calling out after Ethan. She glanced over her shoulder and caught sight of Ethan, listening to the physician with half an ear, his irritation at her escape clear.

A grin lighting her face, Liz slipped into the corridor. Recalling her accident, her gaze strayed occasionally to the floor, seeking out obstacles. She didn't even see the man lurking in a doorway until he detached himself from the shadows and stepped directly into her path.

Liz couldn't quite suppress a shriek of fear as she leapt back from the dark figure. When she recognized Richard Niedan's sour face, annoyance replaced her fear.

He closed in on her like a bulldog. "I told you I didn't

do it. Why did you tell Ethan you thought it was me?''

''I said no such thing.'' She didn't bother to add that she had actually defended him to Ethan. ''Why in the world do you think I did?''

''Because he tore my head off.'' There was the trace of a whine in his offended tone. ''He said he was keeping an eye on me from now on.''

''That had nothing to do with me.'' Liz tried to step around him.

He blocked her way, his expression more menacing. ''You've ruined my life before. I won't let you do it again.''

Anger bubbled up inside Liz and she only just avoided kicking Richard Niedan's shins. ''You falsified data, Richard. You ruined your own damn life.'' She elbowed past him. ''Excuse me.''

His painful grip on her arm hauled her up short. ''I would have substantiated those numbers. I just needed time.''

She pulled away from him, but he just tightened his grip, his baby face a cruel mask.

Tears burned Liz's eyes, but damned if she'd let them fall. ''Stop!'' she whispered hoarsely. ''Let me go.''

Footfalls approached from farther down the corridor, accompanied by the murmur of voices. She heard Ethan's deep bass woven with Dr. Nishimoto's lighter baritone.

After one last pinch, Richard released her arm and stepped back quickly as Ethan and Dr. Nishimoto rounded the curve of the corridor. Dr. Nishimoto continued on, passing them with a cheerful goodnight as Ethan slowed to move to Liz's side.

Liz tipped her face down and blinked away the moisture in her eyes. Ethan didn't miss the gesture, placing a hand on her shoulder. But she refused to answer the silent query, determined to fight her own battles with Richard Niedan.

Ethan's gaze locked on Richard then, the sharp steel of his eyes like an inquisitor's sword. Richard's bluster didn't last long under Ethan's regard. He squirmed and fidgeted, then finally sidled away with a muttered goodnight.

"What was that all about?" Ethan asked.

"Nothing." Liz moved off down the corridor. Ethan was at her side in a heartbeat, his hand nestled at the small of her back.

"You didn't wait for me." His fingers pressed at the sensitive base of her spine.

The warmth of his touch eased away the imprint of Richard's hand, the ugliness of his accusation. Unable to resist his comfort just then, Liz leaned closer, tucking herself under the shelter of Ethan's arm. Her own hand stole up to curve around his waist.

She could feel Ethan's brief hesitation of surprise, then his arm snugged her against his side. They arrived at their quarters that way, only parting to slip through the door that Ethan shut and locked behind them.

"I take it this means another truce," Ethan said.

Liz couldn't help the smile that curved her lips. "I suspect we may need daily truces."

An almost gentle light danced in his eyes. "Maybe a white flag is in order." At her questioning look, he added, "Something to indicate whether we're at war."

She laughed, the soft sound easing the constriction in her throat that Richard had placed there. The gentleness in Ethan's eyes changed, transformed into something warmer, something with an almost tangible sizzle.

Self-preservation urged Liz to flee that look in Ethan's eyes. She edged away. "I'll go change."

She expected one of his familiar mocking responses, but he only nodded, scooping up her nightgown from the foot of the bed. She took it from him with trembling fingers, disconcerted by the image of his large hands on the silky fabric that would soon caress her own body.

A few minutes later, as she gazed at herself in the bathroom mirror, Liz realized their fragile truce would be shattered the moment she stepped back into their room. There on her arm, as vivid as a brand, lay the marks of Richard's fingers. The sleeveless gown would never hide the botanist's handiwork.

Liz puffed out a lungful of air, wondering how to sidestep the scene Ethan would surely make when he saw her arm. Although she felt confident she could handle Richard—if he manhandled her again, she wouldn't hesitate to plant a well-placed foot on his shin—but Ethan wouldn't see it that way. He'd go storming down the corridor, waking all the Bio-Cavers, and batter down Richard's door.

Unless . . . unless she could keep Ethan from seeing the bruises. Unless she could distract him, keep his eyes off her arm until she was safe under the covers. Then maybe to-morrow she could beg some makeup from one of the other women to conceal the purpling outline of Richard's hand.

She pondered what she should use as a distraction. She could pick another fight with him—but that was exactly the kind of conflict she was trying to avoid. She could ask him to retrieve something for her from the lab—but that would only arouse his suspicions.

I could seduce him.

A thrill skittered up her spine at the notion, then settled low in her abdomen. She wouldn't, of course; she couldn't. She was no seductress, didn't know the first thing about tempting a man. But the idea itself, as preposterous as it was, tempted her with its sensual promise.

It would surprise him. Throw him completely off guard.

What better way to keep him from seeing what she didn't want him to see? It would probably end in her making an idiot of herself, but that would accomplish her purpose just as well.

Decided, she flipped off the bathroom light and slid open the door. Keeping her bruised arm inside the doorway, she leaned against the jamb and called out to Ethan where he sat at the desk.

"Can you dim the lights?" She tried for a throaty tone of voice, but to her ears, she sounded like a frog. Ethan's puzzled look confirmed her self-evaluation. ''Lower the lights. My head is still a bit sore.''

He rose and tapped the controls. The light level dimmed to a pale yellow, sending the corners of the room into shadows.

Secure that her bruises would be barely visible, Liz padded toward Ethan, attempting to sway her narrow hips the way she'd seen women do it in the movies. But where the actresses oozed sexuality when they moved, Liz felt like a horse tromping across the floor.

Ethan gazed at her, his expression mystified as she stepped up to him and drew her hands up the front of his soft flannel shirt. Her first feel of him was nearly her undoing, sending her heart into overdrive with fear and excitement. She squeezed her eyes shut to avoid filling her gaze with his broad shoulders, his beautiful, chiseled face.

She needn't have bothered—the image of him was burned into her brain. Her fingers, too, seemed to have the sense of sight, relaying to her an exact representation of his powerful form. The message of his body transmitted itself to her, sending warm honey through every limb, quickening her breathing, teasing a moan from her throat.

She curled her hands around the back of his neck and wondered what to do next. Kiss him? Drag him to the bed, pulling him on top of her? But what then? What if he took her sudden invitation as carte blanche and wouldn't stop when she asked him to? Even worse, what if she didn't ask?

A kiss seemed safe. She drew up on tiptoe, urging his head down to hers. He certainly didn't seem to be cooperating; she felt that she had to bring her entire weight to tipping his head down. Undeterred, she opened her eyes and slanted a quick look up to target his mouth.

One look at his sardonic, mocking smile and Liz jolted to a stop. She snatched her hands free and took a step back. ''Why are you laughing at me?''

His smile broadened. ''I'm not laughing.''

She crossed her arms around her middle, her left hand

quickly covering the bruises. "You might as well be."

"I wasn't, honestly," he assured her. "I was simply wondering what you were up to."

She was glad the low light hid her guilty flush. "Maybe I wanted to try kissing you without being bullied into it. To see if I liked it any better."

His teeth gleamed white in the dimness. "Then by all means, go ahead."

For a moment, she stood transfixed, like prey in the path of a tiger. Then, as surely as that massive feline would snag its prey with a careless paw, his gray eyes pulled her closer, nearer, until they stood toe-to-toe.

This time when she slid her hand around the back of his neck, he surrendered easily to her urging, dipping his head down to her. But he went only as far as she guided him, waiting with lips slightly parted for her to initiate the kiss.

Sudden self-doubt assailed her and she had to close her eyes. She didn't want to see him smirk at her clumsy attempt at sensuality, didn't want to know if his eyes laughed at her. Then, eager to be done with the charade, Liz closed the gap between them and pressed her lips to his.

And realized it didn't matter that she was awkward. Because the simple sensation of kissing Ethan, of sliding her lips across his, sent a shaft of sheer pleasure through her that made her incompetence inconsequential. He might be unmoved by her kiss, but she felt enough for both of them.

Liz traced the seam of his lips with her tongue, feeling the warmth of him clear to her toes. When her tongue brushed against his, a whimper escaped her, a pleading sound that seemed to have come from another woman. Her body urged her to take the next step, to plunge her tongue into his mouth, to taste him fully.

She might have, if he hadn't brought his hands to her arms, slid them up to her shoulders. She couldn't quite hold back the catch in her breath, her shudder, as his palm passed over the bruises left behind by Richard.

She pressed her lips harder to his, hoping to keep his mind

on her kiss and not her brief reaction to pain. But as she'd suspected, he'd been much less involved in the kiss than she. He broke easily from her arms and crossed the room in two strides to slap the lights back on.

Then he returned to her side and lifted her arm to the light. His gaze raked her bruises, one fingertip gently tracing their periphery. Then he raised his cool gray eyes to hers, and the words he bit out held a wealth of danger.

"Who did this to you?"

Chapter Seven

Her first fleeting thought was to lie. Try to somehow pass it off as an accident, the result of another fall. But the mark of a hand was all too clear and Ethan was no idiot.

Liz sucked in a long, slow breath. "It was Richard Niedan."

She'd expected rage; what she saw instead frightened her far more. Murderous intent burned in Ethan's eyes, coupled with a tightly leashed control that made it all the more terrifying.

He'd reached the door before Liz had even had time to blink. "Stay here," he told her, releasing the door lock with swift precision.

Liz hurried after him, catching him a few paces down the corridor. "Ethan." She tugged at his arm; she might as well have tried to pull down the rock walls surrounding them. "Ethan, please, let me explain."

He continued on, implacable, peril shimmering around him like a cloak. She had to stop him, to divert him, or as surely as she breathed, Ethan would kill Richard Niedan.

She overtook him and dug in her heels, planting herself firmly in his path. "Ethan, stop."

He took her shoulders in his hands and put her aside as easily as if she were a doll. Liz scrambled to catch up again, all too aware that the Niedans' quarters were just up ahead.

Liz grabbed his arm and using all her strength, hauled him to a stop. "Listen to me, Ethan." He tried to shake off her hand, but she just held tighter. "Listen to me!"

For a moment, he seemed ready to turn his rage on her, his eyes blazing as he turned on her. His chest heaving, he dragged in air until Liz could see at least a semblance of calm in his face.

He fisted his hands at his sides. "I'm listening."

Assured that he wouldn't bolt again, Liz loosened the circle of her fingers around his forearm. She stepped closer, tipping her head up at him.

"We're only a few days into BioCave," she said, keeping her voice low. "We've already had to deal with the disruption of the destruction in the storage room. If you go in there and deliver a well-deserved punch to Richard's pretty face, that could bring an end to the whole experiment before it even gets started."

"I won't let him batter you." His tone was shot through with a menacing conviction.

"*I* won't let him," Liz said. "He caught me off guard this time, had his hand on me before I could think what to do. If he tries anything like that again, he'll have *my* fist redecorating his nose."

For a despairing moment, she thought she hadn't convinced him, that despite the possible harm to BioCave, Ethan was still intent on expending his rage on Richard Niedan. Intent on dissuading him, she moved her hand up his forearm, her palm stroking soothingly along the hair-roughened skin. His muscles flexed in response, the tension radiating from him.

He wrapped his other hand around the back of her neck, then pressed his forehead to hers with a long exhalation of air. "All right," he said softly, his thumb teasing the short strands of her hair, "I'll let it go, this time."

Her own shoulders relaxed at his capitulation. "Thank you."

His thumb traced lazy circles on her sensitive nape. "But . . ."

She tried to pull back; he wouldn't release her. "But what?"

He shifted his lips to her brow so that she could feel his warm breath feathering her bangs. "Don't ever, *ever* try to hide anything like that from me again."

Liz shivered at the harsh command in his tone. "I won't."

"Then let's go to bed." He pulled away to tuck her under his arm.

She walked beside him, her relief at forestalling disaster pushing aside the alarm she might have felt at the prospect of sleeping with him. She had to get used to the idea sooner or later; she couldn't assume he would wait until she was unconscious before climbing into bed with her each night.

Liz's heart fluttered in a double-time beat by the time they reached their quarters again. When Ethan headed straight for the bathroom to change, Liz slipped gratefully under the covers. She retreated as far over on her side of the bed as she could and turned her face to the wall.

She needn't have bothered. When Ethan returned, he flipped off the light, climbed in beside her and wrapped his arms around her. He pulled her back toward the middle of the bed, secure against his hard, bare chest.

"Goodnight," he murmured into her hair.

Moving tentatively, Liz nestled her hips against him. She nearly bolted at the feel of his erection thrusting against her softness. But he made no move that could be construed as sexual despite the blatant arousal he couldn't hide.

A sense of safety suffused her, confidence that Ethan would take her nowhere she did not wish to go. She could sleep, then, secure in his arms, surrounded by the intimate comfort of sharing Ethan's bed.

Liz drifted off, his rhythmic breathing caressing her cheek.

• • •

Liz woke early as a pale morning light chased the shadows from the room. It had been three days since Ethan had discovered Richard's mark on her arm, three days since she'd made the conscious choice to sleep with her husband of convenience. But although she'd slept safely beside him for several nights now, her sense of security seemed to dissipate with the false morning's light.

Ethan lay sprawled beside her, half on his side, one arm flung over her. The sweet weight of his hand tempted her to edge closer and snuggle up to him as she had through most of the night. But she risked waking him, and if she woke him . . . she doubted he'd be nearly as gentlemanly as he had been during the night.

She turned away from him to free herself from his hand. Even in sleep, he tightened his hold on her, momentarily imprisoning her. Then he sighed, releasing her. She pulled away and his hand dropped from her body, its path across her ribcage and just under her breast sending a frission of awareness through her.

She squeezed her eyes shut for a moment, willing her breathing to slow, the peaks of her sensitized nipples to recede. Then she pushed aside the covers and rose.

In the bathroom, she quickly threw on a rich purple cowl-neck sweater and jeans, then padded back into the room barefoot, sneakers in hand. She checked the clock as she slipped on her shoes—six-oh-four, surface time. Somewhere far above them, the sun rose.

Not quite a week underground, and her inner body clock was already fooled by the artificial illumination that waxed and waned with electronic precision. She could almost believe dawn was breaking through some hidden window. What kind of havoc it would wreak, she mused, if the timers all went out of whack, making morning out of night and vice-versa?

She stepped into the corridor, closing the door quietly before she headed toward the hydro lab. God, she craved the feel of sunlight—genuine sunlight, not the artificial glow of her quarters. She considered a side trip to the common room, just so she could stand beneath the light shaft there. But she had a half-dozen things she wanted to accomplish before breakfast. She'd consider the sunshine her reward for the morning's work.

An hour and a half later, Liz tucked the last of her tomato seedlings into their bed of vermiculite. Activating the pump to flush the growing medium with nutrient solution, she gazed at the neat rows of plants with real satisfaction. To a soil gardener, the plants would appear far too close—each one only about six inches apart. But plants grown hydroponically didn't need to spread their roots out as much and so could be planted closer together.

Liz checked the grow lights hanging over the tank, tweaking one of them slightly to redirect its glow. In addition to the conventional fluorescents, she planned to experiment with metal halide and high-intensity discharge lamps. She'd gotten good results with all three.

Retrieving her digital camera from beside her computer, she slung it over her shoulder and squeezed off several shots of the newly planted tank. She planned to photograph every stage of growth for each of her experimental setups.

"Hello, Miss Lizzy."

Thank God for the strap or her camera would have been shattered on the rock floor. She turned to glare at Noah, who was floating just above the grow tank behind her.

"I'd appreciate a little warning, Mr. Simmons." She watched his booted toes drifting in and out of the grow tank. "And could you light somewhere?"

"Sorry, Miss Lizzy." He sank to the floor beside the grow tank, then his avid gaze latched onto her legs. *"Never thought a lady could look so fetching in a pair of old work pants."*

"What?" She looked down at herself. "You mean my jeans?"

"Ladies sure do dress differently now than they did in my

time.'' He grinned appreciatively. *"Mama would have a fit.''* The thought seemed to please him.

She circled the grow tank containing the mature tomato, pepper, and zucchini plants. Their lush green foliage barely concealed the heavy red, yellow, and green fruit. These plants had been started weeks before lockdown, giving the BioCavers a jump start on the fresh produce they'd need during their time underground.

As she squeezed off shots, he followed, dogging her every step. *"What might that doohickey be?''*

She crouched to photograph the round red globe of a tomato. "A camera. You know what a camera is, don't you?"

He nodded. *"Had my picture taken once, with Mama. Camera didn't look nothing like this.''*

She gestured with the sleek, black instrument. "This one's digital. Instead of developing the film, I can download the image directly to the computer.''

"Computer's that thingamabob over there?'' He pointed to the monitor on her worktable.

"That's part of it,'' she said, surprised he could identify it. "How'd you know?''

"I watch. I listen when folks talk. Don't understand half of it, of course.''

"You understood enough to pull Ethan's wires loose,'' she scolded. "And to wipe his hard drive.''

"That was an accident,'' he protested. *"I didn't reckon passing my hand through the thing would cause a problem.''*

"Just don't do it again, Noah. Not to Ethan, not to any of them. You've caused no end of problems.''

He stared down at his toes, abashed. *"I'm sorry, Miss Lizzy.''*

She acknowledged his apology with a nod, then crossed to the computer to plug the camera into its connection. "If you wait a minute, I'll show you how the pictures—''

"Miss Lizzy.''

She turned, saw Noah twisting his hat in his hands. "What is it?''

"Miss Lizzy," he said again. *"I got to tell you...."*

She waited, watching as he bobbed up a few inches from the floor, then back down. She was surprised the hat didn't come apart in his hands.

"Lordy," he breathed. *"Lordy, I can't."*

With a collapsing of air, he disappeared. Liz stared at the space he'd vacated, worried, uneasy.

Maybe he'd just wanted to tell her again that he loved her. But when she considered the expression on his face, she realized he hadn't looked besotted. What he'd looked was scared.

Noah hunkered down against the curved rock wall in his special place, fairly riddled with guilt. He should've told Miss Lizzy like he intended. Keeping the evil to himself only made things more dangerous for her. He was a danged yellow-bellied coward not to tell her.

But what if it wasn't the monster? What if one of the BioCave folks put that rock there? That Richard fellow, for instance. He'd said some mighty mean things about Lizzy. So mean, Noah had snuck a handful of pebbles into Richard's coffee when he wasn't looking. Made Noah mighty happy to see that cross-eyed look on Richard's face when he'd sucked up a pebble.

Noah snickered a little, remembering, then his laughter faded in the blackness of his tiny cave. It hadn't been Richard. Noah had been there when Richard had opened the door. The rock and broken lumber had already been there.

Noah straightened and drifted around the perimeter of the small bubble of space deep within Hoyo del Diablo. The creature had been quiet for so long. Why had it returned? Because the BioCave folk had come into its domain, had wakened it? No telling what the thing would do. When Noah had come into the Devil's Pit, all unknowing, the monster had killed him. If he didn't tell Lizzy . . .

Maybe the rock was an accident. Lizzy's fall, too. Maybe he hadn't sensed the creature after all, hadn't heard its voice, felt its touch. After so many years listening, he'd imagined the evil thing had returned. And what if speaking of it was enough to call it to them? Maybe it was best to leave the vileness unspoken.

Excuses, danged excuses. Noah hunched back down in a corner of his special cave, ghostly hands locked behind his head. He was a coward and a dang fool besides. If he didn't drum up some courage from somewhere, his dear Lizzy could be in dire danger. His dear Miss Lizzy could die.

When the sight of the plump red tomatoes dangling on one of her mature vines started her stomach rumbling, Liz decided it was time to stop. She checked her watch—just past eight; breakfast must be ready. Saving the data she'd entered in her computer, she hurried from the lab, fingercombing her hair as she went. When she caught herself smoothing wrinkles from the front of her sweater, she forced her hands to her sides. What in the world was she primping for?

She knew the answer to that as soon as she saw him in the common room. Ethan stood beneath the light shaft where several others had gathered. Eyes half-lidded, he tipped his head back to the light, and his broad shoulders strained against the knit of his whiskey-brown V-neck sweater.

Liz paused in the doorway, the sight of him stirring something within her, part pain, part joy. Why did the sun have to glow a little brighter where it touched on him? It lay across him like a mantle, limned his dark hair with gold.

Keeping her gaze on Ethan, Liz crossed the room to stand beside him. She glanced up at him, but he didn't seem to notice her arrival, his gaze still focused on the sunlight. It was as if he was the light's focal point, as if each sunbeam bounced down the shaft, from reflector to reflector, straight to him.

Wendy Nishimoto smiled at Liz from the center of the circle. "Heavens, isn't this wonderful?"

Liz sighed as the sun's rays caught her. "If I'm feeling

like a mushroom after only a week, how will it be after six months?''

The crowd shifted, several people moving away. But Ethan remained, leaning close and placing his mouth close to Liz's ear. ''I missed you when I woke this morning.''

She couldn't quite suppress her smile as tremors shot up her spine. ''I had work to do.''

He brought the backs of his fingers idly up her arm, his thumb just brushing against her rib cage. ''You seem to have work every morning.''

She tried to edge away, but he just closed the gap. ''I have to make up for lost time.''

''Maybe you should rouse me in the mornings,'' he said softly, leaving no doubt as to which meaning of rouse he intended, ''and I could help you.''

She swallowed back a gasp as his thumb skimmed the side of her breast, millimeters from the aching tip. ''Stop.'' Somehow the word turned into a moan.

''Stop what?'' he murmured. ''This?'' His fingers trailed up her arm again. ''Or this?'' His thumb teased her nipple, sending a jolt of sensation clear to her toes.

Her hand shot out and clamped around his wrist. ''That,'' she managed in a strangled tone. She tugged his hand away, grateful he didn't resist.

The clatter of dishes from across the room brought the world back on track. Liz was surprised to see that they stood alone under the light shaft, that the others had already taken a place in the breakfast line.

Ethan slipped his arm around her shoulders, urged her to the food table. ''Hungry?''

Why did everything the man say sound like an invitation to bed? ''Yes.'' Liz wished she could take it back when she realized it sounded like consent.

They took their place behind Matt Smith, their resident expert on animal husbandry. ''Where's Arlene?'' Liz asked. Matt's wife was BioCave's mechanical engineer.

''In the engineering lab.'' Matt served himself some

scrambled eggs. "Trying to repair some of the equipment that's gone belly-up recently."

With any luck, that would be the last of Noah's meddling. As Liz perused the breakfast offerings, Ethan rested his hand lightly on the back of her neck. She swallowed back a sigh of pleasure. "Is that really necessary?"

His hand remained, his palm caressing her nape. "We have to keep up appearances." He pressed his lips to a spot just behind her ear.

Liz couldn't control her shiver. "I don't want you kissing me."

He laughed, the sound a low rumble. "What if you kiss me?"

Heat rose in her cheeks. "That was just . . . an experiment." She stepped away from him so that his hand fell from her neck. "Besides, we're on display." She gestured to the video camera trained on the common room.

He leaned close again. "But the tourists are expecting a show. Just think how it would make their day if I were to—"

But she didn't let him finish, grabbing up two plates and shoving one into his hands. Turning to the food table, she slapped some scrambled eggs on her plate, then moved along in line behind Matt Smith.

"Your hens seem to be doing a good job," she said to Matt, plucking up a corn muffin from the bread basket.

"Doesn't bother them a bit being a hundred feet underground," Matt said. "They just keep on laying."

Liz placed a few slices of ripe tomato next to her eggs, edging forward as she felt Ethan behind her. "It seems a little like cheating to bring six months worth of chicken feed down here."

"What else would they eat?" Ethan reached over her shoulder and snitched a slice of tomato from her plate.

"Hey, get your own!" Liz protested, but he just gave her a playful grin as he popped the tomato into his mouth. Ethan, playful? She eyed him suspiciously. "I've read some studies on hydroponically grown grain."

"Not enough yield." He nudged her with his hip as he reached for a stack of tomato slices. "Anyway, Aaron never intended BioCave to start from scratch. We had to prime the pump to some extent."

"But too much priming and you turn the experiment into a glorified underground camping trip."

"I've always liked camping," Ethan said, "sleeping under the stars."

"No stars, Winslow," Liz reminded him.

"The great outdoors."

"We are most definitely indoors."

He bent his head close to her ear. "Sharing a sleeping bag. Making love in a tent."

Against her will, warmth pooled inside her at the image. "No sleeping bags. No tents."

"We could pretend." His soft, warm breath enticed.

"I'm not good at pretending," she lied, turning away from him and scanning the room for a table. Matt Smith waved at her to join the group at his table and she headed that way, all too aware of Ethan following.

Ethan pulled out a chair for her, then sat beside her, so close that her arm would brush his with each bite she took. She would have scooted away, but there was no space to spare between her and Matt on her left. Liz would have asked Ethan to move, but just then the Jacksons arrived, asking to share the table.

"What do you think of the self-sufficiency issue, Harlan?" Ethan asked as the Jacksons settled into their seats.

"The chicken and the egg issue again, eh?" A grin lit Harlan's dark face. "Should we have started with eggs to hatch chickens to make more eggs. . . ."

"I personally am glad to start with eggs on my plate." Ethan stabbed a slice of tomato from his plate with his fork. "Not to mention the produce from the hydro lab."

As he chewed, Liz found herself mesmerized by the motions of his mouth, the flexing of his jaw. What would that sharp angle feel like under her fingers?

"Liz?"

Ethan's low voice drew her out of her daze. She focused on the succulent bite of tomato that he held out to her, as red as Satan's offer to Eve.

"I have my own," she said, her voice unsteady.

"But I took some of yours," he said, "and I wouldn't want you to go hungry."

She shook her head. "I don't—"

Before she could complete her refusal, he captured her chin with his free hand. Stroking his thumb gently across her lower lip, he coaxed her lips apart. When he brought the treat closer, she didn't resist, opening her mouth, and taking the tart-sweet morsel on her tongue.

Triumph shone in his eyes. "As much as I might want to be Adam to your Eve, Liz, we're not trying to recreate civilization here."

Alarm coursed up her spine that he had read her mind. Liz threw her head back, freeing herself from his grip. "If this is the Garden of Eden, I'd say your role is the snake."

He laughed, genuine amusement clear in the ringing sound. As the others around the table joined in his laughter, he grinned and brushed a fingertip across her cheek.

Good God, he seems almost human, Liz realized as the tenderness in Ethan's eyes sent her into confusion. Even worse, if she wasn't careful, she might begin to like him. A deadly combination if she had any hope of avoiding intimacy with him.

She finished her breakfast quickly, the noise of conversation flowing around her unheard. She needed to return to the solitude of her lab, to consider the roil of emotions Ethan set off inside her. She had to put her feelings back in order.

She escaped from the table with a muttered good-bye, only just evading the touch of Ethan's hand as he reached out for her. She felt his eyes on her as she left the common room, but she didn't look back.

Halfway to the hydro lab, she realized she didn't want to be alone with her thoughts after all. She needed to talk to someone, someone who understood her, who wouldn't make judgments. Doubling back on her path, Liz turned instead toward the communications center.

As she'd hoped, Aaron Cohen was in his office when the connection went through, a ready smile lighting his lined face. Liz's heart ached at how tired he looked, bringing home to her what a toll the creation of the BioCave project had taken on him.

"What can I do for you, Lizzy girl?" he asked, his faded blue eyes dancing.

What could she say? That she'd begun to feel things for Ethan that frightened her? That her heart felt in peril every moment from his lightning changes of mood?

She chose to sidestep the issue. "Nothing really. I just called to chat. How are things going aboveground?"

"Fine. The staff find anything else amiss down there? Like that mess in the storage room?"

Only Noah's mischief. She didn't have to bring that up to Aaron. "Not a thing."

Liz felt a twinge of guilt at Aaron's relieved smile. She was glad when he changed the subject. "So how's my favorite girl?"

She smiled back at him, the familiar ache settling in her chest. "Rose was your favorite girl, you know darn well."

His face softened as he remembered his late wife. "She loved you as much as I do. She wouldn't mind." His gaze became piercing as it fixed on her. "You know I love you, sweetheart, don't you?"

Aaron's intensity surprised her. "I know. If it hadn't been for you and Rose . . ." Liz didn't like to think how she might have ended up.

"As long as you know how I feel."

"And I love you, Aaron," Liz assured him. "Very much."

He nodded, satisfied, then gave her a little wave and signed off. Liz sat back in the chair, feeling a bit less lonely.

"Very touching."

Liz leapt from the chair and whirled to see Ethan standing in the back of the communications room. "How long have you been there?" she asked, her heart pounding.

"Long enough," he said. "Long enough to hear the end of your little tête-à-tête with Aaron."

"I wouldn't call it a tête-à-tête." She didn't understand the dark anger in his tone. "I was just touching bases with him."

"Covering your bases is more like it." He tipped his head toward her. "If you'll excuse me." With that, he turned on his heel and strode from the communications room.

"Ethan!" she called out, running after him. He didn't slow his powerful pace down the corridor, didn't give her any indication that he'd heard her. Before she could call a second time, he'd turned a corner in the corridor and disappeared from view.

What the hell was that all about? After his warm affection in the common room, what had happened to bring back his callous disdain for her? What had she done?

She'd done nothing, she told herself angrily. The problem was all with Ethan, and she was damn well going to tell him so. Her righteous indignation goading her, Liz locked the communications center behind her and headed down the corridor after Ethan.

When the first harsh whisper touched Liz's ears, a chill clutched the back of her neck. She stopped short in the corridor, listening, terror crawling over her like ants. A memory of a memory tugged at her, of a rough, eerie touch, a rasp of sound. Then the whisper came more clearly, and she heard humanity in the desperate sound.

"Help me. Please. Someone help."

Footsteps scraped in the intersecting corridor up ahead. In the next moment, Arlene Smith stumbled into view and collapsed in Liz's arms.

Chapter Eight

Liz sank to the floor holding Arlene, keeping the woman's head cradled in her lap. "Ethan!" she shouted out, praying he wasn't out of earshot.

Arlene struggled for breath. "Crack . . . in the wall . . ." She fumbled for Liz's hands, tugged at them. Her eyes fluttered open. "A gate . . . a gate to Hell."

An icy fist seemed to clutch Liz's heart and she shuddered. Arlene's fingers dug into the backs of Liz's hands as her breath rattled in and out of her throat. Good Lord, could she be dying? "Ethan!" she screamed again. "Dr. Nishimoto!" The rock walls of the corridor seemed to soak up the sound, muffling it.

Where was everyone? She'd just left several of the staff behind in the common room; surely her voice would carry that far. And Ethan couldn't have gotten that far ahead of her.

Arlene opened her eyes again and she looked frantically around her. "Is it gone?" she rasped out.

"You're fine," Liz told her. "You'll be fine."

"Coming . . . coming for me." Arlene struggled against

the confinement of Liz's arms. "Couldn't . . . breathe. . . ."

Liz held her tight until the other woman relaxed again, her eyes drifting shut. Liz kept her gaze fixed on the unsteady rise and fall of Arlene's chest as she fought for each breath.

"Ethan," Liz whispered. "Where are you?"

Silence stretched out in all directions.

It's come back for sure, Noah thought as he circled Bio-Cave's engineering room a third time. *The monster has returned.*

He came up alongside the stretch of wall in the back where a wide crack split the rock. A hissing filled his ghostly ears, and he sensed the flow of something moving from the crack. Some kind of gas, he supposed, fumes which had filled the lab in a few minutes' time.

The woman hadn't been overcome at once. Noah had been watching her, enthralled with the gadgets she had arrayed across her worktable. He'd been amusing himself by fingering the components, shifting them around on the table's surface, when the woman started wheezing. She looked around her, clutching her throat. Then she saw the crack.

She must have felt the monster too, because her eyes opened wide with fear. She went to her knees, arms up to defend herself. Not knowing what else to do, Noah had focused his measly power and gripped the woman's shoulders, urging her to the door. She got it open on her own, then crawled out into the corridor. Noah had closed the door after the woman had left to keep the fumes inside the room.

He stopped his roaming and eyed the crack. Could he stop the leak with his incorporeal self? He stood before the flow, used all his focus to turn back the deadly stuff. But the fumes passed right through him, too insubstantial to be affected by his miserly ability.

Then what could he use to block the gas? He moved about the room, grabbing up bundles of wire, rolls of coarse black fabric, anything he could find to stem the flow. He forced as much as would fit into the four-inch-wide crack, more and more until it seemed the hiss had nearly ceased.

He let himself float back to the ceiling, relieved to have helped, yet still sorely troubled. He'd seen the handiwork of the creature three times now—when it pushed Lizzy in the corridor, when it hurled the rock, and now, when it opened the crack to release the gas. Yet at none of those times could he sense the creature as he had more than a hundred years ago. Lizzy felt it, this woman had. He could see as much in their faces. Yet he could not.

What did it mean? That a dead man could not feel the evil? Yet he had, over the years, sensed the touch of the vile presence, however faint. Then why did he not feel the creature now? Could the monster perhaps only make itself known to one person at a time? Could its power then be limited?

Deep in thought, Noah eased himself through the rock ceiling of the engineering room and back to his special place. As he oozed through the layers of limestone, a whisper seemed to follow in his path.

Noah.

There was no safety, even to the dead. The monster still knew his name.

When help finally appeared, it came from all directions. Liz saw Ethan first, hurrying along the corridor from the direction of the energy center. She couldn't help the tears of relief that pricked her eyes at the sight of him. Then Dr. Nishimoto came from the other way.

Matt Smith followed close on the doctor's heels. "Oh, my God, what's happened?" He bent to his wife. "Arlene, are you okay?"

Liz shifted and rose, letting Matt take her place. Arlene took her first deep breath and opened her eyes to her husband. She seemed lucid at last as she fixed her gaze on Matt. "Hello, love." She dragged in another cleansing breath.

Dr. Nishimoto pulled a stethoscope from his back pocket and knelt to examine Arlene. "How long has she been like this?"

"Five, ten minutes," Liz told him. "I found her right after I left the common room with Ethan."

Ethan's fingers circled Liz's arm. "What happened?"

She shrugged, shaking her head. Arlene, with her husband's help, sat upright and leaned against the corridor wall. She looked up at Ethan. "There was a gas leak in the engineering lab. I didn't notice it at first. Then it got hard to breathe."

Ethan crouched down to eye level with Arlene. "Was there any odor?"

The engineer shook her head. "None."

"Probably natural gas, then," Ethan said.

Arlene locked her fingers with her husband's, as if his touch were a lifeline. "When I got short of breath, I heard the hiss. Then I saw the crack in the wall of my lab."

A gate to Hell, Arlene had said. Liz shivered, remembering.

Ethan raked back his hair with his fingers. "I thought we'd vented off all the pockets in the vicinity. Did you shut the lab door?"

Arlene's brow creased with worry. "I didn't. I couldn't even think straight when I crawled out of there."

"Let's get her to the med center," Dr. Nishimoto said. With Matt on one side and the doctor on the other, they helped Arlene to her feet.

Ethan rose and gestured to Liz. "Come with me. We'd better close up the lab."

Liz stepped up beside Ethan as he took the turn to the engineering lab. "She was pretty out of her head at first. Said some pretty strange things."

"The lack of oxygen, no doubt."

"I suppose, but still . . ." Why couldn't she get a grip on the memory that drifted in and out of her awareness? There was something hidden in her subconscious that linked the recent incidents—her own fall, the broken lumber, the gas leak. But she couldn't seem to put it all together.

When they reached the engineering lab, Liz was relieved

to see the door was shut. "She must have closed it after all."

Ethan didn't seem convinced. "I suppose. Where were you when you first saw her?"

"Where you found me in the corridor."

His gray eyes narrowed on her. "You didn't come down here, close the door yourself?"

"Of course not. I would have told you if I had. I had my hands full comforting Arlene."

Suspicion blossomed in his gaze. "Why did you take so long calling for help? You said you found Arlene when you left the common room with me. I was in the energy center a good ten minutes before I heard you call."

"Then you're deaf," Liz retorted. "Because I was screaming your name like a banshee from the moment Arlene collapsed in my arms."

He shook his head slowly and Liz realized with a shock Ethan didn't believe her. She was almost too astounded to be angry. "Why in the world would I have not called you? I could see Arlene was in trouble, that she needed help."

His eyes burned as if some accusation lurked there, an allegation only barely held in check. Then he compressed his lips tightly and looked away. "I'll go down to the computer center and increase the ventilation to this room. You go grab a couple oxygen masks from storage. Once it's cleared out enough in here, we'll have to investigate that crack."

"Harlan could probably help you with that better than me. I have to get back to my work."

"Harlan's busy tracking down a glitch in the power grid. Delegate your work to Richard. I want you with me."

Liz tamped down the urge to throw a punch at Ethan. He was back in autocratic mode and every fiber of her being longed to rebel. "Fine," she said through clenched teeth. "I'll get the masks."

"Meet me in the computer center." He stalked off down the corridor, leaving her to seethe alone.

Trembling in anger, Liz dragged in breath after breath to calm herself. She stared at the shut door, wondering if Arlene had indeed shut it or if someone else had. But who? Anyone else would have helped Arlene as well. Unless it was Noah. The ghost would have managed to shut the door, but would have been helpless to assist Arlene.

Liz headed off down the corridor, turning right at the intersection toward the main storage room. As glad as she was Noah understood the danger of the gas leak enough to shut the lab door, she was distressed that Ethan suspected her of some nefarious action. How could he not have heard her cries for help, or for that matter, how could the staff members still in the common room not have heard? And when her voice should have caromed off the rock walls, echoing in every room, why did it seem to die just beyond her lips, as if the limestone surrounding her were cotton wool? As if a massive hand had closed over her mouth.

She shuddered as she reached the storage room, her fingers shaking almost too much to tap out the code. She reached inside to slap on the light before entering the room, grateful for the brilliant illumination.

It took two hours to repair the fist-wide crack in the engineering lab. Two tense hours in which Liz wasn't sure what would explode first—the volatile gas in the room or her own hair-trigger temper.

The moment she saw the makeshift repair of the gas leak she recognized Noah's handiwork. But she couldn't tell Ethan, which opened herself up to even more of his speculation. She just suffered his harsh scrutiny in silence as they worked side-by-side filling the opening with concrete patch material.

After they'd finished and washed the last of the concrete dust from their hands, Ethan urged her from the room. "We have to talk."

She didn't bother asking what about. She didn't even bother shrugging his hand off her shoulder. He gripped her so tightly, she'd never shake him free.

When they reached their quarters, Liz was relieved to see

Ethan had stowed away the Murphy bed. She crossed the room and leaned against the opposite wall, arms hugging her middle. He followed right behind her, planting a hand against the wall on either side of her.

"What the hell is going on?" he asked, his gray eyes nearly black with anger.

She resisted the urge to duck out of the circle of his arms. "I don't know any more than you do."

"I think you do."

If she looked away, he'd know she wasn't being truthful. But she was a lousy liar, surely he'd see that in her eyes. "I don't know, Ethan."

He gave her a hard stare before pushing away. "Then how do we explain all the problems?" He paced the small room. "There had to have been a tremendous pressure buildup behind the wall of the engineering lab to open a crack that size. Yet we never detected that pocket of gas."

"Ethan, if I knew the answer, believe me, I'd tell you." It wasn't the whole truth—she knew some of the answers. But there was something more at work here than a mischievous ghost. "Ethan," she said, stilling his restlessness with a touch on his arm. "We'll get through this, I'm sure of it. We've had a few unlucky accidents. It's to be expected."

He covered her hand with his own, enclosing her fingers in his larger ones. "Is it?"

The intensity in his eyes made her take a step back, but he didn't release her hand. "Of course. Surely you didn't expect everything to work perfectly from day one."

His grip tightened momentarily on her, then he loosened his fingers, freeing her. "Maybe I did want perfection. But you . . . you've turned everything upside down."

"What?" She stood toe to toe with him. "What have I turned upside down?" Did he mean BioCave? Or something more personal?

Instead of answering, he strode to the door. "I've got to go." He left, shutting the door firmly behind him.

Liz stared after him, stunned. What the hell was she supposed to make of that? Ethan Winslow seemed to want to blame her for everything that went wrong. Well, the hell with him; she had no intention of taking blame.

She checked the clock—lunchtime had come and gone, but the last thing she wanted to do was eat. She'd head for the hydro lab to check on Richard's progress. Maybe she'd run a few simulations on plant growth. Or link to the Internet for the latest literature on hydroponic gardening. Anything to keep out of Ethan's path.

He wasn't being fair to her. In the silence of the rough-hewn corridors far beyond the main part of BioCave, Ethan had to admit that much to himself. She might be guilty of many things—manipulating Aaron, being out for the main chance, stating the truth as it suited her—but it simply made no sense that she would do anything to imperil BioCave. She had been just as intent on being part of the experiment as he had been. She'd married him, for God's sake, a near stranger. In fact, all she really knew about him was that he was an arrogant son-of-a-bitch who didn't like her.

And he didn't. Or at least, he hadn't. But since coming down here to BioCave, living in close quarters with Liz, he found it more and more difficult to remember to dislike her. All it took was the feel of her curving against him in bed, or the scent of her hair when she leaned close to him, or the sound of her breathing when he eased in beside her sleeping form late at night.

Which was nothing but sexual attraction. Despite the satisfaction he got just holding her while she slept, or the joy he got in teasing her in the common room just to see her smile, the heat he felt for her overwhelmed everything else. It would only take a few nights of plundering the wealth of sensuality her body promised to ease that appetite, then he would regain his equilibrium.

The corridor light had faded nearly to darkness and Ethan looked around him to get his bearings. He'd gone beyond the quarried section of BioCave into one of the natural passageways where lighting had not been installed. He pulled from the back pocket of his jeans the small halogen flashlight he always carried and switched it on. Although he had explored nearly every square inch of Hoyo del Diablo in the course of developing BioCave, he didn't remember coming this way before.

Behind him, he could still see the low-voltage lights that lined all of BioCave's quarried corridors. If he just continued on without making any turns, he would be able to make his way back without getting lost.

So he continued on, reluctant to return to the tedious work of repairing circuits or troubleshooting the energy systems. Hell, they'd barely been down here a week and the routine already grated on him. But if he was honest with himself, he'd admit it wasn't the routine that ground away at him, it was Liz Madison—Winslow, damn it. She always seemed to hang on the periphery of his consciousness, teasing him, one moment soothing, the next arousing. She'd turned the even-keeled six-month experiment he'd anticipated with Cynthia into a hair-raising roller coaster ride.

He laughed harshly as his feet whispered along the rough rock floor of the passageway. He hadn't thought of Cynthia, his erstwhile fiancée, in days. Even now, he could scarcely picture her face. And memories of their lovemaking, always somewhat unremarkable, seemed burned away by fantasies of Liz.

Fantasies of stripping the clothes from her body, with slow care or fast, fiery need. Of brushing his lips along each sleek square inch from the silk of her hair to the delicate arch of her foot. Of feeling her hands on him, stroking along his arms, his chest, his legs, her fingers circling his manhood and guiding him between her parted thighs . . .

Lost in the images, he stumbled on a rough spot on the floor, going down on one knee. Cursing at the jar the fall gave his body, he shifted into a sitting position and shone the flashlight on his leg. He'd torn his jeans and he could see blood oozing from the skin beneath. He supposed it was just what he deserved, coming down an uncharted length of passageway when he was preoccupied and thinking more with what was between his legs than between his ears.

Pushing against the wall to rise again, he cast the flashlight's glow around him. Which way had he come? He focused the beam to the left, searching for something familiar. Was that the direction he'd been traveling from when he fell? He flicked the light the other way. But he didn't recall any of the geological features in that part of the passageway either.

Somehow the fall had turned him all around. He took a few tentative steps to his left, hoping to recognize something. Immediately, a tunnel opened up off to the right. If he'd come that way, he would have noticed the tunnel, wouldn't he? But the angle of the opening, nearly parallel with the one it intersected, would have made it difficult to see. He might have passed it without realizing, especially with the way he'd stumbled.

Turning to test the opposite direction, he strained to see into the darkness. He stepped carefully on the uneven ground, every nerve alert. When he kicked a pebble and heard it skitter across the rock floor, he tensed, then immediately forced himself to relax. No good getting himself on edge. It would only impair his judgment.

Training the flashlight at his feet, his gaze fell on a scattering of rocks on the limestone floor. Those must be the rocks he'd stumbled into, had sent flying across the floor. He bent to pick up a handful and saw with a shock they were peridotite, same as the boulder that had damaged the lumber in the storage room. How in God's name did igneous rock end up in a limestone cave? He stared down at the rough-edged gray-green chunks, trying to find sense in what his scientific mind told him was entirely wrong.

"Ethan."

He stilled, listening. Had he actually heard the whisper? Had someone seen him come down this way and followed him? If they had, they would have called loudly. There was no reason for stealth. Stuffing the handful of pebbles into his pocket, he moved the flashlight from side to side, washing the limestone walls with illumination. Which way? Behind him toward the split passageway or before him?

He stood rooted to the floor, indecisive. A prickle went up his back as he considered the options. He could stay here, wait for someone to find him. Or he could explore farther along the corridor. But which way? He couldn't seem to choose, which was completely unlike him.

"Go to the right." He couldn't precisely hear the words; they almost seemed impressed on his brain. Ethan looked around him, wondering if there was someone nearby. Then he shone the flashlight to the right, looking again for familiar landmarks. But indecision seemed to grip him again.

"To the right, you dang idiot." This time, the soundless directive filled him with irritation. He looked around him, angrily searching for the prankster. There was no one in sight. But his annoyance seemed to have shaken loose his uncertainty. He forced himself to focus and realized the right was indeed the direction he'd come from. His brief moments of doubt had just been a trick of his mind, a product of the dark and his preoccupation with Liz.

Confident now, Ethan continued down the passageway, holding the flashlight out before him as a beacon. Before long, he reached the smooth, quarried corridors of BioCave. Switching the flashlight off, he headed for the energy center and the afternoon's work.

Noah followed along behind Ethan until the geologist reached the well-lit corridor, then drifted off toward his special place. That was a mighty close call. Noah hadn't even realized the creature was there until he heard its voice call Ethan's name. There was no way Noah could have held off the evil thing, but he figured to have a chance to guide Lizzy's ill-tempered husband back to safety. It almost hadn't worked, the man being more stubborn than the most hard-headed of mules.

About to squeeze himself into the minute fissures in the

rock that constituted his passageway to his small cave, Noah changed course and headed off for Lizzy's lab instead. This would be a good time to tell her about the creature, what with Ethan a near goner at its evil hand. Not that Noah would have minded his competition out of the way, but Lizzy seemed to be developing an affection for the sour-faced geologist.

He'd been just about to ease his head through the high ceiling of Lizzy's lab when he felt the first cold touch. It fairly froze him in his tracks, congealed him into the tiniest particle of ectoplasm. There were no words, but in that momentary chill, a clear as a bell message was branded on his soul.

"They are mine."

Like a whipped pup, Noah skittered through hairline fractures and gaseous pockets back to his cave. As he dropped inside the tiny space, he rematerialized and faded several times before he could quite pull himself together. When he'd finally knit his soul back to wholeness, he sank to the floor of his cave and snatched his hat from his head.

It had come after him. After years of cat-and-mouse chase, of being never quite there but never quite gone, the creature had touched him. And told him in no uncertain terms that he was not to tell the others of its existence. And him, yellow goddanged coward that he was, clammed up tight and ran.

And why? He was a dead man, dang it, no one could hurt him now. The monster had long ago taken his body, what did he have left that would come to harm?

Only his soul, he thought, turning his porkpie around and around in his hands. The creature could eat up his soul, quick as you please, if it cared to. And there would be nothing left of Noah Simmons, not even a memory.

Angry with himself, he slammed his hat to the floor. It bounced gently off the rock and floated back to his hand. He would have rent it in a million pieces if he could, just to give his hands something to accomplish. Then shame nipped at the heels of anger and he lowered his face in his hands.

Coward, coward, coward, he chanted silently. Oh, Lizzy, my love, I am not worthy of you.

Chapter
Nine

Liz sat beside Ethan at the dinner table, picking at her eggplant casserole. The first few bites of the tomato and soy cheese–laced concoction had been tasty. But then Ethan had resumed the sensual assault he'd begun in the food line, sitting beside her and brushing his knee against hers at every opportunity. Her dinner quickly lost its savor, as her awareness centered on his touch. It took an effort to keep her attention on the conversation flowing around her.

"There aren't too many passageways that aren't recorded," Harlan was saying. "We could probably figure out from the maps where you fell."

"I don't have a complete set." Ethan dropped his hand to his lap and trailed his pinky along her thigh. "I couldn't pinpoint the location."

Liz sucked in a quick breath of air as she snatched her leg away. "There's a complete package in the small storage room." She stood abruptly. "I'll go get them."

Sliding back her chair, she hurried from the common room. She heard Ethan's deep voice as she retreated, then

129

the laughter of those gathered around the table. Her face burned as she wondered if they were laughing at her. Then good sense stepped in and told her she was just being paranoid.

Ethan had set her so on edge this evening she didn't know what to think. He couldn't seem to stop touching her, whether to brush her arm as they stood in the food line or to rest a hand in the small of her back as they walked to their table. She would have preferred to put some distance between them when they sat to eat, but he didn't give her the choice, guiding her to her seat, then pulling out the chair beside her for himself. He found a myriad of ways to keep his body in contact with hers.

As she tapped out the door code of the storage room, she considered Ethan's behavior tonight. On the surface, his constant sensual barrage seemed like sexual overtures, another campaign in his attempt to conquer her. But at one point, as he drew delicious circles on her wrist with his thumb, she was surprised to see an entirely unexpected look on his face—need. Not sexual need, but something deeper—a need for comfort, a need for connection.

She shook her head as she eased the storage room door open. She'd probably been mistaken. Her interpretation of the expression on Ethan's face was probably wishful thinking. It was something every woman wanted—to be needed by the man she loved. It was true enough for her, even if she didn't love the man in question.

She laughed shakily as she poked her head inside the storage room. That was a horrifying thought—falling in love with Ethan Winslow. That would give him the ultimate power over her. He wouldn't just claim her body with sex, he would take control of her very soul. Then he would probably take great relish in casting her aside when he was finished with her. She dragged in a breath as she flipped on the storage room light. Thank God she didn't love the man.

When she caught herself clinging to the doorway of the storage room, she realized she hadn't quite recovered from the unease she'd felt the day the lumber had been destroyed. Although the wood had been neatly stacked away and the bits of rock swept clean, an aura of fear seemed to hang in the room. No doubt it was just her concern that the room's ceiling was still unstable. But Ethan had rechecked the cohesiveness of the rock arch above her and she knew logically she had nothing to fear. Still, tension seemed to hang in the air, an edgy quality she couldn't pin down.

She pushed away from the door and crossed to the shelf where she'd seen the survey maps stored. Now that she'd entered, her unease lifted. Maybe it wasn't the room itself that caused her discomfort, but something trapped in her own mind, a memory, some bit of information beyond recall. But when she focused on the details of that day, she could only remember her irritation with Richard, vague worries about the safety of the room, annoyance that she didn't have the supplies to complete her experiment. Still, something else lurked in the back of her mind, although she couldn't seem to put her finger on it.

She moved aside a pair of voltage meters and a box of low-voltage halogen bulbs to reach the rolled-up maps at the back of the shelf. Not sure which was which, she grabbed up the whole dozen or so, then had trouble wrapping her arms around them. She dropped two, and the remainder came askew so that she had to set them all down on the floor.

Once she had the main pile neatly stacked, she reached for the two escapees. One had rolled under the bottom of the six-foot-high metal shelving unit and she knelt to reach it. As her hand groped for the vellum roll, her gaze fell on the rock wall behind the shelf.

A crack had opened in the wall. As she watched in horror, the finger-wide split in the rock opened to a yawning fissure. As it widened, a sickly green light seemed to ooze from deep within, as if the very essence of the rock were leaking out.

She whimpered, scrambling back from the shelf, stumbling over the pile of maps in the process. She fell hard on her backside, her eyes squeezing shut in reaction. When she opened her eyes again, her heart fluttered into double-time. The crack was gone, the rock whole again. Good God, she'd imagined the whole thing.

Trembling, she forced herself to crawl over to the shelving and look behind it at the wall. There was a hairline fissure marring the limestone surface. When she skimmed her fingertips along the rock, the line was faint but discernible to the touch. Somehow her wild imagination had seen that minuscule crack and had created a bizarre illusion, no doubt based on Arlene Smith's ravings about a "gate to Hell." She sank back on her haunches and covered her face momentarily with her hands. She'd damn well better pull herself together or she'd be leaving BioCave in a straitjacket.

Bending down again, she snagged the map from under the shelf, then restacked the whole collection. She managed to scoop them all up and, by pressing them against her body with one arm, switched off the storage room light and shut and locked the door behind her. Despite the urge to race back to the common room, she moderated her steps so that she at least gave the appearance of calm as she entered and returned to the dinner table.

She was surprised to see the dishes had all been cleared. She'd only been gone a few minutes. Either no one had had much of an appetite, or they'd wolfed down their meal. Puzzled, she dumped the maps on a cleared spot and returned to her seat.

Ethan leaned close to her as soon as she sat down. "What took so long? Have trouble finding the maps?"

"No, they were right where I . . ." Her gaze strayed to the wall clock over by the kitchen. With a shock, she saw that nearly forty-five minutes had passed since she'd left. "I didn't realize I was gone that long."

Ethan stared at her a moment, his brow furrowed. Then he scooted back his chair and rose. "I put your plate in the oven to keep warm. I'll go get it."

Liz mentally reviewed the sequence of events since she left the common room. Since the storage room was right next door, it had taken less than a minute to reach it, no time at all to open the lock, maybe a minute to find the maps. A few moments to reorganize when she dropped a couple, then she locked up again and . . . Wait a minute—wasn't she missing something? Something in between, something that might have consumed the extra time.

She leaned back slightly as Ethan returned with her dinner, then took up the fork he set next to the plate with an automatic gesture. Her trip to the storage room shouldn't have taken any more than five minutes—*Where had the other forty gone?* She glanced over at Ethan as she took a bite of eggplant. His gaze was steady on her; obviously he was still waiting for an answer. But she just didn't have one for him.

"Daydreaming, I guess," she said around a mouthful of eggplant. "I was probably thinking of some new growing methodology and lost track of time."

He didn't seem to believe it any more than she, but he looked away finally and turned his attention to the maps Dr. Nishimoto had unrolled on the table. Quickly scanning the vellum sheets, he plucked one from the pile. "This is it." He spread the map flat, using salt and pepper shakers to weigh down the corners. "I got as far as here." He tapped the map.

Dr. Nishimoto let out a long, low whistle. "Are you sure about that?"

Ethan nodded. "I remember that split there, the two nearly parallel passageways. I had come along this way." He retraced his path on the map leading up to the intersection. "Why?"

"Look here." His finger on the vellum, Dr. Nishimoto continued along in the direction Ethan had been traveling. "If you had taken that leftmost passageway, you might have ended up here." He pointed.

Liz leaned close to see and her dinner turned to ashes in her mouth. Under Dr. Nishimoto's finger lay a series of concentric roughly drawn circles. *Hoyo del Diablo* was inscribed in neat letters over the circles.

She felt the blood drain from her face. "The Devil's Pit," she said hoarsely. The namesake of the natural cavern from which BioCave had been created. "You could have stumbled in there."

Tension tightened Ethan's jaw as he studied the map. He reached over to take her hand, the strength of his grip belaying the idleness of the gesture. "I didn't."

She turned her hand to link her fingers with his. "But if you had, Ethan, it's nearly a quarter-mile deep, you could have—"

"I didn't." He squeezed her hand to quiet her, then turned to Harlan. "I thought we'd blocked off that corridor."

Harlan nodded, concern in his dark face. "I ordered several tons of rock to be dropped here." He gestured on the map. "I signed off on it myself."

"Somehow it didn't get done," Ethan said. "We'll have to rig up some kind of barrier to keep anyone else from making the same mistake. Who has time tomorrow to help me with that?"

Harlan and Richard volunteered and they arranged to meet with Ethan in the afternoon. Tugging his hand free of Liz's, Ethan rolled up the maps again, putting aside the one of the Devil's Pit. As focused as she was on him, Liz felt sure she was the only one at the table who could see the faint tremor in Ethan's hand.

Liz rose to take her plate to the kitchen, then returned to the common room. Everyone had left except the Vuchoviches, who were donning aprons in preparation for cleanup, and Ethan. He held a rolled-up map in his hand, and he stared down at it thoughtfully. When she approached, he didn't seem to notice her. It was only when she touched his arm that he looked up, his eyes taking a moment to focus on her.

He set aside the map and took her hand. "Let's go."

She had to hurry to keep up with him as he strode from the common room. "Where are we going?"

He pulled her closer as they reached the corridor. "To our quarters."

Slowing, she dug in her heels until he stopped. "Ethan, I can't. It's early yet and I have work to do."

Releasing her, he raked his fingers through his hair. Good Lord, he looked rattled! What could have shaken cold-blooded Dr. Winslow?

She caught his hand. "Ethan, what is it?"

Tucking her arm in his, he urged her down the corridor again. "I'll come with you to the hydro lab. We have to talk."

She moved along beside him in silence, then had to smile when he used his override code to open the hydro lab lock for her. It didn't seem to be in him to step back when he could take charge.

As she entered the lab before him, Liz quickly scanned the room for Noah. He was nowhere in sight, but three bottles of nutrient solution had been relocated to the far side of the room from their spot on a storage shelf. Despite his promises to the contrary, Noah couldn't seem to resist messing with Liz's things.

As Liz crossed the room to retrieve them, Ethan moved along the hydro tanks, looking inside each one. "You've really made an excellent start here."

One bottle tucked in her arm, the other two dangling from her fingers, Liz turned to him in surprise. Praise from Ethan? And it sounded genuine, too. "Thank you."

His gaze met hers, the faint smile on his face disconcerting. "Can I help you with those?"

"No. Thanks." She returned the bottles to the shelf, swinging them into the slots they'd been taken from. "Richard's actually done quite a bit of this work."

Ethan bent to examine the buds on an eggplant seedling. "Under your direction."

Liz detected a question implicit in the statement—was Richard accepting her authority? Was that why Ethan was here? To discuss Richard Niedan? "He's not the most cheerful of workers, but he does what I ask."

"Fair enough." Straightening from his perusal of a bed of

mature bell pepper plants, he walked slowly toward her.

Puzzled, Liz turned to power on her computer. "I need to upload my first week's progress reports to BioCave's website on the Internet. We can talk while I work."

Ethan pulled a high stool over to her computer, leaning over her as she sat in the padded swivel desk chair. "I uploaded my stuff earlier today," he said. Just as he had at dinner, he shifted so he could touch her, his fingers resting on her shoulder. He scanned the monitor. "You've got some nice images. I just sent text."

He began stroking her, and her attention kept straying to his light touch. When she mistyped the computer commands three times in a row, she edged away from him, out of his reach. She was relieved when he didn't try to regain contact. A few more moments of concentrated effort and her files were on their way to an aboveground computer for uploading to the Internet.

She swiveled in her seat toward him. "What did you want to talk about?"

Sighing, he pulled her hand from her lap. "What happened in the storage room when you went to get the maps?"

She blinked. Of all the subjects she thought he might bring up, that wasn't even on the list. "I told you. Daydreaming, thinking about work. At least . . ." Something seemed to dance at the edge of her consciousness. "I guess I was."

She might have expected him to deride her lack of concentration; instead he just looked troubled. "You've forgotten, haven't you."

She shook her head. "It isn't that. I just didn't do anything remarkable enough to remember."

His grip tightened on her hand. "You had a memory lapse, Liz. Just like in the corridor, when you hit your head. Just like Arlene did when the gas leak opened in her lab. Just as I have about getting lost in the corridor."

"What are you saying?"

Enclosing her hand in his, he pulled it close to his lips in what seemed an unconscious gesture. "I've already forgotten most of the details of my experience in that undeveloped part of Hoyo del Diablo. Arlene can't recall anything about the gas leak beyond finding it difficult to breathe. I'll wager you remember next to nothing about your fall. And whatever happened to keep you so long in the storage room is fading fast.''

Even the press of his lips against the back of her hand couldn't warm the chill that passed through her. She wanted to deny what he said, but try as she might, she couldn't muster up much more than a sketchy memory of entering the storage room then leaving it in a hurry. And the incidents surrounding her fall—she had to strain to even remember hitting her head.

She clung to Ethan like a lifeline. ''But what does it mean?''

Elbows on his knees, he rubbed her hand between his. ''I'll need to talk to Benita Jackson—as resident psychologist, she'll have better insight than me. But I'm guessing it's something to do with the confinement of BioCave that's wreaking havoc with our memory.''

''But Ethan, after one week? That doesn't make sense.''

He shrugged. ''Maybe it's a body clock thing, biorhythms. Maybe tricking our bodies with artificial daylight is taking its toll.''

Liz considered that a moment, but something didn't fit. ''Wouldn't the natural sunlight in the common room counteract that? We're not relying entirely on artificial light.''

He pulled away from her and rose from the stool. ''Look, I don't know.'' Pacing the width of the hydro lab, he raised a fist to bang it against the rock wall. Then he turned to face her. ''Something's happening here, something I don't understand. Good solid circuit board connections go haywire, cracks open inexplicably in apparently stable rock walls, and I wander off like an idiot and get lost. And I can't remember a damned thing about it.''

''Nothing?''

He laughed, a harsh sound. "Just one thing. And it's too ridiculous to mention."

She glanced at her screen, saw the upload had finished. Switching off her computer, she stood and moved toward Ethan. "What? What do you remember?"

He stared at the floor a moment, then reached for her, hands cupping her shoulders. "A voice in my head. Telling me the right way to go." He laughed again. "And calling me a 'danged idiot' in the process."

Noah! It had to be. He must have found Ethan wandering in the cave near the pit, had guided him back to safety. She could forgive the mischievous spirit a lot for that one act. Because if Ethan had fallen, if Ethan had died . . . it didn't bear thinking about.

He squeezed her shoulders, shaking her slightly. "What? What is it? You think I'm crazy, is that it?"

He had misinterpreted her silence as some kind of judgment of him. Her gaze roved his face, the uncharacteristic edginess there making her uneasy. Should she tell him about Noah, reassure him that he hadn't gone mad? But he wouldn't believe her. Her confession would probably just make matters worse.

"You're not crazy." Lifting her hands, she pressed her palms against his face. "Your own subconscious knew the right way to go. That's the voice you heard." That was what he wanted to believe, she could see it in his eyes. She'd made the right decision in keeping Noah's existence to herself.

His thumbs rubbed along her collarbone, the motion burning along her skin. "Are you finished? With what you had to do here?" Sliding his hands along her shoulders, he moved them up to curve around the nape of her neck. Now his fingertips lightly stroked her scalp, pulling a moan from her.

"Yes," she whispered, her eyes drifting shut as his fingers delved deeper into her hair. His steady massage seemed to melt every bone in her body.

He brushed his palm against the sensitive shell of her ear,

the sensation enervating. "Come back to our quarters with me."

She forced her eyes open. "But it's still early."

"You can't work all night." His thumb drifted along her scalp. "You need a little relaxation. But not here." He glanced meaningfully up at the camera set above the door.

In spite of herself, her head lolled back at his touch. He seemed to take that as invitation, pressing his lips to her throat, moving them in a hot, wet trail to her jaw, her ear. "Yes," she said, the sound coming out in a moan.

He lifted her then, cradling her body in his arms as if she were no more than a doll. He burned a kiss onto her mouth, then carried her from the lab, deftly hooking the door with his foot to shut it. The thought drifted into Liz's mind that there was something drastically wrong with him carrying her off like this, but then he kissed her again and all coherence fled.

When they reached their quarters, he let her slide to the floor, her hip brushing against his hardness as he lowered her. Then he pressed her against him and the feel of him at the cleft of her legs sent a jolt of arousal through her. God, this was what she wanted, his hands, his mouth on her, her legs wrapped around him as he thrust inside her. It might be the craziest notion of all, and the most dangerous, but she wanted this man almost more than she wanted her next breath.

One hand cupping her hips, the other behind her head, he pressed the tip of his tongue against the seam of her mouth. She opened to him, helpless to do otherwise. His tongue moved in and out of her mouth, mimicking the act she longed for, ached for. Her body screamed for the pleasure he promised.

Backing away slightly, he ran a line of kisses along her jaw to her ear. "Let me lower the bed."

Her fingers dug into his arms as his tongue traced along the whorls of her ear. She moaned, trying to order her thoughts. If she said yes, she was committed—it wouldn't be fair to turn back. But was she ready now, in this moment, to let Ethan make love to her?

She needed the space to think. "Wait," she murmured as his hot breath in her ear turned her knees to water.

He stilled, his breathing harsh. She could feel the impression of each of his fingers curving around her hip. The ridge of his manhood pressed into her thigh, insistent. She shook her head. "Stop, Ethan. Please."

A tremor passed through his body, flashing under her hands like ice. The burn of it against her palms frightened her and she wedged her upper body back so she could look at him. What she saw in his eyes terrified her even more. A darkness, a black evil glow. "Ethan?" she whispered.

He laughed, the raw, throaty sound grating in her ears. His voice didn't sound like his own. "You don't want me to stop, Lizzy. You want to do it . . . do it on the hard rock floor."

What are you doing? Ethan asked himself. *She wants you to stop.* But he pulled her closer again, his arms around her, his mouth covering hers. He didn't want to look at her, didn't want to see the horror in her face. Somehow control of the situation had hurtled beyond his grasp.

It was her fault. The moment Lizzy had laid blue eyes on him, the moment she first smiled at him, he'd been lost. It was no wonder he constantly felt on the edge of madness. No wonder his memory played tricks on him, making him hear things he shouldn't, making him feel things he shouldn't. If he could only claim her body, sink himself inside her, he would be able to get his head straight again. If the damn bed had been down, he would have backed her onto it, had her clothes off before she could gasp a protest, or try to push him away.

She let Aaron Cohen, why the hell shouldn't she let him? The image burst into his mind's eye, Liz smiling at Aaron, her soft voice saying, "I love you." If she would do it with the old man, she would damn well do it with him.

But she wants you to stop! She squirmed against him, and he felt her desperation to escape. But as her softness rubbed against his hard arousal, the darkness seemed to take firmer hold of him, urging him on. *"Ethan,"* it said with the cadence of his breathing, of his rapid heartbeat, *"take her."*

He pulled her more tightly against him. Keeping her body pressed to his, he guided her back to the wall, flattened her against it. He lifted her legs, wrapping them around his hips so that she lay open and vulnerable to him. He didn't need the damn bed; he could have her this way, hard and fast, before she knew what was happening. *"Take her,"* something whispered along his veins, *"she's yours."*

Then she made a sound, deep in her throat. A cry of pleasure? Or a whimper of fear like before?

Dear Lord, he was frightening her! Shame lanced through him, seared through his veins like hot ice.

The whispering voice nearly overwhelmed his remorse, nearly drove him to take her anyway. Before he could take another breath, he tore himself from her and backed away three shaking steps.

"I'm sorry," he said hoarsely. "I shouldn't have—" He scrubbed at his face with a trembling hand. "I'm sorry."

Tears shimmered in her eyes and he wanted to fall to his knees and beg forgiveness. How could she make him so damned weak with just a look? He hated himself just then, hated his lack of control. Good God, what had happened to him? "I won't . . . I can't . . . I'm sorry."

She blinked furiously, but couldn't quite stop a tear from spilling from her eyes. "Ethan," she began.

He heard the edge of pain in her voice, and damned himself again. He moved past her toward the door. "I'll come back later, when you're asleep. And I won't . . . I promise I won't touch you again."

Even as he shut the door behind him, he heard the first shuddering sound of her sobs. He folded his body, crouching beside the limestone wall. His face buried in his hands, he felt like the worst kind of monster.

As he sat there steeped in his misery, he felt something in his jeans pocket digging at his leg. Standing, he reached inside the pocket and retrieved a handful of rough-edged gray-green stone. As he stared at the pieces of peridotite arrayed across his palm, he couldn't for the life of him remember how or where he got them.

Invisible to Lizzy's eye, Noah watched from the highest corner of her quarters, aching to his very soul. Each tear dropping from her eyes seemed to burn right through him, never mind that he was dead and his bones long dust. The wrongness of what he'd just witnessed shook him to the core, made him more afraid than ever.

He hadn't meant to spy, in fact started to bow out the moment he'd seen them kissing. He might not like Lizzy's mule-headed husband, but some things between man and wife should be private. So he'd been about to squeeze himself back inside the rock ceiling when he saw the change come over Ethan.

Noah knew the geologist lusted for his Miss Lizzy, but the way he went for her—Noah could just about taste the wrongness in the air. Lizzy had tried to get away, had pushed, had struggled, but Ethan was like a man possessed. . . .

Noah oozed himself back into the rock ceiling, leaving Lizzy to her tears. He peeked into the corridor long enough to see Ethan walking toward the energy center, a look of horror on his face. Then Noah retreated to his small cave to think. But hours later, nearly dizzy with pacing the tiny space, he hadn't come up with a solution. At least not one a cowardly fellow like himself would have the courage to implement.

Chapter Ten

Liz felt Ethan come to bed late in the night. He lay next to her in the bed, taking great care not to touch her. She sensed his terrible shame in the rigidity of his body, the way his arms lay stiffly at his sides. She didn't understand what had happened earlier, she only knew it wasn't like Ethan to behave that way. She knew, too, he needed her forgiveness and the surest way to give him absolution was to reach out to him.

When she laid tentative fingertips on his arm, he jerked away. She persisted, running her palm up along his biceps to his shoulder and resting it there. It took a long, long time for the tension in him to seep away. Then another long moment before his hand covered hers.

He pulled her into his arms, turning her so she spooned against him. One muscled arm cushioned her head, the other looped over her waist. There was nothing sexual in the contact, just warmth and comfort.

Before his heat eased her back to sleep, he rose up slightly to bring his mouth close to her ear. She thought he might kiss her goodnight. Instead he whispered softly, "I'm sorry."

Liz drifted off to sleep, her heart aching for him.

When she woke, Liz realized from the light level in the room it was well past her usual waking time. Ethan lay facing her, eyes open, a shadow of confusion on his face. He reached out to brush his fingers along her cheek, his brow furrowed. "Something happened last night," he said, his voice a low rumble.

Thank God, Liz thought. Whatever had come over him, it hadn't been right, it hadn't been *him*. He might do everything he could to persuade her into bed, but he would never force her, she was sure of it. She smiled to reassure him, then gave in to temptation and ran her own fingers across his beard-roughened cheek. "I don't know that I've ever seen you before you shaved."

Bringing her fingers to his mouth, he pressed a kiss into her hand. "Because you're out of here by the crack of dawn." His intense gaze bored into hers. "What did I do last night?"

She laughed, sidestepping the question. "Just as well I leave early. That hair is a fright." Playfully, she drew her hand across his tousled hair.

Grabbing her wrist, he stopped her. "What did I do, Liz?"

She tugged lightly until he released her. "Why do you think you did anything?"

Lips pressed tightly together, he glanced away, then his gaze returned to her face. "A gut feeling that I did something . . . wrong. Something bad. But nothing seems to be left but the guilt."

She wished she could spare him. After all the conflicts between them, when she would have happily wreaked all manner of revenge upon him, she still would have saved him from knowing this. Partly because she'd just as soon forget about it herself, but also because she knew, despite his arrogance, this would strike him to the core.

She placed a hand on his chest, momentarily startled by

the feel of the crisp curls there. "Do you remember kissing me in the hydro lab?"

"Yes."

"Picking me up? Carrying me here?"

His brow furrowed. "Yes, I do."

She pressed her fingertips into his warm chest. "What do you remember after that?"

She could see him try to grasp the memory. "I went to the energy center. Came back late." He raised his hand to cover hers. "What happened in between?"

She stated it baldly. "You attacked me."

"What?"

As impassively as she could, she explained the sequence of events. His grip loosened on her hand, then he rose from the bed. He seemed unaware of his nakedness at first and Liz couldn't bring herself to look away. Good God, the man was an Adonis.

Then he grabbed up the jeans that lay rumpled on the floor and drew them on. Lowering himself into the desk chair, he disarranged his hair even further with agitated fingers. He swung around to look at her. "I'm sorry."

"You told me so last night." Liz sat up, letting her silky gown fall to her hips. "Ethan, I don't know what was in control last night, but it wasn't you."

His eyes burned into hers. "That's no damn excuse."

She remained silent a moment, then said, "No, it isn't."

He leaned forward, elbows on his thighs, his jeans gapping slightly where he hadn't fastened the top button. "You need to be clear on one thing here, Liz. I want you. Just the sight of you moving across the room arouses me. Damn, I'd like to crawl into bed beside you right now and throw that gown up around your waist—" He growled low in his throat and pushed to his feet. "I would never take you unwilling, not consciously. But if there's something darker in me, something more evil—"

"No, Ethan."

She might as well have not spoken. "Being underground

might be pulling that out, ripping the controls from my psy-che—''

''No!''

A wild look in his eyes, he turned to face her. Then he subsided back in the chair. ''God, I don't know what I'm saying.''

Liz slid across the bed toward him, perching on the edge. ''We need to talk to Benita,'' she said in a low, even voice. ''There's something going on here neither of us under-stands.''

Pinching the bridge of his nose with thumb and finger, he expelled a long breath of air. ''You're right. And we need another staff meeting. If anyone else is experiencing memory losses, moments of violence...'' The final word seemed dragged out of him. Rising, he dug through the dresser drawer for clean clothes, then headed for the bathroom. His back to her, he paused. ''Announce the meeting for me at breakfast, please. I'll be busy.''

Busy working, Liz wondered, or busy avoiding me? A week ago, she would have been glad he planned to keep himself scarce, but now she looked forward to sharing meals with him, had begun to enjoy his company.

''I will,'' she said softly. ''You'll meet up with Benita in the meantime?''

He glanced back at her over his shoulder. ''Yes.'' Then he entered the bathroom and shut the door behind him.

Liz climbed from the bed and pulled jeans, a long-sleeved T-shirt, and underclothes from the drawer. Too restless to sit still while she waited for her turn in the bathroom, she made up the bed and lifted it back into place. She was ready with a smile for Ethan when he opened the bathroom door, but he didn't even look her way. His hair wet and combed straight back, his face clean-shaven, he muttered, ''Later,'' as he passed her on his way out of their quarters.

Back to square one, she thought. Sighing, she gathered up her clothes and headed for the shower.

• • •

Ethan walked along the row of monitors displaying the status of the energy systems, but the neat tables and charts were a blur. He'd been hiding in there all morning, tweaking and fiddling with the energy balance, adjusting the solar draw here, modifying the electrical usage there. He'd run power diagnostics on all the aboveground windmills, taking each one off-line in turn to determine its contribution to the mix. It was mind-numbing work, all but useless since he'd run through the same processes more than once before lockdown. He hadn't gathered a scrap of new information.

His gaze strayed to the pile of peridotite he'd dug from his pocket the night before and dumped on the workbench beside a monitor. Plucking a shard from the collection, he tossed the pebble up, then snatched it from the air. He could scarcely believe what Liz had told him he'd done, didn't want to believe. Not an inkling seemed to remain in his mind of what had happened. Not one shred of memory. But the shame still clung to him, as if whatever had wiped his mind clean had left it behind as punishment.

Gaze fixed on a monitor, he stumbled over his chair, dropping the pebble and hitting his shins. Even as he spat out an obscenity in irritation, he welcomed the pain. He deserved worse for what he'd done. Grabbing hold of the chair, he dug his fingers into the cushioned back, wrestling with the urge to fling it across the room. The violent impulse shook him and he drew back, willing the tension from his hands.

He didn't know himself anymore. He was a strong man, an assertive man, even arrogant. But somehow the long days underground had infected him with something darker, more frightening. This time in the bowels of the earth had perhaps tapped a potential in him for ugliness, for vileness. He didn't want to think of himself as capable of such an act, but maybe he didn't know himself as well as he thought.

With utmost care, he pulled the chair to him and settled into it. Leaning back against the cushion, he shut his eyes and tried to empty his mind. Anger still seemed to dance on the periphery of his awareness, but whether that rage came from within or without, he didn't know. He let his thoughts drift, images swirling around him until the random memories coalesced into the long-lost face of his mother.

In involuntary reaction, he felt a savage urge to rip the barely remembered image from his mind. His anger shocked him—he thought he'd long ago put aside any emotions centered around the woman who walked out on his father and him when he was four. That he could picture her at all was due only to the fact that in the process of packing for BioCave, he'd come across a photograph of her he'd forgotten he possessed.

Sagging further in the chair, he let the dimly remembered scene return—his mother storming into the house after a month's separation spent at her parents' house. Her shouting at his father that Ethan would be going home with her. The two of them screaming at each other over his head as his mother tried to stuff his arms into the red sweater she'd given him for Christmas. He'd fought her, grabbing the sweater and tossing it to the floor. Then he'd run from the room, yelling he hated her, would never go with her. She'd left without him.

She'd left without him and never returned. He could still feel the anger, mixed with guilt, clamoring inside him. Anger that she would leave him behind, that she stayed away and then died before he could reconcile with her. Guilt that he'd been the one to drive her away.

Irritated with himself, he pushed up from the chair and began pacing the room. It was all old history. His father might have been cold as stone, but life with him had not been so terrible—he had provided Ethan the best caregivers money could buy. And as long as he avoided his father's mistake of marrying a volatile woman like his mother . . .

He froze in his tracks. Good God, he'd duplicated precisely the mistake his father had made. Liz, if anything, was more passionate than his mother, more fiery. And despite their union being a marriage of convenience, his relentless pursuit of consummation was sending him on the same treacherous path as his father.

But how much like his father was he, truly? Physically, his only legacy from his mother were her gray eyes. Mentally, he and his father had the same single-minded focus on problem solving, although his father had pursued business while for Ethan the sciences appealed more. Emotionally— was he as cold a man as his father, as incapable of feelings?

Ethan leaned back against the long, built-in work surface that held the row of monitors. Once, being considered as cold as his father wouldn't have mattered to him. He'd wanted to marry Cynthia for the very reason that their relationship would be placid, easy, without passion. He didn't want a woman reaching beyond his cool façade. But recently, most significantly in the last several days, something inside him had begun to open up, to warm. All because of Liz.

A picture of that little four-year-old boy drifted into Ethan's mind again. He saw the defiance on his face, the anger in his eyes as he threw down the sweater and stalked from the room. But now, for the first time, Ethan remembered the tears of regret that had almost immediately followed, as soon as he'd been out of earshot of the grown-ups. All his bravado had crumpled as he'd thrown himself on his bed.

A warning beep sounded on one of the monitors and Ethan turned to scan them for the problem. He didn't like the vulnerable feeling inside him just then, the four-year-old's memories that had welled up. The last thing he would want Liz to see was that childish weakness. Lord only knew what she'd make of it.

Tracking down the monitor flashing the warning message, Ethan took note of the error code. There'd been a brief power surge in the photovoltaic system. No damage, but he ought to run a diagnostic sequence to double-check. The test wouldn't require his presence in the energy center, but it gave him an excuse to stay nevertheless. He glanced at the wall clock. Nearly the end of lunchtime. He'd stay a while longer, let the common room empty, then go scare up something to eat. After that, he'd be meeting with Harlan and Richard to rig up some kind of barrier in the passageway leading to the Devil's Pit.

Hooking his foot on the chair, he dragged it over and sat at the status monitor for the photovoltaic system. Mouse in hand, he clicked on the icon for the diagnostic program and entered the parameters he wanted for the test. It wasn't until he clicked EXECUTE that he first sensed the wrongness in the room. It tasted of rage and violence, and a bloodred haze seemed to cling to him.

Then a crash snatched him from the strange darkness and Ethan turned in shock to see an oscilloscope had fallen. He crossed to assess the damage, wondering how the hell the heavy piece of equipment could have toppled from its sturdy stand. Shaking his head in disgust, he picked up the oscilloscope, taking care to avoid cutting himself on the shattered glass of its display. By the time he'd tidied up the mess, no memory remained of the bloodred haze.

Noah perched in a high corner of the energy center, watching Ethan lift the broken machine to its table. He should leave, get back to his place before the monster sought him out. He'd gone against its will by distracting Ethan and the thing would be angry. But he had to stay behind to make sure the creature didn't try to go for Ethan again.

The geologist finished righting the machine in its place and returned to his computer. Peculiar how Ethan never saw his ghostly self, even though he'd stood there, plain as day, after upsetting the machine. Noah didn't even have to try to make himself invisible to the geologist. Ethan's disbelief in the spirit world was so strong he wouldn't see a ghost if it danced before his nose.

Nevertheless, the monster seemed right interested in Ethan, had come for him three times now. But where the creature had so easily made the others afraid, Ethan was another matter. It seemed to have other intentions for the geologist. Not to scare him, but maybe . . . maybe to use him. And that was a far more fearful thing to contemplate than any other of the monster's deeds. If it could take hold of a living man, use his body . . . oh, Lord, he didn't want to think about it.

Noah peeked down at Ethan, saw a very ordinary look of concentration on his face. Then he tested the air, the very rock about him for the least inkling of the monster. Once he'd assured himself it was well and truly gone, Noah let his noncorporeal self soak into the rock above him and away.

Lifting his halogen lantern a bit higher, Harlan ran the toe of his sneaker across the limestone floor of the passageway. He bent to pick up a bit of gravel, then turned to Ethan. As Ethan examined the rock in Harlan's palm, his stomach clenched, as if a memory had brushed by him, too quick to catch.

Harlan cupped his palm around the gray-green fragments of rock. "Looks like the rock we dumped down here. I saw it stacked aboveground before it was transported down."

Ethan nodded. "It's peridotite. That answers one question, anyway."

Dumping the handful, Harlan looked quizzically at Ethan. "Which question?"

"Where the boulder from the storage room came from. Apparently, whoever carried it there picked it up from here."

Harlan ran a hand over his short-cropped hair. "Doesn't answer what happened to the rest of the rock we placed here. Work order I signed was for five tons. Where is it now?"

Setting down his own lantern, Ethan leaned back against the limestone wall. Where the hell was Niedan? He, Ethan, and Harlan had met in the common room an hour ago and Ethan had sent the botanist off to gather up some of the broken lumber and a roll of concrete reinforcing wire. Ethan figured they could construct a barrier with the materials. Niedan should have been back by now.

Ethan pushed off from the wall, paced the narrow width of the passageway. "I don't know, Harlan. None of this makes sense."

The sound of footsteps whispered down the passageway toward them, growing in volume. Pushing a dolly ahead of him, Richard appeared at the edge of the circle of light thrown off by their lanterns. "I couldn't find the reinforcing wire," he said. "The Smiths had it squirreled away in their lab."

Irritation lodged in Ethan's gut at the sight of Richard's supercilious expression. He'd never confronted the botanist about his rough treatment of Liz and now Ethan barely suppressed the urge to take a swing at him. It was a stupid, testosterone-driven impulse, but it kept tapping at his conscious mind like pebbles dropped into a steadily filling jar.

Biting back his hostility, Ethan helped Harlan drag the five-foot-wide roll of reinforcing wire from the dolly, then held one end while Harlan unrolled it. While he and Harlan pulled it taut, Richard wove strips of wood diagonally in and out of the wire squares. When they'd finished, they all stood back to evaluate what they'd done.

"Still a bit flimsy," Harlan commented as he tested a finger against the thick wire. It bowed in slightly under the pressure.

"It only needs to be a warning. But maybe if we propped something up on the other side . . ." Squeezing through to the wrong side of the wire barrier, Ethan looked around for a large enough rock to provide support. His gaze fell on a chunk of peridotite the size of his fist.

A prickling skittered up his spine. Bending, he hefted the gray-green rock and tossed it up, then caught it. His thumb stroked the sharp edge on the rock, even as he fitted the piece comfortably in his palm. *What a weapon this would make.* The thought burst into his mind and he found himself looking sidelong at Richard Niedan. One hard blow against the side of his head was all it would take.

"Find something to use?" Harlan asked from the other side of the barrier.

Startled, Ethan dropped the rock, barely feeling it bounce

off his foot. It seemed to beg him to pick it up again, but he kicked the stone aside. He turned to Harlan. "Hand me over that length of two-by-four. There's a good-sized fissure in the wall we can wedge it into."

As Harlan passed the wood over the reinforcing wire barrier, Richard narrowed his gaze on Ethan. "If you don't need me anymore, I have work to do."

With Liz? Ethan wondered. His eyes strayed to the chunk of peridotite lying six feet away. He could still feel its neat, sharp edge, the weight of it in his hand. An image invaded his mind—the rock wrapped in his fingers, his arm arcing through the air toward Niedan's head.

Shaking free of the fantasy, he forced himself to focus back on propping up the makeshift barrier. "Go ahead," Ethan said to Richard as he wedged the splintered end of the two-by-four into the wall crack. "Don't forget tonight's meeting."

By the time Ethan had slipped back to the safe side of the barrier and picked up his lantern, he was soaked with sweat. As he and Harlan headed back to the more developed section of BioCave, he felt a palpable relief, as if his shoulders had been freed of a heavy cloak. When he reached the turn for Benita Jackson's lab, a fog seemed to invade Ethan's brain. Something unsettling had happened in the passageway, something to do with Richard Niedan. But hell if he could remember what it was.

Relief washed over Liz when she saw Ethan at the entrance to the common room. She was afraid that after she'd told him what had happened the night before, he might never show his face. She poked her head into the kitchen where the Nguyens were putting the finishing touches on dinner. "Anything else I can help with?" she asked Trang.

Trang pulled a massive tamale pie from the oven and straightened, setting the hot pan on the butcher block in the middle of the kitchen. "Just take the salad out, if you would. Thanks for your help."

Liz tossed aside her apron and picked up the salad bowl. She quickly set it on the food table in the common room, then sought out Ethan. He glanced her way as she approached, but she could tell nothing from his neutral expression. She smiled as she reached his side, laying a hand lightly on his arm. "Hi."

He tensed, then edged out of her reach. Disappointment settled inside her, followed by irritation. After wanting nothing more than to have him leave her alone, it was so crazy to ache for the temporary closeness they'd had. She stood her ground, refusing to let him see how his rejection hurt her. "How was your day?"

"Fine."

"Any problems getting the barrier up?"

"No."

She waited for him to elaborate. When he didn't, she plowed ahead. "Thought you might have had a problem."

He turned his gray gaze on her. "Why would you think that?"

She shrugged, wishing she hadn't brought it up. "Something Richard said this afternoon when he came back from helping you and Harlan."

Ethan's gray eyes darkened. "What did he say?" There was a taut thread of tension behind the innocuous question.

That you were mad as hell. That you picked up a rock and looked ready to kill him with it.

She forced a smile. "You know Richard. He thinks the world hates him." She kept smiling until her face felt frozen, then inclined her head toward the buffet table. "Shall we go eat?"

In Ethan's face, she could see some inner struggle. Then he seemed to let it go, moving with her to get his dinner. Once their plates were full, they joined the rest of the staff who had pushed together several tables. But although conversation flowed around them, Ethan remained silent. When asked about the night's meeting, he answered, "We'll talk about it later," then returned his focus to his food.

In sharp contrast to his behavior the night before, Ethan avoided touching her. When Liz reached past him to retrieve the salt shaker, he turned to keep his body away from hers. When she brushed her fingers across the back of his hand to get his attention, he pulled his hand from the table out of her reach. His eyes wouldn't even meet hers when she spoke to him.

Was this some kind of punishment—touching her one night, rejecting her the next? If so, who was he punishing? Her or himself?

Determined to pull the answer from him, she leaned close to him to whisper in his ear. "We need to talk."

"Later." He pushed his plate out of the way. "It's time for the meeting." He nodded to Harlan's wife who sat across from them at the table. "Benita?"

Benita clasped her hands before her on the table. "We may have discovered some unexpected psychological side effects of living underground."

"Such as?" Janet Vuchovich asked.

Benita's dark gaze traveled the length of the table. "Unreasonable fear. Memory lapses."

Ethan shifted in his chair. "And violence."

That set off a brief clamor of voices around the table. Liz glanced toward Richard, saw him eye Ethan speculatively as his mouth compressed into a frown.

Benita quieted the noise with a calming motion of her hand. "We don't know if the cause is living underground per se. There seems to have been hardly enough time to incite the extreme reactions we've seen. We're still investigating the possibility of a physical agent such as an underground mold or fungus that could have a hallucinogenic effect."

Richard glared at Ethan. "Meanwhile we're sitting ducks for anyone with violent tendencies."

"We all have violent impulses, Richard," Benita said. "That doesn't mean any of us will act on them."

"Easy for you to say." Richard stabbed a finger toward

Ethan. "You didn't have Winslow with a rock in his hand giving you the evil eye."

Ethan surged to his feet. "You have a hell of a nerve accusing me of violence, after what you did to my wife."

Richard crossed his arms over his chest. "I don't know what you're talking about."

"You grabbed her," Ethan said, lifting Liz's right arm and pointing to the faded mark of Richard's hand. "You left bruises."

A strange expression passed over Richard's face, confusion mixed with a faint guilt. "I never touched her," he said, but doubt threaded through his tone.

Ethan released Liz, then lowered himself into his seat. Quiet settled over the table as the staff seemed to wrestle with the implications of what Benita had said.

Ethan spoke into the silence, his deep voice soft. "Just be aware of what could happen. That your impulses may not be entirely under your control. Until we can find a way to counteract this . . ." He stared down at his hands where they rested on the table. "Just be careful."

Staff members rose from the table, pairing off as they left the common room. Liz watched them—the Vuchoviches murmuring softly to each other in Russian, the Jacksons hand in hand, Dr. Nishimoto and his wife Wendy with their arms around each other—and felt a pang of envy. She longed for that same unity for herself.

When Richard passed, he glanced down at her arm, bewilderment clear in his face. Then he and Phoebe were gone, leaving Liz alone with Ethan. He kept his back to her as he cleared their plates from the table, then carried them to the kitchen. She followed behind him, lowering her voice when she saw the Smiths starting their cleanup. "We need to talk," she reminded him.

"We don't." He shook the food from the plates and slid them into a sink of hot, soapy water. Then he stepped around Liz and into the common room.

Liz caught up to him, grabbing his arm to keep him from

leaving. "I want to know why you've been avoiding me."

He didn't answer for a moment, then he pulled away to face her. "That should be obvious."

She took a step closer, moving into his space. "Tell me."

She could see his jaw work as he stared down at her. "After talking to Benita, I decided it was best we keep our distance."

"I can't believe Benita recommended that."

"She didn't. It was my call."

"Why?"

"You heard Niedan. I have violent tendencies. God only knows what I'd do if I let you get close to me again."

Let *me* get close to *you*? Liz puzzled over his phrasing as she studied his face for a clue to what was going on inside him. Something flickered in his eyes—pain, an old remembered hurt. Insight struck Liz with crystal clarity. "It's not the violence you're afraid of, is it? It's your own damn feelings that scare you."

He took a step back from her. "My feelings have nothing to do with this."

She narrowed the distance between them again. "Then why won't you let me get closer?"

With a shocking suddenness, he grabbed her and pulled her to him, his mouth coming down on hers. His tongue thrust inside immediately and Liz gripped his shirt to keep her knees from buckling. Then just as quickly, he pulled away, putting her at arm's length away from him.

"That is all I want from you," he said, wiping his mouth with the back of his hand. "And that I can get from any woman." He strode from the common room, leaving her reeling.

She didn't move for a long time. She barely noticed the Smiths calling out a goodnight as they passed her, leaving her alone in the common room. His cruelty had chilled her to the core, leaving her numb.

It was no more than what she might have expected from him. She'd known he was a hard, cold man. But in the last few days he'd shown another side of himself, drawing her to him, making her want . . . she didn't know what the hell she wanted. But to act like a human being one day, then to be so vile the next . . . she damn well didn't deserve that kind of treatment.

Angry now, determined to confront him, Liz left the common room and started down the corridor toward the energy center. She hadn't taken three steps when the power went out.

Chapter
Eleven

Utter blackness. It surrounded Liz, pushed against her like a
heavy blanket thrown over her head. She hesitated, one hand
on the rock wall, the other groping for her pocket flashlight.
But she knew where the small halogen torch was—sitting on
the desk in their quarters. She could have kicked herself for
forgetting it.

Should she go forward or back? Did she feel sure enough
of the twists and turns to the energy center to make her way
there in the dark? Or should she stay here by the common
room?

She'd nearly decided to stay when a tiny bead of light up
ahead caught her eye. In black on near black, she thought
she could make out the lines of Ethan's silhouette. She called
out his name, the sound echoing down the corridor, attenu-
ating to a whisper. She strained to hear a response, but the
tricks and turns of the corridor must not have carried her
voice all the way to Ethan's ears. The light began to fade,
as if Ethan were moving farther away. If she didn't hurry,
she'd lose him.

Keeping her hand on the wall, she stepped forward, her feet scraping against the smooth limestone floor. She fixed her eyes on the pale glow up ahead until they burned and watered. Ghosts of light began to play about the corridor, fooling her into losing her focus on the true light. She blinked several times to clear her vision, until tears spilled from her eyes.

When the light winked out completely, she despaired until she realized Ethan must have turned a corner. She picked up her pace a bit, her fingers trailing along the rock wall, occasionally dipping in when she encountered a door. She kept a mental image in her mind of the BioCave layout, counting each room she passed. Here was Dr. Nishimoto's infirmary and next to it, his lab. After that came the research clinic for Dr. Nguyen, Dr. Nishimoto's backup.

Was there another room after Dr. Nguyen's? Reaching out, she searched for another door, but instead her arm dipped into an open space. Swinging her arm wide, she came in contact with another wall and realized it must be a turn in the corridor. Had Ethan gone this way? The faintest flicker of light teased her and she turned, continuing in the new direction.

She faltered after a few steps. Was this the way to the energy center? She squeezed her eyes shut and tried to bring BioCave's floor plan into tighter focus. No matter how she pictured it, she couldn't square the energy center location with the turn she'd just made. In fact, she couldn't remember a corridor here at all. She thought she knew the location of every corridor, but she'd had little to do with building the actual structure of BioCave. Ethan would know every nook and cranny. Perhaps he'd come down this way to repair the power system.

While she'd dithered, the light had disappeared entirely, leaving her in absolute blackness. Torn between turning back and going on, she decided to continue on in the direction she'd started, since that had been where the light had gone. The worst that could happen was she'd have to plant herself somewhere until Ethan restored power.

Fingertips in light contact with the wall, she moved ahead more slowly. As she edged along the corridor, she kept her right hand outthrust to avoid colliding with an unseen obstacle. The blackness seemed to thicken as she went along, growing heavier and harder to move through. She knew it was an illusion, the product of her light-starved senses, but a fine trembling started up along her skin in reaction.

With a force that jarred the length of her arm and down into her body, her right palm slammed into rock. She explored the wall's sharp curve with her left hand, fingers shaking on the sandy-textured surface. Where had this turn come from? She racked her brain, mentally searching for her present location on the BioCave map. But the darkness had stolen her powers of concentration from her.

Turning in the new direction, she crept on, staring into the blackness for a shred of light. Her right hand outstretched again, she thought she saw the outline of her fingers. But it was a mirage, wishful thinking. She could no more see her hand than she could the sunlight a hundred feet above her.

Was she descending? She couldn't be—the excavated corridors of BioCave were all nearly level. Yet she could feel the slope in the walkway as her feet shuffled slowly forward. That could mean only one thing—she'd entered an undeveloped section of Hoyo del Diablo, just as Ethan had yesterday. This might not be the route to the Devil's Pit, but to continue would be foolhardy. Something just as dangerous as the Pit could be just ahead. She had to turn around.

She'd no more than tensed her muscles to turn when a loud bang exploded in her ears. Something rushed against her, shoving her away from the wall. Stumbling and off-balance, she flailed out with both hands, groping for the opposite side. Her fingernails scraped against the limestone as a hard, cold grip took hold of her shoulders and twisted her around. She spun, once, twice, as her attacker struck her, again and again.

"Lizzy," a harsh voice rasped out. The sound insinuated itself inside her, shaking her to the core. *"Lizzy."*

The presence seemed to take hold of her throat, clutching, cutting off her breath. Terror seized her with its touch, freezing her there in the corridor. She was lost, she was forever damned to blackness. It was the end of time for her, the end of all hope.

Damn it, I won't let it take me! Her eyes squeezed shut against the cloying darkness, she dug inside herself for courage, for will. Screaming at the top of her lungs, she tried to throw off her fear. But the thing seemed to swell in the darkness, swallowing up the sound just as it did the light. Hopelessness crowded her again.

"Let her be!" The shout filled the space she was in, rattled around inside her head. She opened her eyes to see Noah floating before her, a faint glow emanating from his form. Anger and stark terror warred on his face as he swung out wildly with both arms. His hands passed through her, but they seemed to snag on something just outside her body, a patch of blackness inkier than the surrounding dark.

Then Noah yanked the thing away from her and she could breathe again. *"Holler, Lizzy, holler for all you're worth!"* She screamed, louder than before, and this time the sound burst out beyond her, released by the deadening blackness.

One last scream and Noah winked out, the malign presence dragged out with him. The thing jostled her as it went, causing her to stumble. As she struggled to regain her balance, her groping hand whacked against the sharp edge of something. She probed with her fingers until they closed around what felt like a wooden shelf. *A shelf? In a corridor?* She reached higher up until she felt another length of wood above the first, then explored lower and found two others. Good God, where was she?

Raising her hands to her face, she pressed her fingertips to her temples. Should she wait here until Ethan restored the lights? Try to find her way back? She could stumble into some hazard if she continued to wander in the dark. It would be best to stay put.

But it might return! a voice inside her shouted. She shook off the horror, feeling behind her for the end of the shelves to the bare expanse of wall beside them. Lowering herself to the floor, she sat rigid with her arms on either side of her, hands pressed against the rough limestone. Emptying her mind, Liz focused on her breathing, on the raspy feel of the rock under her fingers, on the possibility of approaching footsteps. Anything to keep herself from listening for the whispered sound of her name.

The muffled scream went straight through Ethan, nearly tearing him from his frantic search for a break in the energy center wiring. Instinct told him it was Liz calling him and every particle of his being urged him to stop working and search for her. He ignored the clamoring inside him, convincing himself he could help Liz best by restoring the lights.

He passed the flashlight beam again over the bundle of wires just inside the main electrical conduit, his eyes burning as they strained to see in the halogen glare. It didn't help his concentration any when his mind kept replaying what he'd said to her in the common room. He didn't buy her suggestion that he'd pushed her away to protect his tender feelings. Leave it to a woman to interpret a man's acts as somehow related to emotions. But despite his certainty that keeping his distance from her was a worthwhile precaution, he never should have lashed out at her the way he did. That was inexcusable.

He bent closer, fingers separating the strands of wire. If the glitch was somewhere deeper in the conduit, it could take him hours to find and fix the problem. He didn't want to pull wire from the conduit until he'd satisfied himself there wasn't a break right up front.

Relief washed over him when he spied the break, just inches from the junction box. The plastic insulation on the wire looked melted, which suggested a short. But the metal inside the insulation was sliced clean through as if with a pair of wire cutters. That didn't jibe with a short.

A second scream seemed to vibrate the rock wall of the

energy center. To hell with the whys, he had to restore power now. Stripping away the scorched insulation, he quickly joined the two ends of the wire and wrapped the splice in electrical tape. As he headed for the electrical service to reset the breakers, he hoped to hell that was the only fix.

When the lights flared on, Ethan pelted out of the energy center in search of Liz. He nearly collided with Dr. Nishimoto who was just leaving his infirmary. "Did you hear the screams?" Ethan asked the doctor. "What direction did they come from?"

"I'm not sure. Somewhere back the way you came."

Ethan scanned the corridor. "There was nothing . . ." A thread of sound caught his attention, pulled him back down the corridor. With Dr. Nishimoto beside him, Ethan retraced his steps until they reached the storage room next to Dr. Nguyen's lab. A shuddering sob sifted through the locked door. "How the hell . . ."

Ethan rapped out the override code to release the lock, then pushed the door open. The dim corridor light spilled into the room. When he first saw Liz huddled against the far wall, his heart wrenched in his chest. "I'm here, Liz," he said softly. "Brace yourself, I'm going to turn on the light."

When he switched on the light, she buried her face against the brilliance. Ethan crossed the small room in two strides, kneeling to help her to her feet. Shaking, she seemed barely able to stand. "Where did you go?" She groped for him, her hand closing around his arm. "After you left the common room, where did you go?"

"To the energy center. How did you get locked in here?"

"I don't know. I was following you." Her eyes were red-rimmed from crying, the tears so unlike her. She looked around her at the cluttered shelves lining the room. "I saw your light."

"You couldn't have. I'd already reached the energy center when the power went out."

Her grip tightened on his arm. "I saw it. I followed the corridor to the left . . ."

"The corridor doesn't turn that way. It goes straight on, then branches to the right."

"No doubt the storage room was open," Dr. Nishimoto offered. "You must have stumbled into it."

She gazed around her almost wildly at the close-packed supply shelves. "No. It was a corridor. I'm sure . . ." Then, as if all the energy left her, she sagged into Ethan's arms. "Could we go to our quarters?"

Her sudden dependence shocked him. "Of course." He turned her so he could slip a supporting arm around her shoulders. "Dr. Nishimoto can look you over."

"I don't need Dr. Nishimoto, I need you."

She said the last in a whisper, her voice edged with tears. Ethan's stomach roiled at her uncharacteristic vulnerability. Something was terribly wrong when Liz let her weakness show.

Dr. Nishimoto tipped his head toward the door. "You go on. I'll lock up."

Keeping her close to his side, Ethan helped Liz from the room. The Smiths and the Jacksons had gathered in the corridor outside, but he ignored the unasked questions he could see in their eyes. He didn't want to consider why it seemed so damned important; he only knew that Liz needed protecting and if there was nothing else he could do in that moment, he could help her maintain her dignity.

When they reached their quarters he shut and locked the door behind them, then seated her in the desk chair. "Let me make up the bed for you."

"No." She grabbed his arm when he would have pulled away. "I have to tell you now, before I forget."

He dropped to one knee and cupped her chin, bringing her face down to his. "Maybe it would be better if you did forget."

She tugged her chin free. "Listen. I thought I saw a light in the distance, thought it was you. I followed, feeling my way along the wall. Just past Dr. Nishimoto's infirmary, the corridor turned. . . . Damn, I'm forgetting already."

She glared at him as if it were his fault and his heart gave a silly lurch of joy at the return of her courage. "Close your eyes," he told her. "Concentrate."

She did, taking a long breath before she spoke again. "I continued down the corridor. I started to descend—"

"But you couldn't—"

She shook his arm to silence him. "I descended for several paces until . . . until . . ." Her hand began to tremble. "There was something waiting for me in the darkness, Ethan. Something that called my name."

Liz kept her eyes shut, not wanting to see the disbelief in Ethan's face. The memories were fading quickly; she had to get out what she could before they vanished completely. "It took hold of me, cut off my breath. I tried to scream, but the dark swallowed up the sound. Then Noah—"

"Noah?"

Liz's eyes flew open. She couldn't tell Ethan about Noah. The rest of her story sounded so preposterous, he'd never believe the ghost was real.

While she considered what to say, the last of the terrifying images sank beneath the surface of her conscious mind. What had she been about to tell Ethan? Something about Noah— but what? Surely she hadn't been about to reveal the ghost's existence. No, they'd been discussing the blackout, how she'd gotten lost in the corridors and Noah . . .

Looking away from Ethan's intense gaze, Liz raked her fingers through her hair as if the gesture could roust out the lost sequence of events. But her mind remained blank. "It's gone."

"Who's Noah?"

She looked back at him, decided a fragment of the truth would be safe. "Noah Simmons."

"The dead miner?" His brow furrowed. "How does he fit in?"

"I don't know." That wasn't entirely a lie. She forced

herself to release her grip on his arm. "It's all a blur now. What did I tell you?"

He repeated her words back to her. None of it sparked a memory. The experience could have happened to someone else. Agitated, she pushed to her feet and paced across the room. "It's like something from a horror film. None of it sounds real." Except Noah. His face was clear in her mind's eye. She knew the ghost had been there.

"Maybe that's all it was," Ethan suggested, rising to his feet, "something you remember from a horror film."

"An imaginary monster?" She shook her head. "I don't watch horror movies. They scare me too much."

"Then it's more of what Benita described—a reaction to being underground. The total dark probably frightened you, set off some irrational fear inside you."

"I suppose." She pressed the heel of her hand into her forehead, trying to think. In a rush, his words in the common room came back to her. "Except I wasn't scared when the lights first went out. I was angry, angry at you." Glaring at him, she moved toward him, closing the distance between them. "I realize we married as a convenience to both of us, that we'll be parting company at the end of BioCave. But that doesn't give you permission to treat me so shamefully."

"I agree, I was incredibly rude." He folded his arms across his chest. "But what do you want from me? To pretend I care for you? To play the game men play to get a woman into bed?"

"What game?"

"The 'I love you' game. The 'I can't live without you' game. It's nothing but sugarcoating for the primal urges."

She backed away a step. "You don't believe that."

"It astounds me that you believe there's something more to love than an excuse for lust." He took her shoulders in his large hands, his grip inexorable. "At least I'm honest, Liz. I told you what I feel, and it has nothing to do with love. It has everything to do with what I can express to you right now in that bed."

The unvarnished truth in his words set off an ache inside her. Of course he didn't love her. And surely, she didn't love him. She didn't want to even consider the possibility. The longing inside her had nothing to do with Ethan Winslow. It was only the same wishful thinking she'd felt as a child that someone could care for her, could see her as special. She'd thought she'd given up yearning for the love her mother couldn't give her. She'd thought the Cohens' unconditional love was enough. But maybe all this time she'd been searching for something else.

Ethan gazed down at her, his expression impassive. If there were feelings behind his barriers, they weren't for her. She wouldn't be the one to bring down his walls. She tipped her head back, meeting his gaze dead on. "I'm not looking for a declaration of love from you." Somehow the words tasted like a lie on her tongue, despite her determined tone. "I'm only asking that you treat me fairly."

"I will," he said, his thumbs stroking lightly. "No more outbursts. But until we understand what might be affecting our behavior down here, it still might be best if I keep my distance."

She smiled up at him. "You're right here next to me, Ethan. I don't feel the least threatened."

His hands glided along her shoulders to rest warmly at her throat. "You should. At least if you don't want to end up in that bed with me."

Stepping in closer, she spread her hands across his chest. She felt the thud of his heart beneath his thick cotton sweater. "I've already been in that bed with you several nights. I don't recall you doing anything particularly dangerous."

He leaned toward her, his mouth in her hair, nuzzling her ear. "Because I haven't done any of the things I wanted to."

"Like what?" she whispered.

"Put my mouth on you everywhere," he murmured into her ear. "Taste you where you're the sweetest."

She moaned softly imagining his tongue on the most sensitive part of her. "Maybe I want that too."

"You want more, Liz. You want what I can't give you."

He was right, she knew it to her core. But in that moment, she was willing to take only the passion, to let it substitute for her real yearnings. "Never mind what you can't give. Just give me what you can."

He hesitated, then he covered her mouth with his, plunging inside with his tongue. He burned her straight to her toes until she thought she might go up in flames. Then he pulled away, leaving her shivering.

"The bed," he explained when he took in her stunned expression. "Get the lights."

When his demand registered, she turned to the control by the door and moved the dimmer switch down. Behind her, she heard the bed clunk into place and second thoughts rushed in. This is enough, she told herself. As long as she remembered it was only sex, satisfaction of her lust, it would be enough.

But would it be too much? She spun on her heel, saw him standing at the foot of the bed, watching her. "Liz?"

She should tell him she'd changed her mind, bring this craziness to a stop. Then they would both climb into that bed and sleep together as they had so many other nights. But how could she lie beside him even another night wanting him this way?

He stretched his hand out to her in invitation. *You want this, Liz. Take it.* Moving tentatively, she crossed the room toward him and took his hand.

He pulled her to him, his strong hands at her hips, pressing her against the hard ridge of his erection. That was somehow the most exciting and terrifying part, that she had the power to arouse him, that she'd pushed at the edges of his self-control. The urge to escape still lapped at her even as she ached to curl a hand over his hard length and stroke him. Too unsure to do either, she put her arms around him, palms pressing against his back.

He lowered his mouth to hers, this time kissing her gently, lingering over each sipping touch. She wanted his tongue inside her mouth again, but didn't know how to ask. She tested her own courage by sliding the tip of her tongue against his lower lip, then retreating, a shiver running through her at the brief contact.

He turned and lowered himself to the bed, bringing her on top of him. He felt hard everywhere—the tautness of his chest, the whipcord strength of his arms, his powerful legs. She was muscular for a woman, but still he felt leaner, all planes and angles to her softer curves. The contrast delighted her, made her want to explore every inch of him. Especially the jutting manhood between his legs.

He turned again and brought her under him, wedging himself between her legs. Her body responded of its own accord, wrapping her legs around him, pulling him closer to her center. She strained against him, wanting him closer, wanting him inside her. Her clothes chafed her, her jeans feeling suddenly uncomfortable and constricting. She wished they would disappear, her clothes and his, leaving nothing between them.

He tugged at her T-shirt, pulling it free of the waistband of her jeans. Then his fingers dipped underneath, grazing a heated path up along her rib cage to her bra. He teased her with a fingertip, stroking lightly along the underside of her breast, coming near her nipple before retreating. Meanwhile, he pressed kisses along her jaw, her throat, the point of her chin. Her fingers dug into his back as she suppressed the urge to grab his head and bring his mouth to hers.

With the onslaught of sensation came a tumult of emotion, flooding her, filling her mind with half-formed images and her heart with half-finished promises. She felt on the edge of feeling something new, yet long hoped for, long desired. Her mind scrambled to make sense of what was happening even as her body responded. Fulfillment waited for her, urged her toward it. In a few moments, Ethan Winslow would take her there.

When his mouth closed over her breast, his tongue laving her through the silky knit of her bra, she threw back her head in reaction. Her heart sped to an impossible rate and between her legs she felt a pull so near pain she cried out. The emotions within her called out an answer, expanding, encompassing. This was what she had wanted to feel, this was the completion. This was love.

As soon as the thought entered her mind, she went rigid with shock. That was exactly what her mother had thought—that sex and love were the same thing, that if a man were intimate with her he must love her. Sex was how she found her completion, her fulfillment. Sex was also how she ended up with four daughters, all by different fathers.

And Liz had nearly fallen into the same trap. Despite her determination to take what Ethan offered, her insistence that passion would be enough, she let her emotions take control. Good God, even now her heart yearned to believe the lie.

Ethan must have sensed the change in her because he'd pulled away and now he stared down at her intently. "What is it, Liz?" he asked softly.

She was saved from answering when someone pounded on the door and called out from the corridor, "Ethan! Are you there?"

Ethan didn't move, his arms bracketing her body. Her legs were still tangled with his. "Do I answer the door? Or do we continue?"

Another pounding, louder this time. "Ethan! It's Ivan! Are you in there?"

She looked away, the intensity of his gaze impossible to face. "You'd better answer. It sounds urgent."

He hesitated a moment, as if he sensed the turmoil inside her. Then he moved off her, sliding away and off the bed. He raked his fingers through his dark hair, restoring order to the mess she'd made of it. Unlocking the door, he pulled it open, standing in the way so Ivan couldn't see inside. "What is it?"

"I don't know where Janet is," Ivan said.

Liz rose from the bed, tucking her T-shirt back inside her jeans. "Did you check her lab?"

"Of course." Ivan's distress had intensified his soft Russian accent. "First thing when the lights came back on. But she isn't there. I can't find her anywhere."

Ethan glanced at Liz, his worry clear. "You stay here. I'll help Ivan look."

She shook her head. "I'm coming with you."

He didn't argue, just ushered her out of their quarters with a hand on her shoulder. "You've covered everything between here and your quarters?" he asked Ivan. The computer scientist nodded. "That leaves four branching points off this corridor to check."

"Maybe we should split up," Liz suggested.

"No." Ethan's tone was adamant. "We've had enough problems with staff wandering off on their own."

They moved together to the first turn in the corridor, a jog to the left. Liz lagged slightly behind as they followed the junction. The hiss of her name stopped her in her tracks and sent her heart racing in fear. *"Miss Lizzy!"*

She turned to see Noah drifting overhead. "You scared the living daylights out of me," she whispered. Deep in discussion with the frantic Ivan, Ethan hadn't noticed her absence yet.

"I know where the gal is, Miss Lizzy. She's down t'other way."

Ethan turned then, looking back at Liz questioningly. She glanced up at Noah, then back at Ethan. He followed the line of her gaze, but from his lack of reaction obviously didn't see the ghost bobbing against the ceiling. Liz took a sidelong look; Noah was still there. He gestured madly. *"This way, Miss Lizzy."*

In an instant, she put her money on Noah. "I think I heard something, Ethan, down the other corridor."

She turned to follow Noah, trusting that Ethan and Ivan followed. The opposite corridor was dimmer than the one they'd left. Liz vaguely remembered it as an auxiliary access to the communications center. Not one the BioCavers would normally use.

Noah had stopped about ten meters down, still hovering above. At first the shadows hid the still form crumpled on the limestone floor. Then Ivan rushed past her, calling his wife's name and a Russian endearment as he knelt beside her.

Ethan caught up to Liz. "Go find Dr. Nishimoto. Quickly."

She didn't balk at his peremptory tone, hurrying back along the corridor. She hesitated at the main passageway, wondering if she should turn left to go back to the infirmary or right to the Nishimotos' quarters. The quarters were closer, so she checked there first.

Wendy Nishimoto answered her knock. "What's wrong?"

Liz explained quickly. "Is the doctor here?"

"Still at the infirmary. I've got a first-aid kit. You go get Wallace, I'll see what I can do for Janet."

Liz ran back down the corridor toward the infirmary, but it seemed an eternity until she reached the door. Dr. Nishimoto took only a few minutes to get what he needed, but Liz was nearly crazy with worry by the time they made it back to Janet.

Ethan had brought in another light source to brighten the illumination in the corridor. Liz could see all too clearly the gash on Janet's head, the scrapes on her palms. It was eerily reminiscent of her own fall, her own injuries.

Dr. Nishimoto looked grave as he examined Janet. Ivan was close to tears as he clutched his wife's hand to his chest. Trembling, Liz moved closer to Ethan and put her arm around him, needing his stability. "Is it a concussion?" she asked Dr. Nishimoto.

"A bad one," Dr. Nishimoto said. "There's swelling, possibly a skull fracture. She's nearly comatose."

Liz's arm tightened around Ethan's waist. "Will she be okay?"

"Not here she won't," the doctor said. "She's going to have to go back aboveground. Otherwise, she may very well die."

Chapter
Twelve

Liz watched as Ivan and Ethan carried Janet's stretcher into the BioCave elevator and laid it carefully on the floor. Dr. Nishimoto stepped inside and quickly checked the dressing he'd applied to Janet's head wound before he and Ethan stepped out of the car. Ethan stood beside Liz as the doors slid shut on a shaken Ivan and his prone wife.

The remainder of the staff was assembled behind them in the corridor. They were all adults, all well-grounded in their respective disciplines. Still they looked to Ethan for leadership, for guidance. Liz stepped in closer to him, both wanting to feel his support and to offer him her own.

Ethan slid his arm around Liz's shoulders. "Let's all go to the common room."

The group parted to allow Ethan and Liz to go first, closing ranks behind them. They walked in silence to the common room, then headed for the nearest table. Trang Nguyen split off from the group. "I'll go start some coffee."

Liz sat next to Ethan as the others ranged themselves around the table. Emotions simmered just below the surface, a tangible mix of fear, worry, and uncertainty. Needing the connection, Liz reached for Ethan's hand. He turned it, linking her fingers with his. Several minutes later, Trang returned with a tray laden with a full coffee pot and mugs.

Ethan waited for Trang to take a seat next to Qwong before he spoke. "Part of Aaron Cohen's goal in creating BioCave was to experiment with the forming of bonds by a disparate group in a communal situation. We've been down here scarcely more than a week and have experienced more disruptions and difficulties than Aaron or I ever expected."

His hand shifted restlessly in hers. "In the past few days, we've all been tested. We've had little enough time to form the cohesiveness necessary to make BioCave a viable community, let alone endure the loss of two staff members. The question is, will this trauma bring us closer together or shatter what we've built between us?"

Harlan cleared his throat. "What are you saying, Ethan?"

Ethan met the man's dark gaze. "I'm asking if we should continue. There would be no shame in pulling the plug at this point."

There was a moment of stunned silence, then the objections rose around the table. Ethan let everyone speak at once, then he put up a hand to quiet the group. "I had to raise the issue. Just as I have to ask—is there anyone here who would prefer to leave the project now? And in case you need time to discuss it with your spouse, you can put off answering until the morning."

He took care to meet the gaze of everyone at the table, everyone, that is, besides Liz. Oddly, he didn't look at her. Because he felt certain she would stick it out? Or because her opinion didn't matter to him?

She might have thought the latter, except for the tightness of his grip. She sensed tremendous tension in him, from the pressure of his fingers linking with hers to the rigidity of his arm. She wanted to somehow transmit to him her solidarity with him, her agreement with his position. They might conflict on a personal level, might never come to a meeting of the minds in their relationship, but when it came to BioCave and its ideals, they were united.

Liz looked to her left and right, trying to gauge the tenor of the assembled staff. Then she said quietly but firmly, "Ethan, you're in charge here. As long as you're willing to persevere, the rest of us are." There were nods and murmurs of agreement around the table.

His fingers relaxed. "Good. We'll continue. Thank you all."

As staff members filtered out of the common room, he remained seated, his hand still enclosing hers. Liz studied his profile, wondering at the emotions flickering across his face. When he tugged her hand up to his mouth and pressed a kiss to the back of it, the action both shocked and moved her.

"Thank you," he said softly.

"I only said what I honestly believe. I don't know what's happening between you and me, but I do know you can lead this group through just about any misfortune."

He turned to her then, his gray eyes unreadable. "I might be heading up the project, but this is a collaborative effort. I'd call it quits if I didn't have consensus."

His warm breath caressing the back of his hand sent her thoughts scattering in a dozen different directions. She brought herself back in line with an effort. "I have a feeling you'd find a way to get consensus if you had to."

His gaze became more intense. "Am I that arrogant?"

She searched inside her for an honest answer. "Yes. But I think it comes from knowing you're right and bringing others around to seeing that."

"I'm not always right, Liz."

She thought of how low his opinion of her had been when they both worked at GeoCore. Since the start of BioCave, he seemed to see her in a new light, to come to respect her professional abilities. But the relationship between them was still a prickly thing. And she wanted . . . she wanted something different.

"We should go back to our quarters," she said, keeping her eyes on his.

"And?"

She'd almost forgotten what Ivan's frantic summons had interrupted. She wondered what would have happened if Ivan hadn't arrived when he did. Would she have thrown off her misgivings, let Ethan make love to her? And if she had, would she be able to keep her emotions in check? Or would the physical intimacy between them have convinced her she was in love with him?

That was how it had always been with her mother. The first time could be blamed on her mother being young and foolish. Liz's oldest sister Shar had come from that brief union. Liz's two younger sisters were progeny from two other short marriages. Liz had always thought she and Shar were full sisters; it wasn't until her teens when she found out about the one-night stand that had produced her.

Ethan's provocative question still hung in the air. Liz tugged her hand free of his as a prelude to her answer. "I think," she said, eyes downcast, "what we started before . . . we shouldn't finish."

She glanced at him sidelong, expecting anger from him or at least irritation. Instead, guilt flashed briefly in his eyes, then vanished beneath a studied indifference. "You're right. We shouldn't take chances." He shoved his chair back and rose.

"Wait." Liz put her hand on his arm to stop him. His biceps flexed beneath her fingers. "What do you mean?"

The lights in the common room dimmed into low-voltage mode, casting Ethan into shadow. His elusive emotions were impossible to read in the insufficient illumination. "We don't know what set off the violence last night. It could have been . . . arousal."

"No, I don't believe you."

"Nevertheless, we never should have started what we did." There was an edge to his voice Liz couldn't interpret. What did he want? For her to disagree?

"Maybe we shouldn't have. But not because I feel threatened by you."

He raised his hand, stroked her cheek lightly. "Maybe you should." He pulled away and left her in the vast, shadow-filled room.

As she stood alone in the quiet, she tried to piece together the emotions that seemed to lie in tatters around her. Lord, the man made her crazy. She craved his touch, ached for it as she would water for a dry throat, yet it seemed as perilous as an open flame. She could no more withstand Ethan's passions than could a tender seedling bear the brunt of full summer sun.

Reluctant to face Ethan again in their quarters, she started slowly for the exit to the common room. As she turned into the corridor, Noah popped in directly before her, sending her nearly out of her skin.

Struggling to calm herself, Liz took in several long breaths. "You need to find a better way to make an entrance."

Noah wrenched his porkpie from his head. *"Sorry, Miss Lizzy. I saw you looked a bit glum and thought I'd see if I could cheer you up."*

Down the corridor, a door slammed shut. She scanned in both directions to see if anyone was coming. "We'd better go to my lab. Last thing I need is for someone to see me talking to a ghost."

Noah drifted up to the ceiling, floating above her as he followed. Liz looked up at him over her shoulder. "Speaking of which, why couldn't Ethan see you?"

"That's a bit hard to explain, Miss Lizzy."

When she reached the hydro lab, she tapped in the code and opened the door. A quick scan told her Richard hadn't decided to do any late-night work. Swinging the door shut, she quickly disengaged the camera. She heard a little squeak and turned to see she'd caught Noah half in and half out of the door.

"God, I'm sorry." She hurried to open the door again.

Before she could reach the knob, he said, *"No need, Miss Lizzy."*

She watched, astounded, as he strained against the door-jamb, tugging himself into the hydro lab a little at a time. As he yanked the last of his ghostly form inside, Liz thought she heard a *pop,* then realized she must have imagined it.

She stared at him as he made a show of dusting himself off. "How do you do that? Come through the door?"

He settled his hat on his head. *"The honest truth is, I don't come through the door. I come around it."*

"But it was closed."

"But there's an itsy little crack, right here." He pointed where the door joined the jamb. *"I just slip right between."*

"You can't go through the door?"

"Nope."

"But I've seen you come through rock."

"I can't pass through solid rock. But there are cracks all through the cave. I can make my way from place to place by traveling along the cracks."

"One more bit of ghostly lore shot down," she muttered to herself. Too agitated to stand still, she walked along the hydro tanks, checking on her plantings. "Why is it I see you and Ethan can't?"

Noah fingered the turned-up brim of his flat-topped hat. *"Well that might be because you and me are truly meant for each other."*

She looked over at him from between two young tomato plants. "Is that truly why?"

Eyeing his toes, he shrugged. *"No, Miss Lizzy. It's because I know how to make only you see me."*

Carefully she snapped a sucker off a seedling. "But how?"

He screwed up his face as he considered. *"It's a mite hard to explain. I just sorta make myself incon . . . inconpich . . . inconpichus—"*

"Inconspicuous?"

"That's right. Works best with folks who don't believe."

"Like Ethan, you mean." Liz broke a yellowed leaf from another plant. "Could you make him see you if you had to?"

"I don't know, Miss Lizzy. I wasn't trying very hard to be inconpichus tonight, but he just didn't see me."

Which might make it impossible for her to explain Noah to Ethan. So it was just as well she'd kept his existence to herself. "Thank you for helping us to find Janet." She stopped fussing with her plants and focused her full attention on Noah. "But I want to know what happened to her."

With a jerky motion, Noah whipped his hat off his head. *"I don't know, Miss Lizzy."*

Even if he hadn't started mangling his beleaguered porkpie, she would have known from the tone of his voice that he was lying. She rounded the hydro tank standing between her and the ghost and approached him. "You need to tell me, Noah. Our lives could depend on it."

The hat seemed to stretch in his hands as he wrenched it. *"I suspect she fell, Miss Lizzy, and hit her head."*

"I know she fell, Noah. I need to know how." She put out her hand, instinct urging her to lay it on his arm to persuade the truth out of him. But of course his arm passed right between her fingers. A tingling started up in her palm. Good Lord, she'd touched a ghost. "What in the world are you made of?"

He looked down at himself. *"Spirit, I suspect."* Hat hastily planted on his head, he sidled toward the door. *"I got to go, Miss Lizzy."*

"Wait! You haven't answered my question."

He seemed to sink into the floor and Liz realized he'd begun to feed his feet underneath the door. *"I would tell you, Miss Lizzy, if I could. I swear it."*

"Then you know—" But before she could finish the question, the rest of him flowed under the door and disappeared.

Long after he'd gone, Liz stared at the door, wishing she could piece together an answer from what Noah didn't say. When exhaustion laid heavy hands on her shoulders, she fi-

nally left the lab, heading for her quarters and another, completely different, confrontation.

The latest issue of *Science* magazine open on his lap, Ethan
shifted in the bed when he heard the door open. He glanced
at Liz, then returned his gaze to the article on metamorphic
rock formations in Northern Russia he'd been pretending to
read. He really wanted to follow her every motion as she
moved gracefully through the room, slipping off her shoes
and socks, pulling her gown from the drawer before she
headed from the bathroom. When he heard the sound of the
shower running, he burned to rise from the bed and enter
the bathroom, to watch the water sluice off her body as she
cleansed herself.

The water cut off and Ethan could imagine Liz soaping
herself, the lather like lace on her tanned body. Then the
gush of the shower again as she rinsed herself quickly so as
to conserve water. When she turned off the shower for the
last time, he could see her reach across for the towel, the
inside of her arm brushing against her breast, nipples hard in
the cool air. Then she would rub herself all over to dry her
body.

He shut his eyes against the images his fertile imagination
provided, but they followed him there. He surrendered to
them, letting the vivid pictures of what Liz did behind the
shut door play out in his mind.

He was glad for the magazine in his lap when she slid
open the bathroom door. The erection pushing against his
cotton briefs would be all too obvious beneath the thin sheet
covering him. He shifted in the bed, sitting Indian-style to
conceal his reaction to her.

Standing in the doorway, she fingercombed her still-wet
hair, a wary expression on her face. Her nipples peaked beneath her gown, apparent through the thin knit. Damn, he
wanted to cup those breasts with his hands, bury his face
between them.

Flicking off the bathroom light, she edged over to her side

of the bed. She must have finally sensed his eyes on her breasts because she crossed her arms to cover them. That caused them to mound slightly above the neckline of her gown, providing him with yet another distraction.

He dragged his gaze away, forcing himself to stare at the magazine. "Are you coming to bed?"

She didn't answer, didn't move. "Ethan?"

He kept up his pretense of reading. "Yes?"

"I'm sorry."

That snagged his attention. He looked up at her. "What in God's name do you have to be sorry for?"

Although her blue gaze fixed on him, he could see the will it took for her not to look away. "For starting something I couldn't finish."

He didn't insult her by pretending he didn't know what she was talking about. "In the first place, you weren't the one who started it. In the second, you can always say no to me. Always." A faint memory, like a shred of dream came to him just then, and he wondered if he'd just lied.

She lifted a hand to smooth her damp bangs back from her face. He caught the tremor in the gesture. "I'm confused, Ethan. I won't deny I'm very . . . attracted to you."

He smiled at that, considering the more crass way he would have expressed it. "Believe me, the feeling is mutual."

She dipped her head in a jerky nod. "It scares me and excites me all at once."

His body stirred at her evocative words. "But?"

"It's a bad idea."

He agreed with her completely, but something egged him into asking, "Because?"

"Because . . ." She glanced away from him and he knew what she said next wouldn't be absolute truth. "Because our marriage is only temporary. Because Cynthia is waiting for you."

Hell, he hadn't thought of his erstwhile fiancée in days. Tossing the magazine beside him on the floor, he sat up straighter. "What if I told you Cynthia and I won't be resuming our relationship at the end of BioCave?"

She locked her hands in front of her, tension running down her arms. "Would you also tell me you want to make this marriage permanent?"

"Is that what you want?"

She didn't answer immediately and Ethan found himself holding his breath in anticipation. When she spoke he could barely hear her soft voice. "No. Of course not."

Disappointment settled like a rock in his belly at her negative response. He tried to sort out the emotions tumbling inside him—yearning, desire, loneliness. Surely those feelings didn't mean he wanted Liz as his wife forever. It was his ego that wanted their continued union, to give him control over her. But if it was true, the realization was an unpleasant one. That same attitude of his father's was the very thing that drove his mother away.

Anger and impatience arose in him, at himself, at the weaknesses Liz flayed bare with her very presence. He gestured at the space beside him. "Get into bed. I won't attack you."

An answering anger flared in her eyes, but she tugged back the covers and slid under them. She stared down at her hands on top of the sheet. "I want love, Ethan. As ridiculous as that might sound to you, I want to be in love with the man I'm intimate with. *Before* I'm intimate with him."

"Most women do."

She locked her fingers together then pulled them apart, over and over. "Let's just say it's more important to me than most women."

Her statement hung in the air between them, begging the question. He had only to look at the tension in her jaw to know she wouldn't answer. He leaned down to retrieve his magazine, then left it unopened on his lap. He tried to find a way to be honest with her without being cruel, but to avoid raising her hopes.

He reached over and cupped her chin to turn her toward

him. "Love means very little to me, Liz. I haven't experienced much of it in my life. So it's difficult for me to conceive of it."

She opened her mouth, taking a breath as if to argue. He pressed a quelling finger against her lips. "It's not something words can change, Liz. Maybe it's the way I was raised or maybe I'm just built that way. In any case, I come by it honestly—my father was the same. But if you're hoping to convince me the love of a good woman will change everything . . . don't waste your breath."

She pulled back from his touch until he dropped his hand. "Plenty of people have crummy childhoods, myself included. My mother was good at making babies, but not so great at nurturing them. And without a father . . ." She raised her chin a fraction in defiance. "But my sisters made up for what my mother lacked. And my father . . ." Her mouth compressed. "I think I understand love. And I think I learned enough from my mother not to look for it in a man who doesn't have the capacity."

Her words plunged into his chest like a dagger. He slapped open the magazine, then flipped through it so rapidly he nearly tore loose a page. "Good. I'm glad to hear it."

He felt her fingers on his bare arm, as light as a butterfly wing. "I'm sorry, Ethan. That was uncalled for."

The corner of the magazine crumpled in his hand. "Don't apologize. It's better that you understand me."

"Even if you aren't able to love—" Her hand swept down the length of his arm, a slow, stroking caress that stole his breath. "—and I'm not sure I believe that—even so, you're still worth loving."

A knot closed his throat at her soft-spoken statement. He wanted her to take her hand off him, he wanted her to pull him into her arms. Damn, he hated how she exposed his emotions. Was this what his father went through with his mother? Torn between the desire to be cherished and the instinct to protect the soft vulnerabilities inside him?

Jaw set, he shrugged away from her. "You seem to think it matters to me. Believe me, it doesn't."

She withdrew her hand. He was acutely aware of her gaze on him. Then she rose, rounding the bed and heading for the desk. He watched out of the corner of his eye as she picked up a novel she'd left there then returned to the bed. Though he wanted to devour her with his eyes, he only allowed himself glimpses on the periphery of his vision. When he wanted to put an arm around her and tuck her closely beside him, he maintained as much distance between them as he could in the narrow bed.

The words in *Science* magazine were like seeds falling on stony ground. If he'd hoped for a technical jump-start on ideas by reading current literature, he had no chance. Because despite his well-intentioned effort to ignore Liz sitting beside him, he could think of nothing else.

He dutifully read the magazine from cover-to-cover, even esoteric treatises on subjects in which he had not the remotest interest. When Liz finally set aside her book, he sighed with relief at no longer having to keep up the pretense. Dropping the issue of *Science* on the floor, he crossed the room and flipped off the light, then returned to the bed in the dark.

The blackness of the room was a different world. Here he could pull Liz's body close to his, spoon up against her in the night. He could press his lips into the silk of her hair and cushion her head on his arm. He could shut his eyes and inhale her scent, listen to the soft sound of her breathing. In this dark world, he could let himself feel all those unfamiliar, forbidden emotions. Because in the long hours of the night, there were no promises, no commitments, and no one to break his heart.

Chapter
Thirteen

The week following the Vuchoviches' return aboveground passed without incident. Liz let rest the unresolved issues between her and Ethan, knowing more discussion would only disrupt the tenuous peace between them. He was unfailingly polite to her when they were together. Although she saw little of him during the day, he made a point to share meals with her whenever he could. When he touched her in the common room, he made the contact as light and brief as possible, as if to maintain the façade of a loving marriage while still keeping his distance.

But the moment the light went out in their quarters in the evening, everything changed. He pulled her into his arms and held her all night long. He didn't try to make love, although she could feel the evidence of his arousal pressed against her. He didn't even kiss her, although sometimes she felt his lips whispering against her hair or along the nape of her neck. At times his need seemed so powerful she could feel his hands tremble, but still he didn't make a move toward any greater intimacy. If his intent was to drive her mad, his methods were damned effective.

Her only relief from the intensity of the emotions between her and Ethan was her work and Noah. The ghost turned up in the hydro lab at the oddest times. He made an honest effort to warn her of his presence before he popped in, calling out *"Miss Lizzy!"* in a stage whisper before oozing from the ceiling or out from under the door. She'd gotten into the habit of switching off the closed-circuit camera whenever she entered the hydro lab. When Ethan asked why, she told him she found it hard to work under scrutiny and left it at that.

Her interactions with Noah were amusing and uncomplicated. He dredged up story after story of his youth, painting a picture of mid-nineteenth-century life Liz could have never gotten from a book. Much of what he told her she suspected were well-embroidered half-truths, but Noah's company was a relief, a kind of mindless entertainment.

Her time spent with Ethan, on the other hand, drained her. She felt constantly adrift in the palpable tension between them, lost in yearnings she didn't understand, a longing that terrified her. She would catch herself staring at the wall calendar, counting the weeks left of the experiment, praying she'd have the strength to withstand them.

"Miss Lizzy!"

The hissing whisper echoing off the hydro lab ceiling pulled Liz away from her glum assessment of a line of pepper seedlings that were failing to thrive. She looked up, trying to guess where Noah would appear. She'd gotten better at gauging his location from the sound of his voice.

She watched as fingers materialized in the limestone arch just above the storage shelves. An arm followed, then Noah's body rolled out of a hairline crack that Liz would have never noticed if the ghost hadn't just emerged from it. He settled his booted feet to the floor, fussily adjusting his sack coat as if it had somehow picked up a wrinkle as he traversed through the narrow fissure.

He gave her a broad smile. *"How are you, Miss Lizzy?"*

"I'm doing fine, Noah." She gestured at the pepper plants. "I'd be doing better if I knew why these seedlings won't grow."

Drifting closer, he bent close to the hydro tank. *"Can't be wanting water since the little fellas are swimming in it."* He passed a finger through a pale green leaf and Liz had a whimsical notion that Noah might heal the plant with his touch. Instead the shriveled leaf broke off the plant and dropped into the nutrient solution. Noah looked up at her. *"Sorry, Miss Lizzy."*

"No problem." She plucked the dead leaf from its watery grave and tossed it in the trash. "It's just this one row. I suspect the pH is out of whack." She crouched to study the root system of the troubled pepper plants through the acrylic side of the tank. Rather than filling the tank with aggregate to support these specimens, she'd used only a thin layer of gravel on top of wire mesh. Most of the roots were visible in the liquid below the mesh. "Or maybe there's not enough magnesium."

While she examined the frail white roots of the pepper plants, Noah remained silent. She glanced up at him to make sure he was still there and she caught the troubled look in his face. That was nothing new. Whether silent or chattering a million words a minute, Liz suspected Noah was hiding more than he was revealing. But whenever she pressed him, he took a powder.

Typical male. The gender obviously hadn't evolved much in the hundred-plus years since Noah's time. They still only shared what they chose, usually what revealed the least of their true selves. But in Noah's case, Liz couldn't shake the feeling the information he withheld was tremendously important.

She straightened and smiled at the ghost. "Counting the ways you love me?"

She was astonished to see Noah blush. He jerked his hat off and squashed it in one hand. *"I'm over that now, Miss*

Lizzy. I have decided to love you like a sister. A dear, beloved sister.''

She curved her palm against his insubstantial cheek. "That's the sweetest thing anyone has ever said to me."

Amazingly, he turned a darker shade of red. *''Thank you, Miss Lizzy.''* The porkpie was a wad of spectral felt and ribbon in his hands. *''I wish with all my heart I deserved your regard.''*

This was a familiar refrain. Liz circled the tank with the failing plantings and checked the growth in the next one. "Of course you do, Noah." Rounding the tank overflowing with luxuriant growth, she spied on the ghost between the leaves of tomato and pepper plants. He looked guilty again, and Liz wondered for the hundredth time what a ghost would have to feel guilty about. What terrible deed had Noah committed that chased him into death?

''I am a coward, Miss Lizzy,'' he said almost too softly for her to hear.

Peering at him over the tops of the tomato plants, Liz held her breath. She didn't dare ask what he meant, he would only leave. But it was apparent Noah wanted to unburden his soul about something and Liz felt certain it was exactly what was vital for her to know.

"A coward?" she asked, keeping her tone unconcerned.

He squeezed his porkpie between his fingers like a handful of mud. "Because I cannot tell you. . . .''

She moved to the end of the hydro tank, her gaze still nominally on the plants. "Does this have to do with something that happened in your lifetime, Noah?"

His brown eyes widened as he shook his head, then nodded, then shook his head again. *''In a manner of speaking.''*

"Is it the war? Do you feel badly that you didn't serve?"

He blinked. *''The war?''*

"Between the States. I understood from the history you left before you could be conscripted."

His eyes narrowed with anger. *''Is that what Mama said? Because it was her idea to go, seeing as how I was an only son and my mama widowed. Only she wanted me to take her with me.''*

Liz realized her mistake in bringing up the past. In another moment, Noah would launch into another tirade against his mother. Her movements deliberate, she turned from Noah and took up the digital camera. She captured several images of the hydro tanks, both those with thriving populations and the failing rows of seedlings.

"If not the war, then what?" The direct question derailed him from his usual invective over his long-dead mother. It also risked driving him away. Liz continued shooting, never once looking over at Noah.

"That it were only something so simple, Miss Lizzy.'' The sorrow in his tone prompted her to glance up at him. He shimmered and faded briefly then seemed to force himself back into view. Gliding across the floor, he planted himself before her. *"You are in danger, Miss Lizzy. You are all in terrible danger.''*

Then with a squawk, he rubberbanded from the room as if a hand had taken hold of him and snatched him away. Only his fear remained, tangible patches of cold and heat that took a long time to disperse.

Ethan dropped his toolbox into the opening of the waist-high tunnel before him and went on hands and knees to crawl inside. The light he'd hung around his neck swayed from its cord as he maneuvered the short length of tunnel, occasionally banging against the toolbox he pushed along ahead of him. He wasn't the least bit claustrophobic, but he couldn't deny the relief he felt when the tunnel opened on the other side to a larger space.

Aiming the light at the floor, he sought the power box he'd left here on his first visit. He'd wired it to the photovoltaic system with a battery backup, a wasteful bit of whimsy he would be hard-pressed to explain. But when he flipped on the switch, lighting the low-voltage lights he'd placed so far in this cavernous space, he felt gratified with his handiwork. He didn't like to consider what weakness this project might reveal. Instead he focused on its completion.

The chamber was perhaps twice the size of his and Liz's quarters. It seemed smaller, though, crowded as it was with slender stalactites suspended from the ceiling and squat stalagmites rising from the floor. A few columns had formed where the glittering limestone had stretched far enough down to meet its brother growing toward it from below. In between thin, hollow soda straw stalactites peppered the ceiling. Dividing the chamber nearly in two was a translucent sweep of limestone hanging down like an undulating sheet. Its striated surface followed the shape of the ceiling crack from which it had formed. It looked like an angel's wing stilled in flight.

Opening his toolbox, he pulled out the spool of wire he'd brought. Yesterday he'd set the last of the lights illuminating the front half of the chamber. Today he would begin laying out the wiring for the half behind the angel's wing. He had another week if he hoped to finish by his deadline. If he didn't come to his senses before then and disconnect the whole mess. Certainly he had more practical uses for this much wire and the dozens of lights he planned to employ.

But when he straightened with the coil of wire in his hand and surveyed his handiwork so far, he knew he'd keep at this task until he completed it. He'd created something beautiful here. Surely he could offer this to Liz and she would understand. After her frightening experience in the dark, she deserved a gift of light.

She might be angry to have her birthday acknowledged at all. Especially when she found out he'd discovered the date by examining confidential personnel files. He didn't know what had prompted him to bring up her records in the computer center. He'd holed himself up in there the morning after the Vuchoviches had gone aboveground to familiarize himself with the processes Ivan and Janet had set up. But he'd been hard-pressed to make sense of the Vuchoviches' online procedures when his every conscious thought had been of Liz.

That was when he'd pulled up her records. He had the passwords that limited access and as he entered the string of characters, he ignored the guilt he felt. It was hell being with her, a greater torture being apart, but maybe he could satisfy just a fraction of his needs by dipping into her secrets.

Secrets were scarce in her personnel file. It listed her educational background—although there was no mention of Aaron Cohen's footing the bill—and employment history. Her mother's name was listed, as well as her sisters, but she'd filled in the space for father with "unknown." She could have left it blank, but there was a certain defiance in admitting the truth.

And there was her birthdate, only nine days away. He'd immediately decided to honor the day with a gift, but it wasn't until later that afternoon, when he was poring over a map of Hoyo del Diablo, that he decided exactly what the present would be. He'd discovered the angel-wing chamber months ago when they'd first started plotting out BioCave. It would take only the addition of light to turn the space into an enchantment.

He went down on one knee to dig through his toolbox for his wire strippers, pulling the top tray out in irritation when he couldn't find them. But the tool wasn't in the bottom either, which meant he'd probably left it in the energy center. Dropping the spool of wire in the open toolbox, he turned off the lights and returned to the narrow tunnel. It was a damned annoying waste of precious time, but he wouldn't get far without the wire strippers.

He emerged from the tunnel and quickly headed toward the energy center. As he slipped inside, a sudden eeriness crawled over him. He had the sense he'd just missed someone in the room, that someone had just left. But no one but him had access to the energy center. He turned in a circle, looking around him. Everything seemed in order and the wire strippers were right where he'd left them on a workbench.

He continued searching the room as he palmed the wire strippers and stuffed them into the back pocket of his jeans.

His uneasiness compelled him to check on the status for the various energy sources. But as he moved from monitor to monitor, he could see nothing amiss in the displays. All the appropriate wind generators were online and operating at peak efficiency, the photovoltaic and passive solar systems were error-free, the water-based power generators that utilized the two underground streams in Hoyo del Diablo were producing consistent energy. He quickly launched a set of diagnostic programs on the backup windmills and solar systems—no problems.

His gaze strayed idly to the workspace between two monitors and a prickle fingered its way up his spine. Where was the handful of peridotite stones he'd brought back from his foray into the undeveloped area of Hoyo del Diablo? After he dumped them there a week ago, he'd left them as a reminder of what had happened between him and Liz. Although he could remember nothing of what had amounted to an attack on her, the peridotite somehow seemed a symbol of the terrible thing he'd done. If he couldn't recall the event, he could keep the guilt fresh in his mind.

But now nothing remained of the stones but dust. He bent to search the floor; maybe he'd knocked them off the workbench by mistake. But they were truly gone, even the one he'd dropped that day and had never bothered to retrieve.

Somehow, with the absence of the peridotite, it seemed a great weight had lifted from him. Maybe it was best to have the reminder gone. He could find another way to atone for what he'd done. Which was exactly what he'd hoped to achieve with this gift for Liz. Giving the monitors one last scan, he strode from the energy center, locking the door behind him.

No more than ten feet from the energy center, he heard his name called and turned to see Diana Bradshaw hurrying toward him. He watched her impassively and suddenly realized her lush body not the least bit tempting. When had he developed a taste for lean, athletic women? Her smile alone should have sent his mind on flights of fantasy, never mind she was happily married. Diana liked to flirt, but he couldn't seem to work up any enthusiasm to respond in kind.

As she hooked a thick lock of dark blonde hair behind her ear, he saw her fingernails were painted drop-dead-red. Instead of picturing those fingernails on his skin, a different image intruded—Liz's hand resting in his as he painted her nails. The fantasy was surprisingly erotic.

Diana's smile widened as she sidled up to him. "Glad I found you. Aaron's on the line in the communications center. He wants to talk to you."

Hell. Yet another delay to his project in the chamber. He mentally added up the hours until Liz's birthday, wondered if he would have a chance to finish on time. He nodded absently to Diana's chatter as he walked with her, only dimly aware of her fingers occasionally brushing his arm or when she parted company with him at the com center.

When he walked inside and saw Liz there talking to Aaron, the sight of her slammed into his gut. He imposed such strenuous discipline on himself that he never felt the full impact of how much he missed her until he saw her again. In that first moment, he couldn't seem to stop the joy that erupted inside him.

When she turned from the bank of monitors where Aaron's image was displayed, her smile hit him hard a second time. But when it occurred to him that her pleasure stemmed not from seeing him but from her exuberance at speaking to Aaron, something wrenched inside him. In these past several days with her, he'd let himself forget her relationship with Aaron, the prior claim the old man held for her. And even if the ugly rumors weren't true, even if there was no intimacy between Liz and Aaron, *she loved him first.*

It was madness, but in that moment, he felt like a little boy again. Thirty some odd years vanished and he was a four-year-old, watching from his bedroom window as his mother abandoned him. She had loved his father first and her love for him was second-best. Otherwise, why would she have left?

Liz's smile faded and she turned slowly back to Aaron to say good-bye. She rose, but stayed near the chair as Ethan lowered himself into it. He glanced up at her, schooling perfect neutrality into his tone. "Yes?"

Her gaze shifted to Aaron's image, then back to him. He thought she might say good-bye again to Aaron before leaving. But she surprised him. Her hand sliding along his shoulder to the back on his neck, she leaned in and kissed him, once lightly on the cheek, again more lingeringly on his mouth. Then she all but ran from the room, leaving him to calm his heart, to squelch the tremors in his body.

He managed as bland an expression as he could for Aaron. The old goat looked as satisfied as a well-fed cat, his pale blue eyes bright with humor. Ethan glared at him, daring him to say even one word about it. He damn well didn't want the old man asking questions when he himself didn't have a clue about the answers. Hell, that woman had him twisted in twenty different directions.

But Aaron, thank God, didn't pursue it. "Wanted to let you all know Janet's been released from the hospital. It was touch and go there for a bit with the cerebral swelling, but she seems fine now."

Ethan quickly switched gears, grateful to have something besides Liz to focus on. "But she still has no memory of the accident?"

Aaron shook his head. "The injury seems to have caused a partial amnesia. She remembers being afraid, terrified actually. But that might just be because of the fall."

"But it makes no sense." Ethan canted the chair back and rested his feet on the workbench below the bank of monitors. Ankles crossed, he fidgeted one sneaker-clad foot against the other. "The extent of the injury isn't consistent with a simple fall. It's as if someone threw her against the rock wall."

Aaron's brow furrowed. "I hope you're not suggesting someone on the staff might have attacked her."

He jiggled his foot a little harder. "I don't know what I'm suggesting, Aaron."

"But you're talking about a tremendously violent act. You've all been vetted, your backgrounds thoroughly checked. No one among you has that kind of propensity for violence."

A faint memory fleeted through his mind—his hands on Liz, his body forced against her. He felt sick. "Maybe not normally, but if there's something down here affecting us. . . ."

"There's nothing in the literature regarding negative effects of living underground. Hell, men have been living in caves for thousands of years."

"Then it's something else." *Like a darkness inside me I've managed to hide. An evil that took only the right opportunity to emerge.* "I'd like you to arrange for sampling of the exhaust vents."

"What am I looking for?"

Ethan propped his arm on the workbench, then shifted it as something jabbed him. "Any molds, fungus, anything psychotropic in the air supply . . ." His voice trailed off as his gaze fell on what had stuck him in the arm. A bit of peridotite, no bigger than his thumbnail, sat on the workbench. "What the hell?"

As he reached for the stone, Aaron's image suddenly scrambled into static. A moment later, all the screens flickered, the displays dancing with color and light before they, too, dissolved into snow. Tossing aside the rock, Ethan immediately hit the controls to reconnect with Aaron, audio only. But he couldn't raise the aboveground staff at all.

"Hell," he muttered. With all the run-throughs they'd executed before lockdown, he thought he'd worked through every bug the communications system had to offer. Scooting down to the computer at the end of the workbench, he tried another sequence of commands to restore communications, but nothing worked. The lines were well and truly dead. They were completely cut off from the surface.

● ● ●

Noah stared openmouthed at the tiny piece of devil rock on the table next to Ethan. How in tarnation had it gotten there? When he'd followed Lizzy into the room the BioCave folk called "communications," he'd been right at her elbow the whole time. He'd had to concentrate real hard to keep her from seeing him, so maybe he missed seeing him. But that didn't sit right, when he'd been right careful to keep even the least little bit of devil rock away from the BioCave folks, most especially his Miss Lizzy.

Noah angled himself a little closer to Ethan and gave the rock a good once-over. He'd been squirreling away the handful of pebbles in Ethan's lab, one piece at a time. It had been a real bother, because although he could easily carry a rock the size of that boulder that broke Miss Lizzy's lumber, he couldn't seem to lift more than one piece at a time, no matter how small. So it took days to remove all the devil rock from Ethan's lab.

As Ethan shifted from one end of the long table to the other, his arm brushed against the rock, knocking it nearly to the edge. Noah felt certain that piece hadn't been there when he'd first come into the room. Which left only one possibility, one that chilled Noah right down to the core. The monster had brought it here. It needed the rock nearby to work its evil and since Noah had been tossing all he could find into the pit, the creature had learned to bring its own.

Ethan pushed his chair back to the other end of the table and pounded on the thing Miss Lizzy called a keyboard. The moving pictures on the wall above Ethan had all disappeared into little spots of light. Noah knew that was wrong, because every other time he'd peeked into the communications room, the pictures were there. Lizzy had explained how a camera in each lab sent its picture here. Had everyone turned off their camera, as Miss Lizzy did sometimes?

Noah eyeballed the little bit of devil rock and knew different. The monster had something to do with this problem with the wall of pictures. And Ethan looked mighty worried about it.

Noah knew what he had to do—take the devil rock away and throw it into the pit with the others. The creature couldn't keep its power long without it. Noah edged around Ethan, reached for the dark gray-green pebble. Testing the air for the presence of the monster, Noah closed his fingers around the rock. He felt nothing, no doubt because the creature was busy making trouble. So there was nothing to keep him from closing his hand around the bit of rock and carrying it away.

He hadn't lifted the thing more than an inch when he felt the first icy grip of fear. It closed around his wrist, forcing his hand to open and release the rock. In that same moment, the pictures flickered back on the wall, giving Noah a quick view of Lizzy's empty lab alongside the other rooms. He tried to resist the aching hold on his arm, but his own cowardice swamped him and he let go of the rock.

It rattled back onto the table, bringing Ethan's attention back around. Noah realized that in his struggle against the monster, he'd let himself become visible. Ethan stared in shock just a heartbeat before Noah popped from view again. Noah watched, trembling in reaction as Ethan seemed to try to understand what he'd seen. Then the pictures blinked out again, one by one, and the geologist had to turn his focus back to them. Noah floated above him, steeped in self-condemnation. A moment later, Lizzy's shout for help wrested him from his misery.

Returning from the corridor outside the infirmary after calling for help, Liz snatched up a blanket and quickly spread it over Dr. Nishimoto. "Hurts," he gasped, clawing at his chest.

A heart attack? But despite Dr. Nishimoto's advanced age, he'd been in excellent health. That had been a requirement for participation in BioCave. Grabbing a pillow from the examination table, she knelt to ease it under the doctor's head. "Do you have heart problems, Dr. Nishmoto?"

"No . . . no . . ." His head thrashed from side to side in agitation. "Evil . . . evil . . ."

Liz shivered at his rasping tone. "What do you mean?"

"Reached inside . . . reached inside my chest . . . evil . . ."

Her throat seemed to close as horror spilled over her. "What . . ." She swallowed and tried again. "What was evil?"

But he'd lapsed into Japanese, the words incomprehensible to Liz. He whispered one word again and again, *akuma, akuma,* until the syllables were drilled into Liz's brain.

As she shifted on the limestone floor, something sharp bit her knee through her jeans. She moved her leg aside to see a pebble under it, a small grayish-green stone. Her fear for Dr. Nishimoto making her edgy and irritated, she scooped up the pebble and tossed it out into the corridor.

Dr. Nishimoto took in a long, halting breath, then turned to Liz, clear-eyed for the first time. "Nitro tablets. Top shelf of the pharmaceutical cabinet. On the left."

She did as he asked, bringing him the entire bottle of pills. Following his instructions, she broke one in half and helped him slip it under his tongue. Just as the first footsteps sounded in the corridor, the tension in his face eased.

Trang Nguyen appeared first, followed by Wendy Nishimoto and Ethan. Relief clogged her throat and pricked her eyes with tears. Not caring what his reaction would be, she ran to Ethan, wrapping her arms around him as Dr. Nguyen hurried to examine Dr. Nishimoto. Without hesitation, Ethan embraced her.

Wendy had knelt beside her husband, holding his hand as Trang listened to his heart. Wendy held herself rigid and Liz sensed she fought back tears for her husband's sake. Liz tried to imagine how she would feel if it were Ethan stricken but the image so frightened her she couldn't hold the image.

That she'd come to care for him so much so quickly was terrifying in itself. There was no future for the two of them; she only opened herself up to heartache by even considering their relationship could continue past BioCave. But in that moment, she felt so fragile, so vulnerable, she had to allow herself Ethan's comfort.

Trang looked up at Ethan. "I don't like the sound of his heart. He's going to have to go aboveground."

Ethan's lips compressed, his expression grave. "We have a problem with aboveground communications. I haven't traced the glitch yet."

A moment's hesitation, then Trang nodded. "I'll do what I can to stabilize him. But the moment you contact the surface, you tell them to send down the elevator."

With Ethan's help, they lifted Dr. Nishimoto to the examination table. His color seemed better, but from the thready sound of his breathing, Liz knew the doctor wasn't out of the woods yet.

Liz lingered after Ethan returned to the communications center, putting a supporting arm around Wendy. Wendy gripped her husband's hand as if the contact was vital to keeping him alive.

Liz gave the woman a squeeze. "Wendy, do you speak Japanese?"

Wendy's brow furrowed at the odd question. "A little. I've picked up a bit from Wallace over the years."

"Do you know what *akuma* means?"

Wendy's eyes widened. "Why do you ask?"

"Wallace said it several times."

Wendy looked troubled. "I think . . . I think it means, evil spirit."

Chapter
Fourteen

In the end, Ethan traced the problem to a disruption in the power to the communications systems. He had to redirect power from the original source to an auxiliary service. The auxiliary ran off the less-predictable windmills, but in the short term it allowed him to contact the surface, audio only, until he could perform a more permanent fix.

The loss of Dr. Nishimoto and his wife Wendy went far beyond the skills the two offered to the BioCave experiment. Wallace was the revered elder statesman of BioCave, one of its original members back when the project was only a dream of Aaron Cohen's. His wife, Wendy, had been a BioCave booster for years, and as the project's industrial designer had transformed the developed areas of Hoyo del Diablo from dank into comfortably livable. Her sunny personality, too, was a blessing for this sometimes contentious group.

Despite his disability, Dr. Nishimoto kept up a running commentary to Trang Nguyen as he was transported by stretcher to the elevator. As backup physician, Trang had at least a cursory knowledge of the medical histories of the remaining staff. If she lacked a more thorough grounding, it was only because she'd expected to be third in line behind Dr. Nishimoto and Cynthia. She'd spent most of her medical career in research and hadn't worked with patients in years.

Just before they sent the elevator car up to the surface, Wallace gestured to Ethan. Ethan went down on one knee to where the doctor lay on the stretcher. "I'm a stubborn old fool, Ethan, but there's nothing wrong with my heart."

Ethan smiled sympathetically. "If you're trying to weasel out of this trip aboveground, I'm afraid I can't accommodate you."

Dr. Nishimoto waved a hand impatiently. "I mean before the infarction. My heart was as strong as a forty-year-old's. Something happened." He glanced over at Wendy, then back to Ethan. "Ask Liz. Ask her what I said before you all arrived."

Ethan backed away then and let the elevator door close. He parted company with Trang and returned to the communications center and his repairs. But Wallace Nishimoto's words nagged at him the rest of the day.

Liz slumped in her chair at her computer desk, her eyes burning from hours of staring at a monitor. She'd fallen several days behind on data entry and decided to tackle it all in a marathon session at her computer. Now with a push of a button, she could bring up tables and graphs pertaining to any part of her hydroponic projects.

Her eyes blurring slightly, she focused on the time displayed at the bottom of her monitor. Just past ten in the evening. Her gaze strayed to the date and realized with surprise that it was her birthday. She wasn't one to celebrate those milestones—too many years of having the day forgotten by her mother sapped its importance—but she'd made it a point in the past to treat herself somehow on her birthday. Maybe she'd sneak into the kitchen and see if she could scare up a slice of carrot cake from yesterday's dinner.

The loneliness of eating a solitary piece of birthday cake

lanced through her. In the two days since Dr. Nishimoto had had to be transported aboveground, Liz had seen even less of Ethan than before. After he cornered her that day to grill her about what the doctor had said in his delirium, he'd made himself scarce. Both nights since, he'd come to bed so late, she was already asleep. He'd leave so early in the morning, he was gone before she rose.

Damn, she missed him. She hadn't realized how much she looked forward to seeing him at mealtimes, to having him hold her close in bed, until he'd deprived her of even those small pleasures. She knew he was preoccupied with the problems of BioCave, but if he shared them with her, talked to her about their difficulties, he might find them easier to bear. But leave it to a man to want to solve every problem alone.

She hadn't even had the solace of Noah's visits the last two days. He hadn't appeared once, even when she called him. She desperately wanted to ask him about what Dr. Nishimoto had said. *Evil spirit*—Liz shuddered even now, remembering. Because she'd felt a resonance in those words within herself, as if it tangled in her mind with a forgotten memory. Ethan had discounted the doctor's words as irrational babbling, but for Liz they brought a terrifying recognition.

Noah had to know something about it. He'd resided in this cavern for more than a hundred years; he must know every part of it. And he'd hinted that something beyond himself inhabited the dark, had intimated about it a dozen times in a dozen ways. If he cared anything for Liz, it was time he came clean.

Shutting down the computer, Liz realized maybe it was time for her to come clean with Ethan. She had to tell him about Noah, explain to him the source of all the minor problems within BioCave. And it might send them both along the path of discovering if something else threatened them.

Rubbing at her eyes, she left the hydro lab and started for the energy center. With the Vuchoviches gone, Ethan had had to do double duty between the computer center and his own lab. That on top of all the administrative tasks that fell to him as head of BioCave. But he didn't answer her knock at the energy center and at the computer center, Harlan Jackson told her he hadn't seen Ethan all evening. Liz doubled back to check the common room and kitchen. The Nguyens, busy setting up for breakfast, said Ethan had been in earlier. They didn't know where he'd gone, but he'd taken the last of the carrot cake.

So much for a birthday celebration, Liz thought as she headed for their quarters. When she opened the door to an empty room, she felt a keen disappointment. She'd started the search for Ethan ostensibly to tell him about Noah, but she realized it had only been an excuse to see him. Now she hadn't the slightest notion where to look next.

Deprived of her birthday cake, she figured it was time to break out one of the chocolate bars she'd brought with her. She'd brought twelve, two for each month, and had already gone through six. But her twenty-eighth birthday certainly warranted chocolate.

When she tugged open the top drawer of the dresser, her gaze fell on a small packet wrapped in computer paper with a ribbon fashioned from electrical wire. Her name was scrawled across the top of the package in Ethan's impatient hand. A smile curved her lips as she lifted the package and untwisted the wire. She unfolded the paper to find inside not a gift, but a note. *Come to the computer center.* A loopy "E" was sketched below the short missive.

She was astounded. If she didn't recognize the handwriting, she would never have guessed that Ethan would ever conceive of something so . . . playful. Setting down the wire, she took the note with her as she returned to the communications center. Harlan turned to her with a grin and when he saw the sheet of paper in her hand, gave her another tightly wrapped packet. Tugging the paper free from the wire, she unfolded it and read, *There's something for you in the common room.*

Trang and Qwong were waiting for her with another package. That one led to the communications center and another note propped on the lockbox. Several misdirections later, she was standing in a corridor leading to an undeveloped section of BioCave. She assumed she'd made a wrong turn until she saw the square of white paper leaning against the wall. *Keep going,* it said and Liz continued hesitantly down the corridor.

She saw him just as the passageway turned. He stood amidst the glow of dozens of small white lights that had been strung across the corridor and disappeared into a dark space in the wall. He looked completely uncertain and unsure of himself as he watched her approach. Something tightened in her chest as she caught the worried look in his gray eyes, and she wanted nothing more than to hurl herself into his arms.

As she closed the distance between them, she smiled, trying to offer to him all the complexity of what she felt inside. "What is this?"

He flung his hands out to either side in a half-shrug. "Happy birthday, Liz."

Tears pricked her eyes then, but she smiled past them. "Are these my birthday candles?" She gestured at the string of small white lights.

"Some of them." He motioned to the opening in the wall where the lights led. "Come with me."

He dropped to hands and knees and crawled inside. Liz followed after, perplexed and intrigued. A line of lights dotted the dark space, leading to a brighter glow up ahead. When Ethan reached the end of the tunnel, he straightened and put a hand out to help her to her feet. She rose slowly, her heart caught in her throat at the beauty of what she saw.

The tunnel opened up into a high-ceilinged chamber crowded with stalagmites and stalactites. Festooning the pearlescent limestone structures were string after string of the same tiny white lights she'd seen in the corridor. The space shimmered with the soft illumination, like something from a fairy tale.

"Happy birthday, Liz," Ethan murmured again.

She turned to him, tears brimming. "It's incredible. Is this what you've been doing the past few days?"

"For nearly a week. The communications systems problem slowed me down, so I had to double my effort the last few days."

Stepping a little deeper into the chamber, she looked around her again, taking in the incredible fantasy brought to life. "Then this is why I haven't seen much of you."

"Do you like it?"

She looked back at him over her shoulder, took in the intensity of his gaze. It seemed terribly important to him that he had pleased her. She no more understood that than she comprehended why he had gone to such lengths to give her this.

She went to him, clasped one of his hands in hers. "It's wonderful."

Raising his free hand to her face, he stroked her cheek. "Then you like it."

She leaned into his touch. "It's the most amazing present anyone has ever given me."

Urging her head back, he leaned to brush a kiss against her lips. Liz moved her hands to his waist, the warmth of him beneath his denim shirt heating her palms. She wanted to trace the lines of his arms, exposed by the rolled-up sleeves of his shirt. She wanted to explore every inch of his body. Most of all, she wanted him to deepen his light kisses, to dip inside her mouth with his tongue.

But with one more light kiss, he stepped back, one hand lingering on her arm. "Let me show you." His fingers interlaced with hers, he guided her along a path bedecked with lights. "As I worked, I tried to touch the limestone features as little as possible." He pointed to a stocky stalagmite rising from the floor and its stalactite mate on the ceiling. "They're still growing and the oils from my fingers would interrupt the process. Look up there."

Liz tipped her head back to see a thin sheet of limestone hanging like a banner from the ceiling. Lit from behind, stripes of cream, orange, and brown were clearly visible through the sinuous surface. "What is it?"

"A drip-curtain stalactite. It's formed when water seeps through cracks in the limestone. Impurities in the water cause the color banding."

A lacy, glittering structure clinging to the ceiling caught her attention next. "And that?" The delicate spray of white and pale blue looked like a piece of coral.

"Argonite. A crystal formation. Fairly rare."

Like his smiles. His demeanor was so somber so much of the time. Yet he gave her this. . . .

He showed her every feature of the chamber, pointing out columns and soda straw stalactites, explaining how water seeping through the limestone after the cavern is created developed the strange, unearthly shapes. Some of what he told her she remembered from science classes, but the details were new to her. The telling of it seemed to be part of the gift and she appreciated it as much as she did the visual treat.

When they'd finished and returned to the entrance of the chamber, Ethan said, "I'll have to start taking it down tomorrow." She heard the regret in his tone.

She squeezed his hand. "Let me help you."

His mouth curved into a half-smile. "That would be like cleaning up after your own birthday party."

She considered telling him the truth—that spending the time with him would be a continuation of the gift. But she was still afraid to reveal too much of herself to him, afraid of his reaction. "I don't mind. I'd like to help. Consider it my thank-you."

His gray gaze darkened slightly. "I didn't do this to have you thank me."

She closed her other hand around his. "Then why, Ethan?"

He looked down at their joined hands. "It was your birthday. I didn't exactly have access to a mall."

She ought to leave it alone, but something drove her to persist. "But why give me anything at all? It's not as if we were . . ." Truly lovers, she finished silently. Truly husband and wife. "It's marvelous, Ethan. But I can't help but wonder why."

"I suppose," he began, then paused as if he was finding it hard to frame what he wanted to say. "I wanted . . . to make up for everything. The problems with BioCave, the scare you had."

"None of those were your fault."

"And the problems between us."

His last statement hung in the air, bringing up its own tantalizing questions. Like why he felt he had to make up anything to her. And what drove him to such an elaborate atonement.

He tugged at her hand, pulling her to a shadowed corner. He picked up a blanket he'd tucked behind a stalagmite and spread it on the limestone floor. Then he retrieved a napkin-covered plate. "Can't celebrate a birthday without cake."

He sat cross-legged on the blanket, urging her to do the same. He set down the plate and uncovered it, revealing a thick slice of carrot cake topped with a fat candle. Liz put out a finger to snitch some of the creamy icing. "So that's what happened to the last of the cake."

Pulling a match from his shirt pocket, he lit the candle. "Make a wish."

Something in his tone brought her gaze up to his face. He was so skilled at hiding behind barriers, she couldn't interpret the emotions there. But even Ethan couldn't quite conceal the message in his eyes. Yearning, hope. Still, those shreds of enlightenment didn't complete the picture—what did he yearn for, and for what did he hope?

She shut her eyes, spelled out her wish in her mind. *Let me love and be loved.*

Ethan watched as the candle flame guttered and died, sending a wisp of smoke from the still-glowing tip of the wick. Liz's lips were still slightly pursed, and it was all he could do to not take that as invitation. She had a dreamy look in her eyes and in that moment he would have given just about anything to know what she'd wished for.

Reaching into his secret stash, he produced two forks and held one out to her. He positioned his hand so her fingers brushed against his as she took the fork. The tactic reminded him of his randy adolescence, when he would find any excuse to touch a girl. Still, he felt not the least repentant. He gestured to her to take the first bite. "How has your week gone?"

"Well enough." She sliced her fork through the carrot cake, coming up with a huge bite. "I had to pull out a tankful of plants that weren't thriving and start again." She nipped half the chunk of cake from her fork, licking a smear of frosting from the corner of her mouth.

Ethan froze, entranced by the unconsciously erotic motion. Then, with an effort, he focused his attention on the cake. "Talked to Aaron this afternoon." He took a mouthful of the moist cake, watching for a reaction from Liz to the old millionaire's name. Not even a flicker of a response in her face.

She pushed up the sleeves of her royal blue sweater, the lines of her exposed arms a sensual distraction. "Anything new on Dr. Nishimoto?"

"Out of intensive care. They haven't quite pinpointed the cause of the heart attack though."

She took another bite of cake and he watched her swipe a stray crumb from her lower lip. He leaned forward, wanting to take her face in his hands and kiss her. But the issue of Aaron and her relationship to him hung between them. He could ignore it, push it aside, but it never seemed to stop burning in the pit of his stomach.

His conversation with the old millionaire that afternoon had set off the latest wrangle inside him. After they'd finished discussing Wallace Nishimoto's condition, Aaron brought up the subject of Liz's birthday. It seemed he'd hidden a little something for her in one of the storage rooms. Since Liz hadn't come across it yet, he'd asked Ethan to retrieve it. Ethan had found the tiny box right where Aaron had said it would be—concealed in a box of nutrient solution Liz hadn't opened yet. It didn't take a genius to figure out the package must contain jewelry of some kind.

Now the box, with a small gift tag taped to the bottom, sat in the shadows behind him. He couldn't, wouldn't keep it from her. But as soon as she saw the no doubt valuable piece of jewelry from Aaron, his gift of lights would seem trivial in comparison.

Hell, he might as well get it over with. He snatched the box from its hiding place. "Aaron asked me to wish you a happy birthday." He proffered the present. "He wanted me to give you this."

Her eyes went misty as she took the gift from him. They grew softer when she tore the card from the package and read it. When she undid the wrappings and flipped open the jewelry box, she had to wipe the tears from her eyes. "I guess I got my wish." She turned the box toward him.

It wasn't a gaudy diamond ring or jewel-encrusted earrings. It was a simple pendant—a gold key-shaped charm hanging on a delicate gold chain. Exactly the sort of jewelry sold at department stores at a price that would be pocket change for a man like Aaron Cohen. "That's nice," he said uncertainly. Why the tears? Had she expected something more elaborate? Or was it simply that she missed Aaron?

Reaching for the gift card, he gave her a questioning look and waited for her nod of assent before he opened it and read: YOU ARE THE KEY TO MY HEART. A fist tightened inside him as he considered the ramifications of the neatly penned words. Was it simply a demonstration of the affection between two friends? Or confirmation that they were lovers? He could live with the first option, but if the second were true—it cut into him as viciously as a knife.

Hell, he should ask her, straight out, what her relationship was with the old man. Didn't he deserve to know? He was her husband . . . but no, he wasn't really. A legal contract bound them together, not love. Maybe the constancy of love couldn't be counted on, but the termination of the contract could be—they'd agreed to sever it in five months' time.

Unless he refused. The idea startled him. That it had even crossed his mind at all, that he felt such fierce joy in the possibility. To continue with Liz as his wife . . . the rightness of it flooded him. Because he wanted her, because she made him feel alive. He wouldn't have to love her to keep her with him. She wouldn't have to love him. . . .

The fist squeezed inside him again. He pushed his thoughts aside and focused back on Liz. She'd pulled the necklace from the box and was fumbling with the clasp. Pushing aside the plate of cake, he took the pendant from her. "I'll do it." She turned her back to him, dipping her head down, and he knelt behind her. The exposed nape of her neck tempted him to brush his lips against it. He satisfied himself with touching her as he fastened the chain, fingers lingering against her warm skin.

She looked back at him over her shoulder, her neck curving as gracefully as any swan's. Her gaze locked with his, seemed to search his soul. Her lips parted, at once beckoning and dangerous. If she spoke just then, Ethan wasn't sure he would want to hear what she had to say. Because he wouldn't put it past her in that moment to have read his mind and known his deepest mysteries.

He stood abruptly to break the link between them. "It's late. We should get back."

She put out a hand and let him help her up. The out-of-character gesture set him off-balance. When did Liz ask him for help? And as she stood before him, she seemed uncertain, also not quite in synch with the Liz he knew.

"What is it?" he asked.

She wiped her hands on her jeans. "There's something I need to tell you about."

About Aaron? Was this the confession he'd been waiting for? Suddenly, he didn't want to hear it. He bent to pick up the blanket and shake it free of crumbs. "Can it wait until tomorrow? I'm beat.'' Tomorrow he could find ways to avoid her.

''No, Ethan.'' She put out a hand to stop his restless motion. ''Let me just get this out now.''

His stomach churned, but he nodded. It would be better to have the questions answered.

''It's about the problems we've been having.'' She shoved her hands in the back pockets of her jeans.

Problems? How could this have anything to do with Aaron? ''What about them?''

''You're going to think this is nuts.'' She flung one hand out, combed back her hair with her fingers, then stuck it back into her pocket. ''We have a ghost.''

Liz could see immediately that Ethan thought she was crazy as a loon. *''A what?''*

''A ghost. In the cavern.'' Liz took a deep breath before spelling it out. ''The spirit of Noah Simmons is haunting Hoyo del Diablo.''

His eyes went wide before he narrowed his gaze on her. ''Is this some kind of joke?''

''I wish.'' She emptied her lungs in a puff of air. ''He's the one responsible for the mischief in your lab—the wiped hard drive, the broken connections. He's moved supplies around, shuffled paperwork, generally made a nuisance of himself.''

Liz had figured it would be difficult persuading Ethan about Noah, but when faced with his frank disbelief, she realized it might just be impossible. She rubbed at the tension between her eyes, trying to frame a more convincing explanation.

''I know it seems incredible. But I've seen him, talked to him several times.''

''You've been talking to a ghost.''

Liz chewed her lower lip, not liking the worried look on Ethan's face. ''Yes.''

''Once? Twice?''

He was thinking straitjacket for sure. Liz injected as much confidence as she could into her tone. "Several times, Ethan. Mostly in the hydro lab, but also in our quarters and in the corridor. He's the one who moved the rock in the storage room."

He ran a hand over his hair. "Took it right through the locked door, I suppose."

"Actually, no." Liz plunged ahead. "Under the door."

Ethan stared at her. "Under . . ."

Impatient with the course of the conversation, she took his hand and gave it a shake. "Never mind the details. It isn't Noah I wanted to talk about. It's what he told me. He said we were in danger here, terrible danger."

"From what? Him? Assuming I even believed he existed, are you telling me he's responsible for Janet's injury, or the gas leak in Arlene's lab?"

Liz shook her head emphatically. "Absolutely not. The minor mischief, that's his doing, but the rest . . . there's something else at work. Something Noah is so terrified of, he won't say what it is. He only hints at it."

Ethan's skepticism was clear in his face. "Something . . . like what?"

"I don't know. Evil . . . something evil."

He was silent a moment, contemplative. "What did Arlene say—a gate to Hell?"

"And Dr. Nishimoto spoke of an evil spirit."

Liz held her breath, watching him process the possibilities. Then he shook his head. "All of this could as easily fit the scenario we've already discussed—that some hallucinogenic agent is at work. It could explain Arlene and Wallace's unreasoning fear, your own delusion of seeing a ghost."

"Noah is not a delusion."

He scrubbed at his face with his hands. "Hell, Liz, I don't claim to understand what's going on here, but it's pretty damn hard to swallow the concept of an evil spirit."

"Ethan—"

She'd scarcely gotten his name out when the ground suddenly shuddered under their feet, knocking her to her knees. As Ethan reached down to help her up, the ground shook with another spasm, accompanied by a booming roar.

With Ethan's help, Liz struggled to her feet. "What's happening?"

He pulled her close. "I don't know, but we'd better get out of here."

The lights flickered, strobing on and off. Ethan snatched up his flashlight and snapped it on. A moment later, the floor beneath them trembled as another thunderous sound reverberated around them. The lights cut off, leaving them only the illumination from the flashlight.

"Into the tunnel!" Ethan shouted. "Quickly!"

He sent her on ahead of him and as she crawled along. Liz prayed the rock above wouldn't collapse on them. When she reached the far end, she thought her eyes must be playing tricks on her in the dim light.

"Oh, my God," she whispered.

Ethan squeezed in beside her, although the space was barely wide enough for two. Even as he ran the flashlight over the tumble of limestone blocking the tunnel exit, Liz's mind refused to believe what she was seeing. Rock filled the mouth of the tunnel.

Ethan handed her the flashlight. "Get back."

Liz retreated along the tunnel. Turning, Ethan braced his feet against the pile of rock. He pushed against it, straining until Liz could see the veins pop out in his neck. The rock didn't move. He turned back toward her. "No good. Cave-in must be a hell of a lot bigger than what we can see here."

Edging up next to him, she moved the flashlight over the wedged-in stones. She tested one with her hand, managed to pry it loose. The mass shifted to fill the empty space, the whole pile threatening to come down.

"Hell," Ethan muttered. "Can't push it, can't pull it."

Determined, Liz reached for another stone. Before she could touch it, a sound grated on her ears, sent a prickle up her spine. She turned to Ethan. "Did you just say my name?"

He shook his head slowly. Liz stretched out again toward the pile of broken limestone. Her fingers faltered as her eyes sent a horrifying image to her brain. Blackness seeped from between the stones, oozed down the sides of them. It reached out tendrils toward her and Liz started trembling, every muscle in her body caught up in the uncontrollable shaking.

"Lizzy," the blackness called. *"Lizzy."*

Then it enfolded her in darkness and madness took hold of her mind.

Chapter Fifteen

The sheen of terror in Liz's eyes shocked Ethan. The cave-in certainly frightened her—hell, it had sent his pulse rate soaring—but until a moment ago, she'd been coping with her fear. Now something seemed to have taken hold of her, tipping her from sensible alarm into irrational dread.

She groped for his arm, closed her hand around it. He could feel the imprint of her fingernails as she gripped him. "It's coming for us."

With an effort, he tugged her hand from his arm, then enclosed it in his own. "What is?"

"The creature . . ." Her gaze strayed to the tunnel above them, her eyes glassy in the dimness. "No . . . no . . ." She pulled free of him, scrambled to her knees. "It's opening . . ." She pressed her hands up against the ceiling. "The cracks . . . It's all going to come down . . . Ethan, help me!"

Her scream echoed in the narrow tunnel. Ethan turned the light onto the ceiling, trying to see what she saw. "There's nothing there, Liz!"

"Can't you see them? Don't you see the cracks? Oh, my God, pieces are coming down!"

She flinched as if something had hit her against the side of her head. Ethan stared at the intact ceiling, at her scrabbling fingers. At a loss for what else to do, he grabbed her, flung her roughly to the floor of the tunnel. He managed to get his hand under her head so she didn't strike it on the limestone, but the fall jolted her nonetheless. She struggled against him, but he used his greater weight to control her, wondering how long he could hold out if her madness continued.

First her stories of seeing a ghost, and now this. Anxiety dug inside him. Some agent within BioCave had insinuated itself into their minds, acted as a hallucinogen or psychotropic drug. What if the effect was cumulative? What if these crazed episodes of Liz's persisted until they crowded out her sanity?

Desperate to bring her back, Ethan tightened his hold on her. Finally, she stilled, her expression dazed, her eyes on him, but unseeing. She turned frantically to the stones blocking their way back into BioCave, her gaze strafing the barrier. Redirecting her focus to the ceiling, she scanned it quickly before looking back up at him.

"It's gone," she said softly. She glanced again at the ceiling. "The cracks, too."

Ethan dragged in a long breath, then eased himself next to her. "What the hell just happened?"

She brought a trembling hand to her face. "I don't know. Something came out of the stones . . . there were cracks opening in the ceiling." Groping for him, she clutched his hand. "Will it come down?"

Five minutes ago he could have said "no" with great certainty. He wasn't at all sure now, but hell if he'd tell her that. "No. It's stable."

She shivered, her entire body quaking. "The rest of it should have been stable. But it collapsed."

Pulling his hand loose, he grabbed her shoulders, tugged

her close. "It's stable, Liz. Nothing else will fall."

She seemed to take that in. "How do we get out?"

"We'll have to wait for the others to come for us."

Tremors moved along her body. "What if the entire cavern has collapsed? What if they're all trapped?"

He tucked her head beneath his chin. "They'll come for us, Liz."

He tried to relay his conviction with the pressure of his hands, with his voice. The world had turned upside down, he had to find a way to right things for her. He murmured into her hair, "It'll be all right, Liz. It'll be okay. The others know where we are. They'll be along soon to free us. We'll wait for them." He nuzzled her hair as his fingers traced a soothing pattern on her back. "Don't worry. I'll take care of you." And he would, if it took the last breath in his body.

She relaxed, as if the fear had finally surrendered to her will. She drew back and gazed up at him. "I'm sorry."

He hooked a strand of her dark silky hair behind her ear. "There's nothing to apologize for."

Her brow furrowed. "I don't know why I freaked out like that. I was looking at the rock, and I saw . . ." She shivered again in reaction. "What did I tell you?"

"About something coming out of the stones and cracks in the ceiling."

"Lord. All I can remember now is the fear." She pressed a hand to his back, her hand chill even through his heavy shirt. "It's like the other times. Terror, then it all fades."

"Maybe we ought to get out of the tunnel. Move back to the chamber."

One more quick glance at the ceiling and she eased herself out of his arms. "Yes, I'd like to go back."

He let her go first, the flashlight's beam bouncing as she carried it with her on hands and knees. Once they both were out of the tunnel, he took the light from her. "I've got a battery backup in here. With any luck I can get some of the lights on."

Arms tight around her middle, she leaned against the limestone wall. "How long is the battery good for?"

"A few hours. Five, tops." Sweeping the flashlight beam across the floor, he spotted the switch box. He opened the back, and swapped the power source from AC to DC. The lights dotting the chamber came to life, but their glow was only half as bright.

"What if we're not out of here by then?"

Ethan returned to Liz's side, rubbed her cheek with the backs of his fingers. "We can't leave them on all that long. I thought maybe a few minutes to catch our breath, then I'll power off and we can try to get some sleep."

"I don't know if I could sleep."

"It'll make the time pass more quickly until they come for us."

Shadows played across her upturned face, underscoring the worry and exhaustion. Ethan tipped his head down to her. "Hell of a birthday present this turned out to be."

"I wouldn't change a minute. Up until the roof fell in, that is." She tried to smile, but it was a half-hearted effort. "What do you think happened?"

"I don't know. A gas explosion maybe. We won't know until we get out."

"Gas explosion." Questions formed in her eyes—were the others all right? What if they were the only ones who survived? She reached out for him in a jerky motion. "Would you hold me? I just need to be held a while."

As vulnerable as she was, it would be a bad idea for him to do as she asked. Just standing next to her, a million fantasies played themselves out in his mind, all variations of what he'd like to do with her in the isolation of the chamber. It would be worse than crass to take advantage of her in this moment. If he was the least bit noble, he'd put as much distance between them as possible.

Who was he kidding? He had zero resistance when it came to Liz. He wrapped his arms around her, and she embraced him, her hands warming against his back. Blood thundered in his ears as his body reacted, but at the same time contentment suffused him. He could hold her like this forever, for an eternity. In that moment, he wished with all his being he could.

She nestled her face against his chest as if seeking his warmth. As she calmed, her breathing slowed, its rhythm soothing. Then she spoke, and her question shattered his serenity. "Would you tell me about your family?"

His first impulse was to step back, put distance between them. Instead he dodged the question. "You first."

"Mine's a little quirky." He could feel her lips moving against him as she spoke. "Three sisters, all different fathers. Mom was married three times, but none of them lasted long."

He knew that much from her records. "So you share a dad with one of your sisters?"

She hesitated, then said slowly, as if measuring the words, "No. I didn't know who my father was."

He'd read it in her file. Why did he have the sense she wasn't telling him the truth? "Your childhood must have been a little crazy."

Liz backed off a bit so she could look up at him. "It wasn't as bad as some. We didn't see much of my mom since she had to work. But my sisters and I, we kept each other company."

What would it have been like if he'd had a brother or sister? Would it have soothed the loss of his mother? Could a sibling have provided a buffer between him and his father? Or would his father's imprint still be as strong on him?

It was useless to conjecture. He was no longer a fragile little boy at the mercy of his father's cold discipline. He'd made his own way now for years and it did no good to wonder about might-have-beens. It was too late to fill in any missing pieces of his soul. If he didn't know how to give his heart, to love, he also wasn't as vulnerable to hurt as that little boy had been.

He realized she was watching him, her gaze so piercing he wondered if she read his thoughts. For a moment, he felt laid bare to her and he didn't like the feeling. He continued with his questions to keep her focused on herself instead of him. "So you never knew your dad?"

"Not at all, growing up." Again, her response seemed carefully worded.

"You never tried to look for him?"

"No." She was emphatic now. "Never."

Somehow, that didn't fit with what he knew of Liz. He would have expected her to barrel into her past, to ferret out every little detail. If her father was still living, Ethan felt certain she would seek him out. He'd done so with his own mother, simply to have the opportunity to face her one last time, to set the record straight. He'd never had the chance; by the time he located her most recent whereabouts, she'd passed away. It nagged at him sometimes, that unfinished business. But it was really inconsequential to who he was now.

Liz stepped back a pace, her hands lingering on his waist. "How about you? Do you see much of your parents?"

"My mother's dead. I see my father once or twice a year."

"Where does he live?"

"He's retired in Scottsdale."

If she wondered why he saw his father so infrequently when he lived so close, she didn't comment. "What did he do before he retired?"

Ethan gave her the abbreviated answer. "Business."

"But what kind . . ." Her brow furrowed and he could almost see the wheels turning. "Winslow . . . your father isn't Charles Winslow?"

"He is."

She laughed. "Good God, I always knew you came from money, but Charles Winslow . . . he owns half the shopping malls and golf courses in Arizona. Why didn't you have me sign a prenuptial agreement?"

"Should I have?"

He asked the question lightly, as if the answer didn't matter, but he knew he was fooling himself. He desperately wanted to know if his wealth mattered to her.

She shrugged. "I don't want your money. It just surprises me that you didn't do something to protect it."

His attorney would have insisted—if he'd bothered to ask her. In fact, he hadn't given it a second thought. Because he knew Liz had already hooked herself up to one millionaire and wouldn't need his money? Or because, somewhere inside him, he trusted her not to take advantage of him?

But he hadn't trusted her in the least when they'd first agreed on their marriage. Now . . . now he wasn't sure what he felt. Maybe he'd always intended to give her something when they parted, a compensation for helping him keep his place in BioCave. In fact, now that he considered it, he would insist she take something from him. It was imperative she take something of his from their union.

When it ended, that is. He felt cold inside at the thought. To no longer have Liz beside him in bed, sharing meals with him, sparring with him. Time away from Cynthia had never seemed particularly lonely. He always had something else to occupy himself. But Liz dominated his life, elbowing everything else aside so that when she was absent, she was all he could think about.

Was that how it had been with his father when his mother left? Was that why he had closed himself off to friends, his own son? Because his wife had conquered so much of him, he didn't know how to fill in the pieces when she left?

He felt suddenly angry at the control he'd surrendered to Liz already. Before her, women barely touched his life. Like visitors to someone's home, they barely made it past the welcome mat. Liz had burst through the front door, into his most personal, private spaces. Damn it, she would leave a hole when she left.

Hell if he'd let her go before getting something from her. He tightened his hands on her, pulling her close again. Covering her mouth with his, he plunged in with his tongue. In that moment, he didn't care if she was scared, angry, or insulted, he just wanted to take a little of her sweetness while he had the chance.

But she surprised him. She didn't fight him—she willingly opened her mouth to him. She didn't push him away—her arms snaked around his neck and clung there. And now that he had the taste of her on his tongue, there was no way in hell he could pull away. This time, he would take her as far as she let him go.

For a terrifying moment, Liz wondered if the dark evil that had overwhelmed Ethan once before had taken control again. But then she sensed the difference in his touch—desperation rather than domination drove him. His rough kiss sprang from a need to divert her, not to conquer her.

Venturing into his past, his childhood had made him uncomfortable. She'd seen his response to her probing, how quickly he'd turned her questions back to her. He didn't know how to deal with the emotions his past stirred. Physical contact he understood, was probably all that made sense to him in that moment.

But whatever the reason for kissing her, for molding her body to his, she was more than willing. With the cave-in and the terrifying hallucination after, a dark edgy fear that seemed to lurk everywhere in BioCave lapped at her. She felt vulnerable, desperately in need of Ethan's comfort, his warmth.

But feeling him beneath her hands, hearing the rasp of his breathing, the rapid beat of his heart, brought her more than comfort. Her ability to arouse him, to bring him pleasure, filled her with joy. She couldn't deny anymore what she felt for Ethan. The emotions bursting inside her went beyond lust, beyond simple caring. As much as it terrified her to acknowledge it, as perilous as it was for her heart, she loved him.

Elation warred inside her with fear at the realization. Ethan wouldn't welcome an admission of love from her. He would reject it and reject her in the same breath. But if she kept silent, she could have this much from him. She could have this physical joining and to hell with the consequences.

Ethan shifted around, taking her with him as he moved. He leaned against the limestone wall, parting his legs to pull her between them. The hard ridge of his erection burned against her and her breath caught at the feel of it. Her hands at the nape of his neck, she threaded her fingers into his thick hair. His kisses had eased from plundering to sensual, his lips brushing across her mouth, along the line of her jaw, behind her ear. She thought she would melt from the sweetness of it.

Despite the perennial underground chill, heat chased along Liz's skin in the wake of Ethan's touch. His fingers edged beneath the hem of her wool sweater, grazed her flesh along the top of her jeans. A moment before, he'd seemed beyond control. A moment before, he might have stripped her in a heartbeat. But now he seemed ready to take his time, to assure himself she was with him every step of the way.

A part of her wished he would have taken her in a conflagration instead of this controlled heat. It would be easier to be overcome. Instead, this would have to be a conscious decision for her and if she paid later, she would have only herself to blame.

His hands spanned her waist now, thumbs drawing circles along her sensitive flesh. She sucked in a breath as her skin rippled in response and she couldn't quite hold back soft laughter.

"Ticklish?" he murmured in her ear.

"A little."

"Is this better?" He stroked more firmly, moving his hands up until his fingers brushed just below her bra. He took her long sigh as an affirmative answer.

She nestled deeper in the vee of his thighs, enjoying his quick intake of breath at the contact. She brought her hands down the front of his denim shirt, pulled apart the top snap. "I like this. Easier than buttons." She popped open the next one, followed her probing fingers with her lips.

He leaned back against the wall, letting her press kisses

against his bare chest as she opened one snap after another. When she reached the last one, she tugged his shirt free of his jeans, pushed it from his shoulders.

When she moved to press herself against him, he held her away. "We have a little problem here."

She tried to move closer but his grip was implacable. "What's that?"

"I'm allergic to wool. And if I'm not mistaken, that's what your sweater is made of."

"It is." She gave him a challenging look. "So what do we do?"

"Obviously," he said, grasping the hem of her sweater, "we need to get rid of it." He stripped it from her. Liz gasped at the sudden coolness, then moaned as his large hands stroked her.

She melted into the contact, ached to move even closer. "I don't suppose you're allergic to nylon, too."

"Right now I'm not allergic to anything between you and me." His fingers grazed the line of her bra, then hooked the strap and eased it from her shoulder. With her help, he pulled it free of her arm, then did the same for the other. He took care to keep the cups in place so they still covered her. But it would take only the slightest motion to release the front closure and expose her.

But although he toyed with the clasp, he didn't open it immediately. Instead, he slid a finger underneath from the top, millimeters from her nipple. She arched in response, trying to get him to move his finger closer. But still he teased her, barely brushing against her.

Then he shifted tactics, gliding his palms over the silky knit of her bra, making only the briefest contact with her sensitized nipples. She wanted to grab his wrists and pull him closer or strip away the bra herself. She forced herself to wait though, letting the exquisite agony of delayed pleasure roll through her.

But she wouldn't let him get off scot-free. As he teased her, she lifted her hands to stroke his arms, lingering at the sensitive skin at the crook of his elbow. She continued along his biceps to his shoulders, then down the center of his chest. Every line of him was lean and muscular, each plane of warm male flesh more delightful than the last. She experimented with his flat male nipples, teasing them between finger and thumb, gratified at his hiss of response.

Moving her hands down, she stopped at the barrier of his jeans, tracing her fingers along it. Her hands shook—with nerves, with anticipation. She wasn't the most experienced of lovers and the last thing she wanted was to make a mistake.

His grip tightened on her rib cage as she stroked him. "That feels so damn good." His legs trembled from the effort of holding himself up. "Come here," he whispered, the sound hoarse against her ears. He tugged her with him toward the blanket, bringing her to straddle him as he lay down.

He released the catch on the bra and tossed it aside. Now his hardness pressed into the most sensitive part of her, a breath-stealing sensation. Instinct took over, cocking her hips into him in a rhythmic motion.

"Stop . . . God, stop." His hands took hold of her hips to still her movements. "Hell, we'd better slow down." Shifting, he lowered her to the blanket beside him. "We have time. Plenty of time." His hand lazily roamed her back, belying the erotic tension between them. "I want to know what you like."

His fingers dipped low to the small of her back, nearly derailing her train of thought. "I haven't had that many opportunities to find out."

Surprise seemed to flare in his eyes, then he put it aside. "We'll have to find out together, then." He trailed his fingers higher again, bringing them around to her front. Tracing around the curve of her breast, he watched her intently, as if watching for her response.

Her brain scrambled as his fingers neared her nipple, but didn't quite touch. His gaze dropped to her breast, following the motion of his hand. She suddenly felt awkward. "I hope you don't mind," she blurted.

His gray gaze returned to her face. "Mind what?"

"My breasts. They're so small."

He smiled. "Too small to feel this?" he asked as he bent his head to her breast and closed his lips around her nipple. He flicked with his tongue, then scraped lightly with his teeth.

She groaned, unable to offer him more of an answer. He nudged her back against the blanket, settling between her legs as he kept his mouth on her breast. "You're perfect," he said. "Every sleek, lean inch of you."

As he laved first one taut nipple and then the other, she felt a dampness growing in the center of her. She wanted out of her jeans, wanted to wrap herself around him and pull him deep inside her. She writhed under him, trying to communicate her need to him, wishing in that moment he could read her mind. Fumbling with the waistband of his jeans, she tried to edge their bodies apart enough to reach the snap and fly. Then he thrust against her and she thought she would die if they didn't get rid of the damned denim between them.

"Ethan," she said urgently, tipping up her hips, pushing against his hardness, "if you make me wait any longer, I just might kill you."

His low chuckle vibrated against her breast. "I'd rather die of pleasure." He rose and quickly shucked his jeans and briefs. Just the sight of his naked form, his manhood jutting out between his legs sent more wet warmth from between her legs. Her hands trembled as she unbuttoned her jeans. She was grateful when Ethan took over, unzipping them and sliding them down her legs, taking her shoes and socks with them.

Now nothing would lie between them. She ached inside, waiting for completion, for the joining of their bodies. He knelt between her legs, his gaze fixed on hers. Then he leaned over her, hands on either side of her body.

"Are you protected?" he asked.

She shook her head, unable to speak. He reached over and snagged his jeans, pulled a foil square from a pocket. After he'd sheathed himself, he leaned over her again, his manhood at the cleft of her thighs. He entered her slowly, a maddening inch at a time until she thought she would scream in frustration.

Then he plunged in fully, holding himself still for a moment, the strain in his arms apparent. Her body convulsed around him, an involuntary reaction to the exquisite pleasure. She wanted him to stay there forever, but then he began to move inside her and his hard thrusts pushed her closer and closer to a dizzying culmination.

Her hands were restless on his back, skimming over the tight musculature in mindless patterns. She wanted him closer to her, his full weight on her. But he resisted, keeping his body just slightly away. Then he reached down to touch her where their bodies joined and her climax took control of her, driving everything else from her mind. When he reached his own peak, another wave of sensation rocketed through her, bringing her to climax again.

Eyes shut, she lay stunned in the aftermath, every limb weak, her mind drifting in wonder. Joy suffused her, so compelling she felt sure Ethan felt the same. She knew when she opened her eyes to look at him, his barriers would be down, all he held in his heart would be laid out to her.

But when she opened her eyes, only shreds of Ethan's passion still shone on his face. If there had been softness there, it had been thrust aside by older, stronger fears.

She reached a trembling hand up to brush his cheek. "What is it, Ethan?"

For a moment, his yearnings seemed to struggle to the surface, before he smothered them. "One thing, Liz. One thing that has to be clear between us."

She could guess what he wanted to say, and all her ridiculous hopes collapsed. She forced out the words. "You don't have to worry, Ethan. Just because we ... made love, it doesn't mean forever between us."

Lips set, he glanced away, then back to her. "No. It doesn't. But something else you have to understand." He took her chin in his hand. "I'm sure you realize this won't be the only time we make love. We'll most likely continue to be intimate for the duration of BioCave. Because of that, I insist you cut your ties to Aaron Cohen."

She tried to comprehend what he was saying. "What do you mean?"

"You're to have no contact with him, Liz. Whatever relationship is between you ends now. If you give yourself to me, I damn well won't share you."

Chapter
Sixteen

The chill of the chamber, which before had been chased away by their lovemaking, descended again on Liz. She felt cold, cold to the core by Ethan's matter-of-fact tone, the steeliness of his gaze. Where before she felt glorious in her nudity, now she felt exposed and ashamed. She wanted to cover herself, to crawl into a hole somewhere, but Ethan had her trapped, his body still poised above hers, inside her.

Despite her vulnerability, she shook her chin free of his grip. "I won't end my relationship with Aaron."

His face hardened. "Is he that damned important to you?"

Tears clutched at her throat, pricked at her eyes. She set her jaw against them. "He is."

"More important than me."

It wasn't a question. Ethan was too adept at keeping up the walls around his heart to open himself up that way. Yet Liz sensed that somewhere deep inside him her opinion was vitally important to him. But why? Why would he care how important he was to her? So he could know how thoroughly he controlled her? Or because . . . She didn't let herself finish the impossible thought.

She could tell Ethan the truth about her relationship with Aaron, reveal to him what she'd revealed to no one except her sisters. But if all he sought was to control her, what a powerful weapon she would be handing him. And her promise to Aaron would be destroyed.

Aaron's trust had to come first. "It's not a matter of importance," she said carefully. "I feel differently about each of you."

She thought his gray gaze would burn her. "You won't give him up, then."

She shook her head in silent answer. His expression shuttered and he levered himself off of her, turned his back to her. The cold of the chamber bit to the bone. Fumbling for her clothes, she pulled them on with trembling hands, setting her shoes aside where she could find them when their rescuers arrived. He dressed with quiet efficiency, keeping his rigid back to her.

He moved across the chamber to the switch box for the lights. "I'd better power these down. Preserve the battery."

When he flipped the lights off, absolute darkness crowded in. She listened for his footsteps returning to the blanket, but he didn't move. "Are you going to lay down with me?" she asked, not sure if she preferred a yes or no.

The total blackness seemed to stretch his silence into an eternity. When he spoke he seemed to inject an intentional cruelty into his tone. "Once wasn't enough for you?"

She didn't take the bait. "I figured it would be warmer if we slept together."

Only his breathing, unsteady in the darkness, attested to his presence. Then he moved toward her, his footsteps approaching. He felt for her in the darkness before settling himself beside her. His warmth was a relief, despite the tension in his body.

She turned her back to him to spoon against him as they always did in bed. His arms around her, he pulled her close

enough to feel his arousal against her backside. But he made
no move that could be considered sexual, just hooked one
hand at her waist, the other cushioning her head. She realized
he wanted her comfort as much as she wanted his.

Tears stung Liz's eyes. Maybe should have told him. The
truth about her feelings for him, the truth about Aaron. But
at what price? She'd risk her own heart as well as the reputation of a man she'd come to love so dearly. She couldn't
do that to Aaron.

Aching inside at the impossible choice, she drifted off into
sleep and restless dreams.

Ethan felt like a man standing over the wreckage of a fatal
car accident. Even as he cradled Liz's body in his arms, his
emotions seemed as shattered as the rock in the corridor outside the chamber. Never mind his body, so quickly ready for
her again. And here he lay next to the object of his desire,
her heat seeping into him, setting his nerve endings on fire,
waking feelings inside him perilous to his well-being.

She wouldn't give up Aaron. Whatever her relationship
with the old man, she would maintain it. She chose Aaron
over him.

He swallowed back the pain of that, the foolishness of
caring. Ethan had come to doubt any physical intimacy existed between Liz and Aaron. There was love between
them—it was obvious in Aaron's every mention of Liz when
Ethan spoke to him, in the way Liz's eyes softened when the
old man came up in conversation. But Aaron still pined for
his dead wife and Liz . . . it didn't seem possible to Ethan
she could give herself to him so fully, without guilt, if there
was something between her and Aaron besides a deep friendship.

Then why had he demanded she sever ties with the millionaire? Why should he begrudge her a friendship? Because
it obviously meant more to her than a relationship with him.
Aaron meant more to Liz than he did, despite their marriage.
Ethan wasn't enough for her.

And truly he wasn't. He obviously could satisfy her physically. But the kind of connection she had with Aaron, the mutual caring, the love, that was beyond him. She would have to go outside their marriage. If they were to continue, that is, beyond the end of BioCave.

He set his teeth against the sense of longing that threatened to swamp him. It was useless to hope that his marriage with Liz would soothe any of those old hurts inflicted by the loss of his mother, the harshness of his father. If they continued as man and wife—and now that he considered it, perhaps the idea had merit—it would be because it continued to be convenient, not because it was a union of love. Actually, maintaining this marriage with Liz might have advantages. They were well matched physically. He enjoyed her company; she seemed to tolerate his. He had only to get over his reluctance to share her time with Aaron.

Something twisted painfully inside him. He forced himself to examine the feeling. He realized it wasn't that he'd be sharing Liz with the old man, but that Aaron would get the part of her Ethan desperately wanted for himself—her love, her devotion. And damn him, he was selfish enough to demand she give her heart to no man if he couldn't have it himself.

Liz stirred in his arms and he realized his grip on her had tightened. He forced himself to relax and she drifted deeper into sleep. Tipping his head forward slightly, he buried his face in her hair, inhaled her sweet fragrance. He would have to talk to her soon about their marriage. Once they were freed from here, when their life in BioCave got back on an even keel. No doubt it would take a fair amount of argument to persuade her they should continue as man and wife. She would expect love; he would have to convince her otherwise.

He spun the ideas in his mind, what he would say to her, how he would counter her objections. As sleep lapped at his conscious mind, his imagination thrust forward half-dreams, scattered images of a life with Liz. One emotion threaded through it all, calming him into sleep. Love.

• • •

Tension in Ethan's body woke Liz. "What is it?" she asked.

He put a silencing finger against her lips. Rocks clattered in the tunnel. "The cavalry's here."

"Ethan!" someone shouted out. "Liz!"

"Harlan?" Liz cried in answer.

"We're here!" Ethan called. Snapping on the flashlight, he rose and switched on the lights in the chamber. Liz squinted at the sudden brightness after the absolute darkness. She found her sneakers where she'd tossed them aside and quickly pulled them on.

More rock shifted from the other side of the collapse. "Sorry we took so long," Harlan said. "It was a real mess. Are you injured?"

"No, we're fine." Ethan crawled inside the tunnel.

Liz crowded in beside Ethan, felt sweet relief at the sight of Harlan's face through a gap in the rock barrier. "We were nowhere near the cave-in when it happened."

"Thank God." Harlan pushed aside more of the broken limestone and wedged himself a little farther inside. "Are the Smiths with you by any chance?"

Ethan glanced at Liz, then back at Harlan. "No, it's just the two of us."

Harlan's grim expression sent a frisson of alarm up Liz's spine. "They're missing. We haven't seen them since the cave-in."

"You've checked their labs and their quarters?" Ethan asked.

"And the common areas. We've searched everywhere," Harlan said. "The Niedans are still looking. If they don't turn up anything—"

"The Smiths are either somewhere on the other side of the rock fall or . . ." Ethan didn't finish his statement. The alternative was too horrifying to consider. "Is everyone else accounted for?"

"Yeah. Diana Bradshaw's got the link open to above-ground, maintaining a line of communication."

"Did she request help?" Ethan asked.

"She did. But the quake or explosion or whatever it was damaged the elevator. We won't get any assistance from up top until they repair it."

Liz tried to shake off the sense of isolation Harlan's words brought. "Did the power go out on your side?"

"A few flickers, but the system held."

"My connection to the chamber was pretty klugy," Ethan said. "The cave-in must have severed it. Is everyone else working on the cave-in?"

"Trang's in the kitchen, keeping up a supply of coffee and food. The Niedans I told you about. The rest of us are here, clearing away the mess."

Ethan pulled at the rock still blocking the way. "Get us out of here and we'll help you look for the Smiths."

As Liz worked alongside Ethan, tossing the broken limestone down the tunnel, her stomach churned at the thought of what could have happened to Arlene and Matt. When the opening was big enough to squeeze through to the corridor, her concern grew at the sight of what remained of the cave-in. Qwong Nguyen, Benita Jackson, and Bill Bradshaw had formed a brigade to shift rock to one side of the corridor. From the pile that had been moved, she could see that the stones blocking their way out of the tunnel were a fraction of the total mass that had broken from the ceiling. Massive pieces still remained. If the Smiths were trapped on the other side of the cave-in, it could take days to free them. If they were underneath . . .

Ethan immediately bent to heft a chunk of limestone from the towering pile. Liz followed suit, grabbing a smaller piece and wrestling it aside. "How long were we in there, Ethan?"

He checked his watch before reaching for another rock. "About five and a half hours. It's nearly six in the morning."

She grabbed some smaller chunks and tossed them away. It hadn't seemed that long; she'd slept most of that time away. The few times she'd surfaced nearly into wakefulness, the darkness still engulfed her, fooling her into thinking it was still the dead of night. She'd been grateful for Ethan's presence, his warmth.

When the Niedans showed up a short time later to report no sign of the Smiths, a pall of anxiety seemed to settle on the staff. By unspoken agreement, they settled into two brigades and doubled their efforts to move the rock aside. When Trang brought coffee and sandwiches, they drank and grabbed a bite or two as they worked. Liz kept up a silent, frantic prayer that the Smiths would come out of this all right.

When she tugged aside a chunk of limestone and uncovered a dusty sneaker-clad foot, it took her a moment to register what she was seeing. She set the limestone to one side, groped for Ethan. "Look. Is it Matt?"

Trang pushed forward and pressed her fingers against Matt's ankle. "Still warm. I feel a pulse."

"Then he's alive," Liz said, grasping at hope.

"Let's get moving, people!" Ethan shouted, directing the staff over to where Matt lay. They moved quickly to clear off the rubble, but it seemed an eternity before they'd moved enough to expose Matt's body. Arlene lay beneath him as if he'd flung himself over her to protect her. Cocked above him, precariously held in place by a smaller chunk of limestone, was a massive slab.

Liz stared at the huge piece of sheered-off limestone as Ethan and Richard carefully pulled Matt, then Arlene from their near-tomb. As Trang and Phoebe Niedan ministered to the Smiths, Liz took Ethan aside. "If that giant slab had fallen on them, they'd be dead."

"By falling the way it did, it actually protected them from the rest of the cave-in." Climbing back onto the rubble, he bent to examine the limestone boulder supporting the slab. "I don't see how this could have—"

"Ethan, watch out!" Liz cried as the massive rock began to shift. As if it had been held up by an invisible force that only then let go, the slab crashed into the space Matt and Arlene had recently occupied. Ethan jumped back in time, a cloud of limestone dust rising around him.

"Damn good luck," Ethan muttered as he stepped off the pile of rock.

Now that the large piece had fallen, Liz scanned the smaller rock that had apparently held it in place. The way it was shaped, the way it sloped on one side made it seem impossible that it could have supported all that weight. Had it really been chance? Or had a different agent protected Matt and Arlene?

Matt groaned then, bringing Liz's attention back to him. He opened his eyes and immediately looked around him, tried to rise. "Arlene?"

Phoebe pressed him back to the floor. "Right here. Dr. Nguyen's working on her." Phoebe glanced over at Trang, a question in her eyes.

Trang finished her examination of Arlene. "A broken leg for sure. Maybe some internal bleeding. We'll have to get both of them aboveground."

Ethan knelt at Matt's side. "What happened? What were you doing here?"

"Followed Arlene." He reached out for her, took hold of her hand.

"Was she looking for me, or Liz?"

Matt shook his head slowly from side to side. "Something called her . . . called her name. I didn't hear, but she told me . . ."

Dread walked fingers up Liz's spine, poked at a dim memory. "She heard someone call her name?"

Now Matt nodded. "Whispered . . . whispered . . . brought her here. I followed . . . to protect . . ."

Liz bent beside Ethan. "Did you hear the voice, Matt?"

"No. But Arlene . . . was afraid . . . said blackness . . . seeping from the ceiling . . . breaking the rock . . ."

Ethan looked up at Liz, then straightened and pulled her aside. "You said almost the same thing. Blackness seeping from the rock. Cracks in the ceiling." Liz could only nod numbly in response. "How could you both have the same hallucination?"

"I don't know," she whispered, although she suspected at least part of the answer. She desperately needed to talk to Noah.

Just then, Diana Bradshaw arrived to announce the elevator was again operational. Richard and Qwong fetched stretchers and the Smiths were carefully loaded on. Knowing she could be spared, Liz slipped away to the hydro lab. She had a few matters to discuss with a ghost.

Only the tiniest bit of himself out in the open, Noah spied on Lizzy from a tiny crack in the hydro lab ceiling. She'd called his name several times, turning and looking every which way in the room. So far she'd missed him up in the far corner, but his sweet Lizzy just wouldn't give up. Sooner or later, he would have to appear.

He had scarcely the strength to hold himself in the crack, let alone make himself invisible. Since she believed in him so thoroughly, invisibility to her was almost impossible. Maybe he should leave, squish his way along the fissures in the rock back to his special place. But it had been so dang long since he'd talked to her, he couldn't bear it. And it was past time for him to tell her all of it. He'd barely managed to save those folks from the cave-in. He'd had to slip inside that godawful big piece of rock, hold it up for hours with just his will. And being so busy with the rock, he had no way to tell Lizzy where the folks were buried. It seemed like forever before they were found.

Lizzy yelled out his name once more, sounding a mite peeved. He would just have to pop in, show his face, and tell her all he knew. No doubt the creature would just gobble him up for giving the warning, but that would be better than the guilt that burned inside him. He couldn't be everywhere at once protecting these folks. It would be best for them to know the danger, so they could take care of themselves.

Still feeling a mite puckish, he waited until Lizzy had turned her back before he eased himself from the ceiling. Tugging his ankles free, he righted himself. He waited until he was fully formed and had set his porkpie neatly on his head before calling out to her, *"Hello, Miss Lizzy."*

Liz whirled at the sound of Noah's voice and stomped toward him. "What the hell is going on?"

He faded briefly, then quickly recovered. *"I have been remiss, Miss Lizzy, in not telling you."*

She stopped an inch or two from him, anger bubbling inside her. "Tell me now."

He looked about ready to vanish again at her demand, then he seemed to dig in. He leaned close, lowering his voice. *"This cave is haunted, Miss Lizzy."*

"Haunted? Of course it is! By you."

He shook his head. *"Hoyo del Diablo was haunted before I ever set foot inside it. The Indians warned me, but I was too dadblasted ignorant to listen."*

She narrowed her gaze on him, pinning him with her glare. "You tell me every detail, Noah Simmons, and don't you dare disappear until you're done."

He squirmed a little, but he stayed put. *"Before I came to Hoyo del Diablo, when I was alive, that is, I was near dead after crossing the desert, from lack of food and water. I was took in by some Indians nearby."*

Liz thought a moment about the history of Arizona, trying to remember which tribes occupied the area in the mid-nineteenth century. "The Pimas?"

Noah screwed up his face in contemplation. *"Mayhap it was. They nursed me a bit, got me back to health. I asked their medicine man where I might find a little gold or silver, and he told me about the cave. There was treasure aplenty here, he said. But to get to it, I would have to get past . . ."* Noah cleared his throat and leaned close. *"The monster,"* he whispered. As soon as he said the word, he looked around him, fear widening his eyes.

Liz couldn't help herself, she looked around too, but nothing monstrous came roaring into the lab. "Tell me about the monster."

Noah winced at her use of the word. *"Wasn't the Pimas that put it there, was the Indians that came before them. The Hoka . . . Homa . . ."*

"Hohokam?" Liz asked.

"Maybe."

Rubbing at her brow, Liz tried to remember what she'd read about the long-lost tribe. "Hohokam is a Pima word for 'those who have gone.' They disappeared from the area in the mid-fifteenth century."

"That would be them then," Noah affirmed. *"Hoyo del Diablo was a sacred place to them and they put the . . . creature here to protect it."*

"So you came here looking for gold and silver . . ."

Noah nodded. *"And the . . . monster found me."* He shuddered, nearly fading from view before bringing himself back. *"I am not a brave person, Miss Lizzy. And the thought of treasure made me stupid. When I first felt the . . ."* He squeezed out the word, *"monster, I should have turned tail and run. But I kept going until I came to the pit."*

Liz couldn't hold back a shiver. "The history books say you were drunk, that you stumbled in . . ."

"I had drank my last the night before. Shared it around the fire with the Indians." He looked down at his booted toes, then up at her. *" 'Twas the creature pushed me into the pit."*

Trembling started up full bore in her body, and memories rushed in, as if Noah's words had called them all back. Her name whispered, cold hands on her, fissures opening in the wall, a gateway to Hell. She swallowed, digging her nails into her palms. "Tell me how it happened."

He described it all to her, from the first whisper of his name to the endless sensation of toppling down into the pit. He fluttered and faded several times as he spoke, but hung on until the last word.

"So you see, Miss Lizzy, you all must go. You are in terrible danger."

She scraped her hair back from her forehead, wrestling

with snatches of memory as she tried to think. She couldn't remember it all, but Noah's story had brought back enough of what had happened to her to erase any doubt as to his veracity. She glanced up at him. "How do we fight it?"

Noah's eyes opened so wide, it seemed they'd jut right from his head. *"You don't, Miss Lizzy. You get away from it, if you can."*

"We can't just abandon BioCave. We can't give up all we've worked for here."

"Miss Lizzy, if you stay, it will kill you. Surely as I'm standing here, it will kill you dead."

Horror crept inside her at his flat statement. "I'll talk to Ethan, tell him what you've told me."

"That mule-headed idiot don't believe in me. You expect he'll believe in a monster?"

"Then you go to him. Tell him what you told me."

"Won't work, Miss Lizzy. Been right under the man's nose any number of times. He just don't see me."

Liz fought off her despair. "I'll find a way to convince him."

She'd never seen such a sorrowful look on a man's face. *"I love you, Miss Lizzy. But the last thing I want is to see you end up like me."*

"I won't, Noah. You'll see."

Still looking woebegone, Noah started to fade, and this time he made no effort to hold it back. The ribbons on his porkpie clung to visibility a few moments longer until they too disappeared.

Liz tried to hold on to her self-assurance as she gazed around her at the empty hydro lab. But despite her brave promises to Noah, fear gripped the very core of her. She was torn between wanting to deny the truth of what the ghost had said and wanting to run screaming back to the surface. Still another part of her was angry and looking for a way to fight.

She had to talk to Ethan. Once she convinced him, they'd find a solution. She just had to make him believe.

Chapter
Seventeen

He didn't believe her.

When she tracked Ethan down in the energy center, he listened to her recitation in silence, neither asking questions, nor refuting anything she said. He simply sat quietly in his chair looking up at her, his face impassive. If memories of their time in the chamber haunted him the way they did her, he certainly didn't show it. If his body still ached for her the way hers did for him, he kept it well hidden.

Pushing aside the memories and the hurt they created, Liz finished telling Ethan about Noah, about the "creature" that haunted Hoyo del Diablo. She knew without asking he hadn't believed a word she'd said.

Discouraged, she pulled over a stool and climbed onto it. "You think I'm nuts, don't you?"

He didn't smile and seemed to be considering the question seriously. "No. I think you believe what you're saying."

She curled her feet around the rungs of the stool. "Wouldn't that make me crazy?"

His gray gaze was steady. "You're convinced you're seeing what you think you're seeing, hearing what you think you're hearing. But not because they're real, but because of some hallucinogen here in BioCave we've yet to discover.''

Liz wanted to grab hold of Ethan and shake the truth into him. About Noah and the monster, about her own ill-advised love for him. If he rejected her love, it was only her own heart at risk. Denying the truth of the evil force at work in BioCave imperiled them all. She had to find a way to convince him. They had to either end the BioCave experiment now or devise a way to combat the monster.

And since Ethan wouldn't believe the creature existed, that left the option of terminating BioCave. Discouragement settled like a fist in her stomach. "There's only ten of us left, Ethan. With each pair leaving, we lose vital skills. We ought to consider ending the experiment.''

His gaze sharpened on her. "Is that what you want?''

"No, of course not. But it isn't realistic to continue when we're short so many hands.''

"What would be your choice?'' His tone was neutral, but the intensity in his face sent a different message. She had the sense he was asking a question unrelated to BioCave.

"I want to go on, Ethan. To continue the experiment—''

"And our marriage?''

What was he asking? "Yes. The marriage, as long as BioCave exists.''

He gave her a brisk nod. "I've already polled the staff. The consensus is we continue as long as it's practicable. It's doubtful we'll make the full six months, but we should go as long as possible, gathering what data we can. Are you willing?''

As she met his unwavering gaze, she considered telling him no, contemplated demanding they end the experiment here and now. It might mean their very survival if they couldn't find a way to control the evil presence that dwelt here. But there was something in the set of his mouth, the way his jaw worked in unconscious agitation that signaled to

Liz that her agreement meant more than the continuance of BioCave.

She couldn't let him down. She would find a way to battle the creature herself. If she couldn't tell Ethan she loved him, she could at least give him her support. "Yes, I'm willing."

He smiled then, as if he couldn't help himself. "Good. Then I'd like a report from you on what studies you can conduct in the abbreviated time frame. And check in with Benita as well."

She had no intention of discussing Noah with the BioCave psychologist, but she nodded in agreement. Sliding from the stool, she stood before him, bits and pieces of their time the night before whirling through her mind. "Anything else?"

He looked up at her, his businesslike façade slipping a moment before he pulled it back into place. "About last night . . ."

A hand clutched at her middle, stopping her breath. "Yes?"

His gaze fixed on hers as his jaw worked. The silence stretched until finally, the words spilled out. "I had no right to ask you to give up your relationship with Aaron. In fact . . ." He dropped his gaze to his hands, locking and unlocking his fingers together. "I want you to consider something. I don't want a yes or no now."

His tone set off tumult of emotions in her stomach. "What, Ethan?"

He still didn't look at her. "Our marriage. I want you to consider continuing it. After BioCave, on a permanent basis."

Joy exploded in her. He wanted them to stay married! He loved her!

His next words disabused her of her romantic notions. "I've only recently realized the advantages to our marriage. We're reasonably compatible, we're well-suited physically. Continuing the union between us would work as well for me as it would have with Cynthia."

As quickly as the edifice of hope had been built, it collapsed into rubble. She tried to dig her heart out of the hole he had dumped it into, but didn't quite succeed. Hurt laced her words when she spoke. "You want to stay married. Because it's convenient."

Whether he heard the pain in her voice wasn't apparent in his face when he looked up at her. "It would be advantageous for me. I assumed it would be for you as well."

Turning away, she tried to pull together the broken pieces of herself. She felt shattered and incredibly stupid. Damn it, how could she have fallen in love with him? How could she have made herself so vulnerable to him? She tamped back an impulse to strike him, to somehow wipe away the love and the pain in one blow.

Swallowing back her anger and grief, she forced herself to face him. And what she saw there scattered her own troubled thoughts and brought them back together in a new pattern. Not only did the longing in Ethan's face shock her, but the fact that he'd apparently been unable to hide it. He might not love her, might renounce the very notion of it, but some part of him, beyond his physical need, wanted her. The question was, could that be enough for her?

He turned away, and tugged his keyboard over. "Don't answer now. Just give it some thought." The set of his shoulders told her he wouldn't discuss it further.

She left him, and wandered along the corridor with her thoughts in disarray. Ethan's proposal, her unexpressed love for him, Noah, and the perilous creature all battled for prominence. Her heart told her she had to take whatever chance she was given to be with Ethan. Her mind said otherwise, reminding her she'd just be hurt. The puzzle of how to survive the evil amongst them tugged at her, and she realized focusing there would free her from dwelling on Ethan and his cold, stony heart.

Returning to the hydro lab, she gave Richard a halfhearted greeting, then settled herself behind her computer. Once she'd booted it up, she connected to the Internet and spent

the next few hours finding whatever she could about the Hohokam and Native American spirits.

As he ran the energy systems through their paces with diagnostic tests, Ethan returned again and again to his conversation with Liz about their marriage. He thought he'd given
their union a fair assessment, made some good points in favor
of continuing it. But he couldn't rid himself of the nagging
sense that he'd totally bungled things with Liz.

Leaning back in his chair, he scrubbed at his face with his
hands, trying to think. Had she wanted him to profess his
love for her? She had to know that wasn't in the cards. He
found her companionship satisfying, sex with her was absolutely mind-blowing, but beyond that . . . He would never
love her. If he did, he would be vulnerable to her. He would
be opening himself up to hurt, to the potential wrenching
pain of abandonment.

He'd seen his father after his mother left. He'd seen the
icy bitterness his father had sunk into, the bleakness growing
more razor-edged year by year. His father's heart attack last
year seemed more caused by his festering anger toward
Ethan's mother than the disintegrating artery the doctor had
diagnosed.

Loving Liz would leave him open to that same fate. Although . . . over the years, he'd wondered why his father
didn't just go after his mother, why he didn't just bring her
back. Because if Liz promised herself to him, agreed to make
their marriage permanent, he damn well wouldn't let her
walk out the way his mother had. He would drag her back
if necessary.

What had stood in his father's way? Pride? To hell with
that. If there was anything he learned from seeing his father's
bad example, it was that pride could be sacrificed if it stood
in the way of what was right. He wouldn't let pride stand
between him and Liz. He wouldn't let her walk away once
she'd committed herself to him.

But what if she said no? What if she didn't want their

marriage to go on after BioCave? His stomach clenched at the thought. Could he let her go? She'd only agreed to a temporary marriage. He couldn't in all fairness demand she change her agreement.

Then he damn well wouldn't be fair. He wouldn't let her say no. He would bully her into a yes if he had to. He needed her too much to let her walk away.

Needed her. Staring unseeing at his monitor, he shook his head to deny what he felt inside. To deny how damn close loving was to needing.

Liz found nothing on the Internet to help her. The little bit on the Hohokam didn't include anything about evil spirits, and a search on Hoyo del Diablo only told her what she already knew of the history of the cave. There was some tantalizing information on elementals, but it was incomplete and left her with more questions than she'd started with.

Dinner that night was quieter than usual. Each of the remaining staff members seemed lost in their own thoughts. Liz caught Ethan staring at her several times during the meal, as if he were willing an answer from her to his proposal. Out of self-preservation, she had to say no to him, but she despaired that she lacked the courage. She had only enough self-fortitude to keep herself from saying yes. Still, it wouldn't take much of Ethan's company to wear away even that determination.

After dinner, she joined him in their quarters, intent on going over the report she'd written up before giving it to him. But as they sat together on the bed, the question hung in the air between them, mixed with the irresistible tang of desire. She had no intention of letting him make love to her again when matters were so unresolved between them. But her body kept reminding her she had only to say yes to him to enter paradise. If she would only agree, hand her soul over, she could immerse herself in pleasure.

She stayed silent. Her body an agony of arousal, she was too agitated to remain with him. Setting aside the report, she muttered something about checking some data in the hydro lab, pulled on her shoes, and left their quarters. When she glanced back as she strode down the corridor, she saw him watching her from the doorway. She felt his gaze on her every step of the way until she was out of sight.

She continued past her lab when she reached it, then took the first turn she came to. She had a dim idea of walking off some of her restless energy, but she didn't examine her urge to walk on before obeying it. Making each turn without thinking, she didn't notice the lights growing dimmer and dimmer until she caught her toe on a rise in the floor and stumbled. She just barely caught herself from falling. She turned slowly, looking around her, trying to adjust her eyes to the faint light. For the first time, she registered the unevenness of the floor, the collection of stalactites clustered on the ceiling. Somehow she'd wandered into an undeveloped area of BioCave.

"Lizzy."

The whispered name arrowed through her, leaving fear in its wake. The light seemed even dimmer, as if terror had doused them. Fumbling in the pocket of her jeans, she came up with her flashlight and switched it on. The beam stabbed the darkness, driving away its edges.

"Lizzy."

She stifled a moan as she turned back the way she'd come. The creature wanted her afraid; she would have to fight against her fear. Gripping the flashlight, she retraced her steps. The light danced on the walls as her hand trembled.

When she thought she heard her name whispered again, she told herself it was only her breathing, her heartbeat. She was strong enough to fight her terror if she only closed her ears to the sound of her name. But still it insinuated itself inside her, racing along her veins, throbbing with her heart.

"Lizzy."

She squeezed her eyes shut against her horror. When she opened them again every ounce of courage within her vanished. Somehow, she'd returned to the same place as before.

She recognized the uneven pattern of the floor, the stalactites clinging to the ceiling. The creature had taken her in a circle.

Swaying, she tried to think what to do next. But a lassitude had overcome her, freezing her thoughts. Fear battered at her, pushed at her. Then fear solidified into brutal blows as something hit her hard across the shoulders. She shrank from the invisible fists, running down the corridor away from them. They followed, beating at her, pounding her. They knocked her off her feet once, twice, waiting while she struggled back up, then striking again. The creature drove her, hounded her. She couldn't resist its imperative, not when it stole her resolve, her intelligence.

When she saw the pit, she recognized the inevitability of it. Her hand shaking, still clutching the flashlight, she stared at the black maw, robbed of will. This was where it had guided her, what it intended for her. It would take little effort on the monster's part to tip her into the bottomless space.

Like a beacon, Ethan's face swam into her mind's eye. Lord, she loved him. How could she leave him without telling him? Tears tightened her throat, ran hotly down her face. The humanity of her tears seemed to thaw the icy touch of the monster, restored a fragment of her will.

With a hard blow across her back, the creature drove her to her knees. She cried out against it, tried to shake it off. But it struck again, pushing her closer to the edge of the pit. Screaming, she clawed at the invisible force, raw anger battling her fear. Harsh hands lifted her, dragged her. Her screams tearing the air, Liz tumbled into the abyss.

Ethan shifted restlessly on the bed, staring at the issue of *Science News* that lay open on his lap. Every five seconds or so, his conscience nagged him to go after Liz. It took every bit of his will to stay put, especially when his overactive libido added its imagery to the mix. Torn as he was between anxiety over her absence and the powerful lust he felt for her, the *Science News* article on fossilized ammonites might as well have been in Arabic, for all the sense it made.

Hell, the woman made him hard and she wasn't even here. As he tugged at his jeans, trying to relieve the pressure of his swelling erection, something sharp dug at his thigh. He reached into his pocket, then stared at the bit of gray-green stone resting in his palm. A piece of peridotite. Where had he gotten it? He had a dim memory of finding it in the corridor outside Dr. Nishimoto's infirmary.

A sudden chill gripped him and torqued up his anxiety a notch. A wrongness washed over him, nameless and vague, but as real as the slick paper in his hands. Dropping the peridotite onto the floor, he turned to shove his feet into his shoes. Striding from his quarters, he hurried to the hydro lab, needing to find Liz, to assure himself she was safe.

The hydro lab was empty. As he shut and locked the door again, he tried to think where else she might have gone. To the common room, maybe? Or one of the storage areas for supplies? He looked left and right, debating which way to go, unease tightening inside him. As he stood in the quiet of the corridor, he had the sense that someone was calling him, battering his ears at a decibel level too low to detect.

Then as if someone had switched on an amplifier, the voice came through loud and clear. *"Winslow, you mule-headed idiot! Wake up! Lizzy needs you."*

Ethan scanned the empty corridor. "Who the hell is that?"

"Noah Simmons, you fool!"

Noah Simmons. Liz's ghost. Good God, he was beginning to share her hallucination. Feeling a fool for talking back to an illusion, he asked, "Where are you?"

"Damnation! It don't matter. Lizzy's in terrible danger. She needs you now."

Now the anxiety swamped him, coupled with an urgency to find Liz. "Where is she?"

The voice hesitated, then said quite clearly, *"In the pit. And the monster is with her."*

"Lizzy."

Closing her ears to the harsh whisper, Liz clung to the

slim outcropping of rock jutting from the wall of the pit. Farther down, her toes perched precariously onto an even narrower ledge. Her fingers throbbed with the effort to grip the rough limestone, and the shivers convulsing her body nearly shook her loose. A miracle—in the form of Noah Simmons—had stopped her fatal fall to the bottom of the pit; she wouldn't have another. Letting go now would mean certain death.

When she'd first gone flying over the edge, her reasoning mind shut off by the shock of terror, she'd felt the touch of Noah's force almost immediately. He'd slowed her fall, tossed her at the pit's sheer wall, giving her one chance at survival. Somehow her fingers had found purchase, her toes a margin of safety. Crowded by darkness, now she could only wait and pray for rescue.

Ethan, her heart sobbed out. Surely he would come for her when he realized she'd been gone too long. He wouldn't just turn out the light and go to sleep, assuming she'd come to bed when she was good and ready. He had to come look for her. He had to.

"Lizzy."

She squeezed her eyes shut at the evil voice in her head. The creature's touch lingered on her body as iciness on one shoulder, a sharp sensation in the middle of her back. As she fervently prayed Ethan would come in time, she wondered why the monster didn't just finish her off instead of taunting her with her whispered name.

"Let go, Lizzy."

She clutched the gritty limestone even harder. Her heart trembled in her chest in anticipation of another fight with the creature, but damned if she'd let go. Her terror of falling filled her, but the panic she'd felt at the creature's presence had faded. She sensed it had backed off, as if unable to take control of her again. Had it been somehow weakened by its attack on her and now waited to regain its strength? Perhaps it was easier for the monster to cast someone unwitting to their death, but it could not overcome her powerful will to live.

Ethan had to get here soon. Liz kept her eyes shut, so she could forget about the darkness. She would listen for Ethan's approach, attune herself to the sound of his footsteps. When the voice called her, she would pretend it was her heartbeat, or her breathing, or the rhythm of her love for Ethan. She wouldn't let the evil into her soul.

"Your hands are tired, Lizzy. Let go."

Ethan was coming. His footsteps would scrape against the limestone as he approached, he would call down to her from the lip of the pit, he would pull her to safety. She narrowed her heart's focus to one image—Ethan's face. When the creature called to her, again and again, she would turn away.

Lizzy . . . Insidious, the whisper worked its way inside her, loosening her grip. She closed her ears to that darkness, just as she'd shut her eyes, but it had insinuated itself between her and the rock, wedging her hands away, bit by bit. She fought against it, but its pull was inexorable.

"Ethan!" Liz screamed out, a last hope, a last prayer.

As Ethan stared, stunned, at what was left of the barrier he'd constructed with Richard and Harlan, Liz's scream echoed along the corridor. Leaping over the crumpled concrete re-inforcing wire, he resettled the length of rope on his shoulder as he pelted toward the direction of her cry. Noah still directed him, his voice calling out every few feet, but Ethan didn't need the ghost's guidance. He knew in his gut where Liz was and wouldn't waste any time getting to her.

His hand tensed on his flashlight as he neared the edge of the pit. Noah had warned him the creature would be here and damned if Ethan didn't feel it, dark and malign. Anger fountained up in him that it had placed Liz in danger, a white-hot rage.

He dropped to the ground, arms dangling the lip of the abyss as he cast the beam of his flashlight into the bottomless blackness. "Liz! Are you there?"

"Ethan?"

The weakness of her response ratcheted up his fury. That this monster could take her dignity, her fire from her . . . Rage nearly overwhelmed him, then he remembered Liz, that she needed him, that only he could save her.

With trembling hands he formed a loop of rope. He tied the other end around his own waist, then lowered the loop down the rock face. Shining the flashlight into the pit to provide illumination to Liz, he called to her, "Do you see the rope?"

"Yes."

"Grab it. Wrap it around yourself."

Tears threaded through her response. "I can't. I can't let go."

Ethan gritted his teeth, fighting back the urge to climb down after her. "You have to, Liz. Just let go with one hand at a time. Tighten the rope under your arms."

"I can't." Her words were barely more than a whisper.

A fist seemed to have taken hold of his heart. "Please, Liz. I need you to take the rope. Please. For me."

An endless moment of quiet, then he felt the tug as Liz took the rope. His breath caught in his throat at each tiny pull on the rope, thought his heart would rocket from his chest when he heard her gasp, then the clatter of loose rock.

"Are you all right?" he called down into the pit.

"Fine." Nervous laughter accompanied her response. "Slipped a little. The rope's around me now."

"I'm going to pull back. When the rope gets taut, you help as best you can by climbing up the side."

"Right. Ready."

He scooted back from the edge, pulling himself to his feet. Setting aside the flashlight, he took up the slack in the rope, praying it wouldn't fray on the rough limestone edge. Once the tension increased in the rope, he tugged, hand over hand, sometimes feeling her dead weight, other times a lighter load as she crawled up the side.

When her head first appeared above the lip of the pit,

Ethan thought his heart would burst for joy. He kept himself in control until he'd towed her high enough that she could scramble over the edge to safety. Snatching her back from the mouth of the pit, he tugged the rope from her body and pulled her into his arms.

"Oh, God. Oh, God, I thought I might lose you," he murmured into her hair.

"Never. Never. How did you find me?"

"Your ghost brought me here."

"Noah? You saw him?"

He shook his head, and the silk of her hair brushed his face. "I heard him. He guided me here."

Tipping her head back, she smiled up at him. "Then I'm not crazy."

"Or we both are." As he gazed down at her, he wanted nothing more than to cover her mouth with his, to consume her. But something still clung to this place, still roiled within the pit. Ethan knew they wouldn't be safe until they left. He forced himself to back away. "We have to get out of here."

Liz shuddered as if she, too, felt the evil. "Yes. Now."

Grabbing up the flashlight, he tightened his grip on Liz and hurried back the way he'd come. The wrongness dissolved as soon as they reached the makeshift barrier, and did what they could to set it back into place. Wanting a margin of safety, Ethan urged Liz on, down the twists and turns back to their quarters. Once there, he quickly locked the door behind them.

The enormity of almost losing her rushed in, and he stood trembling in the aftermath. He crossed the room and tugged her into his arms, his heart hammering in his chest, his breath catching in his throat. He forced himself to breathe in deeply as he stroked the hair back from her brow. An urgency drove him, compelled him to find a way to bring Liz to him, to keep her with him at his side. He didn't care what the price would be. There had to be a way to keep her from leaving him.

"Liz," he began, struggling to understand the emotions

wrangling inside him. "I don't know what I can give you. I don't if there's anything I could offer that would be of value to you. I know only that I want you." He cradled her head in his hands. "Is that enough?"

Her blue eyes searched his face. "I want you too, Ethan. That's all we have to worry about for now."

Somehow he'd hoped for something else from her, an answer maybe, that only she could provide. But he wasn't even sure of the question, damn it, never mind that it returned again and again to nag his soul. He thrust aside his confusion and focused on the one sure thing. She wanted him. That would have to be enough.

Chapter Eighteen

As Ethan reached over to dim the lights, Liz rolled his words inside her mind. *Is that enough?* On the surface, Ethan had asked her if a physical union between them was enough. It might be, for now, although in the long run it would destroy her. But Liz knew he was really asking a different question, one he concealed beneath the careful veneer he held up to the world.

Am I enough? Ethan had asked. *Am I enough for you?* She heard the unvoiced question and ached to tell him, yes. Yes, you are enough.

He was more than enough for her. Because she loved him with every particle of her being. That he didn't love her back—either out of unwillingness or an inability to love— she would not consider. Her love would have to make up for that lack in him.

He turned to her in the shadow-filled room, the hunger in his eyes sending a shiver through her. No matter what happened to them after BioCave, she would have this night, these moments of passion. No matter how empty she felt afterward, she would try to fill that emptiness with memories.

He took her hand to draw her to him and she couldn't suppress a gasp of pain. "What is it?" he asked.

Turning over her palm, she showed him. The long minutes clinging to the rough limestone had left their mark on her. The skin on her palms, her fingertips, were red and raw, the wounds clogged with limestone dust. Liz gazed down at them in surprise. "I didn't even feel the scrapes until now."

"Come with me." Fingers circling loosely around her wrist he led her around the bed toward the bathroom. Holding first one hand then the other under the faucet, he cleansed her wounds with gentle care. As he dried her hands with soft strokes of the towel, he said, "Dr. Nguyen should look at these scrapes."

She took the towel from him and set it aside. "Later." Raising her hands to his face, she tipped his head down. Their hurried kiss by the pit had not been enough for her; she wanted more.

The beginnings of a beard abraded her tender palms, so she moved her hands to the warm column of his throat. She pressed her lips lightly to his, the smallest taste. A part of her wanted to rush through the preliminaries as they had when they'd been trapped together in the chamber. That would make this less a conscious choice, more an act of urgency. But despite the throb of arousal low in her body, she wanted to feel each heightened step of their lovemaking. She didn't want to be overwhelmed; she wanted to be partner to their intimacy.

He pulled back and with an arm around her, guided her back to the bed. Sinking onto the edge, he tugged her down to sit in his lap. One hand curved around her waist, the other cupped her face, tipping her head toward him. He kissed her, unhurried strokes of his lips, his tongue. He had sensed her need for them to take their time.

Shifting in his lap, she turned to wrap her legs around him. As much as she wanted to press her center into him, she kept some distance between them. She liked facing him this way, her legs around him loosely, her hands free to slide along his shoulders, his chest. She could touch him almost anywhere and watch the play of reaction in his face.

She kissed his mouth, then dragged her lips along his rough cheek, tasting along the way. Following the whorls of his ear, she reveled in his moan, the way his hands tightened on her. He pressed at her lower back to try to bring her closer, but she resisted. She burned at her center, ached for him. But she wanted the pleasure to last as long as possible, for her, for him.

Her thick cotton sweater felt impossibly hot. Grabbing the hem, she stripped it off and tossed it aside. Insinuating her fingers under his lightweight sweater, she nudged it up his body, bending to kiss him in the wake of her stroking fingers. She found one flat male nipple and teased it with tongue and teeth. He tugged his sweater from her hands, tearing it off and throwing it to the floor.

Now she had all of his muscular chest to explore. Fingers spread wide, she glided her hands across his warm flesh, the sprinkling of dark hair only slightly rough on her sensitive palms. She trailed a path to his shoulders, down his arms, glorying in the flex of muscle and tendon. This time when he urged her toward him, she leaned in, pressing herself against him.

"God, you feel so good," he whispered, his mouth close to her ear. He reached between them to the front closer of her bra and released it. Nudging the straps from her shoulders, he rid her of the silky scrap of cloth between them. She edged closer to him, fitting the vee of her legs against his hardness.

"Oh, Lord." He seemed to struggle for breath. "You are almost too damn much for me."

"I want to be everything to you." As she whispered the words he tensed and she realized too late how much of herself she had given away. More than he wanted, certainly. Thinking to repair the damage, she added, "For tonight."

His tension didn't ease. "For tonight," he repeated, the words sounding hollow.

Liz leaned slightly away from him, tried to read his expression. But his hooded eyes concealed more than they revealed. She wished she could reach inside him, take hold of that small precious part of him he hid from the world. Give it succor, bring it joy. The high, unscalable walls Ethan set around himself rejected more than they protected.

But he wouldn't let her in. She might get the barest glimpse of him in the intimacy of their lovemaking, but beyond that . . .

This will have to be enough, she told herself again. It's passion instead of love, but I will make it enough.

When she would have leaned in to kiss him again, he held her away from him. "Wait."

She smiled. "Not too long, I hope."

But his expression grew more serious. "What I said about Aaron—that was foolish of me."

"Aaron is no threat to you."

"But you love him."

"I do." And I love you, Ethan Winslow. She tried to say the words with her eyes, too afraid to say them aloud.

"And I can't change that."

She shook her head slowly. "Nothing you could do would change how I feel about him, but—"

He put a finger against her lips. "You don't have to say any more."

Liz realized in that moment she could tell Ethan about Aaron, that she wanted to. "Let me finish, Ethan. Aaron is—"

He covered her mouth with his, stopping her words. His tongue thrust past her lips, the wet, gliding touch driving a moan from her. Suddenly she didn't want to take things slow and easy, she wanted him now, as fast and hot as possible.

He turned, easing her to the mattress, one hand busy at the button of her jeans. She helped him with the zipper, then squirmed out of the heavy denim. When she fumbled for the placket of his jeans, he pushed her hand aside. "Not yet."

His touch turned lazy, down her bare back, along her hip, over the mound of her derriere. Then he slipped his hand between them, grazing along her belly, sending a ticklish ripple across her flesh. She couldn't stifle a laugh that turned into a long low moan as his mouth found her breast. He pushed her to her back, his lips and teeth and tongue toying with her nipple, sending sensation jolting from her breast to the damp center of her.

Then his roving fingers tangled in the tight curls at the juncture of her legs. He dipped lower, teasing apart her soft folds. He retreated, then moved closer, just the barest touch on the most sensitive part of her. Her legs grew restless, parting of their own accord, so that she lay open to him. Adding to the torture of his fingers, his tongue flicked at her nipple until she thought she'd scream at him for completion.

When his fingers plunged inside her, she convulsed in a shock of surprise. Now his palm rested against her, stroking as his fingers thrust inside. She climaxed quickly, then before she could recover, he took her over the edge again. While she trembled in the aftermath, she groped for him, grasped his sweat-slicked shoulder. "Please, I want you inside me."

He backed away long enough to throw aside the rest of his clothes and sheathe himself with a condom. His first stroke inside her took her breath, seemed to bring her world to a stop. He rested on his elbows, head dipping down, eyes shut, hips still as if he fought for control. Then he pulled out and thrust inside again in a slow rhythm. Liz had to force herself to breathe, so powerful were the sensations rolling through her.

Wanting him even closer, Liz crossed her ankles at the small of his back, her thighs pressing on either side of him. His face sharp and intent, he kept his eyes closed even when she traced her fingers lightly across his lips, his cheek. Was he still hiding from her? Even in this moment of exquisite intimacy? Or did he feel the same burgeoning emotion as she, and had to close his eyes to keep it from overwhelming him?

Endearments lay on her tongue, begging her to give voice to them. But what she felt inside, the incredible love for him, might not be shared. This might be nothing more than a physical union to him, sensual pleasure with nothing beyond it. As much as her heart cried for her to give him her love, she wouldn't do it.

Then the sensations centered between her legs spiraled higher, dug deeper into her nerve endings. She gripped his hips with her hands, trying to pull him closer. In that moment, she wanted not just his physical self inside her, she wanted his heart and soul deep within her own, to be nurtured, cared for. She wanted him to know the beauty she saw in him, the wonder that was Ethan.

Then her body took control, bursting into climax with an explosion of brilliant sensation. As he thrust deep inside her he reached his own completion, every muscle in his body tensing with release. It seemed to take a long time for the slow spiral back to reality, for her body to stop convulsing around his.

He nuzzled her neck with slow, lazy kisses. "Am I too heavy?"

She hadn't even noticed his weight on her. "I like you on top of me. It feels good."

Leaning on his elbows, he still held himself slightly away from her. "Incredible."

Stroking his back, she tried to persuade him to relax, to let go of the tension tightening his muscles. He seemed ready to flee, as if part of him looked for escape even as he ached to be held close. She tried to pull him to her, but he levered off her. "I'll be right back," he said, then headed for the bathroom.

When he returned, he seemed almost hesitant to climb back into bed with her. She took his hand, tugged him down to her until he relented. He lay alongside her, facing her. Fitting her body against his, she continued her soothing touch, keeping her gaze on him, trying to guess what went on inside him.

He stroked her hair back behind her ear, his gray gaze troubled. Had he sensed the feelings she had for him? Did he know she'd fallen in love with him? If he could see that, he might think she expected the same in return. She ached for his love, but understood its impossibility. All the wishful thinking in the world wouldn't make it happen if he didn't have it in him to love.

But . . . was there a chance? Maybe all it took was for her to tell him, to take the first step. Maybe that would be enough to give his heart permission to love her back.

She remembered the fear and horror she felt as she clung to the wall of the pit. Her one prayer had been for Ethan, because she knew when he arrived, he would rescue her. She at least owed him her love in exchange for saving her life. She could be that brave.

"Ethan." She laid her hand against his cheek, kept her gaze locked with his. "I want you to know . . . I love you."

At first his expression didn't change, almost as if he hadn't heard her. Then he looked away and she saw dismissal in that unwillingness to face her. She turned his face back to her. "Did you hear me? I love you."

He wouldn't meet her gaze. "I know you think you do. But you have to know it doesn't change anything."

She swallowed back the pain inside. "You mean it doesn't change how you feel."

"What I feel . . ." He cupped her face with his hand. "What I feel is that I can be a good husband to you. I would respect you, care for you, be faithful. I would stay with you, Liz, stay by your side."

The warmth of his hand sent one message while his words sent another, diametrically opposed. Liz felt torn apart inside. "But you wouldn't love me."

She caught a glimpse of something in his eyes, the longing she thought she'd seen before. Then a curtain seemed to fall. "No. I can't, Liz." His touch on her hardened. "Stay with me, Liz. Tell me you want to continue our marriage.''

Everything inside her urged her to say yes, to take this small fragment of his heart, his commitment. They could have a good marriage, a physically satisfying union. She had no doubt he'd keep his promise to stay with her, unlike her mother's wrong-headed choices in men. They could live their lives together in mutual respect and caring.

But he wouldn't love her. That part of their marriage would be barren and sterile. And what if they had children? Even as she ached inside at the thought of bearing Ethan's baby, she knew it would be wrong to bring children into a loveless marriage.

Tears stung her eyes as she slowly shook her head. ''No,'' she whispered, her throat tight. ''I won't stay with you.''

Liz's words slammed into Ethan's gut with the force of a punch. She'd refused him. She'd said no. Oh, Lord, she was going to leave him. At the end of BioCave, she would walk away and he would be alone. Like that little boy who sobbed into his pillow, he would be left with isolation and despair.

Damn it! He wouldn't let her go. He would find a way to change her mind. If not with love, then with passion. The physical he understood. If he could bring her to ecstasy again, he might force a yes from her lips.

Wild with urgency, he pressed her back against the bed and covered her mouth with his. One hand cradled her head while the other drifted down her body to part her legs. Throwing aside subtlety, he quickly thrust his fingers inside her, seeking her sensitive nub with his thumb.

Her soft sigh dissolved into a moan as he ruthlessly drove her to the edge of climax. Her hips pushed up against his hand, as she wordlessly begged for more. As he thrust into her wetness, he grew rigid with arousal, more than ready to push inside her. Still he resisted, wanting her at a fever pitch.

She reached out for him, grabbing his shoulders, trying to pull him toward her. He stayed apart from her, thrusting his tongue inside her mouth in imitation of the act she craved, they both ached for. She called his name imperiously and he could almost hear the edge of anger in her voice. But he wouldn't give in to her demand, to the clamoring of his own body. He slowed the movements of his hand, easing her toward the precipice, then backing away until he knew she was mad for completion.

"Ethan!" she cried, her hips pushing against his hand.

Trailing kisses to her ear, he whispered, "Stay with me."

"No." The word drifted weakly from her mouth.

His fingers plunged inside her again, driving another moan from her. "Stay with me."

This time she just shook her head. Tears wet her lashes, but he forced aside the guilt knifing inside him. Pushing apart her thighs with his hand, he positioned himself between her legs. The head of his erection nudged at her wet opening. "Stay with me."

"No." The word came out as a strangled sound. Her fingers clutched his hips, the nails digging into the skin. Jaw set, he entered her in one stroke, the sensation of her wet heat screaming through him.

The acuteness of the feel of her shocked him into a realization that he'd forgotten to use protection. Even as his conscience nagged him to pull out, to sheathe himself, dark desperation whispered to him. He took Liz's face in his hands. "If I make you pregnant," he rasped, "you'll have to stay."

Her blue eyes, wet with tears, fixed on his. Emotions rippled across her face—grief, hurt, betrayal. But again and again, love surfaced above the others, setting his own world into turmoil.

"God, I'm sorry," he said and started to pull away. But she held him tight, keeping him where he was. Even as tears wet her cheeks, even as hopelessness scudded across her face, she did not let him go.

In the face of her love, an ache centered in his chest, threatened to clog in his throat. Oh, God, he wanted . . . he wanted . . . The longing gripped him, tried to find a voice, to find words to define itself. But a hand seemed to hold it in place, to block it from expression.

He could only say the words again, and hope, pray, that the truth would show itself. "Liz, please . . . stay with me."

He saw a miracle in her eyes, a softness in her face. She smiled, a gentle curving of her lips. She said nothing, but he found the answer he sought. He thought he might shout for joy, sob in relief. Somehow she'd heard what he couldn't say, saw what he couldn't show.

How far that would take them, he didn't know, wouldn't even consider. He began to move inside her, steady strokes that rushed her into climax. He held back, barely holding on to his control as he drove her to her peak again and again. Then he let go, his seed flooding her, praying for a future hope, a child of hers and his.

Her hands trailed along his back, light traceries of sensation. He felt he could melt into her, he felt so relaxed. Even as he nuzzled the side of her neck, he realized that for the first time he'd let go completely with a woman. He had not held back even the tiniest part of himself.

She hadn't answered him, not in words. Anxiety pulled at him and he began to doubt what he'd seen in her eyes, her face. Sliding his body from hers, he took a breath to say her name. But her eyes were closed and her breathing deep and even. He whispered her name, but she didn't stir, didn't answer. She slept on, well-loved and exhausted.

He smiled wryly. He'd damn well have to live with his insecurities a while longer. Easing himself away from her, he rose to switch off the lights. As he padded back to the bed, something on the floor bit into his bare foot. Feeling for it in the dark, he scooped up what felt like a piece of rock. He remembered the peridotite, tossed aside in his need to find Liz.

As his fingers restlessly turned the bit of stone in his hand, unease tightened in his stomach, pressing in on him. What he thought he'd seen in Liz's face seemed to cloud, to fade. His hand shaking, he set the peridotite on the desk and felt his way back to the bed. But even as he pulled Liz into his arms, as her warmth seeped into him, the triumph of the last few minutes collapsed inside him, replaced with self-doubt.

As Ethan slipped back into bed beside her, Liz woke to muzzy half-awareness. She had felt the surrender in his final release, the way he had at last finally given himself to her. She'd realized in that moment that it wasn't that Ethan could not love, he simply didn't understand love. She was certain he truly did love her, it had been written in his face. He might not yet know how to articulate the words, but it was nevertheless there inside him.

As she snuggled close to him in the bed, curving herself against his chest, his long legs, she considered telling him again that she loved him. With his barriers down in the aftermath of their lovemaking, perhaps he would find a way to express the same to her. But as she laced her fingers through his at her hip, she sensed his tension had returned. He'd been stripped bare earlier and she couldn't fault him for retreating behind his walls again. It would probably take him time to feel comfortable with revealing himself to her.

She lay there in his arms, drowsy and sated, wishing they had started a child inside her tonight. It wasn't the best time of her cycle, but it was still possible. She could hope. Rolling that delightful thought around in her mind, she drifted into sleep.

Chapter Nineteen

Awareness came in snatches for Ethan, like quick-cut images on a television screen. They were jumbled and dissociative, scraps of visual information without sense. It had to be a dream, a roiling nightmare buffeting his subconscious. Nothing else made sense.

There he was in their quarters, Lizzy asleep on the bed, him standing naked by the desk staring down at the chunk of peridotite. Then in the corridor, dressed now, the stone biting into his hand as he gripped it. A scrap of memory of him overriding the controls on the lock boxes for the other staff quarters. A voice in his ear telling him he had to lock in the occupants to keep them safe. Then a flash of him in the energy center, his hand on the monitor, ready to push it from the worktable.

But that couldn't all be real. Because now he stood in the communications center, awake and aware, gazing down at the bit of peridotite on the worktable in front of him. He couldn't remember how he got here, or why those nightmare flashbacks haunted him as if they'd actually happened. He felt an urgency to do something, but he couldn't quite put a finger on what was so vitally important.

He focused again on the peridotite. That was it. He'd dropped it and had been about to pick it up. It was crucial that he take it up into his hand again. His fingers burned to wrap themselves around it.

But even as he edged his hand toward it, another voice screamed at him to back away. It wasn't the ghost speaking to him, it was his own mind making the demand. But even as he turned his attention to that conflicting order, something jostled his elbow, nudging his hand closer. As soon as he touched the stone, his hand closed around it and the darkness descended again.

"Miss Lizzy!"

Liz clung stubbornly to sleep, folding the insistent voice into her dream.

"Miss Lizzy, wake up!"

She might have ignored the summons if her dreams had not shifted into uneasy half-formed images, frightening in their incompleteness. As she bobbed to the surface of consciousness, she became aware of something missing, like a piece of her own heart gone astray. Fully awake, she felt beside her for Ethan, but she knew instinctively before her hand groped across the empty sheet that he was gone.

"Miss Lizzy!" Noah said a third time, his tone frantic. *"You got to get up now!"*

As she sat up in bed, drawing up the blanket to cover her nakedness, she felt terribly sleepy. Wrongness hung in the air, although she couldn't quite grasp where it came from. "What is it, Noah? What's happening?"

Glowing faintly in the dark of the room, Noah stood agog a moment, staring at her bare shoulders. Then he turned his back to her. *"You got to get dressed and come. The monster's loose and it's come for all of you."*

Groggy, Liz fumbled for her clothes beside the bed. As soon as she was dressed, she scrambled over the bed to slap

on the lights. Some instinct stayed her hand and she groped
on the desk for her flashlight instead. She flicked it on and
in the sudden illumination, horror overwhelmed her at what
she saw in the far wall of the room.

A crack had opened in the limestone, finger-width at the
floor and narrowing to a hairline fracture just below the ceiling. The faint telltale hiss of a gas leak spilled across the
room.

"Oh, my God," Liz moaned. If she'd turned on the room
light, she could have set off an explosion.

*"The creature's done this in all the rooms, Miss Lizzy.
You got to find a way out."*

Shaking off her terror, Liz whirled to the door and tried
to pull it open. It didn't budge. "Locked," she muttered,
then pressed in her code to release the lock. A buzz sounded,
telling her the code was invalid. She tried again, making
certain she'd entered the numbers correctly. The buzz rasped
again.

"Damn it! What's wrong?"

Beside her, Noah twisted his porkpie in his hands. *"I think
it was that husband of yours. When he left he did something
to the lock."* She turned and stared at him. He clutched the
porkpie to his chest. *"To all the locks."*

Her blood ran cold. "The monster . . ."

"I think it's took hold of him."

She remembered Ethan's rage when the creature had entered him once before. If it had control of him again . . . She
didn't want to finish the thought. She had to force herself to
think calmly, to figure out a way to bypass Ethan's override.

She turned to Noah. "There's a relay inside the lock
box—like a little switch. Press on it and you can disengage
the lock. Could you go inside the lock box, find the relay?"

"Maybe. Maybe I could."

"Go." She waved a hand at him. "Try."

Squashing the hat back on his head, he rose up and fun-
neled himself into the lock box. The keys clicked erratically
until finally the green light lit and she heard the *kachung* of

the door release. But when she tried the door, it was still locked.

Noah rematerialized and looked at her expectantly. "Did it work?"

The lack of oxygen made her hazy, made it difficult to concentrate. She rubbed at her brow, trying to think. "Go do the same thing on the outside lock. That's where Ethan set the override."

Noah streamed under the door almost before she'd finished speaking. She heard the same series of clicks, this time muffled by the door, then the green light shone on the inner lock box. She twisted the knob and turned, every nerve singing in relief when the door opened.

She hurried into the corridor, then shut the door behind her to block the gas as best she could. "Where's Ethan?"

"Don't know for certain. A bit ago, he was in that place with all them computers on the wall."

"The communications center." She wanted to go to him, but knew they had more pressing business to handle first. "We have to let the others out, Noah. They won't survive long in their quarters."

Liz raced along the corridor, Noah gliding along in her wake. She reached the Nguyens' quarters first and pounded on the door. "Trang! Qwong!" Pressing her ear to the door, she listened for a response. She heard nothing from the other side of the door. "Unlock it, Noah. Like you did the other one."

The process went more quickly this time. Liz shoved open the door, then stood stunned a moment, her flashlight shining on the wide crack in the limestone wall. Trang and Qwong lay on the bed and when she shouted their names again, they didn't stir. Taking a breath of the less tainted air in the corridor, she went inside the Nguyens' quarters and felt for a pulse first in Qwong, then Trang. "Still alive, thank God. Help me get them out of here, Noah."

"I can't help you with that, Miss Lizzy. I'm real good moving rocks and such, but a human being . . ."

Taking shallow breaths, she stared at the inert bodies and tried to order her scrambled thoughts. She might be able to carry the Nguyens one at a time, but then there were all the others . . . God, how could she get them all to safety? Panic gripped her, sapping her will, stealing away her ability to think.

With an effort she refocused her mind. "I'll drag them out into the corridor, then close the door to block the gas as best we can."

Noah floated before her, an earnest look on his face. *"I can go on ahead of you, Miss Lizzy, and unlock the doors."*

Gratitude washed over her. "Good. Thank you. That'll be a big help."

As Noah vanished, she reached down to grab hold of Trang under the arms. Wrestling with the dead weight, she moved the woman into the corridor, then returned for Qwong. Luckily, Mr. Nguyen had a slight build. Liz managed to pull him to safety without too much trouble.

As she swung the door shut again, specks of light danced before her eyes from the lack of oxygen. Feeling again for a pulse in Trang and Qwong, she hurried off to the Bradshaws' quarters. True to his word, Noah had unlocked the door. Bill Bradshaw was already outside his quarters, Diana slumped beside him. He rose from his wife's side as Liz approached. "Who the hell locked the door?"

"I'll explain later. Take Diana to the common room and meet me back at the Niedans' quarters."

As Bill lifted his wife in his arms, Liz propped herself against the corridor wall. Although Bill had shut his door, Liz found it hard to catch her breath. She felt an urgency to find Ethan, to see if what Noah had said was true. That he could have callously locked them all in, even compelled by the creature, cut her deeply.

Pushing off from the wall, she hurried to the Niedans', then the Jacksons' quarters. The creature must have opened the leak in her quarters first, then made its way down the corridor. The Jacksons were barely affected by the spewing gases.

"Go to the common room," she told Harlan and Benita. "Ethan and I will meet you there."

If she found Ethan. If there was anything left of his soul.

She found him in the communications center, standing in the center of the room, his back to her. "Ethan, thank God," she called out as she entered. She rounded a work table, moving toward him.

Then he turned toward her and the spark of relief she'd felt at finding him was quickly extinguished. His gray eyes were flat and empty, and she could see no recognition of her in them. In his hand, he gripped a hammer. Liz's gaze flew to the wall of monitors, and she realized he'd smashed the screen of every single one.

She stared, stunned, at the destruction. "My God, what are you doing?"

Her voice seemed to reach inside him for an instant, because he looked down at the hammer as if puzzled how it got there. He let it slip from his fingers and it clattered on the rock floor. But before his true self could assert itself, the blankness settled in again. He turned away from her and roamed the room, as if searching for something unbroken.

Fear and despair tangled inside Liz. The creature had hold of Ethan, had used him to ravage the communications center. They were blind without the displays, but had he destroyed the communications links themselves?

Somehow the creature had taken the hurt Ethan held so tightly within himself and turned it to rage, for its own evil purpose. She had to find a way to drive the monster from him, to reach inside, to restore him, to heal him. But the only weapon she possessed was her love.

He circled the room, hands fisted, every line of his body tense with the monster's rage. She approached him, afraid of him even as her heart ached. When she stood in his path, forcing him to acknowledge her, she trembled within. "Ethan," she said softly.

Like a wave reaching toward shore, his true self surged briefly to the surface, then receded. His hand shot out and gripped her arm, jerking her toward him. A vicious rage burned in his eyes, terrifying in its malignancy.

His fingers dug into her tender skin and she felt tears gathering. "Ethan, you're hurting me. You have to let go."

His grip loosened briefly, then tightened again. Emotions clashed in his face and she sensed his inner struggle. She had to tap into that, draw on his own strength.

"It's got you, Ethan, the monster's got you. It's feeding off your hurt, your anger. You have to push it away, drive it from you."

The words didn't seem to register. He tugged her closer, reaching out with his other hand. As he did, she heard something clatter to the floor. Glancing down, she saw a bit of gray-green rock at their feet. Ethan gazed down at it, then up at her, confusion in his eyes. "The peridotite. Why . . . ?"

Then the monster seemed to wipe away that brief consciousness. He pulled her up against his body, lowering his head to hers. Her heart felt torn in two as she realized the monster had won. It had complete control now. In the guise of Ethan, it would take her body and wreak its destruction on her as it had in the communications center. At the same time, it would bring its ruin on Ethan, when he discovered what he'd done in the creature's name.

As Ethan's mouth neared hers, she shut her eyes, tears spilling down her cheeks. She waited for his harsh kiss, for his cruel touch. When it didn't come, she looked up at him. She read the battle clearly in his eyes, the stark planes of his face. He was fighting back. He wasn't letting the monster take him. "Liz." He squeezed out her name in a strangled voice. "The peridotite . . . the rock . . ."

Liz glanced down, saw the innocuous bit of gray-green stone. "What . . . ?"

The tips of his fingers dug into her back. "Monster . . . gets its power from it." He squeezed his eyes shut against some inner pain. "May be too late . . ."

Striking out with her foot, she knocked the peridotite across the room. "It's gone. Ethan, do you hear me? It's gone." When he didn't speak, she groped for him, her hands settling at his waist. "Listen to me. I love you, Ethan. I love you. I won't leave you, ever."

Tears brimmed in his eyes as the monster warred inside him. "She left me, Liz. My mother. I told her I hated her, but I didn't." He took a long, shaky breath, careless of the tears streaming down his face. "I love you, Liz. I want you with me forever."

"I love you, Ethan." Meeting his gaze, she willed her love inside him, filling him, forcing out the evil within.

His face sharpened into stark lines as he waged his own war inside, his whispered words, "I love you," repeated in a soul-deep litany. The room around them seemed filled with brilliance as their love seared away the darkness.

She knew the moment the monster was gone. Joy seemed to suffuse Ethan, lighting his face. He smiled at her, all barriers down, walls collapsed. He pulled her into his arms in a gentle embrace, his lips feathering kisses along her brow.

Liz pulled back from him. "You won't let it in again."

He shook his head. "Never. There's no place for it anymore."

"We have to abandon BioCave, Ethan. We have to get everyone back to the surface." She quickly explained to him what the monster had done, while inside him and on its own.

His gaze grew darker as she described each wanton act. "Let me see if I can get a message aboveground. Then I'll check on the air circulation systems, see if they're online."

"Should we send everyone to the elevator?"

He shook his head. "No point until I contact the surface. Better if they all stay in the common room. Go let them know. Send Harlan to give me a hand."

She'd gone barely ten feet down the corridor when a tremor shook the rock walls and floor, sending her to her knees. "Ethan!" she screamed as she tried to regain her feet.

The ground shook again, and a sound like thunder rolled down the corridor. In the next moment, Ethan was there, helping her up, pulling her into his arms.

Liz clutched at him. "Was that an explosion?"

Ethan stroked her hair back from her face, his touch soothing. "Another cave-in, maybe. I don't think the creature is done with us yet."

"We'd better check the others."

Hands linked they hurried down the corridor toward the common room. Long before they reached the entrance, they saw the rubble spilling from it. Just as it had outside the chamber, part of the corridor ceiling had fallen in, trapping the other staff members inside. As they tried to get closer, the cavern trembled again, shaking loose more rock.

Liz and Ethan scrambled back, narrowly dodging a massive chunk. Liz stared at the pile in despair. "We have to get them out." She tugged at Ethan, trying to free herself from his grip.

He held tight. "We can't on our own. We're better off contacting the surface and calling for help."

She knew he was right, but she couldn't bear the thought of her friends trapped, possibly wounded. "There must be some way to find out if they're okay."

"I doubt they'd hear us if we called. And we can't get through that mess."

"Noah could." She tipped her head to the ceiling. "Noah! We need you!" Liz turned, looking from one end of the corridor to the other, searching for the ghost. "He's got to be here somewhere. Noah!"

Finally he slipped from a nearby crack and hovered before her. *"Sorry, Miss Lizzy. Been a bit occupied."* As he floated in the corridor, he faded in and out of view.

"Go inside the common room, Noah. Check on the rest of the staff." He drifted toward the mound of rock, oozing his body in between the stones. Liz glanced up at Ethan. "Did you see him?"

He stared at the spot where Noah had been. "Almost. There was an outline of a man, then it was gone."

When Noah returned, he seemed even more faded. *"They're all right for now, Miss Lizzy. But it seems the monster has been busy in there, too."*

Dread centered in Liz's belly. "What do you mean?"

Noah shimmered before her. *"There's cracks open all through the room. All of them spilling out that gas."*

As he and Liz raced back to the communications center, Ethan did his best to thrust aside the smothering fear he felt for Liz. For now, she was safe, and he would do what he could to protect her. He damn well wouldn't let that monster in again. But the creature's power far outstripped his own. His best might not be enough.

"It can't be in two places at once," Liz said as they entered the com center. "Or take control of two people at one time."

"I know, Liz. I heard Noah."

She rubbed trembling hands together. "I wasn't sure you did."

He turned to her, nudged her chin up so she met his gaze. "Noah's doing what he can to keep the creature away from us."

Tears brimmed in her eyes. "He's weak, Ethan. The monster might destroy him."

"Then we'd better use whatever time Noah buys us."

As Noah perched in a narrow crack between two stalactites in the common room, he couldn't keep from trembling. He'd never been so dang scared in all his existence. Playing cat-and-mouse with the wicked thing he'd spent the last hundred-plus years avoiding was more than a cowardly soul like his could take. But he was his Miss Lizzy's only chance, not to mention the other folks trapped down below him. If this was his last act on earth, he would do what he could to save them all.

No matter it was little enough he could do. He'd been sneaking up on the creature, tweaking its tail so to speak, then squirting away from it when it turned. It had worked for a while—up until it had let loose that mighty pile of rock that trapped those folks. Then the thing was tired, which gave Noah a rest as well. But much as he'd tried to draw it away from the BioCave folks, it would only chase him so far before it turned and made its way back.

What if he took hold of it? Just like he moved boulders and such by surrounding it with his ghostly self, what if he wrapped himself around the monster? He might keep it from mischief a good long time, long enough for Lizzy and the others to get to safety. But that increased the danger the thing might take hold of *him,* pulling him into its evil self. It hadn't done so thus far, which had always seemed a mite peculiar to him. But who knew when it would lose its taste for living beings and go after a ghost.

He would use that trick as a last resort. No telling what the monster could do to him from the inside out. Better to tease it some more, rile it up. Keep it busy, to give Lizzy and that husband of hers more time.

He thought of his special place and longed to sneak off there and hide, leaving the BioCave folk to the horrors of the monster. Would Lizzy come back as a ghost, he wondered, and face him with an accusing eye? The thought made him shudder and he knew he could never do that to her.

Sensing the monster's reawakening, Noah shifted in the narrow crack and sought it out. Grabbing the tiger by the tail, he gave the beast a tug, then dashed away. It came up close behind him, tendrils of it sweeping against it, sending shivers through his ghostly self. Noah slipped through the limestone fissures even faster, terror whipping him along.

He sensed his special cave below him, and yearned to drop inside it to safety. But the creature still pursued, farther away from Lizzy and the others than Noah had yet been able to tease it. As he passed his special place in a blur of speed, joy rose inside him. He was leading the monster away from them! They would be safe after all.

When he first felt the spreading of his ghostly self, he didn't recognize the sensation. Then he felt himself go flatter and flatter, until his limbs stretched too far away for him to feel them. By the time he realized the trap the creature had driven him into, it was too late. He'd been dispersed throughout the limestone too far to recover himself. The monster had turned the trick on him—chased him into an endless crack of minute width. He didn't know where half his being had gone, and the half he remained aware of seemed to seep into the rock like water.

As the world grew dim around him, Noah was grateful for one small blessing. He'd drawn the creature far enough away, at least he'd bought a little time for his beloved Lizzy.

Chapter
Twenty

"Liz, I need more electrical tape." Shoulder-deep inside a control cabinet under the bank of broken monitors, Ethan waved a hand in her direction.

Liz dug through his toolbox for the black tape, then passed him the nearly empty roll she found. "That's the last in your toolbox. We'll have to scout out some more in storage."

Ethan banged his head on the underside of the cabinet and muttered a pungent curse. "Storage room by the common room is blocked. Hope to hell we can find some in auxiliary storage. Damn it!" Ethan yelled as sparks skittered from the open cabinet. A trail of smoke drifted from the wiring. "Wrong connection."

Tension dug into the base of Liz's neck. Ethan had gotten edgier and edgier with each discovery of broken wire and ruined equipment. "How long before we get communications back?"

"Hell if I know. I made a damned thorough job of destroying these circuits."

"Not you, Ethan. The monster." She crouched by the cabinet and laid a comforting hand on his leg. His thigh was rock hard with tension.

"That doesn't make me any less responsible," he said harshly. "If they die, Liz, any of them, I'm the one at fault."

"You shouldn't blame yourself. Your actions weren't under your control."

"But they should have been. I let the thing take control of me. I should have resisted it."

She stroked his rigid leg, wishing she could find the words to soothe him. "Even so," she said, "I love you. Nothing you've done could change that."

He dragged in a long breath, then reached for her, covering her hand with his. They remained that way, the silence stretching out for long moments until he took back his hand to continue his repairs. She stayed where she was, enjoying his warmth. She ran her fingers along the seam of his denim jeans, trailing a path from his knee back to his hip. "At least Noah's drawn the monster away from here." She couldn't feel the slightest sense of its presence.

Ethan moved his leg away from her touch. "I suppose he has."

The words were barely out of his mouth when the lights flickered in a mad strobe, then went out. As blackness closed in, Ethan let loose a long string of curses. Then Liz heard a loud bang as if he'd thrown a tool against the side of the cabinet.

Digging in her pocket for her flashlight, Liz switched it on. Ethan had pulled himself out of the cabinet, and harsh shadows played over his face. "Damn repairs won't do any good without power."

"Is the air recirc still on?" Liz held her breath, listening for the subtle whir of the massive fans. Nothing but silence met her ears.

"No. Hell." Eyes shut, Ethan pinched the bridge of his nose. "We need a battery backup. There's some in storage by the common room. Which is inaccessible."

"Didn't you leave one in the chamber?" Warmth sparked

inside her as she remembered how he'd made love to her there. "We could get that one."

Turning toward her fully, he put his hands on her shoulders. "Could you go alone? While I finish up repairs?"

The thought of traversing the dark corridors alone sent a shiver up her spine, but the intensity of Ethan's gray gaze compelled her to nod yes. He relaxed slightly at her agreement, dropping his hands from her. "Should be a spare flashlight in the drawer over there." He pointed across the room. "Take it—the batteries are fresher. Leave yours with me."

She did as he told her, the urgency in his tone setting off an unease within her. As she handed him her flashlight, she had the strong sense that he wanted her away from him. She wanted to ask, but he turned away from her back to his work without another word.

As she crept along the dim empty corridor to the chamber, her anxiety mounted, her nerves as taut as bowstrings. The scrape of her feet on the limestone floor, the sound of her breathing, whispered to her in the monster's voice. She told herself again and again it was nowhere near. Noah had promised to keep it away from them and she believed in him utterly.

When she reached the site of the first cave-in, her stomach churned as she contemplated climbing back through that pile of rocks into the chamber beyond. Gritting her teeth, she pushed aside a few rocks to widen the opening, then slipped inside. Hurrying along the tunnel into the chamber, she quickly retrieved the battery. Back in the tunnel, she pushed the battery along beside her, then shoved it through the opening in the rock fall.

All the while, tension knotted between her shoulders as she waited for the creature to come for her. But somehow, despite her skittish fear, she still couldn't feel its presence. Perhaps its power had diminished and Noah had been able to take control of it. A cautious joy built inside her as she hefted the battery down the corridor toward the communications center.

"I've got it," she called to Ethan as she went inside. "You know, I think Noah . . ."

Her throat constricted, shutting off her voice when she saw Ethan. He stood at the bank of monitors, hands clenching the worktable below, head bowed. His breathing was harsh and labored, as if he fought for every lungful of air. "Ethan?"

He wouldn't look at her. "Stay back."

Despite his warning, she moved closer. "I brought the battery." She set it at his feet.

"It's trying to come inside me again, Liz. I'm fighting it, but . . ." Tension rippled from him. "If it takes me again, I want you to run, Liz. Away from me, as far as you can go."

She stepped closer, put a hand on his arm. "I won't leave you, Ethan."

He turned his head toward her. "I won't let it hurt you again."

Setting the flashlight aside on the worktable, she tugged his grip loose, drew his rigid body to her. "You won't, Ethan. You're stronger than it is. Because you love me."

A moment's hesitation, then his arms surrounded her. His body shook as he held her close. "I love you."

She pressed a kiss to his cheek. "I won't leave you."

He shuddered, then set her away from him and bent to slide the battery into the control cabinet. "I think I've repaired all the connections. We should be able to at least send and receive an audio message." He hooked up the battery, then tested his jury-rigged circuit. "Hell, still not working."

He looked around him, as if searching for an answer. Then he crossed the room to a storage cabinet and pulled out a roll of paper. He spread it out on the worktable.

"What is it?" Liz asked.

"Wiring diagram for the communications system." He tapped the paper. "There's a junction here that controls lights as well as communication. If the monster severed it, both systems would go."

"How do we fix it?"

"It's a simple enough splice job." He dragged a hand

through his hair, pushing it back from his forehead. "Accessing it is the problem. It's inside an air duct. Too small for me."

"What about me?"

"No way." He stared down at the blueprint.

"Have we got another option?"

"I could bypass that circuit," he said, his tone evasive.

"How long would that take?" she asked.

He wouldn't look at her. "Too long."

"Then I go into the duct."

"You don't know what the hell you're doing. Touch the wrong wire and you could electrocute yourself."

"But the power's off."

"The power's off here, Liz. But the wires inside the conduit are probably still live."

"You'll talk me through it." She lifted her chin, determined.

He grasped her shoulders, kneading with his fingers. His gaze fixed on hers, as if by will alone he could change her mind. "Okay. We'll do it. But you listen for my instruction before you do anything."

Gathering up a few tools, he stuffed them into the pockets of her jeans. The conduit was up near the ceiling with a grill covering it. Ethan gave Liz a boost up, holding her while she unfastened the screws holding the grill. Once it was loose, she handed it down to him, then squirmed inside the duct. There was scarcely enough room to navigate the small space. She had to stretch her arms out before her, flashlight in her hand as she crawled along.

"Are you at the T yet?" Ethan called after her, his voice muffled.

Squinting in the dim light, she could just make out the juncture up ahead. "Nearly there." The tight space seemed to make it difficult to breathe, as if the walls of the duct squeezed the air from her. She wriggled along, making less and less progress with each movement of her body.

Was the duct narrowing as it approached the T? Where

before she could move her body an inch or so from side to side, now she felt wedged into the narrow space.

"There yet?" Ethan's voice came to her faintly, seeming to fade into the metal walls of the duct. She wanted to answer him, but her tongue felt glued to the roof of her mouth. She couldn't have gotten enough air to speak anyway, because the duct had shrunk until she could only drag in the smallest measure of air. The shallow breaths made her light-headed, dizzy. When she sought out the T junction, her vision swam. It could have been a million miles away, or an inch from her questing fingers, she couldn't tell the difference.

A rasping sounded in her ears, in rhythm with her labored breathing. It scraped against her like nails running across a blackboard. In, scrape, out, scrape. Fear rode on the heels of the distant sound, a vague impression of terror that resolved itself into two harsh syllables.

"Lizzy."

Trembling, Liz lay her face against her arms, trying to shut out the monster's call. She tried to focus on Ethan, on her love for him, on his love for her. Still the creature pressed in on her.

"Lizzy."

She felt it along the length of her body, oppressive and dark. She understood now that it wasn't the duct that had narrowed, but the monster that had closed in on her. It stripped away her courage, her sense of self, and sought entrance into her very soul.

"Lizzy."

She closed her mind to it, closed her heart to it. But it seemed to claw at her, closing in on her like a fog. She heard a hissing, felt a wisp of something brush against her left cheek. Turning in that direction, she saw the duct had split, exposing a crack in the rock behind it. Her mind fuzzy, she realized gas must be spilling into the duct from the crack.

"I've come for you, Lizzy."

Still she resisted. She felt a flash of gratitude that it had come for her and not Ethan. Then it flayed bare that weakness and sent into her mind a vision of Ethan sprawled on the floor of the communications center, struck down. Tears flowed hotly down her cheeks as she realized the creature had gone to Ethan first, had finished him before it came to her.

"You are mine, Lizzy."

She tried to shake her head to drive away the image. She wouldn't believe, not until she saw his body with her own eyes. The monster sketched another picture in her mind, even more gruesome, adding frightening details to what it had shown her before. Setting her jaw against the wickedness, she forced herself to edge a millimeter farther along the duct. "I love you, Ethan. I love you." She repeated the words over and over, drowning out the monster's voice.

"Miss Lizzy, I'm here!"

Her eyes flew open at the sound of Noah's voice. One moment the duct was empty, then he seemed to explode into it. His ragged brilliance blinded her a moment, then she fixed her gaze on his face, inches from her. "The creature . . ."

"He tricked me, Miss Lizzy. Thought I was a goner, for sure."

"Ethan . . . is Ethan okay?"

"Mad as a wet hen, last I saw him. Don't you hear him yelling?"

The monster had receded slightly at Noah's arrival. She could just make out Ethan's shouts. Relief drove a sob from her throat. "Noah, you have to keep the monster from Ethan."

His face, floating before her, turned grave. *"I know what I got to do."* His hand snaked toward hers, scudded above it. *"I hope you'll remember me kindly, Miss Lizzy."*

Then he reached toward her, seeming to grab at something around her. He clutched tightly, tension in his face, strain in the line of his arms. Then it felt like a blanket were being dragged from her shoulders, a rough covering that scratched against her as it was removed. Even with the sharp pain, she felt lighter and lighter, as if her world were expanding. She could breathe a bit more easily and the duct seemed to widen around her.

Now Noah held a clot of darkness between his hands, a knot of something vile. His fingers glowed where they gripped the blackness, as he squeezed and pressed the thing tighter and tighter. It resisted his pressure, now growing in size, now shrinking, fighting Noah's every effort. Liz reached out once, wanting to somehow help the ghost take control, but Noah shouted, *"No!"* and she snatched back her hand.

Each time the monster swelled, Noah faded slightly. Then he would redouble his efforts, brightening inside the duct, a flare of stunning light. When Noah brought the dark thing inside the globe of his cupped hands, his fingers extended like a cage, he drew it closer to him. His arms strained against the creature's pull, as it scrabbled against the ghost, once nearly escaping his grasp.

As Noah brought the inky darkness to his middle, he glanced up at Liz. *"I love you, Miss Lizzy."*

Tears clogged her throat as she whispered, "Thank you."

Then Noah took the thing inside him. As his form swallowed the last of the blackness, the ghost seemed to fold in on himself. He burned brighter for one last instant, then with a silent implosion, Noah fell in on himself. A moment later, only the ordinary light of the flashlight illuminated the duct. There, just beyond her fingertips was the T and the junction box.

"Liz!" Ethan's shout echoed along the metal ductwork, rang in her ears. "Are you all right?"

She shook her head, trying to clear it. The crack still yawned beside her, still spilling out gas. Then that part hadn't been an illusion. Taking a breath, she called out weakly, "I'm at the juncture."

He yelled instructions to her, telling her to remove the casing, then explaining how to handle the wires. She worked silently, tears filling her eyes, spilling down her cheeks. Her vision had closed down to the field of view of her hands and sleep wanted to close her eyes. But she kept doggedly at it, even when her trembling fingers could barely manipulate the last scrap of electrical tape around the wires.

When she made the final connection, she laid her head on her arms, exhausted. Dimly, she heard Ethan calling to her, telling her the communications systems were operational, that he'd contacted the surface. But she couldn't seem to lift her head as the gas still poured from the fissure. Regret flooded her—that Noah had sacrificed himself for her, that she wouldn't see Ethan again. Then sleep took her inexorably into darkness.

In the next few hours, Ethan felt he'd died a thousand deaths. First, when he heard nothing but silence from the duct where Liz had crawled, then when he couldn't force his too-large body inside to reach her. The rescue team seemed to take forever to come down, then the young female paramedic who climbed in the duct after Liz was gone so long, he wondered if she'd been overcome as well. When finally they pulled Liz to safety, he thought he would go mad at the sight of her so silent and still on the stretcher.

Now he sat beside her hospital bed, watching her, his gaze fixed on each rise and fall of her chest. She'd yet to wake from the coma they'd found her in. A weight rested heavily inside him as he gripped her hand, the coolness of her skin sending terror to his very core.

He raised trembling fingers to rub at his eyes. He couldn't remember how long he'd been here. Two days? Three? He'd only been dimly aware of the other BioCave staff coming to visit, joining him briefly in his vigil. They all knew they owed their lives to her. Without Liz, they all might have died in the common room when the leaking gas filled the space, driving out the oxygen.

God, please don't let her have paid with her life.

As Ethan bent over her hand, Aaron Cohen stepped into the room and moved to the other side of the bed. Ethan realized he didn't care what Liz felt for the old man, if only she would wake. If she opened up her eyes and told him she didn't love him anymore, he could even accept that, if only she would live.

"How is she?" Aaron asked.

"No change." Ethan rose and bent to brush his lips against her cheek. "I love you, Liz," he whispered.

Reaching across her, Aaron laid a hand on Ethan's shoulder. "I'm so glad you two found each other."

Ethan's throat grew tight. What the hell good would it do to love Liz if she died?

With an effort, he swallowed back his anger. She'd opened up his heart again. That was worth something, even if . . . He didn't let himself finish the thought.

When she first stirred against his lips, he didn't register the significance of it. Then he felt the sigh of her breath against his cheeks. "Ethan?"

He looked down at her and joy exploded in his chest at the sight of her blue eyes meeting his. "Thank God," he murmured.

Aaron was grinning from ear to ear. "Hey, Lizzy girl. You gave us a hell of a scare."

She smiled up at the old man, her expression sweet and loving. "I wouldn't do that to you, Dad."

As the significance of what she'd said rocketed through Ethan, Aaron bent to peck a kiss on Liz's brow. The old man straightened, and for the first time Ethan saw the resemblance between him and Liz that would have been obvious if he hadn't been busy being such an idiot.

"I'll give you two some time alone," Aaron said, giving Liz's hand a pat as he left the room.

Liz smiled up at Ethan, her gaze roving his face. "I wanted to tell you. About Aaron, I mean."

"I know. I just didn't want to listen."

Her brow furrowed. "It was just one night between him and my mom. He and Rose were having problems. Shar's dad had just walked out on my mother. Right after it happened, he admitted it to Rose."

"She forgave him."

Liz nodded. "I guess it was rough for a while. But their love overcame it. When Aaron found out about me, Rose accepted me as her own daughter."

He raised her hand to his lips. "I understand why you wanted to keep it secret."

She sighed, her eyes drifting shut. "Noah's gone, Ethan. He sacrificed himself to save us from the creature."

"Then I owe him a debt of gratitude. Because he saved you." Wanting to assure himself she was here, and alive, he touched her—stroking her hair back from her brow, caressing her cheek with his palm. "I love you, Liz."

"And I love you."

Gazing down at her, his world complete now, Ethan felt her love suffuse him, washing away the old hurts. "Forever, Liz," he whispered. Then he drew her into his arms and held her against his open, loving heart.

If you enjoyed
NIGHT WHISPERS
you won't want to miss

The More I
See You

by LYNN KURLAND

Coming in October from Berkley Books

Chapter
One

Jessica Blakely didn't believe in Fate.

Yet as she stood at the top of a medieval circular staircase and peered down into its gloomy depths, she had to wonder if someone other than herself might be at the helm of her ship, as it were. Things were definitely not progressing as she had planned. Surely Fate had known she wasn't at all interested in stark, bare castles or knights in rusting armor.

Surely.

She took a deep breath and forced herself to examine the turns of events that had brought her to her present perch. Things had seemed so logical at the time. She'd gone on a blind date, accepted said blind date's invitation to go to England as part of his university department's faculty sabbatical, then hopped cheerfully on a plane with him two weeks later.

Their host was Lord Henry de Galtres, possessor of a beautifully maintained Victorian manor house. Jessica had taken one look and fallen instantly in love—with the house, that is. The appointments were luxurious, the food heavenly, and the surrounding countryside idyllic. The only downside was that for some unfathomable reason, Lord Henry had decided that the crumbling castle attached to his house was something that needed to remain undemolished. Just the sight of it had sent chills down Jessica's spine. She couldn't say why, and she hadn't wanted to dig around to find the answer.

Instead, she'd availed herself of all the modern comforts Lord Henry's house could provide. And she'd been certain that when she could tear herself away from her temporary home-away-from-home, she might even venture to London for a little savings-account-reducing shopping at Harrods. Yet before she could find herself facing a cash register, she'd been driven to seek sanctuary in the crumbling castle attached to Lord Henry's house.

There was something seriously amiss in her life.

A draft hit her square in the face, loaded with the smell of seven centuries of mustiness. She coughed and flapped her hand in front of her nose. Maybe she should have kept her big mouth shut and avoided expressing any disbelief in Providence.

Then again, it probably would have been best if she'd remained silent a long time ago, maybe before she'd agreed to that blind date. She gave that some thought, then shook her head. Her troubles had begun long before her outing with Archibald Stafford III. In fact, she could lay her finger on the precise moment when she had lost control and Fate had taken over.

Piano lessons. At age five.

You wouldn't think that something so innocuous, so innocent and child-friendly would have led a woman where she never had any intention of having gone, but Jessica couldn't find any evidence to contradict the results.

Piano lessons had led to music scholarships, which had led to a career in music that had somehow demolished her social life, leaving her no choice but to sink to accepting the latest in a series of hopeless blind dates: Archie Stafford and his shiny penny loafers. Archie was the one who had invited her to England for a month with all expenses paid. He had landed the trip thanks to a great deal of sucking up to the dean of his department. He didn't exactly fit in with the rest of the good old boys who clustered with the dean and Lord Henry every night smoking cigars into the wee hours, but maybe that's what Archie aspired to.

Jessica wondered now how hard up he must have been for a date to have asked her to come along. At the time he'd invited her, though, she'd been too busy thinking about tea and crumpets to let the invitation worry her. It had been a university-sponsored outing. She'd felt perfectly safe.

Unfortunately, being Archie's guest also meant that she had to speak to him, and *that* was something she wished she could avoid for the next three weeks. It was only on the flight over that she'd discovered the depth of his swininess. She made a mental note never to pull out her passport for anyone she'd known less than a month if such an occasion should arise again.

But like it or not, she was stuck with him for this trip, which meant at the very least polite conversation, and if nothing else, her mother had instilled in her a deep compulsion to be polite.

Of course, being civil didn't mean she couldn't escape now and then, which was precisely what she was doing at present. And escape had meant finding the one place where Archie would never think to look for her.

The depths of Henry's medieval castle.

She wondered if an alarm would sound if she disconnected the rope that barred her way. She looked to her left and saw that there were a great many people who would hear such an alarm if it sounded, but then again, maybe she wouldn't be noticed in the ensuing panic. Apparently Lord Henry funded some of his house upkeep by conducting tours of his castle. Those tours were seemingly well attended, if the one in progress was any indication.

Jessica eyed the sightseers. They were moving in a herd-like fashion and it was possible they might set up a stampede if she startled them. They were uncomfortably nestled together, gaping at cordoned-off family heirlooms, also uncomfortably nestled together. Lord Henry of Marcham's home was a prime destination spot and Jessica seemed to have placed herself in the midst of the latest crowd at the precise moment she needed the most peace and quiet. She had already done the castle tour and learned more than she wanted to know about Burwyck-on-the-Sea and its accompanying history. Another lesson on the intricacies of medieval happenings was the last thing she needed.

"—Of course the castle here at Marcham, or Merceham, as it was known in the 1300s, was one of the family's minor holdings. Even though it has been added to during the years and extensively remodeled during the Victorian period, it is not the most impressive of the family's possessions. The true gem of the de Galtres crown lies a hundred and fifty kilometers away on the eastern coast. If we move further along here, you'll find a painting of the keep."

The crowd shuffled to the left obediently as the tour guide continued with his speech.

"As you can see here in this rendering of Burwyck-on-the-Sea—aptly named, if I might offer an opinion—the most remarkable feature of the family's original seat is the round tower built not into the center of the bailey as we find in Pembroke Castle, but rather into the outer seawall. I would imagine the third lord of the de Galtres family fancied having his ocean view unobstructed—"

So could Jessica and she heartily agreed with the sentiment, but for now an ocean view was not what she was interested in. If the basement was roped off it could only mean that it was free of tourists and tour guides. It was also possible that below was where the castle kept all its resident spiders and ghosts, but it was a chance she would have to take. Archie would never think to look for her there. Ghosts could be ignored. Spiders could be squashed.

She put her shoulders back, unhooked the rope, and descended.

She stopped at the foot of the steps and looked for someplace appropriate. Suits of armor stood at silent attention along both walls. Lighting was minimal and creature comforts nonexistent, but that didn't deter her. She walked over the flagstones until she found a likely spot, then eased her way between a fierce-looking knight brandishing a sword and another grimly holding a pike. She did a quick cobweb check before she settled down with her back against the stone wall. It was the first time that day she'd been grateful for the heavy gown she wore. A medieval costume might suit her surroundings, but it seemed like a very silly thing to wear to an afternoon tea—and said afternoon tea was precisely what she'd planned to avoid by fleeing to the basement.

Well, that and Archie.

She reached into her bag and pulled out what she needed for complete relaxation. Reverently, she set a package of two chilled peanut-butter cups on the stone floor. Those she would save for later. A can of pop followed. The floor was cold enough to keep it at a perfect temperature as well. Then she pulled out her portable CD player, put the headphones on her head, made herself more comfortable, and, finally closing her eyes with a sigh, pushed the play button. A chill went down her spine that had nothing to do with the cold stone.

Bruckner's Seventh could do that to a girl, given the right circumstances.

Jessica took a deep breath and prepared for what she knew was to come. The symphony started out simply. She knew eventually it would increase in strength and magnitude until it came crashing down on her with such force that she wouldn't be able to catch her breath.

She felt her breathing begin to quicken and had to wipe her palms on her dress. It was every bit as good as it had been the past 139 times she had listened to the same piece. It was music straight from the vaults of heav—

Squeak.

Jessica froze. She was tempted to open her eyes, but she was almost certain what she would see would be a big, fat rat sitting right next to her, and then where would she be? Her snack was still wrapped, and since it really didn't count as food anyway, what could a rat want with it? She returned her attentions to the symphony. It was the London Philharmonic, one of her favorite orchestras—

Wreek, wreek, wreeeeeek.

Rusty shutters? Were there shutters in the basement? Hard to say. She wasn't about to open her eyes and find out. There was probably some kind of gate nearby and it was moving thanks to a stiff breeze set up by all the tourists tromping around upstairs. Or maybe it was a trapdoor to the dungeon. She immediately turned away from that thought, as it wasn't a place she wanted to go. She closed her eyes even more

firmly. It was a good thing she was so adept at shutting out
distractions. The noise might have ruined the afternoon for
her otherwise.

Wreeka, wreeka, wreeeeeka.

All right, that was too much. It was probably some stray
kid fiddling with one of the suits of armor. She'd give him
an earful, send him on his way, and get back to her business.

She opened her eyes—then shrieked.

There, looming over her with obviously evil intent, was a
knight in full battle gear. She pushed herself back against the
stone wall, pulling her feet under her and wondering just
what she could possibly do to defend herself. The knight,
however, seemed to dismiss her upper person because he
bent his helmeted head to look at her feet. By the alacrity
with which he suddenly leaned over in that direction, she
knew what was to come.

The armor creaked as the mailed hand reached out. Then,
without any hesitation, the fingers closed around her peanut-
butter cups. The visor was flipped up with enthusiasm, the
candy's covering ripped aside with more dexterity than any
gloved hand should have possessed, and Jessica's last vestige
of American junk food disappeared with two great chomps.

The chomper burped.

"Hey, Jess," he said, licking his chops, "thought you
might be down here hiding. Got any more of those?" He
pointed at the empty space near her feet, his arm producing
another mighty squeak.

Rule number one: No one interrupted her during Bruckner.

Rule number two: No one ate her peanut-butter cups, *especially* when she found herself stranded in England for a
month without the benefit of a Mini Mart down the street.
She had yet to see any peanut-butter cups in England and
she'd been saving her last two for a quiet moment alone.
Well, at least the thief hadn't absconded with her drink as of
yet—

"Geez, Jess," he said, reaching for her can of pop, pop-
ping the top and draining the contents, "why are you hiding?"

She could hardly think straight. "I was listening to Bruckner."

He burped loudly. "Never understood a girl who could get all sweaty over a bunch of fairies playing the violin." He squashed the can, then grinned widely at the results a mailed glove could generate. Then he looked at her and winked. "How'd you like to come here and give your knight in shining armor a big ol' kiss?"

I'd rather kiss a rat was on the tip of her tongue, but Archibald Stafford III didn't wait for the words to make it past her lips. He hauled her up from between her guardians— and a fat lot of good two empty suits of armor had done her—sending her CD player and headphones crashing to the ground, pulled her against him, and gave her the wettest, slobberiest kiss that had ever been given an unwilling maiden fair.

She would have clobbered him, but she was trapped in a mailed embrace and powerless to rescue herself.

"Let me go," she squeaked.

"What's the matter? Aren't you interested in my strong, manly arms?" he said, giving her a squeeze to show just how strong and manly his arms were.

"Not when they're squeezing the life from me," she gasped. "Archie, let me go!"

"It'll be good for research purposes."

"I'm a musician, for heaven's sake. I don't need to do this kind of research. And you are a . . ." And she had to pause before she said it because she still couldn't believe such a thing was possible, given the new insights she'd had into the man currently crushing the life from her, "a . . . philosopher," she managed. "A tenured philosophy professor at a major university, not a knight."

Archibald sighed with exaggerated patience. "The costume party, remember?"

As if she could forget, especially since she was already dressed à la medieval, complete with headgear and lousy shoes. And it was an afternoon tea for the vacationing faculty of Archie's university. Why they had chosen to dress themselves up as knights and ladies fair she couldn't have said. It had to have been the brainchild of that nutty history professor who hadn't been able to clear his sword through airport security. She'd known just by looking at him that he was trouble.

If only she'd been as observant with Archie. And now here she was, staring at what had, at first blush, seemed to be one of her more successful blind dates. She could hardly reconcile his current self with his philosophy self. Either he'd gotten chivalry confused with chauvinism, or wearing that suit of armor too long had allowed metal to leach into his brain and alter his personality.

"I'll carry you up," Archie said suddenly. "It'll be a nice touch."

But instead of being swept up into his arms, which would have been bad enough, she found herself hoisted and dumped over his shoulder like a sack of potatoes.

"My CD player," she protested.

"Get it later," he said, trudging off toward the stairs.

She struggled, but it was futile. She thought about name-calling, but that, she decided, was beneath her. He'd have to put her down eventually and then she would really let him have it. For the moment, however, it was all she could do to avoid having her head make contact with the stairwell as Archie huffed up the steps. He paused and Jessica heard a cacophony of startled gasps. Fortunately she was hanging mostly upside down, so her face couldn't get any redder.

"I love this medieval stuff," Archie announced to whatever assembly there was there, "don't you?"

And with that, he slapped her happily on the rump—to the accompaniment of more horrified gasps—and continued on his way.

Jessica wondered if that sword she'd seen with the armor in the basement was sharp. Then again, maybe it would be just as effective if it were dull. Either way, she had the feeling she was going to have to use it on the man who chortled happily as he carried her, minus her dignity, on down the hallway to where she was certain she would be humiliated even further.